KAYAVAN RISING

THE KAYAVAN CHRONICLES - BOOK 1

Published by: RBF Books

Kayavan Rising

ISBN:
979-8-9897644-3-3

For information address author.MariaGrace@gmail.com

Author's Website: **RandomBitsofFascination.com**

DEDICATION

For my husband and sons.
You have always believed in me and made this world a reality.

Chapter 1

Leaves and debris swirled around her, caught in the irresistible grip of the level four winds. Dark clouds roiled overhead, blackening the sky to nearly midnight. Ozone, humidity, and anxiety permeated the atmosphere, driving all sensible creatures into hiding.

That said a great deal about her right there, didn't it?

"Ari! Arilyn Lysand! Get inside now!" Mama shouted from the front door of the tiny, egg-shaped pod house, her voice barely audible over the roaring tempest.

"I'm right here, making sure the storm shutters stay tight this time." Ari tightened the locknut on the gray steel shutters a final quarter turn, slipped her tools back into her belt kit, and fought her way through the first burst of cold rain to the front door.

Mama slid it shut behind her, leaving a spreading puddle in its wake. "Is that any way for a full-grown woman to act, riding the storm's edge like that?" She parked her hands on her hips, wind-whipped hair clinging to the side of her face.

Everyone said she and Mama looked too much alike, petite—no, that was what polite folks said. Ari was just short and angular, without Mama's soft curves. With sharp, clear brown eyes and tousled dark curls, sometimes looking at Mama was like looking at a perpetually irritated version of herself.

"What do you expect? You're the one who likes to remind me I was born on the day Kayavan's star began rising. More or less guaranteed I'd always be on the edge of a storm 'cause of that." Ari ran her fingers through her mop of damp curls, slinging drops of water on the smooth industrial gray flooring.

"I'll never forget the fierce storm that day. Seems like there's always been a storm following you." Mama smiled and shook her head. "Get yourself cleaned up before you take a chill. I'll make us some tea."

Tea? Lovely. That meant she wanted to talk. And not the pleasant sort of companionable chat to while away a stormy evening. Tea meant there were serious things to be said. Things Ari probably didn't want to hear.

Sighing, she crossed the few steps from the front door to the tiny bathroom. Every surface wore white tile, while glaring, too-white lights glinted off the polished finish. Barely large enough to accommodate the necessary toilet, sonic cleaning station, and a bare-bones clothing recycler that should have been upgraded years ago, "efficient" seemed insufficient to describe the level of function crammed into so small a space. Ari tossed her work clothes into the recycler and set it to print up something soft and comfortable, which would help her sit through Mama's upcoming lecture.

Yes, Mama had suggested it would be a conversation, but Ari's perspective definitely wouldn't be welcome.

The sonic shower drowned out the sound of the howling winds, replacing it with the itchy-prickly sense of scavenger ants crawling along every inch of her skin. She rubbed her bare shoulders with both hands, but the sensation persisted. It might not be so bad if she actually felt clean after the sonics, but only the faint dust left on the floor after it was done gave her any indication she wasn't leaving the stall unchanged. Maybe she'd go out in the rain before it got too much worse, just for the sense of a proper cleansing. Someday she'd be able to afford the luxury of a real water shower.

When the shower stopped, the howling winds resumed and storm-driven debris slammed into the side of the house, hard enough to feel like the house would roll with the impact. That wasn't going to happen. The anchor points, which gave way in order to absorb impact, would only go so far. They would hold fast against the storm.

At least they always had in the past. There had been a lot of storms to hold fast against.

Three steps out of the bathroom, almost into the cramped living room, Mama handed her a mug of tea, not a cup, suggesting this was going to be a long "conversation." Excellent.

Mama didn't like things on the wall or decorations cluttering up the place, so there were none. With the windows shuttered, and the lights turned on to full brightness, the room felt sterile, cold, and sparse. The pungent industrial cleansers Mama used did little to dispel that sense.

She beckoned Ari to join her on the worn couch. Ari would rather have curled up on the ragged chair across the room. Even if it was hardly farther away than the other side of the couch, it still felt like there was more breathing room there.

"I swear the wind sounds like the Hell Cat's roar, calling departed souls out to walk Laythe's Woods." Mama glanced over her shoulder at the shuttered window.

"To find their final place of rest." Ari drew her knees up close to her chest, wrapping her arms around them to cradle her tea. The familiar lumps and bumps of the old dirt-brown couch only served to remind her she was about to get a lot more uncomfortable. "You say that every time the storms come at the comet's appearance. Why are you so attached to those old myths?"

"Kayavan's star, dear, you have to get it right. When his star rises, he sends the storms to keep Pogo, the Arch Soul Catcher, and his soul catcher minions from dragging the newly-awakened souls to Abadon's Gates." Mama winked. She really loved those stories.

"What I've never understood is why the storms would hold back the soul catchers, but still allow the souls to find their way to Roque, the Arch Key Minder, and his minions at the Great Maze."

"Do you always need an explanation for everything?"

"Haven't you wondered how anyone can be prepared to answer Roque's question to enter the maze leading to Celios? Or to answer the lesser key minders at the Maze's every junction to finally earn the key to Celios? And another thing—"

"All right Arli-girl, that's enough. Why do you always do this?" Mama set her mug on the tiny steel table next to her side of the couch. "It's like you intentionally look for storms to lead in—"

"Like the arli fireflies that came out to warn us this storm was coming, right?" A loud thump—something frighteningly large hit the house. "Why do you always tell me that? Why am I always at fault when someone doesn't like what I say?" Or think. Or feel.

"That's what we need to talk about."

Of course it was. Ari winced as something else crashed into the house. Maybe the storm was reaching level five now.

Mama leaned in close. "Get those hackles of yours down and listen to me. Really listen to me. This is important."

"I'm listening, Mama." She met Mama's insistent gaze to prove the point.

"Good. It's time you start acting like the grown woman you are." Mama leaned back and crossed her arms over her chest as though she were talking to a little girl. Mama knew very well how upsetting that particular posture was.

So much for not wanting Ari's hackles raised. "How can you say that? I've been working at the Yard full-time since I was sixteen. Nine years now. How is that not being an adult?"

"I know you work hard. I appreciate it. I'm not faulting your work. But it isn't always enough to work hard, you have to work smart, too."

Ari bit her tongue. Mama was not the person to be lecturing about smart choices.

"I get it. You don't think it was a wise choice for me to retire from the Comfort Guild and settle with Joco. But you weren't around in those days. It was what I wanted. Both to leave the Guild and to settle with Joco. He wanted me and I, him."

"Despite the fact he already had an equal partner in Bithy?"

"That partnership was a business arrangement, and everyone involved acknowledged that. A person can only have one equal partner. Settling with him gave us both what we wanted. I'm happy with the life I've had with him. I've been free to leave it at any time, without the entanglements an equal partnership would have had. And ... I've been free to have Sander's companionship, too. It has been an advantageous arrangement for all of us."

"That may be how you see it, but it's always been a little different for me." Even if Bithy wasn't supposed to be jealous, everything she did screamed of it, coloring every interaction she had with Ari.

"Yes, Bithy has been a storm of her own for you. That's part of the reason neither Joco or Sander has claimed any connection to you—if Joco claimed you, it would have been the Hell Cat's own party, and Joco would have refused the support he offered for you if Sander had."

"So which one of them was it who seeded me?"

"I understand, it's been hard not knowing."

"That's not the word I'd have used for it." Ari touched the little scar behind her left ear, the one Sander had put there when he officially declared there was no connection between them. Joco's near-constant reminders that there was no connection between him and her hurt almost as much as that burn. It wasn't supposed to, but it did.

"Trust me, it's best for now that you let the matter rest. It'll all come out when it needs to. Don't go poking into a trask's nest like that when you don't need to."

It wasn't the first time Mama had told her that. Ari rolled her eyes.

"You're right, they've been harsh with you. But knowing who seeded you would only have made it worse—for everyone. They're both difficult men and it doesn't take much to get their backs up. Sander's full-blooded Theran, and that's the way they are. If you'd grown up with him on Thera, it would have been the same. And Joco—he's not the warm, soft type, but he's a good man, a good Guild Master. People have made him the most powerful Guild Master on the whole of Lighten. Do you realize what that means?"

That people were brutish and stupid and couldn't identify a problem unless it bit them on the nose like the venomous trasks she wasn't supposed to stir up. "Apparently not."

Mama pinched her temples and shook her head. "He's got a lot more to manage than a regular person. Nearly all those things you resent so much about him are because of that."

"Like him being cheap, controlling, and resistant to anything new or even just different than his precious Guild standards?"

"Frugality has kept body and soul together for so many in the Transport Guild. That's how he lives, that's how he teaches his people to live."

"Frugal is one thing, but stingy and cheap is another. And for everyone that admires Joco's frugality, I promise you there's at least one more who says he's a cheap soul catcher who doesn't—"

"That's enough." Mama slapped the couch cushion. "You are so focused on keeping that ridiculous ship Sander left you flying, that you ignore the bigger things around you. If you would only adhere to the Guild rules like everyone else does, Joco would give you those flight clearances you say you want so badly. You realize Lighten's in a very precarious place, don't you? As a settled moon, it's not like we have the say that Thera and Dextra have in the system. The fact that we orbit the twin planets doesn't seem to make either one of them particularly willing to claim an equal connection to us. They barely recognize our independence and consider us primitive, second-class citizens, settled by second-borns with no inheritance and outright criminals desperate to leave their planets."

"We're considered primitive because Joco and the Guild Master before him have fought to keep out new technologies—"

"Joco is fighting tooth and nail to keep us independent from both Dextra and Thera. We've been through that—"

"That was a long time ago, Mama. Things have changed. The Dextrines and Therans aren't like that anymore."

"Perhaps not the Dextrines so much, but I still don't trust their new prattle about system unity. And Therans, they never change." Mama meant Sander. And if he was standard for a Theran, she was probably right.

"Joco restricts modern technology that would put us in a better position to compete with both planets. He refuses to give flight clearances to anyone he hasn't certified himself. We can't even make modifications to our own ships without the Guild shoving their noses right up our—"

"He is trying to ensure our transport systems are safe and remain under local control. That hasn't always been the case. You don't understand what it was like then."

But "then" was in a time before Mama had been born. It wasn't like she knew firsthand, either. There was no one still alive from those days to give perspective on what was truth and what was opinion. And there were plenty of opinions. Not all of them agreed with Joco.

"I know you don't like his methods, but there are quite a few of us who believe that what Joco has done for Lighten as a whole is critical to our future. We support him." Mama sighed, that big long-suffering sigh she must have learned from her mother before her. "And you're fighting him at every turn."

"You believe that, but it looks different from where I sit. Those flight clearances you say I *want*, I've outright earned. I've ticked every standard to have earned them, and he still won't budge. How is that right? He uses that to limit me to the lowest-paying jobs in the Yard. If I didn't take the off-Records work—"

"Have you considered he limits you because you refuse to follow Guild standards? How can you expect him to give you more freedoms if he can't trust you with what you have? And exactly how much off-Records work—"

"And another thing, the drowned parts. Every part, down to every screw and nut, has to be Guild-sanctioned, even if there are others that are just—"

"It is a safety issue. If parts aren't regulated, ships won't be maintained properly, and we all suffer. The Guild Master before Joco had to deal with a transport system that was falling apart because of unregulated parts and so-called improvements to existing vessels. Lighten had earned the reputation for being primitive—you could barely get from downtown Paxton to the Ship Yard without seeing half a dozen broken-down transports with their passengers hoping to catch a ride back to civilization. That's what not regulating such things got us."

"There're other ways to accomplish that without the Guild keeping us from even breathing without their approval. Not to mention that there's no reason to force me to pay the Guild for maintenance, repairs, and adjustments that I'm perfectly capable of accomplishing myself."

"Don't get started on that again. You're not qualified to make adjustments on ships, as you call them. You're thinking too well of yourself. Pilots reckoning they were mechanics and technicians was one of the things that got us into so much trouble before Joco and his predecessor."

"So, we're stuck in the past, making do, while Thera and Dextra laugh at us for being primitive and backward, and the Raiders run roughshod over all of us."

"All that modern technology you're going on and on about isn't keeping the Raiders away from Thera and Dextra. Joco's limits are necessary until Lighten develops our industry and resources enough so that we won't have to rely on Dextra and Thera. Once we achieve that—"

"You really believe things are going to change then?" Ari stared straight into Mama's eyes.

"Things would change for you if you'd button up and fly right. Do you understand how your rebellion is a genuine threat to Joco?"

"No. That's Joco being resentful of what he hasn't been able to control." Ari rolled her eyes and turned aside. "This little arli-bug, as he's so fond of calling me, is no threat to the mighty Transportation Guild Master. I fly a barely third-rate cargo hauler on insignificant runs. No one pays attention to that."

"You're wrong."

"Then someone's been spying on me and taking word to him, 'cause there's no other reason for anyone to pay any mind to me. Palmer—"

"Speaking of Palmer—"

Now it was Ari's turn to slap the couch. "No, I'm not having this conversation again. You know what he is, and I'm not having him."

"You may want to reconsider that." Mama's expression shifted.

"I don't much like the look on your face. What's going on?"

"Joco's losing patience with you and isn't willing to have you about without someone to keep a close eye on you."

"What have you been telling Joco about me?"

"Not me. More people than you realize are aware of your rule-skirting. He's been willing to tolerate it because I'm here with you, to keep it from going too far. But ... well, you need to realize how much you owe him. He's given me a lot for your support. Not to mention, he helped you learn to fly, gave you work before you were of legal age. He's paid forward a great deal on your behalf. Is this really the way you want to treat him for that?"

"He paid forward the bare minimum of hospitality—I know you don't see it that way, but I do. And yes, I do appreciate the bare minimum, it was more than nothing, but I hardly think that means I should settle with his partner's hot-tempered, drunken son because of it."

"Do you have any idea what's going to happen if you continue to thwart his authority and dodge his rules behind his back? What do you think that's paying forward? Keep on this path, Ari, and Joco is going to cancel all your credentials and throw you out altogether. And I won't be here to do anything about it. You have to consider your future."

Ari started and blinked several times. "You won't be here—what do you mean?"

"I'm sure you've noticed things haven't been easy with me and Joco for years now."

He hadn't come around in quite some time, and life had been much more pleasant for it.

"I've picked up with Sander again—"

"The same man who up and disappeared for five years? And you're good picking up with him again? Just like that?"

"My affairs are none of your business, but no, there was a great deal more to it than simply disappearing. All you need to know is I'll be leaving with him in a few weeks. And it's a situation where you can't join us."

"Where is it you're going?"

"I can't tell you. Not won't, can't."

Ari bit back a dozen different responses.

"And that's why you need to settle with Palmer, at least for a little while, to sort out what you're going to do next."

"No, I'll move to the workers' dormitories. There are open berths there." With little more than a sleeping pod and a storage locker to call her own, it wouldn't be much, but she could get by for a while that way.

"I'm not sure Joco's going to allow that."

"Then I'll leave the Yard and find work elsewhere."

"Without Joco's support or recommendation, those opportunities are going to be few and far between. And, more than likely, far worse than life with Palmer."

"I don't need that controlling, arrogant—"

"You don't know what you need. You don't know what the Guild, what Lighten needs. And yet you stand ready to push your own agenda, regardless of who it hurts. How can you be so selfish? You complain about what Joco has paid forward—what about you? Have you considered the kind of hospitality you have offered him?"

That was a punch to the gut, and Mama knew it. No matter how hard Ari worked to extend hospitality to everyone, it was never enough, especially when Joco was involved. There was nothing that would satisfy, nothing that would please, no effort would ever be enough. "You may believe in all you've said about … about everything. But I don't. I can't. And I won't. Thank you for the warning, but I'm not settling with Palmer." Ari stood, hands shaking, and set her mug on the floor. She crossed the few steps to her room to retrieve her boots and work jacket.

"Where are you going? We're in the middle of a level four storm. It's not safe. You can't—"

"I have to. I can't breathe in here anymore." Ari stuffed herself into her jacket and boots and slid the door open just far enough to slip out into the raging winds.

Cold, stinging rain tore at her face, pummeling her in wind-driven pulses that screamed loud enough to drown out her own thoughts. She pointed herself with her back to the wind and let it propel her into a blind run along the narrow path, paved with permeable concrete, which would float on the waters as they rose. That would keep her safe from the flooding swamp as long as she stayed on the path, and the storm itself would keep the dangerous fauna at bay. She shivered as the rain saturated her jacket. It was cold, yes, but not dangerously so. Not yet. At least she would be able to breathe.

A sudden downdraft surrounded her with the pungent, chlorine odor of ozone. Lightning flashed and thunder cracked so close, her skin prickled and tingled.

Splintering ... groaning .... Crack! Only immense trees made that sound!

She ran ahead, away from the sound, as something massive crashed through the surrounding trees.

Metal squealed and folded with a hideous crunch.

She stumbled as she turned. The pod house collapsed under the weight of an enormous tree.

Chapter 2

THERE WAS LITTLE WORSE than being forced to sit, blind, deaf, and dumb in the passengers' cabin, while pilots less competent than himself fumble-fingered their way through their job. The little transport might look like a luxury model from the inside with high-end fittings, comfortable seats, and plenty of leg and shoulder room, not to mention he was the only passenger in the eight-seat cabin. But what mattered right now was the contents of the engine compartment and the cockpit, and neither one seemed up to his standards.

Matteo Sennet muttered his exhaustive list of expletives under his breath, recited in alphabetical order. A solid way to keep his mind off the Raiders breathing down their necks.

Abadon's Gates ... Aimless maze-wanderer... Arrogant soul catcher's arse ...

His module—not the cockpit, they were as tight-lipped as Roque the Arch Key Minder about everything—warned him that the ship had entered that swath of space between Thera and Dextra that hovered outside the jurisdiction of both. The most dangerous place in the Kayavan System.

Smarter pilots would have avoided this region, instead flying in Lighten's shadow as it circled the twin planets. But no, this crew had something to prove, though only the Key Minder knew what it might be.

For the love of life and limb! Yes, it was a longer path. Yes, Lighten's defenses were primitive compared to Theran and Dextrine technologies, but primitive defenses were still better than being exposed in a father-forsaken, poorly shielded, unarmed ship.

For the love of life and limb. Father-forsaken. Those set his expletives out of order. He'd have to start over.

That or storm the cockpit and take over flying himself.

But he wasn't qualified for this model and wouldn't be able to do much, even if he took the pilot's seat. That was probably intentional. Cracking, splintering shards—also out of order.

The emergency klaxon shrieked, like it had at graduation …

Uncle Artain waited in line, near the entrance to the amphitheater, brushing dust off the sleeve of his dark suit. His way of implying he was surrounded by substandard company. Matteo, in his formal, all black cadet uniform—the last time he would wear it—stepped up to escort Artain to his seat.

"I do not understand the meaning of this demonstration," Artain grumbled.

"It is a show of honor to our patriarchs—or those who are standing in for them."

"Don't go on about that. Father could not clear his calendar to be here. By all rights, Wroxton Academy's administration should have rescheduled for him."

"Here is your seat, uncle. I will see you after the ceremony."
Matteo proceeded to the seating reserved for the graduating
cadets. To the space reserved for the top graduate.

At one time, he'd dreamt of Grandfather seeing him in this
place, giving the valedictory address. But Grandfather couldn't
be bothered. His absence did not diminish Matteo's accom-
plishments—or so he would tell himself until he believed it.

Wroxton Academy's headmaster called the audience to or-
der...

Klaxons blared. Blasts of weapons fire bombarded the sta-
tion. Screaming—so much screaming.

Chaos.

"Raiders have been sighted. Take emergency precautions."
An artificial voice droned through the cabin speakers. The
kind of voice that made him wonder if there were actual
flesh-and-blood pilots in the cockpit.

Matteo fastened his emergency straps as the cabin lights
dimmed and an oxy-mask and blanket dropped into his lap
from an overhead compartment.

Exactly like the ones they'd used at graduation.

Matteo mustered cadet teams for their emergency assign-
ments—getting nonessential personnel to the safe rooms at the
heart of the station. They dispersed through the terrified sea of
visitors.

Power failed and emergency lighting and life support kicked
in. Dark, cold, heart pounding, hard to breathe. Still had a
job to do. His team gathered their charges and wrangled them
to the safe room, where oxy-masks and blankets helped relieve
their most immediate needs.

Too many visitors packed into the safe room. No other choice.

"Prepare for sudden course change and turbulence. Passengers are not to leave their seats unless directed to do so by
the crew."

Matteo settled his oxy-mask in place and fought to breathe
normally. Not like he did when the school staff had ordered him

and his team into the safe room, to be locked inside, trapped. Like he was in this ship.

Uncle Artain? Matteo checked his module. Artain had not checked into a safe room.

Module tracking located him. A group must be trapped in a secondary corridor.

Two volunteers from his team followed him through dark, cold, smoky corridors. Past the dead—several whom he knew, their faces etched into memory.

They were burned, probably exposed to spewing, broken control conduits. Nothing could have helped them. But their faces were locked in cries for help.

They pulled pry bars from emergency lockers on the way to a jammed bulkhead door. The pounding, the voices of the trapped.

They smashed the locking mechanisms with the sharp end of pry bars and forced the door open.

Two dead visitors tumbled through, but the living pushed them aside to flow out like floodwaters through a breach in a dam.

No Artain.

Matteo forced his way inside, though his team struggled to pull him back. There, in the dark corner, on his knees, struggling to breathe. Matteo dragged him out. His teammates rushed in to help. They half-carried, half-dragged Artain to a med station.

Poisoning from the ruptured control lines. Not just Artain. All of them.

But they'd gotten aid in time. Barely in time. Many hadn't.

The faces. He kept seeing their faces.

Swallowing hard, Matteo snugged his well-padded safety straps, clutched the plush armrests, pressed his heels into the rich carpeting, and began cursing from the end of the alphabet backward. That should distract him from the fact that mediocre pilots and a foolishly chosen flight plan meant he might not make it home at all.

Uncle Artain survived and returned to Dextra. He would, too.

Matteo cycled through his list three times, backwards, forwards, and from the middle, alternating forward and back. He'd have to keep that tactic in mind for particularly difficult circumstances. And he needed some fresh expletives—had to find a fresh source soon since his Wroxton Academy buddies were all now graduated and flung to all corners of the Kayavan System.

He had just finished cursing his ancestors to Abadon's Gates at the point of the soul catchers' bows when the ship touched down at Newbry Space Port, Dextra's premier interplanetary port, conveniently located in Tegris, the capital city of his home territory, Timnon.

"Landing protocols complete. Prepare to debark." The artificial voice was so calm and friendly.

Good thing he couldn't see the speaker, lest he punch it for the mere satisfaction of it. Matteo escaped his safety straps, gathered his personal effects, and hurried down the long, white boarding bridge.

"Matté!" Benton Sennet, Matteo's favorite cousin and best friend, jogged to meet him. "Point for that dramatic entrance." He pulled Matteo into a back-slapping handshake, near enough that he could hear Beny's heart pounding. Still tall and lean, Beny had filled out across the shoulders since they'd last met face-to-face.

"Don't blame me. I would have had better intel on the Raiders to plan my route getting here." He raked his hair back from his forehead. "I think things are worse than Grandfather wants us to believe."

"Not exactly news there. Come on, let's get out of here. We can talk more privately. I've got a flitter and pilot waiting. Where do you want to go first?" Beny pointed down the empty, white corridor of Newbry Space Port's private wing.

"To see Mom and Dad." The emptiness was equal parts comforting and disconcerting. Transportation hubs were supposed to be populated, weren't they?

"I figured as much. Did I ever tell you how predictable you were?"

"Nice to hear I have some redeeming qualities."

"Really. What are those?"

He cuffed Beny's shoulder. They wound their way through the maze of empty white corridors to the ground transport pick-up point. A sleek, late model flitter, replete with the latest in technology and comfort, waited for them. Beny had spared no expense to welcome him back. Jet black, with long elegant lines, it had the grace of a Raptor fighter ship, and, if he knew Beny, the durability of an armored personnel carrier wrapped in polished metal, like a huge gemstone. The sort of vehicle he'd always dreamt of riding in as a boy.

The inside was every bit as extravagant as the outside, with leather and polished wood interior fittings, soundproofing to keep the outside out, and full-surround media screens should they want to treat themselves to the illusion of some place new. It even smelled luxurious. It was hard to pinpoint why, but it did.

Beny pulled out his module and sent destination information to the pilot, offering Matteo a reprieve from dealing with people, even if it was only for a few minutes. Beny had a gift for taking care of people, which was why, to Grandfather's chagrin, he went into medicine, not politics.

Matteo dropped his bag on the floor at his feet, fastened his safety strap and melted into the deep, soft seat. The dark window tint blocked the bright afternoon sun and heat, making the flitter a quiet little haven apart from the rest of the world's demands. He closed his eyes and sighed.

He really didn't need to watch the scenery as they traveled. It wasn't as though Tegris would have changed much since his last visit. Capital cities, at least on Dextra, had an amazing propensity to avoid change.

How long had it been since he could just sit and breathe?

"I read about what happened at graduation. I'm so sorry. I wish I could have been there."

No, he wasn't going to look. He couldn't handle the expression Beny would be wearing right now. Concern mixed with the guilt that there was something more he could have—should have—done. Matteo threw his arm over his eyes. "Just as well that you weren't."

"How bad did it get?"

"Had to get all the guests into lockdown. Cadets mustered to guard the perimeter while the professionals dealt with the threat from the air. One campus facility took a direct hit, but it wasn't occupied because of graduation. But it was close enough to the amphitheater that the graduation ceremony might have been the actual target." He let his arm fall from his face and glanced at Beny. "I'm really glad you weren't there."

"That was a cracking memorable way to end your tenure at Wroxton Academy."

"Par for the course. It started in crisis, and ended in crisis, and seemed pretty much like jumping from one crisis to the next all the way in between." Matteo scrubbed his face with his hands.

"It was cruel of Grandfather to ship you off like that so soon after the accident."

"What else could we expect? He's never been known as a fount of kindness and compassion, has he?"

"No, but considering Wroxton's reputation, he outdid himself with that. Was it as bad as they say?... You never really said. I guessed it earned its reputation for a reason, but ..." Beny tried to catch his gaze, but Matteo turned aside. Beny would see far more than would be comfortable for either of them.

There was a reason Matteo had never talked about it. "You guessed right. If a bit conservatively."

Beny gulped hard and leaned closer. "Worse than that? What went on there?"

He was not prepared for the full answer to that question, and Matteo was not going to burden him with it. "The Theran military runs on Vigilance, Valor, and Victory. Anything that gets in the way of that—"

"Like compassion, tolerance, understanding?" Beny whispered.

"Pretty much. Those take second, third, or fourth place to the key tenets of Theran life." Matteo rubbed his shoulder, thin hard scars under his fingertips, a memento from Wroxton he'd always carry.

"Kayavan's bones, Matté, I wish I'd known."

"Best that you didn't. It would have made you soul catcher crazy. Not to mention, since you were left here to deal with the family's insanity, you had enough on your hands." Matteo huffed and pulled himself up a little straighter. "I made it out the other side, and with a few useful achievements to show for it. So, there's that, right?"

"Advanced standing in statistical systems modeling, interplanetary strategic organization, and supply chain security is more than a little useful. And you earned pilot's clearances on the side. You definitely weren't slacking there."

"Glad someone thinks so." Matteo forced a laugh.

"You know better than to give Grandfather's grousing any credence." But he criticized Beny as much as he did Matteo, and it bothered Beny more. "Given any thought to what you're going to do now?"

Matteo bit his tongue. Beny was not implying he was going to sit around and do nothing like Grandfather would. "Things with the Raiders are getting worse, as my flight here proves, and all the posturing about Dextra, Thera, and Lighten being separate, unconnected entities isn't helping. It took all of us to make them, it'll take all of us to take them down."

"That's going to be a hard sell. Therans are impossible to work with and Lighten insists on primitive technology for reasons I can't begin to understand. It's hard to believe that trying to work with them has any hope of succeeding."

"I hear that a lot. But truth is, I'm convinced we're hopeless if we don't."

"I imagine you've already worked out how you're going to single-handedly bring the whole system into harmony, working together to conquer the foe, and live happily ever after." Beny cocked his head and lifted an eyebrow, as if to suggest that was not what Matteo was intent on doing.

What was wrong with having big goals and an even bigger imagination on how to accomplish them? But maybe now was not the time for discussion. Beny was by his nature an optimist, but even he had his limits. "Of course. And tomorrow, I'll abolish all political matchmaking, and set us all free of that dreadful practice."

"You don't dream small, do you, buddy?"

"Why bother unless you're going all in, right?" He turned to peer out the dark-tinted window. If Beny got a good look at his face now, there would be far too many questions that he wouldn't want to answer. Far too many.

The flitter touched down in a private berthing hangar, a generous structure of steel and concrete, nondescript from the outside, a place that encouraged one to overlook it. A very admirable quality. Better still, it was quiet and nearly empty.

The flitter slid into its berth as though it were a natural habitat. Beny's module pinged with a signal declaring it safe to exit the craft.

It was tempting to stay inside the safe little cocoon for a bit longer. But that wouldn't be fair to Beny.

"You want me to go with you?" Beny touched Matteo's shoulder.

"I'd rather have some time alone with them if you don't mind."

"No problem. I'll wait here, then, and work on dinner arrangements."

"Please, no, I'm not up to a big party." Matteo squeezed his eyes shut and tried to temper the grimace seizing his face.

"I promise, only a few people who you actually want to see. Remember, I'm the one you can trust with these things. Yes?"

"Yeah, I know. But ... oh, all right. Just don't blow that reputation now." It wasn't fair to worry that Beny would, but too many others had, and it left a mark.

"I got your back." Beny slapped his shoulder as Matteo ducked out.

Matteo paused beside the flitter and took in the cold angular efficiency of the concrete hangar, with its regular, and mostly empty, berthing places, each marked with a painted white number and yellow wall stripes to assist the auto-parking features present in every vehicle. Faint traces of chemical exhaust hung in the air, not yet scrubbed away by the low-roaring fans in the ceiling above. How many times had he walked this hangar, this pathway? Too many to count. And there would be countless more such journeys in the future.

Fifty-eight steps to the hangar exit. Warm afternoon air embraced him as he stepped into the incongruous green space surrounded by Tegris' large, imposing, modern architectural marvels, hemming it in, containing it and those who dwelt there.

Sixty-three steps from the door, down the tree-lined gravel path through the quiet, manicured park. Fifty-six more steps to the little path into the "natural" woods, the only sound the crunch of the gravel underfoot.

Though the woods might be called "natural," they were still a meticulously curated creation of master gardeners, resembling a natural thicket enough that he could pretend. He would have to get away from the city soon. Tegris was nice enough, but it had nothing to the untouched, unspoiled glories of his father's hunting lodge, deep in the Resprith Mountains. That's where he needed to go. Soon.

A polished white marble mausoleum, complete with half a dozen intricately carved columns, ironwork doors, and the Sennet name engraved over the lintel, peeked through the impeccably groomed trees, manicured into an artful submission to the expertly crafted marble monument.

And there went the semblance of natural.

Matteo pressed his thumb to the lock plate on the iron doors. With a solid click, they parted and invited him inside. The echo of his footsteps on the marble floor called forth the deep loneliness that he usually managed to keep filed, tucked away in a little box within his chest, pretending it wasn't even there. Discreet lights near the ceiling came on to light each segment of the hall as he passed through, welcoming him into the tomb of his ancestors.

In theory, the space had been designed to fill one with awe and reverence. But the truth was, he hated this place.

A short flight of steps took him downstairs into the crypt proper. Mom and Dad rested near the foot of the steps, the traditional resting place of the crypt's newest occupants. Eventually, they would be moved to a less prestigious spot, as they were replaced by newly departed souls. He sat on an ornate marble bench near them, staring at their names engraved on the end stone of the burial vaults. Audra Sennet. Durand Sennet. Their formal titles, as well as their dates of birth and death, were etched below their names, but those didn't really matter.

Those names said everything. At least to those who had known them, they did.

"It's been fifteen years, now, Mom, Dad. You've been gone longer than you were here with me. And I really hate that." He swallowed back a painful lump in his throat. "I just graduated Wroxton Academy, with my advanced standing studies. I defied Grandfather, and I studied all the organizational and modeling subjects you taught me to love, not the political sciences that he had wanted. And I became a pilot, just like I told you I would. A good one. I did my studies for you, but I fly for myself. I know you would have wanted that."

He covered his mouth with his hands, rocking lightly on the bench. "Wroxton was hard, Dad, really hard. I understand why you didn't want me to go there. I didn't have a choice, though. I promise you, I won't send my children there, assuming I have any. But I learned a lot. Not all of it what I wanted to learn, but I hope I can put it all to good use. "

He braced his elbows on his knees and laced his hands behind his neck until his heart stilled enough to continue. "I'm back now, but don't ask me what's next. That's the Key Minder's own question. You know, they used to call me Roque the Key Minder back at school. Apparently, I got your knack of asking tough questions, Mom. But they accuse me of being like you, too, Dad. I haven't let go of your ideals, believing that unity is better than isolation. And no, it's no easier an argument now than it was when you left.

"I'll be meeting with Grandfather to talk it over next month. His schedule is too busy to be bothered until then. But maybe it's just as well, I need some time to process a lot of things." He leaned back and dragged his sleeve across bleary eyes. "Whatever's going to happen next, I hope I can make you proud."

"I'm sure you will." Beny laid his hand on Matteo's shoulder.

"I didn't hear you come in."

"I didn't mean for you to." He sat beside Matteo. "I miss them, too. I've never stopped resenting them for dying and cheating me out of the escape they provided me from my parents."

"I know they meant a lot to you, too."

"I still want to be like them when I grow up." Beny leaned his shoulder into Matteo's.

"Me, too." He tipped his head sideways to glance at Beny. "Would you hate me if I told you I've always resented that it was Mom and Dad in that accident, not your parents?"

"Not at all. You might be the guy we're all supposed to look up to as the paragon of all virtue, but you're still only a man, right?"

Matteo laughed because if he didn't, he would find himself lost in grief all over again. "How do you do it? Always come up with the right thing to say? I always stick my foot in my mouth and make it all the worse trying to pull it out again."

"Part of my job, I guess. But don't, you're the one doing all the heavy lifting."

Somehow, hearing someone acknowledge it suddenly made the weight real. His shoulders sagged.

"You holding up all right?"

"About as well as can be expected. Not as much as I'd like, though."

"Going hungry won't help. How 'bout we meet up with Niles and Bryce for dinner?" Beny glanced at his module. "They've confirmed that they're available, and they're waiting on the details on where to meet."

"Their wives, too?"

"Your choice? It can be cousins only or cousins plus, whatever you're up for."

"Only them, though, not your sisters ... sorry, foot in mouth but—"

Beny silenced him with an open hand. "No need for apologies. I know them even better than you do, and no, not them. You'll get your fill of them soon enough, I'm sure."

"I think just the four of us for right now. I'm ... too raw for better company."

"Then us four and no more it shall be." Beny tapped his module and slid it back into his chest pocket. "I booked the private room at our favorite pub, where no one will bother us."

"And they still have all the privacy guards up?"

"That's why it's our favorite. Let's go before you get so deep in your own head that I can't get you back out. And promise me, you'll try to enjoy yourself a bit. Doctor's orders."

"Only for you, Beny."

Chapter 3

Sunrise was the right time for a soul's last honors. Some said it was because the sky wore the bright red of mourning. Tradition said that color directed the departed souls away from this realm and into Laythe's Woods to be chased by the soul catchers to Abadon's Gates or find their way to the key minders at the Great Maze leading to Celios.

Others argued it was because it was early enough in the day that the swamp's heat wouldn't make one grieve the memorial as much as their loss.

Ari stared into the sky. The night's darkness had been driven back in a sky painted red and orange and gold. The planets that Lighten orbited winked in the first light of day. Thera peeked above the horizon, while Dextra bowed to the inevitable, retreating below. Today, Kayavan's star rose high above Thera, almost as though Kayavan himself noticed the lack of attendees and sought to make up for it.

Perhaps it was fanciful to look at it that way. But at such a time, one was entitled to find meaning where one could. Or at least one should be. Besides, Mama would have appreciated the notion.

Mottled clouds cluttered the brilliant, crimson sky. The slightest cloying-hot breeze, carrying the heavy, sweet scent of the honey vines that climbed the nearby trees, encouraged the bay's waters to sway the long ceremonial dock, heaving it this way and that, enough to remind one of the uncertainties of all things.

Or at least that was what the sweaty, overdressed officiant said. Long pants, long shirt, waistcoat, coat, neckcloth, and a hat, all black, as though that made things official somehow. At the very least, they should have been mourning-red.

Ari's fingers chafed as the unfinished wooden handle of the commemoration basket, holding gifts of flowers and fruits for the departed, forced splinters into her calloused palm. Impossibly tall and lean, Joco seemed unperturbed as he held the other side. His weathered, tanned face glistened in the heat. His red shirt, already soaked with sweat, clung to him like a jealous lover, like his first woman, who left for downtown Paxton on a matter of imagined urgency to avoid Mama's final remembrance.

It wasn't so odd for a man's equal partner to attend his lover's memorial. Really, it was just good manners. Which explained Bithy's absence. And her daughters'. They always followed her lead.

It didn't explain why the boys kept away, though. Mama had always been kind to them, all six of them, mothering them when Bithy was too busy with her own business to bother. No doubt Bithy had threatened them with whatever it took to make sure Mama's farewell was a lonely one. A jealous trump card Bithy played at the very end. She had won the last hand.

For all her imperfections, Mama hadn't deserved that.

The breeze changed direction, and the red scarf Ari had tied around her neck over her drab green shipyard coveralls slapped her across the face. She jumped, nearly losing her grip on the basket.

"Stop woolgathering, Arli-girl. Show your mother some respect," Joco hissed like an angry swamp lizard whose nest had been disturbed. Not a patient man on good days. Today was not a good day.

One day, Ari would snap back when he jumped on her that way. Tell him exactly what she was thinking.

But not today.

Still, it was Bithy's brood he should be saying that to, not her. But that would never happen. His first woman's spawn, all seeded by other men before he and Bithy partnered, did little wrong in the world and had their places in life secured. Favors never bestowed on the woman he actually cared for, or her child.

Not the time to be dwelling on that, either.

Somber in the way a man was paid to be in such a moment, the officiant trundled toward them, the dock heaving and bucking with his every step. Another part of the show—no one who made a living on the docks could truly be such a lumbering oaf.

He took the basket from them and recounted the myth of Kayavan. The progenitor of all in the Kayavan System lived, died, then was called forth by the Hell Cat's roar. He wandered Laythe's Woods, avoiding the Arch Soul Catcher's arrows and dodging the Arch Key Minder's questions, refusing to end his final journey, to stay forever with the Hell Cat and watch over his progeny. Thus, Kayavan became a star that would regularly visit his children.

The officiant pointed to the faint traces of the Kayavan comet and the Hell Cat constellation that stood out against the dim cloud of stars known as Laythe's Woods, a forced dramatic emphasis in his memorized speech. Perhaps trying to make up for the lack of any feeling or soul in his words and give Ari a chance to create a worthwhile memory of this event.

Ari and Joco muttered the called-for responses, their voices the only ones speaking for the dead.

Drown it all! Mama should have better than this. She might have been a settled-for lover, who offered no equal value in their relationship, but she was the one Joco turned to for comfort and understanding. That was worth something, wasn't it?

The officiant scattered pink-speckled flower petals and the tiny, tart red swamp fruits that Mama had loved along the gray-green water's surface. Tiny fish rose to nibble at the offerings, pulling them below the surface, symbolic of the end of the traditional month of remembrance.

Now was the time she was supposed to cry. If only all her tears had not already been spent weeping alone in the night, where none would pretend to share her grief or decide when she had grieved enough. She dabbed the corners of her eyes with her mourning scarf. That should be sufficient to satisfy Joco.

The officiant would not care.

They followed him back to shore, before the sollerts—Lighten's most famous export, unofficial mascot, and official fiercest predator—gathered to feast on the burgeoning mass of fish. The little ones would attract bigger ones, until the water was full of threat to life and limb, separated from them only by a swaying, undulating dock underfoot.

At least their staggering and lurching as they hurried back would make a good show of their grief in the Records, if anyone decided to check them.

But who would? Maybe the shadow that ducked behind the trees on the bank. The one that looked like Sander. How did he feel now, after waiting so long, that his plans with Mama would never come to fruition?

Not her problem.

The officiant lumbered back to his climate-controlled office, while she and Joco turned away to the barren landing field, empty but for the flitter they had arrived in. A reminder of the empty exercise the memorial had been. But it had been the best she could afford when Joco, true to form, refused to contribute to the effort with the same hollow excuses he always used.

Not frugal; he was stingy and cheap. He claimed he would pay her back later.

But just how long was a "later"?

Joco thumbed his module to open the ship yard's flitter, sweat beading on the planes and angles of his chiseled face. Technically a commercial transport, with "Paxton Ship Yard" emblazoned in large blocky black letters across both sides, the oblong, ocher-yellow vehicle sat on half a dozen squat wheels that would retract once they took off. It looked like a striped summer beetle at the end of the season, when they were ragged and worn and ready to molt and bury themselves underground to wait for the next time the red swamp fruit trees bloomed.

Joco did not appreciate the comparison, so she kept the observation to herself.

He stood beside the flitter, glaring over the top of it, one of the advantages of being taller than anyone had a right to be. "Straight back, nothing fancy. There's no needing any o' your showing off today. Too much work to be done. A big storm's coming in, and we got to leave for the Championships as soon as it passes."

"It's not too late for you to book passage to Anara on a proper private transport. You'd be more comfortable that way." Maybe, just maybe...

"No point in paying for the luxury when you can do the job for me. Besides, you've been doing a lot of work on that old ship and questions are being asked. I'd like to see the answers firsthand."

"I'm not done with all the work it needs."

"Get it done before the storm." He didn't have to add "or else"; his tone carried the threat effectively.

Drown it! Drown it! Drown it! She ducked into the pilot's seat, ignoring the smells of old sweat and humidity that lingered in the cabin. "It'll be ready. Everything will be ready."

"See that it is, Arli-girl."

Did he have to call her that now?

Joco folded his lanky frame into the confined flitter seat and shut the door, elbows and knees barely fitting inside. He tucked his chin to his chest and closed his eyes. Not sleeping, his way of saying he wanted to be alone in himself for a while.

Just as well, there wasn't much to say.

Preflight checks helped settle the undercurrent of irritation prickling under her skin. The flitter was old, which meant simple, basic, stripped-down, but it still flew, so Joco wasn't about to retire it. No, he liked to keep the old ships flying as long as they could. Hard to want to retire them when the Guild, and thus he, profited from every part made for them. Not only was the Yard flitter old, but it lacked the luxury systems to ensure an easy and comfortable flight. Not hard to fly per se, but hard to fly comfortably. That was her job.

But for all that, the compact economy of the control board was pleasing, and more importantly, easy to reach for someone not technically tall enough to pass pilots' quals. Another one of Joco's excuses for not assigning her to fly the bigger haulers, the ones that came with better-paying jobs. Bloody annoying when those ships were virtually identical to what she was already flying.

Paying for the memorial, such that it was, had left her accounts looking lean. She'd have to press him about extending her flight clearances again soon.

But not today.

She stabbed the power control a little more forcefully than she should, tearing the fragile yellow membrane over the switch. One more thing she'd have to fix before Joco noticed it. The control board came to life with blinking lights, gauges, a flood of information that intimidated most commuter flyers. Which was why they preferred autopilot models that would get them from here to there in safe, local corridors where the biggest surprise was a drunk flier veering out of its assigned corridor.

Those were the least of her worries.

She scanned the readouts. Everything looked good. All systems solid enough for this flight. Maintenance would have to come soon, but not today. With three taps, she filed the flight plan with the local control.

And ... approved. Best get moving before Joco got restless.

A few bumps under the wheels to get to the takeoff zone. The engine hummed, then whined, complaining that it should have to fly again after so short a respite. Balky little thing. But it obeyed her touch and leapt into the air, happy to settle into a slow—ponderously slow—navigation plane back to the Ship Yard, where nothing "fancy" would be demanded.

She would save "fancy" for paying jobs.

Distraction, she needed some distraction to keep from losing her mind at this pace. She flipped on the news feeds and turned the volume down low. Better that than being alone in her head right now.

After an extended absence, the Kayavan comet has once again revisited our skies. Many have been calling upon the Kayavan legend to explain the unusually active storms we have been seeing ...

And those were the same folks that believed that sollerts could leap out of the swamp, sprout legs, and chase them down. She flipped to another news feed.

Fleet needs pilots!

No, enough of that. If Joco heard that, he would come apart at the seams.

Reliable sources warn of increased Raider activity near the Firen Mine works headquarters in the High Jipny Desert...

Old news. The Raiders were everywhere these days, but they'd been hitting Firen Mines especially hard. When she needed news on the Raiders, though, it was the pilots' chatter feed she needed to listen to.

And the latest from Anara, home of the Lighten Ring Fighting Championships...

Finally, something worth listening to.

For the first time this year, representatives from Dextra and Thera will participate in exhibition bouts against some of Lighten's top fighters. It will certainly be interesting to see what they can do against our top warriors.

Warriors? Ring fighters were scrappy soul catchers who she wouldn't want to cross paths with if they lost a match. She glanced at Joco, who didn't stir—but they were athletes, not warriors. The Raiders, they were warriors. The kind who killed without hesitation, the kind she'd rather not share airspace with. Big difference.

We have received official confirmation that the much-anticipated match between Mining Guild Master Brels Da and Transport Guild Master Joco Hol will take place.

After Joco's near loss to rival Danz Bek...

It wasn't a near loss. Joco lost the fight but won the election, something no one believed could happen. But Danz—

...led to rumors that Joco might be unfit for the ring and possibly his seat as Guild Master. But we're certain all that deadfall will be swept away as we watch Joco and Brels, the premier fighters of our day, take it to the ground in the final climactic match of the Championships.

The bookmakers are already declaring it will be too close to call a favorite. It's going to be a match to remember for sure.

"Damn right." Joco muttered. "Gonna be dodging the Soul Catchers at Abadon's Gates when I get through."

He wasn't exaggerating. They'd be lucky if he didn't spend a day or two in hospital before he was declared fit to fly back.

"Good thing I've got a light touch with fragile cargo."

He snorted and settled deeper into his seat.

It was true, though. There was no one with a softer touch than hers—takeoffs and landings that passengers and cargo barely felt. Joco was willing to admit that. But her other skills, like outflying Raiders in the shipping lanes and in the restricted travel corridors no one was supposed to fly in—that, he'd never give her credit for. If he did, he'd have to pay her for them, and cheap was his way of life.

Joco avoided thinking about the Raiders whenever he could, though it was getting harder and harder to get away with. Lighten's Security Corps couldn't adequately defend the shipping lanes, especially those around the mines. Chatter feed sources said the Security Corps blamed Joco for restricting the advanced fighter ships they needed. He insisted they should be classed as "transport vehicles," not weapons, and therefore controlled by Transport Guild import limitations. Old Lighten tech wasn't equal to keeping up with the Raiders. Other chatter threads went further, suggesting it might be Joco's fault if the Lighten economy took a hit from all the disrupted exports.

All issues well above the pay grade of a little arli-bug who should follow the rules and keep her place and stay away from "big things," as he called them. Not that she was bitter about that.

Arli-bug had been a cute nickname when she was small—even if no one else liked the tiny fireflies that led in the storm fronts. They were brave enough to dance along the storm's leading edge. When she was a child, she'd hoped to be that brave someday.

Unfortunately, the name stuck, and became her honest name, the one everybody used and knew her by. Being a storm-bringer didn't mean brave to them. It meant annoying.

But maybe it fit. So many of the off-Record jobs took her right to the edge of the Raiders' reach, and they were the biggest storm of all right now. Funny how Joco hated her taking off-Record jobs, but wouldn't lift a finger to provide anything that would relieve her of the necessity. One of those things that somehow made sense in his head, or perhaps his pocketbook. Hard to tell which.

... will be the match of a lifetime. And the results may be felt for that long.

While the rest of the Kayavan System may call us savage, everyone knows that the way a man fights in the ring is the best judge of his character to lead. And we're all waiting to see what the ring reveals and how it informs the election. Who knows, the next Chairman of the House of Guilds, possibly even the next President of Lighten, will be decided in that ring...

Joco snapped the news feed off.

Chapter 4

MATTEO SENNET WAITED AT the end of the long hall, leading to Clan Lord Timnon's office, deep in the heart of Tegris' political district. The artificial "fresh air" scent that the environmental systems pumped throughout burned his nostrils and left a cloying taste in the back of his mouth. Only yesterday he had returned from the hunting lodge and still knew what fresh air smelled like, and this was not it. An ornate portrait gallery that featured each of Timnon's Clan Lords and Ladies, in order of their service, with a white information platform beneath each portrait, detailing the high points of each reign, lined the walls. Somber blue carpet, thick and velvety, edged with a handspan-wide gold border, dampened the sound of footsteps as it encouraged one to continue all the way down the hall.

If he did not stop at any of the portraits, it took sixty-five seconds, walking at an appropriately brisk pace, to get to the office from here. And since he knew every posted detail of each of those Lords' service to their clan, and many that were not, he had no need to stop.

No point in showing up at the office one second before he had to. He checked his module. Three, two, one. He took the first step.

No matter how quietly he walked, he could feel the disapproving glare of each of those Clan Lords and Ladies, boring into his back. Was that a trick of the artists or his own imagination born from knowing what those people had been like?

Sixty-five seconds later, he studied the mammoth door separating him from his destiny. Broad white columns held up a carved wooden door header with the clan crest and the broadly recognized Dextrine motto: *Duty. Honor. Family.* above it. So out of place in the otherwise-modern design. But it was traditional. So, it was necessary. Such was the Dextrine way.

His module alerted that it was time for the informational briefing, as it had been noted in the invitation. Not an invitation, it was a summons, no point in pretending anything else. And it would not be a briefing—more like a cross between a lecture and an interrogation. He rolled his eyes and tapped the door signal to the left of the columns.

The door slid open, nearly silent in its motion. In theory at least, the sudden appearance of the grand interior of the office was supposed to elicit the proper sort of reverence and awe for the office of the High Lord in those who were given the honor of entering.

It elicited something, indeed, but a sense of honor? That was arguable.

Armed guards, probably the traditional pair of bonded spouses, in garish traditional uniforms with a feathered cockade atop shiny white helmets, a Timnon-blue—a dark shade of saturated blue, reminiscent of military colors, but standing out with an air of royalty—frock coat with gold buttons, and black pants too tight to allow the wearer to accomplish much of anything, stood at attention on either side of the door. Lord Timnon had taken great pride in standardizing that color. Through the years, several variants of Timnon-blue had appeared, signaling an unacceptable disorder in the Clan. One the current Lord Timnon's efforts had set to rights—a story told with pride during many official gatherings.

The guards carried flashy weapons, but the charges were kept in a locked box on the other side of the office. Stupid move in many respects, but in some ways, it made sense. Given that these particular guards were chosen for their looks—to be an attractive set of bookends—not their marksmanship, it was for the best.

Matteo had checked. He wouldn't stand on the firing range with either of those two clods, much less depend on them not to shoot the very person they were tasked with protecting. Not that anyone had ever asked for his opinion.

The joy of dealing with Dextrine Ranks.

The guards saluted, and he strode past with a cursory nod. They should have required documentation. It didn't matter that they recognized him. Sloppy.

The inner hall was thirty-seven steps long, a narrower corridor than the last. The deep red walls were lined with paintings of Timnon Clan achievements. Architecture, universities, industry, spacecraft in the Dextrine Forces. All testaments to Timnon's contributions to Dextrine civilization.

As if no other clans had been involved in those achievements.

No, that was not a helpful thought. Focus on the Timnon-blue carpet, follow the gold line to the next set of doors.

Less ornate and more practical, though painted the same bright white as the other doors, these were made of blast-reinforced Lighten steel. He pressed his palm to the pad and waited for the biometrics to process. The reading took longer than usual, twenty instead of fifteen seconds. Odd, later he would have to sort out why.

The doors slid open to reveal another pair of armed guards, most likely spouses, blocking his way. Dressed in black tactical gear and armed with working weapons, they were less dressy and more functional than their compatriots at the first doors. Some comfort there.

"Honored Clan Lord Timnon is expecting me." Matteo presented his module.

The rightmost guard inspected Matteo's identification while the other reviewed the schedule. "You are to be shown directly in, sir." Both guards bowed.

Of course he was. The guard must be new at his job. Otherwise, he'd already have known that.

Patience, patience. It wasn't fair to blame the poor sot for being new at his post. Lord Timnon would make his errors clear to him soon enough, no point in adding to the misery.

Matteo nodded and counted to himself as he marked the beats of the formal entry protocol. Bows, salutes, presentation of weapons for inspection, and, at last, an escort to the final inner sanctum doors.

There was a protocol for everything that involved Dextrine Ranks. Including breathing—thankfully, that one was rarely required. But he knew it in case anyone asked. Matteo could hold a determined Key Minder at bay, reciting all the protocols branded on his memory.

Damned lot of good it had ever done. But it was a clever party trick. There was that.

The inner guards saluted and opened the final doors. He glanced at the module. A new record this time, just over five minutes to get through the guard stations. The process seemed to get slower every time he was summoned.

Matteo brushed a bit of dust from his black—intentionally not Timnon-blue—uniform sleeve, the garb of a proud honor graduate of Wroxton Military Academy, and sucked in a deep breath. Time to face the Soul Catcher.

Fifteen regulation-length steps took him to the massive carved wooden desk, where Clan Lord Timnon waited for him.

Twice the size it needed to be, the office existed as a temple to Lord Timnon's importance. Rebuilt according to the Clan Lord's own specifications, it was a testament to how much he thought of himself. Sweeping white arches held up the night-blue ceiling five meters above them. Lighter blue walls extended twelve meters from the entry door and six meters to either side. One might have settled a small village in that space.

Viewscreens lined the walls, dark for the moment, but when important guests attended him, Lord Timnon set them to play continual loops attesting to Timnon's achievements and influential members. Noting the inaccuracies of those portrayals was not a good way to earn Lord Timnon's favor.

Every piece of furniture was oversized, handcrafted heirloom, and hideous. The amount of garishness gathered into a single space strained the eyes and one's sense of incredulity all at once. A remarkable feat, that.

The old man behind the monstrous desk wore a smart Timnon-blue suit, designed by whoever was the top designer of such things this season. It had been tailor-made for him, as was every one of his garments, and it showed. His white neckcloth was tied in a simple knot today. Was that preference or current style? Style, more likely.

If Lord Timnon's face had ever been kind, that aspect had been long since banished from his repertoire. His severe, lined visage managed only two expressions, one sincere—disdain for everyone and everything, and one insincere—a neutral mien that could be interpreted as approval, support, or whatever else the political situation required. Short silver hair framed an otherwise bald head, with shaggy white eyebrows that all but curtained sharp, observant blue eyes.

His face drew into tight knots and lines as he gazed at Matteo. Then he rose with greater strength and purpose than his looks suggested, and circled Matteo several times, searching—as he always did—for any irregularity in his uniform, any flaw he could correct. "You are late."

A favorite place to begin the tirade. "Check the Records on the guard station. I was precisely on time. It is not my fault that the new guard dithered about letting me in."

Lord Timnon wrinkled his nose and sniffed. "Quite the confident answer. Bordering on impertinent."

"I will accept responsibility for what is mine to control. If you wish more than that, train your guard better." Matteo avoided the old man's gaze.

"Still strong-willed as ever, you unlicked cub." Lord Timnon turned on his heel and returned to his seat.

"Greetings to you, Grandfather." Matteo clacked his heels together and bowed.

"I don't want a Theran salute, no matter what you learned in that splintering military academy." He rapped his knuckles on the polished desktop.

Matteo stood at attention in front of the desk. "You mean the one you personally selected for me? The one you chose because a 'proper' Theran military education would suit your purposes? Sir."

Grandfather glared.

"Perhaps you should have considered the implications of sending me to a place whose political views did not match your own."

"That will be enough from you, Lord Heir Timnon." Grandfather slapped the desk. "I don't need any more of your lip. I thought they taught you discipline at that academy."

"That they did, sir." With any luck, his jacket hid the twitch in his shoulders.

"Then show it in the presence of those who outrank you."

"Sir, yes, sir." Matteo saluted and clacked his heels.

Grandfather snarled and pointed across the room to an oblong white conference table, suitable for seating ten, but with only two chairs set out today. "Enough playing soldier. I expected it would be out of your system after you earned your advanced standings at Wroxton.... Go sit down. We have a lot to cover and not much time."

Matteo took his place at the far end of the table and flipped on his module's transcription function. The best way to cover himself when Grandfather forgot or changed his mind about Matteo's instructions. He would have preferred to trust his Clan Lord. But keeping Records had become a way of life.

Grandfather made the typical show of seating himself at the head of the table, then fiddled with the media controls until the transparent central screen dropped from the ceiling to bisect the table. Not only would it play Records visible on both sides of the table, it also allowed Grandfather to keep watch and ensure Matteo did not become distracted.

"To remind you of the history of the situation ..."

It was going to be a long afternoon.

Two hours later, Grandfather paced the long edge of the table, launching into his third repetition of the same material. If anything was worth saying, it was worth saying three times.

Matteo hunched over his module, pretending to take notes. The odds on the final qualifying match of the Planetary Championships of Lighten's Ring Fighting league had just shifted in favor of the Firen Miners Guild's entry. There was just enough time to place a small wager to make the contest a little more interesting.

"Lord Heir Timnon, are you listening to me?" Grandfather smacked the slick white table with his fist, his silvery Clan ring clattering hard enough to loosen the huge blue gem bearing the family crest.

Matteo jumped, thumbing his module to a new screen. Find the notes, find the notes ... "Yes, of course. You were saying that ..."

"You only have the future of the Clan, of Dextra itself, on your shoulders and you—" he snatched the module from Matteo's hands, "—seem more concerned about the odds on a third-rate Lighten contest than your role in your planet's future! The fight you should be interested in is the one that threatens to destroy the system as we know it."

So sarding dramatic. "I'm not convinced blaming the current Theran administration for the Raider attacks—"

"You are misrepresenting Thera's role in the origins of the current situation. Their traditional Conquest Mandate has resulted in—"

"I know, the Old Guard Therans must conquer everything they don't already control. Always have been that way, always will be. And the only difference between a Traditional Theran and a Progressive one is what they think they have a right to conquer."

Lord Timnon glowered, probably because he could not correct the description.

Matteo drew a deep breath. Calm, he needed to remain calm. It was not as if they didn't renew this conversation every time he came back from Wroxton. "But insisting that we have no connection to them, that we are not of Theran blood, only strengthens the argument that we might as well be their next conquest."

"How dare you suggest they would even consider such a thing? We are more than their equals in every way. They would not risk—"

"Have you forgotten what happened after their last great war, what, seventy-five years ago now? They exiled the fringe group who claimed they were the only 'True Therans'. The ones who insisted the Laws of Conquest gave the right to take whatever they wanted. 'No True Theran would refuse the opportunity to take what they could.' You remember that battle cry?"

"Have you forgotten that I was alive when all that happened? I remember it well. That's what led to the movement to recognize Dextrine Identity, which I proudly support to this day. We

must distinguish ourselves from those primitive warmongers."
Grandfather lifted his chin and squared his shoulders.

"Have you forgotten, or are you ignoring the repercussions of
that movement? It only solidified the exiles into the Raiders we
face now, and it made us a legitimate target for conquest in their
eyes." Matteo slapped the table, which might not have been the
best choice, but even his self-control had limits.

Grandfather threw up his hands—a sure sign he was losing
patience. "Our stance had nothing to do with the formation of
the Raiders. It was the Theran government that gave us—"

"Seventy-five years ago. The progressive administrations have
been working for the last fifty years to change that. Their political philosophers have developed a modern understanding of
the nature of Theran identity that recasts the Laws of Conquest
into a mandate to explore and settle space, not to conquer the
settlements they've already established."

"Dextra is not a Theran colony."

Not this again. "Where do you think the population of Dextra came from? The Dextrine Diaspora from Thera was an actual historical event pointed out in our own history Records."

Lord Timnon's face turned colors that would have alarmed
his doctors. "The intervening two centuries have been enough
for us to become a separate and distinct people. It is time that it
be recognized."

"As soon as we convince ourselves and the rest of the system
that we are entirely separate from the Therans, the Old Guard
Therans are going to be breathing down our necks, slavering at
the opportunity we're presenting to them."

Grandfather hurled the module onto the table. Good thing it
had been made to military specifications. "More nonsense you
learned from Wroxton Academy and their bloody progressive
leadership. Dextra will never rise to its full glory until we throw
off this ridiculous notion that we are Theran."

"I appreciate your perspective, but you fail to take into consideration the real problems—"

"Enough of your attitude, you naïve little lordling. I will not discuss this further." He pulled himself up to full height and towered over Matteo.

Best enjoy that while Matteo was still sitting down. For the last five years now, when Matteo stood, he looked down on Lord Timnon. "Then what do you wish to discuss? Sir."

"Your duty. I have an assignment for you. One even you should be able to accomplish." Grandfather rolled his eyes and stomped back to his seat.

"What do you believe my newly-complete Wroxton education has fitted me for?" What were the chances it would be anything remotely related to his study in statistical systems modeling, interplanetary strategic organization, or supply chain security? Or flying? That was the most likely option.

"You will do your duty to your Clan and homeworld as my representative to that dressed-up bar brawl that passes for politics on Lighten."

"And decides their political future." There might be something said for letting men brawl it out to decide who would run the planet.

"Uncivilized barbarians—"

Who were once settlers from Dextra and Thera, which Grandfather also conveniently forgot. "Who own the rights to the richest resources in the Kayavan System."

"Savages don't deserve any of it."

"You are sounding very Theran. The Conquest Manifesto: Suffer not the barbarian his own state. For he wastes on a night of debauchery what a son of Thera would grow into a thousand fleets, therefore—"

"That is enough out of you. Study the briefing materials for all of the scheduled meetings and events. We need to strengthen our connections among the Guilds there." Grandfather stabbed his module, and a detailed schedule appeared on the screen.

Matteo's module pinged. No doubt all the documents Grandfather wanted him to study. "Wait, what's that bit about an exhibition bout on the schedule?"

"The Lightens have opened the event to Theran, Dextrine, and even Fleet combatants. You fought at Wroxton, so you will represent us—"

"I am not sure that's a good idea." Matteo pinched his temples.

"So, they just gave you championship standing, then? You are not up to the task?" Grandfather rolled his eyes and sneered.

"I will not dignify that with a response. The issue is that the styles are so different—"

"All the information you need is in the briefing packet."

"I will go to your meetings and parties and make nice to those who pass for Rank on Lighten, but—"

Grandfather's face started changing color again. "Ignorant and ill-mannered though they may be, you would do best to control your attitude. They are smart enough to know when someone looks down on them."

"And they haven't noticed your attitude?" Probably should not have said that.

"I did not ask for your opinion. Everything I do, everything I plan, is for the benefit of the Clan. You have no idea how to manage a Clan and no right to an opinion on how I do so."

Matteo slammed his hands on the table and stood. "Perhaps if you allowed me to function as a proper Second to you instead of shipping me out—"

"You will have that training when I decide you are ready and not a moment sooner. It would behoove you to stop grasping—"

"Grasping? Grasping? No, you can look at my cousin Patryce if you want to see grasping. She's been trying to displace Benton as Heir to the Family leadership. That is grasping." Matteo stood and leaned his hands on the edge of the table. "I graduated as valedictorian of the top military academy on the whole of

Thera, which you picked for me because it was the most difficult, brutal establishment in the system. Then I returned for
advanced honor studies there, with more top marks, and yet
your favorite parting remark remains a threat to disinherit me
if I displease you? What more do you want of me?"

"Obedience, the ability to follow orders for the good of the
Clan. Do what you are told on Lighten, and I will put plans in
place for you to take your place as Second. *Duty. Honor. Family.*
Remember what you are about out there and the weight that
rests on your shoulders. Show me you can do that, and I'll give
you that position."

Lovely promise, that. But how much integrity would it cost
Matteo to see it fulfilled?

Chapter 5

THOUGH THE TRIP BACK to the Paxton Central Ship Yard only took a quarter hour, Ari had to wake Joco when she landed in the broad cement-paved field near his office. His soft snoring was the only compliment she'd hear towards her feather-soft landings, but it was nice to have that much. Waking him was like poking a needle-wasp's nest. He hated that anyone would see him fall asleep so early in the day.

He scowled at her, grunting something about berthing the flitter for the storm and that he would come by later to see that her hauler was ready for the trip to Anara. Then he sauntered off to whatever other business he had to accomplish. If the winds were with her, that would keep him busy the better part of the day. She didn't need him breathing down her neck.

She logged the flitter's maintenance needs on her module and sent them to the Yard Chief, Palmer. Chances were she'd be assigned the work, but, oh, the storms that would follow if she took it on herself to get the job done. It was procedure, and procedure had to be followed. A convenient cover when Palmer wanted to be in control as much as Joco.

Or at least he did when it gave the Yard the look of propriety on the surface so that no one was tempted to look any closer.

Not the sort of thing one commented upon out loud.

Still, getting the flitter into its hangar and battening down the Yard for the storm, that wasn't merely procedure, it was essential. Ari settled into the pilot's seat and guided the beetle-looking vehicle to the long, squat hangar building at the far west side of the yard property. With all edges rounded against the wind, the oblong green structure looked like a great egg sac from which fully formed flitters would hatch in the storm's wake.

All small, local-use vehicles had to be tucked away out of the winds before stormfall, which made a great deal of sense, even if it was far more challenging than it sounded. Her berth assignment flashed across her module, and one of the ground crew waved her through the broad open hangar doors into the space where too many vehicles had been shoehorned in, like enormous books jammed into inadequate shelving.

Exactly the way Joco liked to do things. Funny how he left his fingerprints on everything.

Bay 36 was a right pain in the ass to get into. Drowning hangar was meant to have only thirty-six bays, front, and another thirty-six in the back. But Joco organized it to have forty on each end. Those eight extra bays only fit tiny ships, so they didn't bring in that much profit. But why not pull in that extra rental revenue?

If he'd had to pay the maintenance on all the scrapes and assorted damage jamming in those four extra bays caused, he might reconsider. But as long as it was someone else's problem, he'd ignore it. And, of course, Bay 36 was the worst.

Which was why it had been assigned to her. Set in the middle of the row against the far wall, with two rows above and two rows below and just this side of being—technical-ly—large enough for the flitter, only two pilots ever berthed in that space, and the other kicked up such a storm when assigned to it, he rarely had to set in there.

She patted the control panel and whispered, "Don't get balky on me, little beetle, you'd like a solid nap, so tuck in nice and sweet for me." Did it help? Not the ship, but it helped her find the right frame of mind.

Although the flitter had working proximity sensors that should have assisted the process, she flipped them off. Too much beeping and shrieking and otherwise making a spectacle of a simple parking job one could accomplish by feel alone.

She guided the flitter down the row. The tricky part was lining up the vertical. A bright yellow sensor stripe on the wall that the proximity sensors sighted on was worn away by clumsy parking jobs so frequent no one bothered to repaint it anymore. The trick was there—a large bolt that lined up with the seam between the side window and door. One more landmark to mark the horizontal, a gash in the wall from yet another clumsy parking job. That one lined up with her shoulder. Now a little scoot to the right, and she was tucked away all nice and tight.

She popped the door and inched her way to the slide pole down to the hangar floor. She couldn't help but feel like a book falling from a bookshelf when she did that.

Hangar Chief Reed, one of Bithy's many daughters, ap-peared as Ari's feet hit the ground. Reed was tall and lean, and bent whichever way the wind was blowing, but always toward Bithy. Her drab-green Yard coverall hung from her shoulders like a flag from a pole on a windless day. "I've got three more parking jobs needing done—" She glanced over her shoulder. There were indeed three more vehicles waiting that had not been there when Ari arrived.

"Got to do maintenance on the hauler before stormfall. Joco wants to fly out as soon as we've got the all-clear." Ari tried to step around her, but Reed cut her off.

Reed huffed and folded her arms across her flat chest, glaring down on Ari. Trying to be authoritative or intimidating, or some such thing, but she only succeeded in looking annoyed. "I've only got two on parking duty and neither of them—"

Ari raked sweat-matted curls back with her fingers. "Get your brother, he can manage. Hawk's always boasting he's the best pilot in the Yard."

"Really, you're going to do that to me?"

"Unless you're willing to recycle my hauler's old junction box for me—"

"I can't do that." Reed frowned and her cheeks filled with a string of epithets she struggled to hold back. "The subscription on that part has run out, and I can't print new ones until it's re-upped."

"Joco expects me to fly him out right after the storm. The maintenance has to be done before I can take her out."

"Joco has to approve the subscription renewal, and that will take days." Reed wasn't wrong about that. When it came to spending approvals, things moved painfully slow.

"Then give me access to the equipment shed." Ari folded her arms and matched Reed's posture.

"Drown it all, Arli. You'll only print something not fit for transport use. You can't use those parts in anything but the equipment they're rated for."

"I understand that."

"But you're going to do as you drownin' well please, ain't ya?" Reed rolled her eyes and muttered under her breath. She looked so much like a gaunt version of Bithy when she did that.

"I ain't taking out a ship that's overdue for maintenance."

"Then you should take another ship."

Which would defeat Joco's stated purpose for flying with her. The Hell Cat herself would demand payment for that! "And you should have been at Mama's remembrance."

Reed flinched and glanced over her shoulder toward the imposing house where Bithy and Joco lived. "You know why I couldn't."

"And you know why I can't take another ship." They locked eyes, agreeing on what could not be spoken.

"Why are you always leading in a storm, Arli?"

And why did Reed always bend in the wind? "I suppose there's a reason that's my honest name. But arlis only lead the storm 'cause they get shoved out in front of it."

"Paying Joco forward like this is gonna cost ya, right? You're breaking some of the Transport Guild's clearest rules."

"And what's he paying forward by forcing me to do it? Why doesn't anyone question him?" Ari clamped her jaws shut. Getting baited into the conversation always went sideways.

"You could settle with Palmer like they've been wantin' you to." Reed blinked several times as though she believed that a good option.

"Go manage your own drowned parking. I have work to do." She dodged Reed and hurried away.

"Fine, it's your own wings that's gonna be plucked. I'll open the equipment shed." Reed pulled out her module and stabbed at the screen.

"I swear, if you relock it before I get my part, I'll take every one of those ships right back out of the hangar and a few more, to boot."

Reed looked about to counter, then shut her mouth. "It's done. But I've warned you and won't have this storm coming down on my head." She trudged off toward her office.

That was too easy, which, of course, meant that the berthing would be worse than Reed let on. Ari sent the printing instructions to the equipment shed—she had thirty minutes to kill while it printed. Just as well that she had ships to park.

Reed had lied. There were four, not three, ships that needed parking. The fourth was tucked away in a corner, where the last pilot to try berthing it had left it in frustration, door still open. All four spots were in tight corners at the end of the hangar, and none of those ships would technically fit in those spots. At least they wouldn't if anyone else tried to get them in.

Each one proved every bit as much a pain in the ass as Bay 36 had been. One even took two attempts to wedge in, something that almost never happened.

Ari dusted her hand on her pants and found her own hauler in Bay 23, its permanent address, tucked among the Yard's flitters so that proper paying customers wouldn't notice the bedraggled little craft. It was silly to be so fond of a beat-up, cobbled-together excuse for a ship, but they'd been through a lot together since Sander had started her flying in it, and eventually gave it to her outright.

The gray cargo hauler—an old Acoling industries model they no longer made—didn't look like much on the outside: an old-style boxy profile with a sharp nose and a flat hatch in back, dented and bruised from experience. With a skim coat of neutral gray paint covering the skin and no name on the side, only a tiny number to identify it across the stern, the ship was easy to ignore. She wasn't much on the inside either—a patched-together mess of mismatched parts, many not legal transport parts—that didn't seem to belong together. The battered little ship had seen more than her share of storms and still remained flightworthy.

A little like her pilot.

Maybe a lot.

Of course, there were plenty who would argue with her. Ari chuckled as she tapped the hatch code into her module and mounted up. May as well get it out and opened up for work.

The black-paved maintenance field stretched out between the hangar and the parts, maintenance, and equipment sheds. Surrounded by the heavy trees and foliage of the swamp, it was empty in anticipation of the storm, so she took the choice spot by the sheds. Assuming Reed did as she promised, Ari should be able to pick up her junction box in a moment and could get to work. Strange feeling, to be alone in a place that usually teemed with so much activity, one could hardly find a spot to put down.

The afternoon air tasted like incoming storms, hot and cold at the same time, with the green flavor of rain and the heavy, rancid essence of swamp underneath. A suffocating blanket of humidity hung in the air, an oppressive change from the mourning-red sunrise only hours ago.

Somehow, it already felt weeks away.

She opened the junction hatch on the side of the hauler, removed the old part, and headed to the equipment shed. Under low dark ceilings, squat brushed-metal boxes jammed the shed, the smallest only two handspans wide and tall, the largest as tall as she was and twice as long. Some top-loading, other front-loading, all their front-mounted control panels blinked in standardized yellow letters, asking for instructions or announcing part status. Chemical smells, sweetly bitter and thick, hovered like storm clouds. Not the sort of place one hung out, at least not if they enjoyed breathing.

"Did you get the parking finished?"

Ari jumped.

Reed looked up from the module she read as she perched on a tall, rusty metal stool in the corner. What was she doing here?

"Is my part printed?" Ari dropped the old part into the recycling hopper that fed the extracted raw materials back to the printers.

"There was already a part in-process that had to finish, but yours is halfway done." She pointed at the nearest printer's control panel.

Waist high and an arm length long, the printer vibrated with its efforts. The yellow countdown flashed fifteen minutes and below it, the ID number of the part being printed.

At least, it was the one Ari wanted. "There were four ships to park, not three."

"Did they all get in?"

"What do you think?"

Reed scowled. "I ain't got time for this."

"And I do?"

"Watch your lip with me, Arli-girl."

"Or what? You'll tell Joco, and let him deal with me? Go right ahead, but you'll have no more help berthing flitters from me."

"What bug's crawled up your butt today?"

She waved the ends of her tired red mourning scarf. Reed scowled.

Both their modules screamed. Ari pulled hers from her belt holster and polished grime from the screen with her elbow. Scattered storm warnings over the next few hours. Full stormfall, level three, after that.

Could be worse.

"I'm warning you, the storm over these parts is gonna be worse than the one coming in." Reed shoved her module back in her hip pocket.

"You plan on bringing this to Joco?"

Reed raised an open hand. "Don't put that on me. Audits on the prints are coming up and Palmer's farmed them out to Digits, who is sure to notice. If you kill the print on this now, it can be recycled, and no one will notice."

Squalls and storms. That was going to be a problem. "I've got no choice. I need it before the storm hits. If the hauler isn't ready by the time Joco comes by to check, he's going to take it outta my hide."

"Fine, it's on you, then. I tried, remember that." Reed trudged off, muttering under her breath.

She wasn't a bad soul, just utterly rule-bound and lacking in any creativity. And dependent on Joco. That wasn't a character flaw ... but it tended to make one less agreeable.

Digits came by his honest name for a reason. He was merciless with numbers and data and all things one could put on a spreadsheet. And he had a way of making those spreadsheets tell their secrets like a drunk miner in a bar. No doubt Palmer had missed something important on the last audit, and Joco had to bring in someone competent. That was going to make it a lot harder for her to find workarounds.

Harder, but not impossible.

Thunder rumbled in the distance.

She'd have to figure out that problem later. The printer dinged three times. Step one finished. She released the rucksack-sized part from its substrate and brushed off some of the dust. She flipped the printer into reset mode lest someone would have a fit that it wasn't ready to go when they needed it. It hummed agreeably until the front panel read "ready."

What were the chances the junction box would test out right straight out of the sonic cleaning? She wrestled the awkward oblong part into the nearest sonic cleaning booth, barely large enough to contain it. Tall, white, and covered by a heavy curtain, it resembled a sonic shower a little too much for comfort. The inevitable whine of the cleaner set her teeth on edge and ran prickles along her skin—like the sonic showers she hated. But it was cheaper and faster than the acid bath. Sonics also left the parts a little rougher around the edges. But often as not, that was a good thing, making up for missed tolerances in the print.

Especially with parts not approved by the Guild for vehicular use.

An annoying whine signaled the end of the sonic cycle. She grabbed the tester, with its wild array of cables threatening to attack like an angry swamp monster, and wrestled it into an embrace with the junction box. Slow, why was it always slow to read when she didn't have time to waste? One green light; two, green; three green, and one yellow. Within tolerances. Probably have to be replaced sooner than the Guild-approved part would require, but it would work.

She put away the tester and headed back to the maintenance field with the part.

Dark clouds rolled in across the sky, and with them, the first of the arli swarms. A small collection of the tiny fireflies, but enough to be seen against the dark sky. Dainty yellow and green flashing lights darted and danced overhead. In the larger clouds, there were sometimes as many as eight colors.

Those who knew said changes in pressure and humidity drove the arlis from their usual solitary hiding places, and the pressure along the storm front drove them along ahead of the weather. Something about being a group of their own kind triggered their mating instincts, which resulted in the frenzied aerial dance of light and color before the rain scattered them into hiding again.

But to everyone else, the arlis were tiny, annoying little insects, who led in the storms. Sometimes by hours, sometimes more than a day, but storms always followed.

That's what Reed thought of her. That's what they all thought of her. Arli-bug, Arli-girl, it was all the same: their own personal storm-bringer.

And she'd had enough. Chills slid across the back of her neck.

She had tried on that thought before, just to test the fit. Then it had itched and prickled and poked, refusing to settle into place. Today, though, it laid itself across her shoulders like a new jacket, tailor-made to fit.

Lightning flashed across the clouds, thunder following on its heels. Get the hauler done, now. She'd have time to try out that new thought later.

An hour later, she buttoned up the ship's junction hatch. There wasn't much sun left, and the arlis danced overhead, higher than any other insect ever flew, now denser than before. Maintenance complete, the hauler would pass inspection, as long as the inspector didn't have a stick up his ass about checking the numbers on the parts she'd used to accomplish the process.

The ones Joco hired usually didn't.

Ari patted the side of her craft, sweat sheeting off her face. It was hot in the maintenance hatch, even without the sun beating down on it. Especially when trying to jimmy a part into a place that wasn't meant for that spot. She dried her face on her sleeve.

There was enough time to get the hauler berthed and herself back to the dormitory before the blow hit.

Heavy footsteps approached. Lovely.

"Have the storm warnings addled your mind Arli-girl? What you doing, still working on your ship?" Joco stopped and towered head and shoulders over her, bared arms crossed and bulging with wiry muscle.

She matched Joco's stance, craning her neck to look up at him.

This wasn't the first time they'd postured this way. He liked to think himself a force to be reckoned with, especially in all things happening in his shipyard and the Transport Guild.

And he was.

For most people.

If the booming voice and imposing height didn't cow them, the knowledge that he was Transport Guild Master and still held a top rank among the Lighten Ring Fighters assured he got his way most of the time. He was used to that, expected it, and got not a little touchy when it didn't happen without question.

He was often touchy with her.

"What does it look like? I'm getting her ready to fly you to the Championships. Like you wanted." She turned her back and sealed her tool box.

"I saw you coming out of the equipment shed. What parts did you use?"

"I replaced the one that needed maintenance. You want to take her up and test her out? You always say a ship won't fly right if that part's not Transport Guild-approved." She gestured toward the open cockpit.

He glowered. She was playing a dangerous game, forcing his hand this way. Either he had to fess up to the Guild's convenient falsehoods that assured their control over all aspects of transportation, or fly her ship and admit that it flew right. It was a no-win for him, and he knew it. He clutched his forehead and growled. Most people ran when he did that.

Distraction, that was the safest course. "Are you going to take her up or not? Stormfall's nearly here, and the dormitory is going to button up soon. If I don't get there in time, I'll be locked out of my berth and dinner, to boot."

"About that—" he laid his hand on her shoulder, heavy and warm, "—take dinner with us tonight. Ya turned your mother over to the sunrise this morning. It ain't right for you to stand alone after that, especially with stormfall coming in. No one should stand stormfall alone. You got a place with us."

Why did he have to say that? With his eyes so full of warmth, like those things were true.

"No." She set her jaw and turned her face aside, bracing.

"What do you mean?" How quickly his voice lost its warmth.

"You know as well as I." She turned back to him. "I don't have no place anywhere near Bithy or her brood."

"You can't expect Bithy—"

"To be polite? Not to be a jealous, vindictive sollert-cow?"

"You don't talk about my partner that way." She ought to pay attention to the threatening edge in his voice.

"I will if it's true. She was horrid to my mother, and still is horrid to me. She couldn't even bring herself to come to the last honors, nor none of her brood. What do you call that?"

"Practical. They were working—"

"Funny how you support them doing that, but refuse to give me the clearances I've earned so I can support myself. You keep throwing Palmer at me, when I can fly every damn ship in this Yard. I've been ready to fly prime-level jobs for years now—"

"I will not discuss this. I got my reasons. It's not for you to question them."

"You think keeping me poor and unnamed is going to make me go to Palmer's door, all quiet and obedient? You've known me since Mama birthed me into your hands. Nothing ain't never going to make me that kind."

"That's enough, girl. Ya ain't gotten too big to feel my leather across your back."

She flinched and turned away. It wasn't the sort of thing one forgot—especially when he wouldn't hesitate to make good on the threat. "I've got to berth the hauler. Then, I'm going home."

"You don't need to, I told you—"

Something in his voice made her look back at him. A flicker of warmth, a hint of understanding. He was grieving Mama, too. The only one in that house who did. He didn't want to stand that stormfall alone.

There was something to be said for sharing such a time, making a memory there, amid a storm, to sustain them through the next one.

"Besides, if you would give Palmer a chance. He's changed—"

She jumped back. Insensitive, boorish, brute—and those were Palmer's best qualities. He was the kind that would never change. "No. I don't need another storm." She turned her back and walked away, Joco's gaze burning across her shoulders.

Joco meant well, or at least she wanted to believe that. Truly wanted to believe it. But it grew harder with every storm.

She climbed into the hauler and trundled it back to Bay 23.

"Cutting it close there, Arli," Reed met her at the base of the side pole as she locked up her ship.

"Don't know how to do it any other way, I suppose." With a nod, she slipped out as Reed locked the hangar up behind her.

Ari's module screamed again. Fifteen minutes until stormfall at the yard. Not much time left to get home. She jogged from the hangar, through the maintenance field, slowing only as she turned down the little trail through the imposing draping trees toward the residential zone.

Small white houses for the section chiefs, miniatures of the dormitories, dotted the sides of the trails. A few larger houses for the division chiefs were set apart, away from the others. And the largest, the Yard Chief's, sat away from them all, overlooking all the residential zone.

Palmer lived there.

Bithy's eldest son—not Joco's, she came to him with all her children—served as Yard Chief. The squat, stout, spit-and-image of his mother, Palmer did what Joco asked, having not an ounce of imagination or creativity, no ability to think for himself. To be fair, it was exactly what Joco seemed to desire in those who worked for him.

But Palmer would never be accepted in Transport Guild leadership. That required all the traits that Joco discouraged. The ones he'd tried to beat out of her, but failed.

Not that she wanted anything to do with leadership in any of the Trade Guilds.

Or with Palmer.

She trotted faster past his house towards the dormitories.

Four long workers' dormitories lined the sides of the trail, sleek, white, capsule-shaped industrial fabrications, with steel-shuttered windows, and mounted on flood-resisting, floating concrete slabs. They buttoned up tight during the storms, held fast in the wind, and stood up to nearly anything a storm could slam against them.

She checked her module. Still had a few minutes before the dorms would lock up.

She increased her pace past them, past the main kitchen and medic station and recreation hall, all variations on the white capsule theme, where the woods encroached upon the flood-resistant slabs that would rise with floodwaters and keep the structures above all but the most severe floods.

A narrow, overgrown trail to the left, behind the medic's station, led to a small dock, where Joco kept a personal motor boat for fishing and sollert hunting. Would permission to use those be the next things Joco denied her? The sollerts she bagged were, more often than not, what kept enough food on the table to keep body and soul together.

She sucked in a deep breath of hot spongy air.

Even if Joco footed the bill for her fuel, she'd need to hunt after the Championships. The ship would need work after the trip, and even if she didn't use Guild-sanctioned parts, it would be tough to cover all the costs. Especially if she had to pay off Reed to look the other way while she fabricated them.

What was left of Mama's tiny pod-house came into view. Once a compact, off-white egg with windows nestled in the dense vegetation on the smallest possible flood slab, it was now a mangled heap of scrap metal, scarred where Mama had been pulled from the wreckage. Plain, basic, and efficient, but it had been home. As modest as it was, it still might be some time before she had such a place to call her own again.

Ari kicked a rock out of her way. It skittered into the underbrush. An angry yellow-striped trask, all teeth and claws and spit, drove her back from its nest. The last thing she needed now was a bite from a pissed-off venomous lizard. Not the time to be stupid.

The wind picked up and heavy clouds enveloped the woods in viscous darkness like the swamp's murky waters. Ari turned back and ran for the dorms as the first fat raindrops fell.

Chapter 6

MATTEO STRODE DOWN THE long, sleek corridor of the Newbry Transport Center's private wing. One hundred and twenty steps' worth of glass and tile and steel, no furnishings, no media screens, just a walkway, smelling of industrial cleansers and recycled air, stretched out before and behind. His footsteps ricocheted off the hard surfaces, filling up the empty spaces. Dark windows lined both sides of the passage, allowing those within to see outside, but none, even the media drones that were forbidden within Newbry's boundaries, to see inside. It was nice to be out of the public eye, at least for a little while.

He glanced to his left. "So, you got assigned as my handler again?"

"I hate it when you put it that way. Just because I'm the one best able to goad you into attending meetings you'd rather not attend doesn't mean I'm your handler." Beny huffed and attempted to glower, something he rarely did well.

They looked enough alike that they might have been brothers—one of those things Grandfather liked since he thought it made the Clan give a strong impression of unity, that their circle was strong and stable. Tall, broad-shouldered, well-built. They had the angular Timnon nose, and prominent cheekbones in common, too. But Beny inherited his rich olive skin and nearly black hair and eyes from his mother, making him the more attractive of the two. Matteo's unremarkable, standard-issue, neither-light-nor-dark-nor-colorful features made him far easier to lose in a crowd. At least one that didn't realize Ranks were present.

"Be honest, Beny. You hate it when I'm right." Matteo tugged his casual, sand-colored banded collar jacket over darker slacks. The garment printer hadn't been calibrated correctly, again, and everything was slightly off, chafing and binding already. Why did uniforms always print truer to size?

"Well, that, too." Beny chuckled, rolling his eyes. He was the kind of man who always looked comfortable and easy wherever he was, whomever he was with. One of his most admirable and irritating traits.

"He always sets you to ride herd on me when he doesn't trust that I'm going to follow orders." Matteo patted the module in his chest pocket containing lists of those orders.

"No. Sometimes he does that for the media value of seeing the Clan and leading Family heirs walking out together as though they were in lockstep with each other." Beny raised his hands with a flourish.

"In lockstep with him, you mean. You and I have never been in contention—"

"But Dad and Grandfather have."

"You have a penchant for understatement."

"That's why he wants to put the attention on us, to give the impression the other isn't happening. And thus, I'm going to the fights with you." Beny elbowed Matteo and winked.

"So, he didn't tell you, did he?"

"Tell me what?" Now he had Beny's attention.

"Oh, you're going to love this. I'll tell you everything once we get the privacy shields up inside the ship, though. This is supposed to be a high-security, private zone, but ..."

Beny's eyebrows rose and he almost, but not quite, asked anyway. But he shut his mouth and pressed his lips hard, curiosity rolling off him in prickly waves. It would be interesting to see how well he'd predicted Lord Timnon's latest demands.

An elegant relief filigree on an arch to their left—not a simple sign—marked their assigned docking terminal. Did the designer believe that was the way to elevate the interior, or were they concerned that Ranks could not read? Not a question he wanted an answer to.

A male and female pair of white-uniformed attendants approached, looking young, uncertain, and intimidated. Must be new hires. The usual crew here was so accustomed to the Ranks who regularly traveled through, they'd have been on a first-name basis if the scandal of such informality would not have brought an end to all Dextrine civilization.

"Lord Heir Timnon, Lord Heir Sennet?" The blushing blond attendant barely looked at them, the tremor in his voice breaking any illusion of professionalism.

Who else would they be? But no, Matteo forced a neutral expression onto his face. It wasn't their fault that they were new and hadn't mastered all the proper forms. "The ship is ready for us?"

"If you will thumbprint here, you are welcome to board." The attendant held out his oversized module toward them, and they pressed their thumbs to the screen.

In tandem, the attendants gestured to unadorned white double doors behind them. A green light flashed over the doors, and they slid open with only the barest whoosh. Matteo and Beny strode through, shoulder to shoulder, in lockstep.

That Record would make a great shot for the Media—who weren't even allowed in this wing, but would probably get their hands on the Record, anyway.

One day, he would not have to constantly be aware of these media moments, of the way everything he did would somehow offend his ancestors and find its way on to every screen on Dextra. But that wasn't today.

Grandfather had assigned them one of the smallest Timnon Clan transports housed at Newbry. For the best. A larger ship would have invited more company, which Matteo would rather avoid. The journey from Dextra to its moon, Lighten, was long enough to be unbearable if he had to play nice and make polite, politic conversation for the duration.

The passenger cabin, appointed in shades of Timnon-blue and gray, would have held four. But two of the cushioned seats had been stowed, allowing him and Beny the shoulder and leg room that they both needed to take a deep breath. Four windows with privacy shades, all drawn, perched above shallow, wall-mounted bins to stow any personal gear they might carry. Low-pile blue-and-gray-striped carpeting covered the floor and the walls up to the lower edge of the windows, dampening sound and affording a warm, comfortable sort of feeling throughout. At least that was how the official portrayal of the craft described it.

Matteo was much more concerned with who and what was in the pilot's cockpit, which was, of course, locked to him. He wrestled himself into the gray woven safety straps that were always this side of chafing. "Might want to get your webbing on, too."

"Not again." Beny followed suit, with far less finesse. "When is Grandfather going to let you fly us yourself?"

"Not soon enough. But in this case, I can't. Lightens want their own flight clearances. I couldn't get cleared for their airspace in time for this trip. Their Transport Guild has those locked up tighter than the Prime Minister's daughter."

Matteo opened a compartment between the two nearest windows, revealing a small control panel. He pressed his thumb to the pad, tapped in clearance codes, then confirmation codes. Finally, the fool thing came to life, and he set the industry-standard privacy filters in place.

"So, we can talk now?" Beny stared at the panel.

Matteo shook his head and pulled his module from his pocket. Several taps later, it hummed and whined, then blinked red.

He went back to the wall panel, input several more codes and repeated the process until the module blinked green. "Cracking Media is getting smarter."

"What now?"

"Got wind of it right before we left. I updated all the jamming sequences." He held up his module. "I've got a handy little bit of ware on this that can identify when something is breaking through."

"Dare I ask where you got it?" Beny cocked his head with a knowing look.

"No, it's not standard, nor is it likely to be. And yes, I got it via a personal contact's contact. Never met them, though. They call themself 'Longshot Digits.'"

"Sounds like someone Lord Timnon would not approve."

"Who does he approve?" Matteo tucked his module back into the inner chest pocket of his jacket.

"Any chance you can share that with me?"

"My guy tells me it's not quite ready for distribution, but I'll ask. I'm on the beta test list, helping shake loose the bugs. I'm told that the alpha testers have already made certain that it doesn't let more Media through, so I'd rather get any extra level of protection I can, buggy or not. Getting the next release may cost you an endorsement, though. Unofficial, and not leaked to the Media, of course."

"Seems fair. If it will shut down the watchers, I can endorse that." Beny made that face, a blend of disgust and frustration, that he usually wore when they discussed the Media.

Three soft dings rang from a hidden overhead speaker. "Prepare for takeoff. Secure your safety straps and stow all loose objects in the available bins." The AI voice somehow reassured him that no one was inserting themselves into their conversation, even as it attempted human inflection in its statements.

Matteo checked his webbing and pointed to Beny's. "Trust me, Grandfather hires pilots as political favors. You want to strap in."

Beny adjusted his straps. "No wonder you're grumpy."

The engines whined as the transport taxied down the runway and leapt into the air. Not the worst takeoff he'd ever experienced, but one that would have embarrassed him if he'd been responsible for it. One could tell a lot about a pilot by the way they took off and landed.

Beny grimaced and pulled a packet of green tablets from his coat pocket. He popped several into his mouth, swallowing them dry.

"It wasn't that bad. Lightweight."

"Maybe not to you." Beny returned the remaining tabs to his chest pocket. "So, distract me and spill, what's the deal about this trip? Are you supposed to meet with Iantha? As I recall, Cobel Clan's got their Evering Industries in that joint venture with the Firen Mines—something about refining the ore before shipping to bring down costs. I heard she was supposed to be onsite there now. The Firen Headquarters Complex isn't too far from Anara—that's where they're holding the Championships, right?"

Matteo snorted and rolled his eyes. It kept his less kind thoughts to himself. "Do you really think he wants me meeting with my betrothed, without a chaperone—"

"You mean spy."

"Yes. And no, he is not sending me to talk to her."

"By which you mean that you intend to see her, anyway. Which is most likely why he didn't let you know about this in time to get your flight clearances."

"For a 'mere medic,' you're pretty smart." Lord Timnon did not approve of Beny's choice of career. Far too earthy and personal, lacking in the dignity expected from the High Ranks.

"I'm not a mere anything."

"I agree. Keep in mind, it's still better than the things he calls me." Matteo laced his fingers behind his neck and stared at the padded gray expanse overhead. "And yes, I intend to find a pilot to get me down to Firen HQ sometime during the fights. There're always fliers looking for side jobs while the matches are going on. And in the interest of pleasing Lord Timnon, I've done my research—"

"Of course you have. If I didn't know better, I'd swear you don't change your silks without researching it first."

"Keep it up. You remember we're sharing a suite, right?"

Beny raised his hands in mock surrender.

"I've even heard that the Transport Guild Master's pilot is connected to him somehow, not clear on all those details. But if she flies him about, she's got to be good, and if I can get her to pilot for me, then we'll have a connection—"

"What sort of connection?" Beny's eyes narrowed.

"The kind I won't be ashamed of the Media finding out about." The snarl Matteo added at the end wasn't for show.

Beny blew out a sharp breath. "You had me worried there for a moment, sounding like my father—"

"Don't you ever make that comparison." Matteo gritted his teeth until they hurt.

"Deep breath, Matté, deep breath. I didn't mean to step on an open sore."

"Well, you did. Don't go there. My father didn't play those games, and neither will I."

"Which is why you're my role model and Grandfather's bane. 'The monk among us', that's how you're known among us lesser Family Ranks. Your reputation is safe." Beny cuffed his shoulder. "Remember though, it is possible to be too strait-laced. I worry about you sometimes."

"If you had the Media on one side, spying on you, waiting for anything it could use to spice up the feeds, and Grandfather on the other, looking for yet another reason to disinherit you, you might see it differently. Remember what happened the first time I looked at a girl Grandfather hadn't picked out for me? Took her family years to recover from that smear campaign. And let's not forget the scandals your father has graced us with, and the near miss your sister Cortly had recently. I could also point you to Ranks in every other family who have opened themselves and their Clans and Families to a world of complication because of their ... indiscretion. That's the current euphemism, yes?" Matteo leaned back and closed his eyes. "Look, I know you're not sure you approve of my way of avoiding scandal. But it works for me. So just go with it, please." If Beny's parents had what Matteo's mother and father did, he might understand better.

Or he might scoff that Matteo was clinging to an impossible ideal and making his life all the more difficult. Which was true, but also not up for discussion.

"So, if Grandfather's not sending you to make nice with Iantha, and you're not planning to make illicit connections with the Guild Master's daughter, why are we headed to Lighten?"

"It's not merely Lighten we're going to, but the Ring Fighting Championships, my friend." Matteo raised his brows and cocked his head.

Beny's jaw dropped. "No, you're kidding. He really did it? He got you into the exhibition fights?"

"They still aren't allowing non-Lightens into the competition, but he thought it would be good for us to make a showing."

Beny dragged his hand down his face. "And that's why he sent me along! Damn it all. I would have packed my kit if I'd known."

"Don't have much faith in me, do you?"

"That's not fair. You held top rank in the Wroxton Academy league, which was tougher than the professional leagues, but I haven't forgotten how many times I patched you up from the trainer's pit. No one escapes the ring unscathed. What is he trying to do—"

"Teach me a lesson with someone else's hand, I suppose." Matteo shook his head. Not the sort of thing to dwell upon too long. "Which lesson, take your pick. For what it's worth, I understand there's a fully-stocked kit in the rear hold with our luggage."

"At least that's something. I'll have to go through it as soon as we land and figure out where to get what I'll really need. That kit won't be packed to my specs."

"A fully-stocked operating room wouldn't be to your specs."

"Not for a ring fight, it wouldn't." Beny pulled out his module and stabbed at the screen. Probably making his first list of the trip. He liked lists. "Do you know who you're fighting?"

"One of the current open class champions. He's from the Firen Mining group. As I understand, fighters hold championship rank for three years, then rematch or retire. This guy, Phalen's the name, is starting his second year." Matteo sent Beny an image and dossier.

"Phalen, Phalen." Beny mouthed words, not polite ones, as he scanned his module screen. "I'm sure you've seen all this, too. He's fighting a totally different style to ours, not playing by the same rules we do. And this guy is cracking good, to boot."

"Thanks, yes, I noticed."

"You're at a real disadvantage on this one. Grandfather realizes this, right?

"Maybe, but it wouldn't matter to him." Matteo pinched the bridge of his nose, cringing in anticipation. "He wants me to throw the bout."

"You're. Joking."

"Nope." He smiled a tight-pressed smile at Beny's almost comical outrage. Clearly, he was not as accustomed to this game as Matteo was.

"How exactly is that supposed to be a good thing? Lord Timnon never accepts a loss."

"He didn't explain, of course, it's not like he ever does. But I did a bit of reading..."

"Another one of your deep data dives? Oh, never mind, what else are you going to do when you're busy not getting yourself in trouble?"

"Did you forget data analysis was my secondary study at Wroxton? It seems Timnon is trying to get in bed with Firen over some rare ore deposits—I'm less sure about the details than I am that he's trying to make a deal of some kind. But something about the Evering connection isn't making it easy. He didn't say that, but I get the sense that's the case. My guess is he thinks that letting them show their dominance in the ring will make them easier to negotiate with, more willing to cut another deal with Dextrines."

"Which is the opposite to everything he has ever said." Beny stared at his module for another moment, then slipped it back into his pocket.

"He's been doing that a lot lately. It might be that I'm listening more now or—"

"Something is really wrong? I have some strong opinions on that—"

Matteo held up an open hand, pointed to his ear, and shook his head. "Understood, enough said." Some things one could not be too careful about, even with the latest privacy ware in place.

"Seriously, though. Are you okay with this whole fight scheme? I remember what your Academy bouts were like, but by comparison, these matches get brutal."

"The exhibition matches are supposed to be 'bloodless' matches, as defined by their rules. So, it will still be brutal, but we shouldn't come out too damaged. Not like the ones used to decide political seats."

"Can you imagine if we did things that way?" Beny's wry smile dissolved into a deep chuckle. One could only imagine the pictures in his head.

"There are moments where it doesn't seem like a bad idea. I can think of a few Clan leadership transitions that would have had a better heir inheriting if we did that."

"You can't believe that. You're trying to get under my skin."

"You make it easy." But it was still true.

"Even when you're being a small-time soul catcher, I'm still glad to have you home." This time Beny's smile was genuine.

"You may be the only one."

"That's not fair, Niles and Bryce and their Ladies are. Uncle Artain and Aunt Terease were very welcoming, too."

"His attitude has changed a great deal since graduation." Matteo suppressed a shudder and shook his head to drown out the memory of the screams.

"For the better, which I never would have thought possible. I'm sorry that my parents and sisters decided it would be better to suck up to Grandfather, though."

"I don't like that Cortly and Patryce are trying to convince Grandfather to put them in direct line for succession. And not for the reasons they expect."

"That would be a disaster. Those two may have taken political science as their schooling track, but they've found that falling in line with Family Sennet and Clan Timnon's politics and policies is very rewarding." Beny's face wrinkled like someone opened a case of rotten offal in the cabin.

"I'd hoped they'd be able to get their heads out of the Clan archives and look at the bigger picture."

"You've always been the idealist, haven't you?"

"Is it too much to ask for Dextra, or at least our Clan, to quit navel-gazing, for a single generation?"

"I expect so." Beny leaned back in thoughtful contemplation of the ceiling.

Matteo joined him. "You realize I would have been at your graduation—it killed me missing it."

"It's okay, really. Lord Timnon, exalted personage that he is, was asked to deliver the address. He made it all about him. He had the stage so long, the actual ceremony had to be abbreviated because of the honor he did us." Beny let the bitterness coat his voice like a rare seasoning, something only brought out for the most privileged company.

"Well, I'm proud of you. We don't have many full-fledged physicians among the Ranks. Lord Routel is the only one. It's cracking impressive what you've done. Especially since you had to stand up to Lord Sennet and Lord Timnon to do it. That by itself would be enough to earn my respect."

"Don't go there. I'm heir to only the Family Lordship and Dad's a lot younger. I've got time for a career before I step into his role. So, it's a lot easier for me to get away with it for a little while. Not like you, who's likely to make Clan Lordship his entire life's work." Beny refused to meet Matteo's gaze.

"When we get through on Lighten, I'm kidnapping you for a week, off the grid, at the hunting lodge, just us, no one who can order us around, and no media feeds." There, they would have a long, private conversation about all these things.

"If I hadn't intended to patch you up after your bout, that would be enough to bribe me to do it." Beny's smile had a wistful edge. "Sounds like you've got a plan that includes pissing Grandfather off that's going to require you to play duck-and-cover."

"Nope. Not this time. The trip to the lodge will be entirely about celebrating you and the life you'll get to have that I'll be jealous of. So, what do you want to do there?"

Three soft chimes filled the cabin. "Passengers, check your straps and return all items to stowage. Emergency course change, effective immediately, and sudden emergency maneuvers are possible." Reassuring AI voices were most certainly not reassuring.

"Splintering soul-catching Raiders!" And once again, Matteo was not at the helm.

Chapter 7

As LEVEL THREE STORMS went, this one was hardly memorable. The floating concrete foundations under all the structures rode out the floodwaters with little trauma, the waters only half as deep as the slabs could handle. Since all the Yard structures were storm-resistant, pod-shaped structures. A few broken windows from shutters left open made up the majority of the damage. Certainly, there would be broken limbs and other debris, but nothing the clearing equipment they kept on hand couldn't handle.

Far more noteworthy was the list of job leads her search returned. *That,* she would remember, especially considering how Joco insisted job hunting would be a futile effort every time she brought it up.

Curled up on the hard, utilitarian couch in the equally utilitarian dormitory common room, she studied the list on her module while the final bands of the storm passed. Finally, the module's all-clear shriek sounded.

On the one hand, she had more options than she expected. On the other, many of them—*Fleet Needs Pilots!*—were unappealing as a drowned swamp rat, floating bloated on the stagnant waters. Who wanted to recruit into the mangy, ragtag operation that pretended to police the airspace to counter the Raiders' threat? Run by Therans who shouted *Vigilance! Valor! Victory!* at every turn, the joint-effort Enforcers Corps couldn't seem to work out their own internal strife between Lightens, Dextrines, and Therans, much less effectively hold a line against the Raiders.

Although running passengers for the local comfort houses was not much better, the chances of getting shot at while earning a living were lower with them than with Fleet. So she'd keep that option open. As a last resort. There were those who still remembered Mama working for the Comfort Guild and she didn't want anyone getting mixed up as to her chosen profession.

The mines, both Firen and Devlin, needed cargo pilots. Although both mining groups were at odds with Joco and his policies, those were still her best options. Even if they were located in the deep desert, at the very Gates of Abadon itself, at least there she had a chance to be judged on her merit. It would be easier to get them to consider her if she had more aboveboard jobs for references, though. Was that why Joco refused to assign her those? She'd never considered that before.

Her module pinged. Time to get Joco to the Championships. She'd come back to her options once he was safely about his business in Anara.

She headed back to her compartment with its sleeping pod, footlocker, a shelf above it, and three wall hooks alongside. A quick change into her flight gear: drab pants made from the same heavy canvas as her matching flight jacket, with a snug white knit shirt and pants beneath, and her favorite worn-in work boots. All pilots seemed to wear some variant of the combination, making them universally recognized in the system.

She pinned her unruly dark curls into a knot at the nape of her neck, fitted her belt knife into its sheath and her module into its holster, then checked the knife in her boot. Everything was where it should be. She grabbed her rucksack from a hook, shoved a change of whites and silks and a few other necessities inside. A thumbprint locked her compartment, and she was off.

Hot humid air hit her like the steam off a boiling pot. Thick, oppressive, heavy, like it always was after a storm.

"Where ya going, Arli?"

Ari stiffened, but maintained her pace past the residential zone. If she slowed, Palmer would take that as an invitation to talk. "Busy now, Joco's waiting."

"Ya gots time for the Yard Chief." He caught up to her and jogged to keep pace. Stout and squat, like his mother Bithy, he breathed as heavily as he sweated.

Why was he wandering the residential zone right after a storm? It wasn't like he was part of the aftermath crew. Had he been in his house watching for her to come past? Or amused at the prospect of watching the crews work? Both were possible. "You going to explain to Joco why his transport is late?"

"We ain't finished with that bit of business—" Drown it all, his breath reeked! Was that beer or that distilled engine-degreaser he brewed?

"I am, I told you. I ain't interested, and that's the end of it."

"Well, I ain't finished with it."

"Then go talk to yourself, I got no time for this."

He growled. "When you get back..."

She waved him off and broke into a run. Doubtless, he would dog after her like a hound after a bone when she returned. But she would deal with that then. Maybe she would have a new job at that point and would never have to consider settling for Palmer, or anyone else, again.

That was a bit optimistic, but hope, at least sometimes, was a good thing.

Luckily, Reed had the hangar clear, and Ari pulled her hauler out of Bay 23 without incident. Better still, the inspector was already waiting for her in the preflight yard and passed the ship without looking twice at it or the new junction relay. Just as she had expected.

She opened the rear cargo hatch and stowed her gear. If Ari had been alone, she would have tucked it under one of the passenger seats. But regulations said baggage should be properly stowed, so today it would be.

Now a final check of the cabin, if the compact affair could rightly be called that. Joco could barely stand inside, his head brushing the ceiling. Arms extended, he could almost, but not quite, touch both interior bulkheads. The passenger seats were close enough that the passengers might brush knees if they were much taller than she—which was close to everyone. But it put everything at her arms' reach, which was exactly as she would have it.

She ensured the extra padding she'd installed on the front seat Joco would use was secure and that the new settings on the seat would give him a little extra space to stretch out. The new media screen she'd installed flipped out of the way when not in use. Hopefully, it would help keep him distracted. He might be tolerable today, but, especially if he lost to the Mining Guild Master, it could be a long, miserable ride home. Even if he won, he'd still be hurting, and anything to make the trip easier was worth it.

She maneuvered herself into the pilot's seat and filed flight plans with local control. The oversized control screen she'd installed front and center on the dash below the viewscreen and above the control stick was an expensive, Guild-rated part. Made sense when it was the one that would attract the most attention. A little reprogramming of the standard controls allowed her to adjust the display to bring up any single system she needed, or a customized layout of several sets of controls or readouts, organized the way she liked them. Two additional screens tucked into slots beside the main screen, to be pulled up to allow her more system readouts and controls available at once.

Not forbidden by the Transport Guild, but the overwhelming mass of information interspersed with touchscreen ship controls was not considered best practice. Better keep as much as possible on auto presets with as little visual clutter as possible.

Winds be with her, the new screens should keep him distracted enough not to fiddle about with trying to inspect any of the hauler's innards. That was where she tucked away all the parts co-opted from other equipment designations: construction equipment, recyclers, environmental systems. There was even a piece from a commercial dishwasher that had made its way into her cobbled-together mass of mismatched parts. Yes, Joco and the Guild at large would come apart at the seams if they knew.

But really, what sense was there in using an expensive Guild part when a standard machine part would work quite as well at half the cost, sometimes less? Especially when one didn't have any funds to spare.

The Guild's official stance, declared in bold lettering in all their Records, explained that their parts were the only ones safety-rated for vehicular use and failure to use them could be considered a criminal act if there were to be an accident. Even if there wasn't, any Guild member caught using non-Guild parts would face immediate revocation of their flight and maintenance credentials with little hope of reinstatement. That was the real threat. The Guild—Joco—liked the profits of the monopoly almost as much as the control the monopoly exercised over the powerful mining interests.

With every aspect of transportation limited, the Mining Guild had to play nice with Transport to get their products out, their people in, and their territory protected, all with technology that was out of date and not up to the demands being made on it. Seemed like Transport would make more by allowing the best of Dextrine technology in, but asking why they didn't had proven to be a very bad idea. Little wonder the truce between the guilds was so uneasy.

They could have their little power pissing match. As long as she could keep flying and make sure none were the wiser for her shortcuts, then the storms would batter other shores. She flipped the hidden switch that locked all the maintenance hatches and access panels. That should keep prying eyes out, and she could claim that the panels had gotten stuck. The ship had taken so many beatings, it was easy and convenient to believe that brand of fiction. And if she could keep Joco distracted with the new media screen or with her creative, but still legal, programming, then he was unlikely to look further for things to complain about.

Annoying, but better than the alternative.

She settled her headgear into place and flipped on the local pilot chatter feed. If there was anything important to know, she'd hear it there first.

Raiders near Firen Headquarters Complex in the High Jipny desert. Drown it. That wasn't far from Anara. Best adjust flight plans—

Heavy steps thundered into the hauler. "You ready to go? Meeting with the Ag Guild shifted again. Earlier now."

"How early?" Further remarks she could and should keep to herself.

Joco fell into the seat next to her, dropped his bag on the floor beside him, and kicked it underneath his seat. His short-cropped dark hair was wet and plastered to his head, not with sweat—he must have just showered. He smelled like cleansers. "Top speed, and I should get there in time."

Lovely, he was running late, and it was now her problem. She closed the main hatch. "It would be better to use the express flight lanes, then."

"Stick with the flight plan we agreed on, no need for the tolls."

"They are faster and safer."

"No. Just do what we agreed." Joco wrestled his safety webbing into place.

"There's Raiders—"

"Ain't gonna be none in the main corridors. Now go, girl."

Not going to be worth arguing with him. On the bright side, if they ran into Raiders, then he would have to acknowledge her skills as a pilot. Assuming it didn't get them killed.

The main cabin speakers crackled. "Paxton 23, this is local control. Flight approved, cleared for takeoff."

"Go, go, go!" Joco waved at the dashboard.

"Sit back, and don't tell me how to fly." She began her preflights, not looking at him.

He grumbled so loud he might have sprouted spines like a pricklefish. He would rather be the pilot in charge and hated anything that reminded him his failing eyesight had grounded him. Even worse, he hated for someone else to be in control. Which was why the other Yard pilots demanded double and triple rates to cart him about. She hadn't yet worked up her nerve to try that, but maybe after this...

She guided her ship down the taxiway, lifting it off the ground with barely a twitch. Her hands danced over the smooth, responsive touchscreen controls before her. "We'll be in our navigation plane in three minutes. The traffic may slow us down, though."

"Do what you need to get through it." He clapped his forehead. "Keep it legal. I ain't paying your enforcer's fines."

He said that often enough, but what he meant was don't get caught. He leaned back, tucked his chin, and closed his eyes. That way, he could claim not to have seen anything untoward by his pilot.

Convenient.

But what he didn't see wouldn't leave him twitchy. There was that. Just as well, the navigation plane was jammed with putzy flitters on autopilot and large public transports with little incentive to be efficient.

Time to be resourceful. Which meant things he wouldn't want to see, starting with removing the proximity sensors from her control screen and shutting off the automatic alarms. She knew where her elbows and knees were and didn't need the drowned ship nagging at her to keep legal distances. She reset the rest of the control screen with her favorite array of external sensors to pick up unusual activity on communication bands and environmental sensors—ones that she'd tuned to her own specifications.

One more thing. She flipped a discreet switch on the control stick to set it to high sensitivity, which would allow her to dive and weave through the cluttered navigation plane like an arli dancing over the waters in the moonlight. She made headway through the traffic without leaving a wake behind her, nor any sign that her modifications were wildly off spec for her cargo hauler.

A soft buzz from the touchscreen, under her right hand. Traffic Enforcers ahead. She dropped her speed and shoehorned herself into the main traffic way, closer to the hulking public transport than she would have liked. She could almost hear its pilot calling her any number of colorful things.

Once past the enforcers, she resumed her dance again until they left Paxton's airspace. Away from Lighten's capital, the traffic cleared and permitted a substantial speed increase. Much better. "You can open your eyes now. There's space to breathe."

Joco lifted his chin and opened his eyes. "What's our arrival time like?"

"Assuming nothing interesting happens, I'd say under three hours."

"See that nothing interesting happens."

"You realize that's not all up to me, right?"

"Trouble stays off the main lanes. Arli, you know that." The tone of his voice suggested simply declaring it would ensure it would be so.

"Wishful thinking, Joco, wishful thinking."

"How much trouble have you been seeing on your runs?" He sat a little straighter and looked at her like this was the first time he had heard that. It wasn't.

"Not enough to keep me from flying them."

"That isn't an answer. How much?"

"Enough to know where to fly and where to avoid."

He slapped the hard armrest and snorted. "I want a straight answer."

"That's as straight as I can give you. It's not exactly what one includes in the logs, now is it?" She tossed a quick glare in his direction. "That would put the information in the Records. And that would be bad for the Guild." It was nice to throw the line he used on her so often back at him.

He harrumphed and growled under his breath. "You don't keep—"

"No, I don't." Yes, she did, but if she admitted it, he would demand to examine them, and that would have led in a whole new storm system.

"You should. What kind of pilot don't keep their own Records? I taught you better than that."

She clenched her jaws. Best not say any of the things nearest the tip of her tongue. She might not have a great deal of sense, but every once in a while, she could keep from wandering into the slipsand.

Thirty long minutes of chafing cold silence followed.

He cleared his throat. "When we get to Anara—"

"You want me to take the western approach to the arena and drop you at the second entrance, away from the foreign visitors. Then you want the hauler parked in the fourth lot on the south side, so we can make a quick exit after all is said and done, avoiding any media that might be there."

He grunted. "And after that, I want you to keep to the hauler, stay out of the stadium."

That might be the stupidest thing she had ever heard. She drew several deep breaths before the urge to tell him so passed. "Do you have any idea how hot it is on those lots? I don't have climate control to handle those temperatures while on the ground. It ain't just uncomfortable, it's plain not safe."

Joco muttered something about why she always had to be difficult. She glowered and left the rest unspoken.

"Can't you see? I'm trying to protect you." His boot beat an uneven rhythm on the bottom edge of the nearest bulkhead.

"Certainly not from the deep desert heat."

"There's a lot more than that to be worried about."

"Such as?" Yes, she really was going to force him to come out with it.

"You don't understand the way things are. To start with, your ship is barely legal to fly and anyone looking too close may yet decide otherwise. There's those looking to take advantage of you with that ... or other things."

"And you don't think I understand that? I've got all the Records to say that the ship's passed inspection right before we left. If Paxton Ship Yard credentials aren't enough, then there's a much bigger problem than me."

"It's more than that, and you know it. I've kept you safe in the Ship Yard. Bithy's boys watch out for you—which you don't appreciate nearly enough."

What he meant was that she didn't appreciate Palmer enough. And he was right. She didn't appreciate him at all.

She worked her tongue along her teeth. He was right on one count. Joco cowed most of the Yard hands too much to bother harassing a little arli-bug. Most, but not all. And it wasn't Bithy's brood who dealt with them either. But Joco wouldn't believe that she was smart and capable enough to do that. "It's not like I have a name or connections for anyone to be interested in." She touched the round, flat burn scar behind her left ear.

"Sander did that, not me." Joco's voice rang with the same disgusted tone he used for anything related to Mama's other man.

Technically, that was true. Sander had officially marked her nameless. That's why she was Lysand, using her mother's name. "You've done nothing to change it."

"I gave you your honest name, what more do you expect?" He shifted in his seat—a guilty conscience, or concerned how it would make him appear before the election that would follow the fight?

Either way, he did not want her to answer that question—for so many reasons. She pressed her lips hard and kept her eyes on the viewscreen.

"Ya got no experience with the way things are out there, Arli. The yard hounds are all bark, with you. None of them dare lay hands on you."

If only he knew—there was a reason she always had a knife, most often two. And Sander, not Joco, had been the one to teach her how to use it.

"But that ain't the way things are elsewheres. There are those who would see you as a way to get connected to me, name or no name. And neither one of us need that."

There he had a point, a miserable, painful, gut-wrenching point. But a point.

Especially if he became Chairman of Guilds. That was a valuable connection that some might be dumb enough to think they could gain through her, even if she was without his name. Maybe Sander thought that when he first connected with Mama. It could be that he got that connection with Joco, in a strange way. Sharing a woman could do that. But it was not the sort of thing she could ask about, or ever truly wanted to know. It was enough, though, to leave her certain that anyone looking for her favors was not to be trusted.

Joco clutched his forehead. "Keep to the pilots' lounge, then. I mean it. I got enough on my hands and no bandwidth left to pull your little ass out o' the fire."

"The pilots lounge, then. I can do that." Actually, that was an excellent place to look for job leads.

"And don't be—"

"I understand!"

"Don't be talking to me that way, I can still—"

"I understand that, too." No point in telling him she'd walk Laythe's Woods before that was happening again.

"Do as you're told and stay outta trouble, girl." He stomped for emphasis.

An alarm screamed.

"What sorta storm are you bringing now?"

"This shipping lane is being plagued by Raiders. I told you that before we took off. I rigged the pollution sensor to pick up—"

"What'd I tell you about that?"

"Fine, there, I turned it off." Instead, she'd turned the sensor to vibrate the left lower quadrant of her control pad. "You happy?"

"Stop pretending to be more than you are, girl. Straighten up and fly to standards. When we get back, I want everything about this ship refit to Guild specification. Then we'll talk. I got a solution for everything, but first I got to get through this." He shook his head and rubbed his temples.

Don't ask, don't ask. Whatever it was, she wouldn't like it. But her left hand was buzzing with pollution sensors picking up fuel residue traces that only Raider fliers left, and she couldn't afford the distraction now.

Chapter 8

DURING THE EXTRA-ORBITAL PORTION of the flight between Dextra and Lighten, they picked up a full Fleet escort. Whether the armed escort was necessary could be a matter of definition. The need to be present for High-Ranking Dextrines, whose support Fleet always courted, would have made the show—and it was quite a show—necessary in some eyes.

Were they under actual threat of Raider attack, though? Debatable at best, considering they were in a portion of space where both Dextrine and Lighten defense forces patrolled.

Contacts Matteo retained from Wroxton Academy, now established in careers in both the Dextrine Planetary Guard and Theran Space Armada, had independently assured him that their planned travel corridor showed no sign of Raider activity, nor did they have reason to expect that would change soon. So there was that.

Poor Beny had lost all color in his face when the first announcement about "evading Raiders" came through. He'd never come face to face with anything unfriendlier than the Dextrine Media, which, while vicious in their own right, limited their weapons to bullying with opinion pieces, and putting terrible spins on unflattering Records.

To be fair, it was probably as unsettling to the transport pilots as it was to Beny. Though all Timnon pilots were required to have advanced training in defensive flight maneuvers, none expected to use them.

To date, the Raiders had not penetrated the Dextrine planetary defense grid, to the point many believed it couldn't be done. Which was, of course, Lord Timnon's position, despite Matteo's best efforts to disabuse him.

All of which left Matteo questioning the reality of the "threat" and motivations for the show that was made of it.

"Final approach to Lighten atmosphere. Prepare for entry," the AI voice droned again.

"If you've got any more of those green tabs, this is where you're going to want them." Matteo adjusted his safety harness.

Beny pulled the packet from his pocket, chewed half of them, and groaned. "How do you do this? Seriously, how?"

"I suppose the same way you manage the blood and guts that are part of your world. I can't fathom how you can do what you do."

"Fair enough. Seeing the impact the Raiders are making for myself gives me a new appreciation for the problem." Not that Beny had actually seen anything, but for now, they could go with Beny's impressions.

"Remember that. I may call on you the next time I have that conversation with Grandfather. He seems to think the Raiders are a Theran problem, below our notice. He would rather argue whether or not we should consider ourselves Therans than deal with the reality of the situation."

Beny opened his mouth to reply, but the jolt of the transport penetrating the atmosphere shut it for him. He closed his eyes and gripped the armrests as his face took on an unhealthy green cast.

There was no rush to finish that topic of conversation. They would have the whole journey home to debate Grandfather's politics and philosophies.

Matteo leaned back and clamped his hand around the armrest, teeth gritted, tongue firmly held in check. If only he had a viewscreen or instrument readouts instead of leaving him blind and deaf, having to trust in the competence of Grandfather's appointees. As soon as he had comm-net access again, he would file his own paperwork for Lighten airspace flight clearances and researching what might be done, from the right side of the law, to hurry the documents along at top speed.

The cabin speakers buzzed and the AI voice said, "Making final approach into Anara." A screen dropped from the ceiling. "Please enjoy this message from the Lighten Tourism Guild."

"They've organized into a guild now? Interesting. The last I read, they were still trying to establish themselves as a separate industry." Beny stared at the screen. The distraction would do him good.

"The Lighten Tourism Guild welcomes you to Anara." The female AI voice had shifted to a prerecorded message. With a hint of a Lighten accent, it was just enough to add local color, but not so much as to make it difficult to understand. But the intonations were all wrong, making Matteo cringe. "As you approach, if you look out your windows or viewscreens you may find it difficult to identify the Anara metroplex."

They got that right. Flat desert landscape with few signs of occupation, save what appeared to be a massive landing zone and several fields of parked ships surrounding a moderate-sized, low domed structure with what seemed to be four commodious entrances at the poles and median of the dome.

"One hundred years ago Anara was a small mining claim in the Firen Mining Group. Seventy-five years ago, its real value was discovered."

Beny leaned toward Matteo. "It failed as a mine and someone was trying to recoup their losses."

"Purchased as an experimental venue by the Entertainment Guild, it has become the premier entertainment destination on Lighten. The High Jipny Desert offers a remote yet central location where travelers can find something to suit every taste." The AI's voice emphasized "every" with a sultry lilt.

Matteo grimaced. Focus on the facts being correct, that was the thing. The High Jipny Desert was dead center of the single major land mass on Lighten, making it central to everything, but the terrain made it remote. A truly novel feature.

"Far enough from civilization that those who can afford to get here think they can't get caught doing whatever is skirting legal back home," Beny murmured into his fist.

Matteo snickered. He wasn't wrong. Dextra had enough of its own entertainment complexes. Anara couldn't be too different.

"Because of the challenges of Jipny's extreme climate, Anara's developers faced special obstacles which led to the development of significant building innovations. As a result, Anara is the largest underground complex of its kind in the Kayavan System." This time the voice emphasized "underground" in the same, now incongruous, lilt.

"I think it's the most recent addition to the complex that's made it the record holder. Makes me wonder how the formation of the Tourism Guild is connected to all this." Matteo chewed his bottom lip. Would the Raiders see this as an attractive target because of the remote location? Or was it too big for them to tackle at the moment? Hard to guess.

"And the fact you'd even think to ask that is why you need to be the one to take Grandfather's seat."

"With an army of Hospitality Specialists, versed in *every-thing* Anara has to offer from ecotourism opportunities to fine dining, sports of *every* variety, both recreational and *professional*, to on-stage entertainment to suit *every* taste, our staff is available to assist our guests find the perfect experience, anytime day or night. Welcome to Anara, we hope you enjoy your stay." The media screen retracted into the ceiling, which seemed for the best as the innuendo had escalated to an absurd degree.

But maybe Matteo was oversensitive to such things.

"They forgot to mention the business conference center, the gaming facilities, and a few other specialties represented in their offerings." Beny winked.

"Did you really need to go there?"

"Just looking out for you, don't want you to miss out on the real Anara Experience." Beny elbowed him. "Relax, you know I'm—"

The ship jolted hard enough to knock Matteo's module out of his hand.

"Clumsy useless fliers—no excuse for that in this class of ship." Matteo closed his eyes and muttered under his breath, cursing in alphabetical order.

"You've added a few new ones to the list."

"Gotta keep things fresh."

"I'm taking notes."

"Don't go teaching those to any of your sisters, especially Cortly or Patryce. Grandfather already blames me for being a bad influence on them and teaching them their most inappropriate behaviors."

Beny spat a chuckle. "If only he knew where those really came from."

"The less said on that the better." Matteo contorted himself to retrieve his module and made a show of turning off the privacy ware.

Beny sighed.

The air seemed to turn stale and heavy as they resigned themselves to the inevitable need for decorum once again.

"Please remain in your seat with your safety webbing securely fastened until we have come to a complete stop at the Premier Entrance to the Anara Complex."

"You ready for this?" Beny asked.

"No, that's why I need a handler, remember?"

The hatch opened with a blast of desert-hot metallic-smelling air that snatched Matteo's breath away as he freed himself from the safety webbing and headed out. Ferocious sun beat down on them with an intensity that made an interrogation from Grandfather seem mild. So, this was Lighten's greeting. Trying to make a point, perhaps? A little reminder about how insignificant Matteo was here?

Grandfather would appreciate a place that did that; probably try to have him assigned here as some sort of liaison the next time Matteo crossed him.

He preceded Beny down the ramp more because Beny was still trying to get his feet under him than from any matter of protocol. Still, it made for a good show for the Media, Matteo leading the way for the Clan or some such rot.

Shimmering heat rose from the pale-gray paved ground that led into a debark field for ships bearing less significant passengers. In the distance, past rows and rows of personnel transports, large and small, the pavement disappeared into the too-bright sky, a wrong enough shade of blue to be disconcerting.

Beny's jaw dropped, and he panted slightly. He'd never been off-planet before and it showed. The experience took some getting used to, no matter how much one prepared.

Everything here was a few degrees off from both Dextra and Thera. The sky should have been bluer. The air tasted wrong, and wasn't quite satisfying to breathe, making it tempting to breathe hard and fast like Beny. The sensation would pass, thankfully, but those first few minutes could be truly anxiety-provoking. Lighten's gravity was slightly lighter than at home—that's why the first settlers to Dextra's moon had dubbed it Lighten in the first place. Or so the story went.

For all that the texts said Dextra and Lighten shared the same atmospheric and planetary conditions, they didn't. No more than Dextra and Thera did. Knowing that helped get one's expectations in order and feel more comfortable in the new space. Beny would figure it out soon enough. It was one of those things you couldn't tell someone. They had to sort it out for themselves.

A white-uniformed team of three hospitality specialists, two women and a man, approached the end of the ramp, checking their modules as they walked. No doubt double-checking the details of their charges. A brute squad of standard-issue security guards flanked them. Six matched guardsmen in sand-colored paramilitary uniforms, armed with an impressive array of modern-issue arms, both lethal and not.

How much would it take for him to shake their company?

"Lord Heir Timnon, Lord Heir Sennet?" A white-uniformed woman stepped forward. Her tailored skirt and short-sleeve jacket stood up crisp and perky in a climate where lesser garments would slump into a heap, begging for mercy from the oppressive heat. With her dark hair tied back in a tidy knot and a fine sheen of sweat covering her face, she held her module before her, as though it might offer answers to questions she didn't yet know how to ask. Questions like: What is the proper greeting for a High-Ranking Dextrine heir?

Luckily, Beny was not any more insistent on those forms than Matteo was. Now, if Grandfather had been with them, they would have been spending the next hour dealing with the grave offense that had been committed.

"This is our first time to take in the Championships." Such a wonder to watch as Beny smoothly took over. This was the sort of situation where he shined, and Matteo was only too happy to let him, which often gave the impression that Matteo was prideful and aloof. Better that than uncertain and socially awkward.

"It is our honor to be your hosts." The woman laced her hands together and dipped her head.

The local greeting, if Matteo remembered the briefing correctly. Technically, the correct response would have been taking the hospitality specialist's hands and placing them against his cheeks. That was not going to happen, though.

The Media would run with such images and in mere hours, they would be implying secret dalliances and worse if he permitted such personal contact. Far less dangerous to risk offending the locals.

Considering how often Dextrine Ranks gave offense to those below them in society, it was more or less expected, and thus not media worthy. So, he followed Beny's lead and bowed from his shoulders.

"We have a private box prepared for you at the arena and a suite in the Lodgings Wing where you may be assured privacy and comfort. As soon as your modules are connected to the Anara private network, a thumbprint will allow you access to all the lock codes on your accommodations. You will also find maps and schedules to all public and conference events, including those sponsored by the trade guilds and consulate."

Matteo pulled out his module and confirmed his access. What a pleasant surprise. He had been warned not to expect Lightens to be efficient. The first prejudice to fall.

"My direct call codes are in your diplomatic packet. Please contact me if you have any questions or requirements that have not been fulfilled. My assistants will be available to help you with *anything* you might require." She gestured to the matched pair of white-uniformed "Hospitality Specialists," according to their name tags, standing slightly behind her. Hopefully, that meant they would be administrative support, not offering other sorts of hospitality.

While those sorts of professional favors might be far less complicated than more personal ones, Matteo's life was already far too complicated. Though, at times, it might be tempting, it still was not enough to risk the outcomes if something were to go even slightly sideways.

"What of the training and ringside facilities?" Beny asked. "Lord Heir Timnon is scheduled for an exhibition bout at some point, but we have not been provided those details."

"That information is provided to each of the fighters or their manager if one is designated."

"Lord Heir Sennet is my trainer and fulfills the role of a manager in this case," Matteo said.

"I understand." The lead Hospitality Specialist tapped her module and Beny's pinged. "Trainer's clearances and documents have been added to your Records, sir."

Beny, diplomat that he was, didn't check. He just nodded.

"Your security detail will accompany you throughout your stay with us, as will my team and I. While we do not anticipate any problems, caution is the first precept of Vigilance, is it not?"

Ah, vigilance. *Vigilance, Valor, and Victory.* Thera's favorite three-word cheer. Had someone done enough research on him to realize he'd been trained at a Theran military academy? Vigilance indeed.

Unfortunately, this all meant that he would be under much tighter watch than he'd hoped. No question he had Grandfather to thank for that. So, getting out for his little "'quest," as Beny called it, might be more difficult than he'd hoped. But he had slipped the watch of far more highly trained guards than these.

"If you will follow me, please, we have a brief facility tour, and then we will show you to your suite, if, of course, that is agreeable." She bowed, albeit awkwardly. Clearly, that was not a familiar gesture for her. But she tried and ought to be respected for that.

"That would be most helpful," Beny gave the appropriate twitch of his head, not a full nod, but an acknowledgment that would save Matteo from having to respond.

All the years at Wroxton had left Matteo's skills at this sort of thing rusty. Not that they had ever been that good to begin with. The military protocols that ruled Wroxton were far less subtle, and subtle had never been Matteo's strong suit. Best have Beny continue to lead on this.

They followed their assigned hospitality specialists, flanked by their security team, to an arched portico that sheltered a wide door into the facility. Vents along the arch pumped cooler air into the portico, easing their transition from the desert heat to the chilled and humidified environment inside. Just through the doors, they paused, giving Matteo's eyes a moment to adjust from the blinding brightness outside to the dimmer artificial light within.

A long stone-tiled hallway, lined with screens displaying diverse images of the Anara complex and the attractions it offered, led them to an impressive bank of elevators built into a round column that was most likely at the center of the dome he had seen on the landing approach.

"These are the Premier elevators," the lead hospitality specialist said. "Use your thumbprints to access them. They can be identified throughout the complex by the carved sandstone trim around the doors." She ran her fingers along the intricate filigree carvings. "Once your party is inside, they will not admit other passengers until you have been delivered to your destination."

"Excellent." Beny nodded again.

A bit high-handed, but especially appreciated, considering the hazards of being in a confined space with unknown personages for any length of time. The Media could get very creative on slow news days.

The hospitality specialist touched the print pad and the polished bronze doors slid open to reveal a spacious elevator lined with polished wood panels and lit with a filigree of lights built into the ceiling. Gaudy, but fitting for an entertainment complex.

Half the security team entered first, then Beny and Matteo, then the hospitality specialists and finally the rest of the security team. That's why the elevator was huge. And now rather crowded and stifling. Hopefully, they would reduce the security team to a more reasonable number after the initial show of hospitality was over.

Fast and smooth and with a far better landing than their pilot had achieved, the elevator came to a stop and disgorged their cumbersome party into a substantial common area. Soaring ceilings arched overhead in a web of steel and stone whose artistry would have fit an art museum. Below their feet, a stone mosaic subtly indicated traffic flow and even a suggestion of lanes to keep directions of travel separate.

Not as rustic and primitive as he had been led to believe. So much for Grandfather's briefings on the hardship of Lighten's accommodations. Another prejudice to be set aside.

"This is the Premier central hub for the Anara Complex. Each spoke of the hub will take you to one of the main wings, each designated by their own color: Sports, Dining, Performance, Gaming, Conference, Lodgings, Administration, and Support Systems, where you will find a fully-equipped medical center, a library, equipment rentals, and tour planning services. All locations in a wing are designated by the wing color and a number. The numbers increase as you get farther from the hub. Interactive map screens are available at every intersection, should you need them. But our team will be with you for your entire stay, so you can rely on us to ensure you find your destinations easily."

Translation: full-time babysitting. Matteo swallowed back a sigh.

"If you will follow me down the green Lodgings Wing, your suite awaits." The hospitality specialist gestured to her left.

Encased in their living security cocoon, they reached their Dignitary Suite, which they were assured was the finest accommodation Anara offered. Beny politely declined a tour of the suite. Best to keep everyone but him and Beny out of the space. With the Suite Support office across the hall, the aides could easily be reached if necessary.

Beny closed and locked the door behind the departing hospitality team, leaning hard against it, fingers pressed to his lips.

Matteo pulled out his module and set the privacy ware. It took several tries before the happy green blink assured them they could breathe again.

The grand living room, huge when one considered it was an underground facility and space was at a premium, had been primed with artificial "fresh air" scent that was especially noticeable in that it smelled nothing like the outside air when they had landed. Not unpleasant, but not a natural smell. Decorated in varying shades of white—who knew there were so many versions of white, and all of them a questionable choice for decorating a room to be lived in?—the suite boasted soft, comfortable seating clustered near a media screen, a wide desk in the far-right corner, next to a door leading to one bedroom. A kitchen wall and dining table occupied the left side, along with another bedroom door. The most prominent feature, though, were the floor-to-ceiling false windows taking up the entire back wall.

Advanced viewscreens displayed a feed from what a local artist deemed to be the most attractive view of the outside. The trick to a good artificial window was displaying the right frequency for the sunlight, and these did that well, making it easy to believe they were not a hundred meters underground.

"So?" Matteo fell onto the center of the nearest couch and sprawled, taking up as much space as he could. Not a dominance move. He had to shake off the sense of confinement soon or he might well lose control of his tongue. Beny didn't need one more thing to manage.

"Better than the expectations I'd been given. The staff here clearly knows their business, if not all the intricacies of Rank protocols. I could see coming up here sometime and taking in some of the ecotourism opportunities I saw listed. I'm a lot more interested in meeting with the Tourism Guild rep now, for certain." Beny dropped on the opposite couch into a somewhat more polite sprawl.

"When I'm in a better mood, I'm sure I'll agree with you. Maybe if we're on a private visit they can pare back the entourage to less than a battalion."

"I imagine you've already been planning your escape from the babysitters so you can pursue your side quest?"

"You know me so well. I've managed to find the staff map for the complex. " He called up files on his module and handed them to Beny. "Apparently there are service corridors connecting everywhere to everywhere else. I registered as Matteo Sennet, a visiting pilot, and they gave me clearances into most of them."

"You're lucky they didn't connect your name to who you really are."

"I'm not the only Matteo Sennet on Dextra, and the pilot credentials are genuine and don't include titles, so it worked. At least for now. I should be able to get down to the pilots' lounge easily enough on those. Once the luggage arrives, I'll have my gear that should make me look like an ordinary Dextrine pilot—didn't want to have Records of printing that up here—"

"You are taking paranoid to new levels. You know that, right?"

"Not at all. You remember that weekend I took off my last term at Wroxton?" Matteo sat up a little straighter. "I printed up a decent suit so I could try a new restaurant. Some moron let the Media get hold of that information. Imagine my surprise to learn that I was having a clandestine rendezvous with a secret lover that evening."

"Grandfather dragged you from one end of Laythe's Woods to the other over that, I imagine."

"Putting it mildly, yes. And if you'd been on the receiving end of his ire as often as I have, you'd be as 'paranoid' as me."

Beny laid a long-fingered hand over his eyes. "I'm sorry, I should have remembered that."

"Yes, you should. Give me the benefit of the doubt, please. I need you on my side here." That was a little more forceful than he meant to be. This was Beny, after all.

"I am. Really."

"Then cover for me on this one. My exhibition round isn't for a couple of days. That should give me plenty of time to be out and back before I'm noticed."

Beny tapped his module and stared, crestfallen, at the screen. "And what about these meetings Grandfather has us scheduled for?"

"'Us' is the operative word here. The first meeting is coming up in a couple of hours, the first few actually. We'll go to those together. After that I'll dip out for a bit—claim a stomach bug or something. They are common enough after travel and strange food, right? You keep doing the dutiful heir thing, and keep the show running. I'll be back as soon as I can, before the important Trade Minister's dinner. Yeah?"

Beny scrubbed his cheek with his hand and blew out a long breath. "You realize how much you owe me for covering for your sorry ass, right?"

"You know I'm good for that debt."

"You always have been."

Chapter 9

JOCO LOOKED SO PEACEFUL asleep, snoring softly, head cradled against a broad gray strap of safety webbing cocooning him in his well-padded seat. Despite having space for two more passengers, Joco's presence filled every corner of the hauler, critiqued every centimeter of her crammed-with-too-many-readouts control panel, and disapproved of every innovation aimed at making her a better, safer flier. That was a lot of presence for a single man. Such a shame to wake him.

"We're down." Ari poked his shoulder with all the wariness one approached a sleeping sollert.

He snorted and rolled away from her as much as the webbing permitted, knees and elbows constrained in the compact cabin. "I ain't got the energy for your games. Tell me when we're there."

Must be enjoying his nap, or more likely, he had his earpiece in and had an audio version of his notes for the meeting playing. Even with the ample media screen she had provided, reading would have been taxing, and the extra-large print would have been a visible admission of his worsening vision, something he avoided at all costs. Would have been nice to realize that before she'd gone to the effort and expense of installing it. But there would be other paying passengers who would appreciate it, so there was that.

"I'm not joking. Open your eyes. You've got fifteen minutes before your Ag Guild meeting." She poked him again.

He snarled, opened one eye, and strained to sit up straight. "Damn. How long've we been down?"

"Just pulled up to the Standard Entrance." She pointed to the crowded metal archway hung with easy-to-read rust-colored letters spelling out "Welcome to Anara." People flowed from every direction toward those words. Getting through that crowd was likely to make him late. Why did he refuse to use the less crowded Prime or even Premier entrances? As Guild Master, he should be entitled—

"You should have woken me sooner. I needed time to get prepared. You land like an arli on a raindrop—it's unnatural." He fought his way out of his straps.

From him, that was a compliment. Mostly. Her landings were unnaturally delicate, though. Enough cargo breakage fines did that to a pilot. She hadn't had a single bumbled cargo in years. Not that he would know that, considering most of her jobs were off-Record.

She opened the hatch. Heat rushed at them in a suffocating wave, replacing the lighter cool air with its unmistakable weight. "It ain't that hot. No reason you can't—"

She mouthed '*no*' and shook her head. "What are you so damned afraid of? I'd sooner fly back to Paxton."

"That's the thing." He smiled. "Why don't you do that, then? It's better than—"

"You going to pay the extra fuel? Upfront?" If he didn't pay it upfront, that was the sort of thing he'd deny ever having agreed to.

He scowled and glanced over his shoulder at the crowded entrance.

"That's what I thought. Are you ashamed to be associated with me? I don't get it."

His eyes bulged, and he threw his hands up, brushing the ceiling. "That's the problem, you don't. You're used to being sheltered under my watch. I don't want to see you taken advantage of."

No, he did not want to be taken advantage of through her. But he wouldn't appreciate her pointing that out. "Doesn't it help that I promised to keep to the pilots' lounge? All the Lighten pilots are Guild members, and they owe you loyalty."

"I suppose." He clutched his forehead. "But in the pilots' lounge there'll be Dextrines and Therans, and storm-shorn Fleet pilots who'd use you without a second thought."

"Drown it all! No one's getting a connection to you through me. What do you think I'm going to do? Cozy up with the first pilot I meet?"

His eyes narrowed, but thankfully he didn't say what he was thinking. It wasn't as if she couldn't guess.

"I ain't given you any reason to think that of me." She turned aside. "I saw enough of what cozying got Mama. I want no part of that kind of comfort." Drown it! Drown him! She never meant to say that.

Why did he get to her like that? Drown that, too!

He huffed something that sounded like he was satisfied. "Don't let anyone on this cobbled-together heap of scrap, for no reason. I don't want no one getting the idea I approve of how close you are to violating Guild standards."

If only he knew she'd crossed that line long ago, he'd never have let her off the ground in the first place.

"Heard." And she heard, but she sure as storms wasn't going to agree, and would have the Records to show she hadn't.

He stomped out, and she shut the hatch behind him.

Sweat dripped into her eyes. She dragged her sleeve over her face. Best get out of the heat before she got into real trouble.

She guided the hauler down the taxiway to the fourth lot on the south side of the arena, near the Sporting Wing, where a fighters-and-staff-only exit would allow a quick and private departure, should he deem it necessary. Which essentially meant if he lost, or was too injured to present a solid Media image for the upcoming election.

What was that on the floor? Sollert shit! Joco left his bag. She probably ought to take it to him, but after that little show, he could find his own way to get it himself. She was a pilot and not a porter, and today she'd act like one.

She retrieved her rucksack from the cargo hold and locked up her hauler. Leaning against the dusty hull, she pulled out her module. What folder had those instructions? There. Check-in at the Staff Security station, Basic Entrance. A friendly line-map appeared under the directions. Seemed simple enough. She ambled toward the enormous arena's Basic entrance at the far edge of the debark field.

Paved in light-gray, lightly-textured concrete, formulated for minimal thermal expansion, the debark field stretched out a kilometer in every direction. Ships of every description lined up in neat rows along the field, each row marked by a tall, thin utility pole that held Recor-keeping equipment and lighting. In the distance, several transport shuttles, like determined millipedes, crept down the rows, picking up and dropping off Anara's guests. Few had any interest in braving the heat to walk to the arena entrance.

But Ari had even less interest in being packed into an over-crowded vehicle with a driver she didn't know, surrounded by excited tourists. Walking was far less taxing.

The same sun beat down on her as it had in Paxton. But somehow it was so very different. Many joked about the dry desert heat being different from the cloying humidity endemic to the Paxton Swamp region. But apparently the jokes were true.

So light and thin it seemed almost sharp, desert air was easy to breathe. Not like the heavy spongy air of the swamp. But her lips had already grown parched. This heat had the attitude of a predator lying in wait, lulling prey into complacency with its feather-light touch.

She understood the swamp, with its predators, slipsand, the bloodsuckers, and storms. But this place made her wary. That wasn't a bad thing. She picked up her pace.

The crowd at the Basic entrance was as extensive as the one that swarmed around the Standard, but more unruly. It seemed the designers had expected that by building immense stone columns to surround the base of the metal arch, painted with "Welcome to Anara" in gigantic white letters, that would withstand the press of the throng. Many group tour services utilized this entrance, especially those that started the tour by opening the onboard bar.

White-uniformed hospitality specialists paired with discreetly armed guards ushered the crowds into lines and encouraged them to watch the screens hanging throughout the portico that teased at the wonders Anara had to offer. For the most part, the efforts at distraction worked and kept the visitors from becoming too short-tempered.

It wasn't as though she had plans that would suffer by waiting in this crowd, but the sight of "Staff Check-In" on the far right, almost beyond the portico's shade, buoyed her spirit. No line. Only one bored-looking guard stationed there. Perfect.

She dodged around the crowd and made it to the station without anyone following with the idea that it was a shortcut to avoid the proper line.

"Which crew?" he asked, not looking up. Despite the shade, sweat covered his face and his dark hair was stuck to his head. His sand-colored short-sleeved shirt and matching slacks showed the dust as much as they did the sweat. The only thing that looked clean and fresh about him was the sidearm in his belt holster.

She cued credentials on her module and held it out. "Paxton Yard."

His head whipped up and his jaw dropped as he scanned her credentials. "Joco's staff?"

"Does pilot count as staff?"

"Yes, it does." He tapped his module. "Give me a second, and I'll get you approved for the pilot's lounge. What's your flight handle?"

"Paxton 23."

"That checks out. Come on, my shift's ending, and there's my replacement. I'll walk you down to the pilots' lounge." He beckoned her to follow him to a smaller door, beside the crowd entrance, that opened to his thumbprint.

Cool, climate-controlled air blasted her so hard she shivered, barely able to see in the far-dimmer-than-sunlight interior.

"You'll get used to that in a minute. It's always a shock coming in from outside. A different feel to the way climate control is used in the swamps." He straightened his shirt and slicked back his hair as they paused in the tight vestibule. "This way."

He opened a second door into a crowded corridor, thrumming with the noise of people and music and air circulators and more people. Bright screens covered every vertical surface. Tour-group meeting points flashed in company colors, attracting tourists like moths.

Twinkling blue lights topped the map screens, making them, and the hospitality specialists that flanked them, easy to find. Red lights indicated interactive informational screens that, if they were to be believed, would be active anytime day or night, and provide quick and accurate, individualized solutions to all visitor problems. The rest of the screens, like the ones outside, advertised the entertaining wonders of the complex with something to suit every taste and desire.

Except, apparently, the desire for quiet.

"Overwhelming, isn't it? You get used to it, though." The guard motioned her down a corridor, near the sleek tiled wall. "The different wings fan out like wheel spokes and are color-coded to make them easier to navigate. Lodging is the green corridor, between Dining in blue and Support in red. Sporting wing is yellow. Cross corridors link the wings and are marked with the colors they connect. The closer to the central hub, the more posh the facility, the deeper, the more posh."

"I imagine the pilots' lounge is at the end of the green spoke, surface level?"

"Give the little lady a prize."

"I may be little, but 'little lady'? Really?" She clenched her fists at her side.

He winced, as he should. "Sorry, no offense intended. Spent so much time among the tourists, I kinda forget my manners among my own kind."

"What do they call you—I can read the name tag, but what do the ones who know you call you?"

A slow smile bloomed that encompassed his whole round face. "Marsh. They call me Marsh."

"I like that, rather homey. I'm Arli." She laced her hands in front of her chest and dipped her head.

He took her hands and pressed them to his cheeks. "You're the first to use my honest name since the Championship crowds landed. You have no idea how cold it is to be among those who don't know you and have no desire to. Thank you for your hospitality."

"Please accept the hospitality of what I have, according to your need."

"I receive your hospitality with gratitude, and offer what you need according to what I have." He extended open hands to her.

She pressed his hands to her cheeks. "I am a stranger here and appreciate your hospitality."

They both stepped back and smiled. It wasn't much, but it was nice to have someone she knew here, even if it was only a name.

"And for that," he grinned, "I'm going to tell you a secret. The packet you got says pilots must sign in and out of the lounge whenever you enter or leave. But taking side jobs is a thing and crew bosses ain't always in favor of their folk taking those jobs. In fact, I hear that if you're looking for such opportunity, there's someone already waiting for Paxton 23 to check in."

Who would care that she was here? Maybe someone she'd already done work for? There were some pretty satisfied customers in her history. "You've got a workaround?"

"Yep. The check-in pings off your module whenever you use the main doors. There're service doors that don't take a module ping when they're unlocked and they get left unlocked as a matter of practice. Take those gray-tiled service corridors and ..."

"Nice."

"I'll give you access to the service map when we ping into the lounge." He jerked his head, and they continued down the green corridor.

"That seems like an awful big favor for calling you Marsh."

He threw back his head and laughed. "There's been a bit of a pool betting whether or not Joco'd be flying himself in. Finding you means I win." He looked over his shoulder and winked. "Any idea why he's having a pilot bring him in?"

If word got round about Joco's vision issues, that could affect his media image, no matter the outcome of the fight. Was that part of the reason he didn't want her seen? It made sense.

Marsh did not need those sorts of details, though. "Considering he's going to be Chairman of Guilds at the end of the

Championships, there's a heap o' work to be done. Figured time would be better spent getting ahead on that."

"That's some ego he's got then. There's even odds on the fight and the elections."

She shrugged and bobbed her head in a neither-yes-nor-no. "I suppose you gotta have big balls to run a guild, much less all of them."

"Makes sense." Marsh seemed a little disappointed, but whatever he'd won from his bet would make up for that. "Lounge is here. Commercial pilots only."

He stopped at a pair of plain green metal double doors that matched the green of the hallway. No sign marked the entry, not even a thumbprint pad. Interesting. Few tourists were likely to make it this far down the Lodgings Wing, so few who did not belong would try to enter. Making it so unnoticeable only improved that passive level of security.

Marsh looked up and pointed at a small light over the left edge of the door. It flashed twice, and his module, then hers, pinged a polite little notification. That was how they secured the doors. The doors slid open, and a low hum of human activity poured out.

The vast room spread out in all directions around the door, divided without walls, into spaces for different uses. At least a hundred pilots milled about inside, and it only seemed half full.

"Over there's the service door I mentioned." He pointed to a green-painted doorway tucked in the far corner nearest the wall of—were those real windows or artificial ones showing a view of the debark field?

"Yes, those are real windows, some of the few in the facility. Most are artificial and the views on them strictly managed. They tried that in the lounge at first, but discovered pilots get twitchy if they can't see the weather directly." Marsh chuckled.

"We tend to be a pretty twitchy lot." And that was a polite way to describe it.

He ushered her a few more steps inside. The doors shut behind them, enfolding them in the lounge's embrace. Though loud, it differed from the tourist mayhem outside. These were people relaxing off duty, not frenzied to make the most of an expensive excursion in a flurry of frenetic energy. She drew in several deep breaths.

"You feel it too, don't you? That's why I sneak back here whatever excuse I can get." Marsh elbowed her softly, then gestured to a wide screen on the wall behind them. "That's where all the announcements and basic information are posted. The code for the side job board is on the crawler at the bottom of the screen. Register on the board and enter your constraints. There's an automatic system to match you up with jobs." He turned to the other side of the room and pointed out a long service window with evidence of a fully-staffed kitchen beyond.

Off to the left, near the windows, a forest of tables, large and small, basked in the sun. Maybe a third of the tables were filled with chatty groups, some with solitary pilots studying their modules. Nothing like the long, noisy tables of the Yard's food service building.

"Fresh cooked food's always available at that window there, courtesy of the venue. Real stuff, not the industrial heat-and-eat slop. Gonna grab something while I'm here. You pilots get the best of the staff provisions. Hard not to be a little jealous, but I suppose if it weren't for pilots, Anara couldn't function. The rest of us are easily replaced." He rolled his eyes and shrugged.

"Never really thought of it that way. I work at the Paxton Ship Yard. Pilots are as plentiful as swamp water there."

"Not so around here. Maybe one day Anara will be able to negotiate with the Transport Guild to have their own squad of pilots, but I ain't holding my breath on that one." He pointed toward a door to the left of the kitchen window. "Those doors lead to sleeping pods. Shower room is at the end of that hall. There are a couple of comfort rooms, if that's your fancy. You need to register medical clearance if you want access, though."

What would worry Joco more, comfort room access or the side jobs board? Tough call.

"The lounge is open all hours—lots of crews are on different time maps, so there's coming and going all the time. There's gaming feeds and media feeds available on the screens in the corner opposite the windows, if you want them, and plenty of space for good old face-to-face conversation, which I'm told your kind doesn't get much of."

"You're right about that. Thanks, I appreciate the hospitality." She laced her fingers before her chest and dipped her head.

He tossed a jaunty salute and headed toward the food counter. Not one for formalities, it seemed. But, all things considered, was that a fault? Probably depended on who one asked. For her, it was one less obstacle to fitting into an unfamiliar place, so it was positive.

She wandered toward the windows, oriented herself against the landmarks outside—oh, that was so much better, so easy to lose a sense of direction in the complex. That weight lifted. She surveyed the room.

Even for those without uniforms, it was clear who belonged to whom. The Lighten crews, even those in company uniforms, appeared casual and easy to approach.

The Dextrines, always, always, always conscious of Rank and Clan, mostly remained aloof and organized themselves by those invisible lines that divided them. It seemed they would talk to others, but always returned to their safe home base, a cluster of upholstered chairs and a matching couch near the windows.

The Therans, even the smaller ones, managed to be big and bombastic, and wearing some shade of black. If allowed, they would have taken up most of the space in the lounge. Their egos needed room to breathe.

No Fleet pilots today. That was just as well. For all their quirks, the rest were generally decent enough. One never knew about Fleet.

She scanned the link to the side jobs board and filled in her parameters, her rates, and her ship size. Hopefully, the job Marsh hinted at would pop up. Maybe something would come of that. Perhaps a useful connection that could lead to a job away from the Ship Yard. That might be far-fetched, though. She wouldn't hold her breath, but any extra funds would come in handy, paying off Mama's last expenses.

If Joco found out about any side jobs, he'd have her walking Laythe's Woods for it, though. Especially if it meant taking passengers.

So she'd have to make sure he didn't find out.

"You been here before?" A pilot wearing the distinctive rusty red of Firen Mines sauntered up. Like many of the miners, he wasn't physically large, all wiry muscle and sinew, his features sharp-chiseled. His presence more than made up for his modest height.

There were two kinds of miners. He was the sort that could go either way. He might be a total tunnel-snake, complete with fangs and venom. Or he could be the stubborn-as-rock-but-decent sort, rough around the edges but willing to offer hospitality. Hard to tell from here.

"Was supposed to be here last year but storms kept us at bay." She turned to face him, and his hazel-green eyes met her gaze with no hesitation.

"That was a splintering shame." He looked her up and down, a smile creeping across his face. Not handsome, but good-looking, and he knew it. "Who do you fly for?"

"Paxton Yard. You Firen, like your uniform?"

He cocked a brow and nodded, tapping the logo on his jacket. "I'm Pogo."

Her eyebrows climbed high. "Enforcer, then?" What other position could a man bearing the Arch Soul Catcher's name as his honest name do?

"You can be sure I still fly often enough, though. Now's your turn." He folded his arms over his chest.

"They call me Arli."

"You fly at the edge of the storm often?"

"As much as there's call for."

"I respect that. If you ain't afraid of the storms Raiders bring, and you're looking for new skies, Firen needs pilots. We're a better outfit than Fleet." He laughed again. "You Paxton 23?"

"You the one Marsh warned me about?"

"Warned? That's an awful strong word." He winked.

"He mentioned someone might be looking for me. Why?" She folded her arms and matched his posture. He wasn't as tall as Joco, but she still had to look up at him.

"Word gets around—pilots live in a small world. I'm looking for a particular breed of pilot who can handle passengers, cargo, and challenging situations, who isn't afraid of ... new things. What I've heard suggests you may be one."

Her skin prickled like a storm front approached. There was something he wasn't saying. But then again, that was usually the case with the jobs she got.

"Let me see what you can do, and if you're a solid fit, there could be a decent job with Firen for you."

"That's a pretty snap judgment if you only want a single trial run. You know nothing about me."

"You'd be surprised." His lips curled into a wry grin.

So drowning sure of himself. Was that attractive or intimidating? Both, definitely both. "I don't much like the sound of that. Care to explain?"

"Right to the edge of the storm. I like that. We can get a drink, and I'll answer whatever you want." He led the way to the mess counter.

All manner of beverage flashed on the menu, but no intoxicants. Made sense. She picked up a bottle of red swamp fruit juice and wandered to a pair of chairs around a small table near the window. "So, you were going to explain something to me."

He popped the lid on a bottle of non-intoxicating malt brew and dropped comfortably into the chair, spreading to take up more space than he needed. "Not as good as the real thing, but they don't need the liability of drunk pilots." He raised his bottle in a salute toward the mess counter.

She nodded and drew a long sip of juice. Tart, slightly sweet, with a refreshing, thin aspect and a shocking bright pink color. A little girly to look at, but with a surprisingly powerful sour pop at the end. Palmer had once said it reminded him of her. "So?"

"So, yes. What do I know about you? You're from Paxton, saw your ship come in, and you checked in through security as Paxton 23."

"I suppose it's not surprising for enforcers to keep track of that sort of thing."

"The ship you flew in on isn't a passenger transport, but a cargo hauler, and a near-ancient one at that. So, you're not flying commercial passengers. Paxton 23 has a rep for flying an old ship like the Hell Cat out of Laythe..."

She nearly dropped her bottle.

He enjoyed that a little too much. "Didn't realize anyone had noticed?"

"A bit surprised." Was this what Mama had warned her about?

"Given almost all the Paxton-based guests flew in commercially, and the ones that didn't prefer to travel luxury models, you must be flying the Guild Master. And I expect you're his daughter."

The juice's sour notes filtered through her bones, leaving her fingers and toes curling. "You may be right on a few of those points, but no, I don't have his name, and I can offer you no connection to him. You're chasing one blistering storm if that's what you're looking for."

"No worries, I don't need a connection. Brels wouldn't likely approve, anyway."

Mining Guild Master Brels' own pilot—what were the chances? Someone Joco would not approve of her meeting.

"You've got your own guild master on your wings? I'd expect him to travel with an enforcers' contingent."

"What I don't understand is why you're the only one in Joco's party." He cocked his head with raised brows.

"He likes to travel light."

"You mean he's cheap?"

"Your words, not mine."

"Loyalty. I approve." He saluted her with his drink.

Her module pinged—a response to the side job posting. She was supposed to meet with her potential employer in the side room in ten minutes.

"Job offer?"

"Might be."

"Don't want to get in the way of paying jobs. But, see if you can get approval for me to fly along, see what you're made of. Don't really care about the destination. Just need to see you in the cockpit, stick in hand." He winked.

"A job interview, then? On the back of a paid job?"

"We can call it that."

It probably wasn't the smartest thing to invite him along. But if he was good on his promise, it could be the opening she needed. "Is there a call code I can reach you at?" She raised her module.

He tapped his and touched the corner to hers. "That will get you to me. Only active for the next few days."

"Understood." She rose, gathered her juice, and headed for the side room.

Chapter 10

MATTEO TOSSED BENY a quick wave as he headed into the service corridor. A waist-high green stripe identified the hall as part of the Lodgings Wing. Narrow, with low ceilings, cool recessed ceiling lights, and gray-tiled walls, no normal visitor was likely to mistake this hallway for guest accommodations. Wearing basic pilot's drab, half a size too big, and walking with a bit of a slouch, he looked no different to anyone else traversing these corridors. Amazing how common garments could make such an effective disguise. Dress and act ordinary. That was all he had to do to disappear into the background. At least it worked often enough to be a viable option.

Grandfather hated the notion that any Rank of his Clan could appear "ordinary." Beny's reasons for disliking that disguise were at least better founded. It was a security risk. But some risks were worth taking. This side quest was one of those.

If he was lucky, he could get out and back in unrecognized, with the news feeds none the wiser.

That was too hopeful. Definitely too hopeful. Grandfather would know what he'd done by the time they got back. And there would be a key minder's price to pay. But that still wasn't as high as the price he'd pay if he didn't do this.

He glanced at his module again. Paxton 23 had replied to the message and was waiting for him in meeting room three attached to the pilots' lounge. Flying a nondescript, old-model cargo hauler could be an ideal way to get there and back, with little attention drawn his way. And if the pilot was connected to the Guild Master, it was the sort of connection that might be useful later.

His module's navigation buzzed, suggesting he was near a turning point, a plain service door, unmarked, like the rest of the corridor. Not a door he'd likely open without some other indication it was the right one. The module pinged to reassure him of his course, so he passed through it into another gray-tiled hall, with several small doors on the right and left and a larger service door at the end that, according to the map, would lead to the pilots' lounge.

Yes, checking out the pilots' lounge first was procrastinating, but getting the lay of the land wasn't a bad plan. So, he took a quick tour of the well-designed lounge. Not luxurious, but comfortable and practical. No question, Anara appreciated the role pilots played in the facility's success. Nothing like plying pilots with free food, lodgings, and some basic entertainment to ensure there was a ready supply of transport. Not luxurious enough to be considered unseemly or illegal, it was likely the kind of thing Lightens would consider under their rubric of hospitality. Not that he understood that very well, but it sounded right. Either way, a real win-win for both sides.

He picked up a bottle of cold black tea from the mess counter, glanced at the announcement board, and steeled himself for meeting with the pilot who might usher him into a new control over his own destiny—or utter disaster.

Might want to curb the dramatic streak a bit.

He headed back to the service corridor and paused outside the door marked "3." Just "3." That was all it said. No decoration, no further explanation. That was all.

What did one do now? Knock, wait, call out?

The door clicked and swung open. Did it pick up a ping from his module based on the meeting arrangement? That made as much sense as anything. Either way, it seemed appropriate to interpret that as an invitation to enter.

He pulled the door open a little farther and stepped in. Bright white-tiled room, barely large enough to count as a room, not a closet, much brighter than the tunnels had been. The air was slightly stale, that of a clean room that didn't see much use. Who'd want to spend much time there with the comfortable pilots' lounge steps away? A simple white table with matching resin chairs on either side, and a wall display screen added to the not-a-closet impression.

"Paxton 23?" he asked.

The pilot—a tiny woman drowning in an undecorated, drab flight suit—stood. "Yes, I am."

Her voice was pleasant enough, though her tone was crisp and businesslike. Good sign. Dark, tousled curls, which had come loose from a knot at the nape of her neck, framed her face. Her face was girlish, but the way she carried herself, she was no child. And her eyes, a unique clear golden brown he'd never seen before, sparkled with energy. She was pleasant to look at, but not distractingly so, the sort who would not stand out in a crowd. Ideal.

"I'm Matté." Inviting anyone to use his personal name, much less a nickname, was uncomfortable, especially with a woman, but it's what a regular pilot would do. Necessary to play the part. Just being ordinary.

"Dextrine?" She sat down and gestured for him to do the same. "The accent gives you away."

He wrenched open his bottle and sipped bitter black tea. Stronger than he preferred, but it was something to do with his hands while he figured out what to say. "It always does. You fly for the Paxton Yard?"

"Is that important?"

"It would give me a sense of whether you can do the job I need."

"You're asking for references, then?" Her expression suggested she would rather have been asked that directly.

He should have done that. Bad time to revert to his Rank training to demonstrate his importance by not coming out and simply saying things. "Yes." That actually hurt to say.

"The Yard doesn't keep Records for the private jobs its pilots fly. I have a reference list, if you need, but the Yard won't acknowledge it." She tapped her module and the screen to his left came to life.

Impressive list, divided between passenger and cargo runs. Routes to all territories on the single inhabited land mass on Lighten, and extra-planetary to Dextra, Thera, and some of Thera's orbital stations. Lots of experience to claim. But was it true?

"Those three at the top have links I can give you to check references. But a lot of my customers want their private runs to remain private. If that's not enough, then you'll have to find someone else." She shrugged as though she meant that.

No hard sell? Interesting. "You're the only one who registered my destination in their acceptable routes." He fought to keep his tone negotiation-neutral.

"I'm not surprised. You sure you want to go there? That flight path has had Raider activity not long ago and has been seething with pretty significant dust storms recently. I'll have to ask for a hazard pay rider to the contract." She called up a local weather report, confirming her claim about the storms, with a split screen showing an up-close-and-personal of what those storms looked like.

For the love of the ancestors! So those warnings about not going out into the desert without a guide had not been exaggerations. "I've got something I have to deliver in person."

She leaned back, eyes narrowed with a gaze that peered right into one's soul. Few ever dared look at him that way. It was disconcerting and a little exciting. "How legal is this delivery?"

"It's information, and completely legal. I'll attest to that in writing if you need. I'd fly it myself, but I'm still waiting on Lighten clearances to come through."

"Let me save you the temptation to wait on them. Those things take months at best, if you have all the right bribes in place. If you want to fly in Lighten airspace next season, you might have clearance in time. And even if you did, you wouldn't want to fly that corridor if you don't have experience in the winds and weather we get. Any local pilot will tell you the same."

"I've heard there is a pilots' chatter feed. Can I find you in that?"

She rubbed her knuckle along her chin. "It's considered private, and takes a while to be granted access." Chewing her lip, she stared at her module. "But it's a reasonable way to check up on me. I could give you access using my module, in this room only. See if you can find what you want that way. Would that suffice? I won't snoop over your shoulder or anything, you're free to search whatever you want. I won't censor anything."

"That seems reasonable." Not ideal. He'd have preferred his own access, but considering he didn't have Lighten clearances, it made sense that he wouldn't be welcomed in private conversations.

She opened the site on her module and cast several maps and additional weather reports on the wall screen. "I'm in, and you can have a poke about. Don't post anything under my identity, all right?"

"Of course." He took the module from her. She scooted back from the table and studied the data on the wall screen. Naturally, those maps were of the Firen Mining Headquarters region, where he wanted to go. The topography was pretty challenging—he hadn't realized it before, with rapidly changing elevations, and high-level wind patterns that could make the flight pretty tricky.

She glanced at him, then to her module.

Right, right, not the time to get distracted. "Paxton 23's your call sign, yes?"

"Yes, all my private jobs are under that sign." She turned back to the maps and scowled at the weather forecast.

He tapped a sophisticated analytic search into the pilots' channel and waited for it to churn through. Was the feed that slow, or was there that much on her? One eye on the module—an industry-hardened, basic model, designed to be nearly impervious to impact, electrostatics, and water. It had none of the frills he considered necessary, like built-in privacy and security features.

A triple beep announced the conclusion of the search, revealing many references to her flights and a number of discussion threads. A lot of information for a pilot with limited customer references. "Kayavan's bones!"

She turned over her shoulder to catch his eye. "Is that good or bad?"

He blinked hard and waved her off, skimming several long discussions. Interesting, a little alarming, but mostly interesting. "You've got a rep for getting the job done well and pissing people off in equal measure."

"Can't say that surprises me. People can get pretty touchy when it comes to how they like things flown." So calm, the way she said that. Hard to know what to make of it. Professionalism or indifference, both, neither?

"What do you think pisses them off the most?" Yes, it was a loaded question. No, it was not polite and only bordered on appropriate, but the answer would tell a lot.

She pressed her lips as though trying to decide how to answer. Finally, she shrugged. "If you want things done by the book, with no room for creativity or innovation, then I'm not the pilot for you. I don't look like much, but I'd put good money down that the number of flight hours I've logged this year is at least twice what you have. All woefully underpaid and strictly off the books. My ship don't look like much, either, but I have it kitted out especially for evasive maneuvers and amped-up shielding custom-built for Lighten's ... conditions."

"None of that regulation, I suppose?"

"Not a bit of it. But I'm alive and my cargo gets to where it belongs, in one piece, so there's that." At least she didn't mince words on the matter. "If that's what's important to you, then I might be your pilot. If not, there are others who can do the job for you."

"There's suspicion that you are the Transport Guild Master's daughter." The chatter feed was rife with it.

She rolled her eyes and grumbled under her breath. "He ain't claimed me. So don't put stock in any connection there."

Interesting. She wasn't trying to capitalize on a connection or convince him she was the pilot for the job. "Your flight clearances are through the Paxton Yard, though?"

"That's what the Paxton in Paxton 23 means. If you're worried about my ship, it's passed all required inspections as of this morning. I'm happy to show you the official forms from the Yard, no problem. If you don't want me to do the job, fine. But let's not waste time dithering about, yeah?"

"What are your rates?"

She pulled up another screen, this time a chart including distance, type of cargo, including passengers, extra fuel, and hazard fees. Next to it, she posted a standard written contract. "Read those over, and let me know your decision. I can give you a ten percent discount if you agree to a second passenger on the trip, a Firen miner who needs a flight out that direction."

"Another passenger?" That made it easier. If—when—Records of the trip got out, then having another passenger would quell rumors of impropriety. And if the miners trusted her skills, that was another mark in her favor.

And his gut approved. That was the most important thing. A pilot had nothing if they couldn't trust their instincts.

He studied the contract and fee schedule. "I can accept that, including the other passenger."

"Half due now, half along with any hazard charges due on our return."

"That's fair. Send me the transfer codes, and I'll get you the first half." He probably should try to haggle her down, but if she lived up to the reputation he saw in the chatter feed, her work would be well worth it.

Not to mention no other pilot seemed available to get him there. His trip to Lighten would be a complete waste if he didn't get to Iantha.

"Weather reports suggest first light tomorrow is the best time to head out. Will that work?"

"First light tomorrow. Done."

Her module pinged with the funds transfer. She glanced at it and nodded. "I'll make the arrangements. Pick you up tomorrow at the private lanes of the embark fields, near the Premier entrance."

She rose and bowed. Like a proper Dextrine—she bowed. Thank goodness she did not expect all the face and hand touching of a Lighten greeting. Perhaps this would be more tolerable than he feared.

"I'll see you at first light."

Chapter 11

SMALL AS THEY WERE, the pilots' lounge sleep pods were still better than trying to sleep in the cargo hauler. She'd been assigned a top row corner pod, similar to the berths she often wrangled flitters into before a storm. A ladder of sorts had been molded into the sleek composite wall, a matte, Lodgings-green surface, lined with hatchways just large enough to allow one to slide into the mildly cleanser-scented, downward-sloping pod.

A comfortable sleeping mat lined the pod's floor. A control pad along the side managed environmentals and a media screen that slid down from the top wall and locked the pod from within with a thumbprint. The sliding panel opposite the controls revealed pillow and blanket, and a spot to stow and charge a module. Not an extra handspan of space anywhere. Strictly utilitarian. But with a locker nearby to stow her gear and a locked hatch over her head, it felt safe, clean, and comfortable.

And there were showers. Real water showers. The sort that marked the height of luxury in the deep desert. She'd trade a spacious, well-appointed room for a real shower anytime. Sonics never left one feeling quite as clean.

Hair still damp around her ears, Ari stowed her rucksack back in a thumbprint-activated locker and picked up hot tea and a fragrant sausage-stuffed roll from the mess counter. To their credit, the freshly prepared, aromatic food left her mouth watering and stomach aching to break her fast. Nothing like the dining hall at the Ship Yard.

Despite the sun peeking over the horizon in the dark before dawn, the expansive pilots' lounge was every bit as active as when she had retired last night. Screens along the back and side wall flashed with information feeds, reminding everyone that with Kayavan's star rising, storms would be unusually powerful; entertainment feeds divided between sports and dramas that felt a little too close to home to be enjoyable; and games whose players and observers engaged with fierce concentration. Pilots tended to be intense about whatever they did.

Some faces and uniforms were familiar from yesterday. But it seemed like a fresh crop of ships had landed, and their crews were now unwinding from their flights. Though she was often around the Yard pilots at home, this was different, with a subtle sense of comradery and fellow-feeling that did not exist when everyone was looking over their shoulder, waiting for Joco to appear scowling from the shadows.

She sat down at one of the small tables near the windows in time to catch the sunrise blossom across the desert in a glorious showing that the Records couldn't capture accurately. Blue skies fading into violet and red, suddenly breaking open into a sparkling sun filling the horizon. So unlike the sunrise over the swamp.

The hot sausage roll melted in her mouth. Not preserved and reheated into a rubbery semblance of what it appeared to be. Anara was investing in getting pilots excited to return, despite the difficult flight corridors and weather. That was another avenue to search for work, the Tourism Guild's Anara routes. Chase that up when she returned.

She took a long sip of tea and pulled out her module. Just enough time to file flight plans and get the hauler to the designated spot with a few minutes to spare. Maybe get the interior tidied up a smidge.

The interior wasn't dirty per se as much as it was a cluttered, tight fit. Joco could not admit the important difference. Every bit of equipment she'd added improved performance, shields, or sensors, even if it impinged on comfort. All of which, unbeknownst to her until yesterday, gave her a unique reputation among her peers.

That notion was going to take some time to digest. It was such a contrast to what Joco had always told her. All of which were considerations for later. She had a ship to move, flight plans to file, and preflight checks to get underway.

Outgoing traffic proved sparse, ideal for her purposes. Making getting the hauler ready for departure smooth and efficient.

Three soft raps sounded on the hull, next to the passenger hatch. "Arli?"

She opened the hatch only enough to peek through. "Pogo?"

"Going to let me in?" Still wet behind the ears from his own luxurious real water shower, he wore Firen's signature rusty-red flight suit and carried a small bag of food from the pilots' lounge.

"I'm sure you've guessed my ship's a little ... irregular .... If I let you in, I need your word that you will not carry word of it—"

"Strictly between us. I'm no fan of Joco's, if you hadn't guessed." He met her gaze, unflinching.

It was a risk, but she had to go with her instincts. "Come in."

He climbed in and surveyed the deceptive chaos lining the interior, jaw agape. "What blew up in here?"

She could hardly blame him. All her touch-sensitive display screens were open along the dash, right below the viewscreen, every centimeter covered with some readout or control. A few manual switches and gauges peeked out between the screens, an eclectic mix between outdated and up-to-the-minute tech. Well, it was up-to-the-minute if one considered that she'd recently cobbled it together herself from the depths of her own imagination and the spare parts she could afford.

Additional storage lockers fit like a puzzle behind the two passenger seats all the way to the rear hatch. The luggage hold boasted its own set of reconfigurable lockers to accommodate a variety of cargo. Ugly, but very efficient, and reasonably comfortable, to boot.

She shrugged. "I don't carry flammables or live animals. Anymore."

He laughed into his fist. "Seems like a good idea. Gotta admit, this isn't what I expected from the outside. This a model from the Acoling lines?"

"A very old one and I never promised it would be new or pretty. I can promise that it all works. Very well."

"Let's say I believe you, which is a stretch at the moment—" Pogo took a few tentative steps inside, alternately staring and scowling.

Another knock. "Paxton 23?"

"Come in, Matté."

The big Dextrine, wearing oversized flight drabs, his damp sand-colored hair clinging to his forehead, nearly in his eyes, ducked to enter the hatch and stopped, jaw dropping. He wasn't staring at her ship.

Pogo's hazel eyes bulged.

In unison, they pulled shoulders back, chests puffed, posturing like fantail cocks. So sarding familiar ...

"Drown it!" She squeezed her eyes shut and pounded her fist on the armrest of her seat. "You're pilots, but you're fighters, too, and you've got a bloody bout scheduled, don't you?"

"So it seems." Matté sighed and shook his head.

"Neither of you have been completely straight with me." She slid out the hidden step she'd fitted underneath her seat to help her reach the upper panels and stood on it. Better, she didn't have to look up at them now. She glowered at Pogo and pointed at Matté. "Why don't you tell me who he is?"

"You're going to love this." Pogo chuckled, and he rubbed his fist into his palm. "He's only the heir to the largest clan Lordship on Dextra, Lord Heir Timnon. Top graduate of Wroxton Military Academy, reigning champion in Theran Academy-style wrestling. Betrothed to Lady Iantha of Corbel Clan, a political union, I might add. I expect you're heading out this way to an unapproved liaison with the Lady."

Matté scowled.

"Better than smuggling," she muttered. "Your turn, Matté, who is he?" She pointed at Pogo.

"He's Piers Phalen, Chief Pilot for the Firen Mines Enforcers and part of Guild Master Brels' personal security detail. He's in the second year holding championship status in his weight class. He co-owns a successful mining claim with his brother, and has designs on expanding their claim, and unless I miss my guess, making a name for himself in Guild leadership down the line. He fights classic Lighten-style, with particular emphasis on his ground game. Against a higher weight-class opponent, his strengths are—"

"Nice. You've done your research, I'll give you that." Pogo tossed a quick salute.

"So now you know us, what about you?" Matté pointed at Ari, looking far too smug and pleased with himself for that.

Arrogant trask.

"There I can help." Pogo folded his wiry arms and cocked his head, winking at her. "You get what you paid forward. She is Arilyn Lysand, honest name, Arli, flight designation Paxton 23. She's known to fly anything with wings and has the reputation of a hell cat in the air. She's the daughter of Transport Guild

Master Joco Hol's second woman. Though Joco doesn't claim her, it's widely believed that she's his daughter and he'll broker that connection into—"

"You can stop right there. He claims no connection to me, and I don't expect that changing. If that's what you're looking for, then you may as well cancel this flight as you ain't gonna find a connection with Joco through me. He makes his own connections, doesn't take them through anyone. Didn't I make that clear already?"

"So, he's saving you for some sort of arrangement like the big guy's?" Pogo jerked his thumb at Matté.

"Don't go there. If you want to fly, sit down, strap in, and shut up. Otherwise get out. Takeoff window opens in five minutes."

Matté sidled into the seat beside hers and strapped in.

Pogo took the seat behind her. "Show me what you've got. I don't care about your connections. I need pilots."

"You good flying with each other? I don't much like rival fighters sitting shoulder-to-shoulder in close quarters." She didn't bother turning to face them. They'd more than likely laugh at her.

"No point in wearing ourselves out before the show, yeah? Besides, pretty boy ought to arrive presentable for his lady." Pogo's seat creaked as though he were already leaning back, lounging comfortably.

Matté grumbled under his breath. "I don't want that out in the media."

"Behave yourself, and it won't happen." She leveled a potent stare over her shoulder. "Right, Pogo? I can't imagine that Brels would much like the idea that one of his bodyguards can't control his temper or his mouth, would he?"

Pogo snorted while Matté suppressed a smile. Nothing like a little leverage to keep everyone playing nice. Matté settled into his seat, doing what he could to avoid her unorthodox equipment arrangement.

She strapped in and finished her preflights. "Paxton 23, ready for takeoff."

"Proceed to runway twelve." The voice crackled through the cabin speakers.

"Here we go, gentlemen. Tighten your straps. You won't feel the takeoff. We're supposed to be clear from storms until midmorning. But no telling what's going to show up in the flight corridor." She guided the hauler down the taxiway, feeling each bump and crack in the pavement as they trundled along.

"What approach are you taking?" Pogo leaned against his straps to peer at the navigation panel and maps displayed on her leftmost control screen.

"The Klouis Canyon corridor has the least likelihood of an ambush." She pointed at the spot on the map.

"You don't like the Shoburn Heights route?"

"No. That mountain chain makes a great hiding place for Raiders."

"But the Klouis Canyons are wide and deep enough to hide—"

She huffed and glanced over her shoulder at him. "Raiders aren't finesse fliers. They stay out of that section of the canyon. They can't handle the updrafts."

"How do you know?"

"Squalls and storms, you are stubborn! Shut your mouth, sit back, and study the sarding Records, you'll see what I mean." She returned to her controls.

Pogo muttered under his breath as he tapped at his module. Clearly, he wasn't accustomed to being argued with. "I see what you're saying. Not sure I agree, though."

"Then when you fly, you can pick your route. If you want out—"

"No, you're pilot today." She could almost hear him raising his hands and backing away, muttering as he went.

"Remember that. Prep for takeoff." She stroked a worn, smooth spot on the control panel beside the control stick.

"Show 'em what you're made of, old girl." Beside her, Matté's brow creased, but he said nothing.

Smart man. Every pilot had their preflight rituals. Not all talked to their ships, but maybe they should. "And we're airborne."

"Nice, very nice. You give lessons? I know a few who could use some." Matté nodded.

"Color me impressed." Pogo whistled softly. "Hardly felt that. You do many passenger runs?"

"When the need is there. More often fragile cargo—just no live animals—never again." She shuddered. That memory would always do that to her.

"I've never done livestock." Matté chuckled. "The mind boggles with the complications that go along with it."

"The skin crawls. What was it?" The seat creaked—Pogo must have been leaning forward.

"Swine. It was memorable." She adjusted her sensors, shifted the extra displays for comfort, and rearranged her readouts from her takeoff patterns to standard flight controls.

"What did you do there?" Pogo's safety webbing creaked. Probably trying to get a better view. Twitchy fellow.

"I like to put up everything I need at a glance, but that changes between takeoff, flight, and landing. So, I move the displays and controls from the built-in dash controls to these and switch things around as I need."

"Is that a Paxton standard?" Matté leaned in and studied the array of panel displays.

"You have a problem with it?" She didn't quite control the snarl at the end of that question.

"No, I like it." His long, elegant fingers hovered over the nearest displays. "Those are standard screens strung together?"

"I know specialty panels give better resolution, but they're finicky to install and they get balky if you want to display something that isn't native to the hardware. I like the flexibility of putting any readout in any spot." Ari shifted the readouts around. No, it wasn't necessary, but who could resist showing off to someone who could appreciate the customization?

"That's got to simplify maintenance, too." The passenger seat squealed as Pogo adjusted it forward. He leaned over her shoulder, so close she could feel his breath on the back of her neck.

"That it does." She turned her head, nearly nose to nose with him. "Back off, a little. I like to breathe."

"You do your own work?" Pogo reached for one of the panels.

She slapped his hand back. "Best way to make sure it gets done right. Seriously, back off."

"I haven't seen too many customized ships. Much less this personalized. What else have you got? If you don't mind my asking, of course." Matté sounded more fascinated than judgmental. Not the way the Transport Guild responded to the idea of her off-spec tweaks. Drown it all, though, this was exactly what Joco didn't want her showing off. But it could get her the job she needed, so ... "Nothing's proprietary, but not much of it is likely to please inspectors with a case of the grumpies."

"I won't come back and use anything against you." Matté lifted an open hand in pledge. "And I'm sure Pogo will keep me honest to that."

"Damn straight, I will. Firen pilots have little loyalty to the Transport Guild, not with all the shackles they put on us." Even if Ari already knew it, it was a relief to hear. "I'm interested in what might be applicable to our systems."

"Seriously? This is swamp engineering at its finest, born out of a mixture of scarcity and necessity. It's nothing to be proud of. "

"Why don't you let us be the judge of that?" Pogo released his safety straps and edged in between the front seats, encroaching on her space, oozing a contagious enthusiasm.

"Where do you want me to start?" She threw an elbow into his side. Hopefully, he'd get the hint.

"How about the readouts and work from there?" Matté pointed at the nearest display.

"I like having everything right out in front of me where I can take in the whole picture at once, so I rigged this series of screens plus a little display-shift routine that sets up the patterns I like best on command." She shifted the display to reveal full system performance, then shifted again to a full sensor display, then a mix of navigation and traffic patterns. "I'd rather have all the details instead of the summaries when I can. Most find it overwhelming, though."

"I can see why." Pogo whistled through his teeth. "I'm starting to understand your reputation."

That didn't sound positive.

"There are some real advantages, especially for seeing patterns that don't show up in the summaries. I do something similar when I'm working a complex analysis." Matté tapped his fingers along the side of his jaw. Itching to mess with the touchscreens, no doubt.

"And since I'm running most systems close to their limits, I need to keep tight eyes on the performance reports." Might have been better not to have admitted that. If those details got out, she could be in real trouble.

"Show us those performance screens again." Pogo leaned into her shoulder. "Was this a standard hauler before you started in with it?"

She threw another elbow and shifted the display. "Not sure, my mother's man who had it before me tinkered with it, so no telling. Everything was old and out of date when I got it. Now, some parts I can't get print specs for anymore. And some are so drowning expensive and need added consumable materials that I substitute others instead."

"But it passes inspection?" Pogo asked.

"Most inspectors only check for performance, not under the hatches. So, yes."

"So, the pressures on those lines—" Matté pushed up against the armrests to get a better view of the far left-hand screen.

"Wonky as Laythe's Woods, as you noticed. But I've replaced the pressure conduits, too, so that these readings are within tolerances."

"But what does that do for steering?" Pogo asked.

"There's a reason no one else tries to take out my hauler. They think I have it tuned that way 'cause I'm bitchy about anyone else flying her. Which might also be true. But—"

"Tough to steer doesn't sound like an improvement." Matté rubbed fingertips across his mouth.

"She's slicker'n snot. But that lets me get through spots that are impassable to most other pilots."

"What does that do to your speed?" Matté asked.

She glanced at him with a raised eyebrow. "Do you think I'd fly hobbled?"

Pogo laughed, slapping the back of her seat. If he did that again, she'd throw the next elbow somewhere he wouldn't appreciate. "I like it. How much improvement?"

"Never ran her full throttle, to be honest, but she can move. Chomps down fuel like a hungry sollert, though. So, I hold her back as much as I can."

"No clue how a hungry sollert eats, but sounds nice to have in a pinch, though." Matté's tone seemed a mix of impressed and uncomfortable.

"Where'd you pick up these tricks?" Pogo asked.

She laughed, trying to make it sound more gracious than bitter, though that never really worked. "No one is going to claim credit for that. Seriously. All I did was throw out the rules, read the manuals on the parts I had available, and put the puzzle together. Gotta keep the inspectors from examining her guts, though. They have little imagination and no sense of humor." A distinct whine pierced the cabin. She shifted the readouts. "Damn Raiders. Get back in the safety webbing."

Pogo dropped back into his seat and wrestled into the webbing. "What are you scanning for?"

"You identify them sooner if you scan for their fuel residue. They use stuff no one else around here does. You can find it on the pollution control sensors."

"Not their shield frequencies? I thought you could hear those on the comm channels." Matté pushed back into his seat and snugged his straps.

"By the time you sort out those you're too close to outrun them." She retuned her sensors. "These traces are old, but I don't like it. I'm going to switch routes. If they were here before, they're likely to come back at the wrong sarding moment."

"Going back to the Shoburn Heights approach?" Pogo asked.

"No, gonna take my own back roads approach." She switched the left screen to a navigation layout with weather, maps, and atmospheric condition reports. "No one expects traffic off the designated flight corridors. So, as a rule, there's nothing hiding in the rocks. And flight control usually forgives getting off designated paths when there's Raiders involved."

"You're flying awfully low for all the rocks in the way." Pogo sucked in a long breath. "Seems like you could use some extra eyes."

"Either of you can manage a nav station?"

"Of course," they both said.

"What about comm?"

They snorted.

"Okay, then. You can be helpful. Adjust those media screens near your seats, and I'll put something useful to do on them instead of the usual brain candy."

"Seriously? You can do that? You flying with extra crew?" Pogo knocked the back of her seat as he adjusted his screen. Worse than a man twice his height. Inconsiderate or clumsy? Had to be inconsiderate. Champion fighters weren't that clumsy.

"No. But Joco can get twitchy when someone else is flying, and giving him something to do is better than tranqing him."

Matté swallowed a laugh. "Got some family who'd be better passengers that way."

"One can only imagine," Pogo muttered. "Okay, got the screen set, what now?"

"Switching stations now. I've still got access here, but nav is now fed to the back screen and comm to the right. You got them?"

"Got it. Oh, you've got one of the new nav interfaces, too. Nice, I like."

"Matté, watch the comm for something that sounds like a nav-grid marker signal putting out a three-cycle ping. Sending you a sample to match to."

"Got it. Mind if I turn up the sensitivity?"

"Fine, just don't tune it below my original sensitivity settings."

"Three-cycle nav ping—haven't heard of that. Those pings are two- or four-cycle," Pogo said.

"That's what makes the three-cycle hard to pick out. Listen to the pilot chatter. It's being talked about."

"How do you filter out all the nonsense? There's so much garbage on that channel."

"A few solid keywords'll do it."

Pogo groaned under his breath. "You willing to share those?"

"Later. Yes. Focus now. This next bit is a bit tricky. Get me a course suggestion for the route I sent you."

"Right. Immediate path coordinates established. You ought to be able to see them."

The path coordinates list appeared between her map and the atmospheric conditions outputs. "Thank you." She checked his plan, and it matched hers. Nice to have that validation.

She didn't need the help. But they both seemed less twitchy having something to do. Exactly like Joco. Pilots were the worst passengers. Always convinced they could do the job better than you. And always wrong. She ducked around several stony landmarks, smooth and easy, as it should have been.

"You're cutting that awfully close." Pogo's boots ground against the deck plating. Miners had a reputation for being especially twitchy.

"You make that look effortless." Matté whistled under his breath.

"Means a lot coming from another pilot." And it was true. Pilots rarely voiced appreciation for another's skill. Stupid, but that was the way of things. Egos were fragile beasts.

Matté leaned in toward his screen. "I'm getting something on the comm. Got it tuned up high, so could be a false—"

"No, I'm seeing it, too. Signals are getting stronger now." Like nav-marker signals would if she were approaching them. All the known markers were already pinging in at the proper distances. So, those were ships—Raider ships—headed their direction. "Plot me a course three degrees west in the lowest plane possible. I'm setting my cloak to mimic a low-level sandstorm. As long as they don't get a visual on us, we should be effectively invisible." But they needed to get out of visual range fast.

"Got your course for you. Cloaking as a sandstorm? Can those systems do that?" Pogo asked.

"Now find me a spot to hide. You ever noticed what sandstorms do to weather readings? Throw out the right kind of static and you look like'em."

"Parameters for hiding? About the static—you willing to share the—"

"Yes. Later. Hide now. Ideal is an overhang we can duck under. If not that, a cluster of rocks our size or bigger that I can get between."

"How tight can you manage?"

"Tight enough you could reach out and touch our neighbors."

"Be serious."

"You try berthing too many ships in too little hangar before a storm. I don't even scratch the paint, at least not most of the time."

They both snorted. Good, a sense of humor was a valuable thing at a time like this. Keep them from thinking too hard about her explanations.

"Found you two choices. One of each."

Nice to have options. "Get me a course to the rock pile that goes past the overhang in case I need it."

"On it."

"Those three-cycle pings are getting stronger. Looks like another has joined the conversation, too," Matté said.

"Damn, they may have noticed us. Make sure your straps are tight, gentlemen, I'm opening her up, it could get bumpy in here." She tightened her own safety webbing.

Funny how they jumped to follow suit when she did that.

"That's it, girl, you've been itching to show your stuff. Now's your time." She eased the speed up until the hauler rumbled under their feet.

"Can she hold this speed?" Matté stayed focused on his panel.

"She ain't about to shake apart, if that's what you mean. But she's an old girl and you gotta give her leave to complain about things."

"Coming up on our first hiding spot. Do you think it's too obvious?" Pogo asked.

She pulled back the speed and circled the first of the Shoburn Heights, a small dusky-red mountain, that looked like it had been randomly dropped from the sky into this spot, away from its fellows. "It's a tight enough squeeze that no one in their right mind is going to try it, so yeah, it looks good. A whole bunch like the last parking job I did before I headed out. What's the clearest approach?" She'd already sighted it out, but they'd have more confidence if they thought they had some control.

"Sending it now."

Nope, her plan was better. He probably wasn't going to like that. "Might want to close your eyes if you're the squeamish type. Otherwise, hold on and hold your breath. Don't distract me." She flipped off the parking sensors and divided a three-hundred-sixty-degree view across all the screens. Study the space. Just another parking job.

"That's not what I sent!"

"I know, now shut up." She wheedled and nudged and shimmied the craft into the space, like a mud crab scooting into the rocks to hide. A tiny bump when they came to rest, and that was that.

"Kayavan's bones, woman! I swear you've got ice in your veins." Matté muttered. "I'd have lost the bet on that one."

"Make that two of us."

"Not sure if that's a compliment or not, gentlemen." She reset the screens, her fingers dancing over the cloaking controls. "I'm matching the cloak to the magnetic signature of the rock here. Unless they can get a visual, no one will ever notice us."

"Do Raiders fly low enough for that? Our patrols haven't noticed it," Pogo said.

"I've never seen them do it. Doesn't mean they won't, but I've never seen it."

"What's the plan if they do?" Matté asked.

"Run like the Hell Cat herself is after our souls."

Chapter 12

MATTEO GLANCED AT PHALEN, eyebrow raised. Running seemed like a reasonable option, but calling for enforcer backup seemed like a solid addition to the plan.

Phalen scowled a moment, then nodded. "This is home territory for me. I've got people in place for this sort of thing."

"Enforcers, right." Arli's voice was tight and laced with distrust. "You got a secure channel our friends out there won't pick up? Last chatter I saw said they'd broken the latest Firen codes."

"Sand-scoured tunnel-snakes!" Phalen slammed his fist on his armrest.

Nice, a new addition to the expletive list. "I might be able to help. We've got some protocols that haven't been broken yet." Matteo kept his voice very soft. Getting a suggestion like that accepted was all in the tone.

"Dextrine? Some of those have been compromised, too." Arli focused on her screens, but something in her posture suggested she was trying not to glower at him.

"These are new in the last few weeks ..."

"Those should be solid. But will those get through to Firen resources?" She turned to look at Phalen.

"Questionable. We might not even have those protocols yet."

"I can get through to Lady Iantha at the Firen Headquarters facility. She should be able send forward it to your enforcers from there." He handed Phalen his module. "Here, put your message in. I'll put in a priority packet and push it out."

Phalen scowled, working through several frowns. In all fairness, Matteo would have had the same hesitation had the situation been reversed.

"I get that you don't like exposing your security measures this way. But neither do I. I'm not asking more than I'm giving."

Phalen huffed and entered a message for the packet. The message was coded, but then again, so was Matteo's to Iantha.

"Our guests are getting closer, and they seem much more attentive than the last set I encountered." Alri switched displays. Pollution levels would give her a sense of how close they were; detailed topography of the canyon might reveal some new options. "Make sure your people have enough to ID us. We don't need them shooting us by mistake if we need to run."

"Already done," Phalen muttered.

Matteo hit Send and pressed back into his webbing. "Sent. Asked for receipt confirmation, so we can hope to hear something soon." No sense in mentioning the just-in-case packet he'd coded for delivery to Beny if he didn't cancel it in the next twelve hours. He'd put that emergency packet together some time ago, but this was the first time he'd ever felt the need to use it. "Does this happen often out here?"

"Here and there," Phalen said.

"A lot more than that." Arli shook her head and muttered something more colorful under her breath.

Would have been nice to have heard that well enough to add to his list, assuming he survived to use it later.

"Really?" Phalen seemed taken aback.

"Yes, really. Usually, I don't get myself pinned down like this, but I've had runs where I had to cower in dark places and sit tight over twelve. There's a reason I include hazard contingencies in my contracts."

"Not trying to be an ass here, but why haven't I heard more about that?" Phalen asked.

"Reporting those things is bad for the Transport Guild, and you pretty much can't fly on Lighten if you're not on their good side. It's not healthy for careers to make too much of it. Not even the Lighten Security Corps try crossing those lines. But we pilots talk to each other. You got to know where you need to pay attention and what to listen for."

Phalen snarled more creative invectives that Matteo would have to add to his list. Dust storms and tunnel-snakes made for some interesting imagery. "Another thing you'll give me details on?"

She heaved an exasperated sigh and rolled her eyes. "When there's no longer someone with firepower breathing down my neck."

One couldn't blame Phalen, though. It must be like discovering all those secrets the Family Patriarchs were keeping that would have been splinteringly useful to be aware of before one made an ass of oneself in front of important company. "What I don't understand is why they would bother with us? This was a last-minute side-booking, no one should have gotten wind of it."

"That is the question, isn't it? Makes you wonder how information is getting out." Phalen bounced his fist off his chin.

"Hate to bruise egos here, but it is as likely to have nothing to do with you fine folks. I've heard suspicions they're building some sort of outpost right under Firen's noses and using Firen's defenses to cover themselves." Arli returned to her controls.

Phalen growled under his breath, cursing the ancestors three generations back of everyone in Firen's defense department.

Phalen could deal with Firen, but Matteo would have to get that suspicion leaked to his own people, starting with Iantha. After he dealt with his personal business with her. His module buzzed. "Message received. Enforcers alerted, deploying immediately."

"ETA?" Phalen checked his module.

"Nothing promised, but maybe thirty minutes."

Arli chewed her lower lip. "We should be able to sit tight that long. Matté, I'm routing the pollution sensors to your panel, too. Could use an extra pair of eyes on them."

The screen closest to Matteo split with the communications array taking up two-thirds on the right, and the concentration gauge and directional compass of the pollution sensors on the remaining left-hand portion. Was it her idea to use those sensors in such an unconventional way?

"Pogo, I want navigation out of here, as many options as you can give me. By the time we need those routes, we won't have time to find them. The question is, how close do we let them get before running like a bait-bug from a hungry hen?"

Phalen snorted out a laugh, one of those laughs one tried to contain, but couldn't.

"I know, I'm swamp, and it shows." She shrugged.

"I've seen a hen after a bug. I think the description fits. Though, I don't mind telling you, I don't love being the bug in that story." Phalen folded his arms across his chest and sank back into his seat. "What kind of arms do you think they carry?"

Arli pulled up the chatter feed on one of the front screens. It would take the Arch Key Minder himself to get answers out of that mess! How did one even find a conversation thread in that unlabeled, untagged, uncategorized nightmare? She tapped in what must have been filters and maybe a few keyword parameters and sent it all back to Phalen's screen. "Unless it has a blade, weapons aren't my strong suit. I've filtered that feed, see what you can make of it."

"So, you like bladed weapons?" Given her expression, that might have been a stupid thing to say, but small talk never had been Matteo's strong suit.

"Firearms are heavily restricted around here. If you're not a registered enforcer or part of the Lighten Security Corps, it's almost impossible to get the printing specs for them. When you need meat on the table, blades are handy to get your own."

"What do you hunt?" Phalen didn't look up from the feeds. Apparently, he needed small talk as much as Matteo right now.

"What else do you hunt in the swamp? Sollert." She seemed to duck away, as though she didn't want to talk about it.

Phalen either didn't see or ignored the hint. "What's your best catch?"

"Intentional or not?"

Phalen peeked up, a perplexed look on his face.

"Okay, I'll bite, how does one hunt unintentionally?" Matteo tapped a discreet search into his module's Lighten diplomatic packet that he hadn't had time to read through yet.

Sollert, see also *Native Lighten fauna*

Legless reptile, apex predator native to the Lighten swamp regions. Major export product, a foundation of the Lighten economy.

Extremely aggressive, with a venomous bite, an unrecorded number of deaths are attributed to them each year. Estimates suggest the numbers could be as high as several thousand. Sollerts do not survive captivity. They are not found outside of their native environment.

Exported products include: meat, hides, teeth (sold as gems), venom, and internal organs (for medical research.)

"After a storm, you can find some huge ones out by the shipyard docks. If you're smart, you keep away from there. Not everyone is smart."

"And they need rescuing?" Phalen frowned and returned to his reading. "Fools."

"That's the kind of thing you want to pay forward, ya know."

Matteo'd heard that phrase before, and it seemed important. Might as well look into it, since the packet was already open.

Pay Forward, see *Hospitality*

Hospitality, *Lighten*

(1) A social artifact of meteorological and geological conditions on Lighten.

(2) Lighten means of avoiding "debt" (see additional entry) by "paying forward." A Lighten will spontaneously give "what they have" to one who has not asked to avoid obligation in the future when they receive similarly from another.

(3) A Lighten expectation that if they offer what they have when they have it, their needs will be similarly met in the future.

Yeah, that was more important than he'd expected.

"Who'd you rescue?" Phalen asked.

"Hard to say, it was like the eye of a shit-storm. Some folks from Refuge City visiting Paxton let their kids play in the floodwaters. One of the little ones fell in, and by the time all was said and done, there were half a dozen in the water trying to get him out before some of us locals got wind of it and hauled their asses out of the water with sollerts still attached." She rubbed her right shoulder, grimacing.

"You get bit?"

"The little one made it out safe. The rest of us all took some damage or another. Important thing was no one died that day."

"I've heard those bites are worse than tunnel-snake venom."

"Never met a tunnel-snake, thanks. Sollerts don't have venom, but they scavenge anything, so their mouths are vile and if their bite doesn't kill you, the infection might. You don't play around once you get bit—straight to the medics or you're gonna meet the sunrise."

Apparently, the packet was wrong about a few things.

"I've heard that. Not looking to find out for myself."
Phalen leaned forward on his elbow. "How big was it?"

"Big enough most of the teeth required trade registry and
there were a lot of little ones that didn't, to boot. The hide
was top-quality, spotted, which is pretty uncommon, and
with so many hands on board, we even got the meat harvested
before it turned. Got a sarding good return on that effort,
even though it got split so many ways. Still not the way I'd
like to pay the bills."

Matteo tapped yet another search and brought up several
media pieces on sollert rescues that seemed to match her
story. Those things were monsters! Flesh and blood monsters,
complete with dagger teeth, slimy skin, and vicious person-
alities. Not like the marketing images used by exporters of
popular sollert products to Dextra. Sure as his ancestors'
disapproval, those were not what he wanted to hunt.

An uncomfortable silence fell, and he put away his module
lest they wonder what he was doing with it.

"So, you going to call on your girl, big man?"

Of course, it was only fair that Phalen would put him on
the spot now. "Lady Iantha is not 'my girl.'"

"Forgive me suggesting something so plebeian. Sir. Or do
you prefer the use of your full title?" The start of a sneer
turned up the side of Phalen's narrow lips.

"Here and now, I'm Matté. Beyond, sticking with title is
the best way to stay out of trouble. The Dextrine Media is
always looking to be offended. Firen doesn't need that kind
of press." No one did actually, except the Media who made it
their blood and bones.

"So, Matté, if she's not your girl, then what is she?"

"My betrothed."

"What exactly does that mean?" Arli asked.

"Probably a political match, like the one Joco made for his
daughter last year. If I remember right, he claimed her equal
partner as connection when the partnership was announced."

"Dove isn't Joco's daughter. Bithy brought all of her children, ten of them, into the partnership with Joco."

"And he accepted them?" It would be quite a man who accepted that many children he did not have genetic connection to, even on Dextra where "family" was a value like Therans shouted *Vigilance, Valor, and Victory*.

"Not until he's gotten them usefully matched." Phalen indulged in a full-bodied sneer.

"That's rather cold." Arli looked at her hands in her lap.

"You're the one who's very clear that he isn't connected to you, despite your mother being his second woman. Study the Records, and tell me what you think. He might not come right out and say he's not connected with his partner's brood, but it sure looks like it from the outside." Phalen's tone made his opinion clear. "Dextrines aren't the only ones who play those alliance games."

Strange to think that it was the way of Lighten as well. Considering how often Lightens were considered uncultured primitives, it seemed odd to think they could be so similar. And yet another prejudice shattering.

"Are you comfortable with that sort of partnership?" Arli asked softly. Not the way people usually asked that question.

Nor was it something anyone needed to know. "That's an awfully personal question."

"Of course, sorry." She dodged away from his Clan Lord glower and attended her screens. "Do you see that?" She pointed.

Phalen jumped up and leaned over her shoulder. "Yeah, I'm not much liking it. How much closer do we let them get?"

Splintering shards! He should have been paying attention to those pollution readings instead of taking offense.

"Strap in, we're getting out of here. Matté, look for Pogo's people on the sensors. I'm sending you their fuel pollution signature. We'll head toward them if we can, otherwise—"

"Got them!" Matteo sent her the coordinates.

"Plotting course—"

"Hold on, gentlemen, we're about to find out how fast she can run." She tightened her webbing and eased the ship from its hiding place.

When your pilot did that, it was wise to follow suit. Matteo pressed into his seat and snugged down his straps painfully tight.

The hauler's engine hummed and whined—sounds it probably wasn't supposed to make. But all the performance readouts he could make out from his vantage point suggested it was functioning within safe parameters.

Her hands danced over the controls, with a calm that all his flight instructors demonstrated. One that was supposed to take decades to master.

She was petite, which made her look young, but even taking that into consideration, she couldn't be older than he. He'd been flying from the moment he was legal, over seven years now, but his confidence didn't match hers.

Was she that good, or had she started well before she was legal? That made sense, really. Even if Joco did not claim connection to her, she grew up in the Ship Yard. Of course, she wouldn't have waited until it was legal to learn how to fly.

But none of that meant that her skill wasn't real. Real and a bit unsettling to witness in an actual situation, not a sophisticated academy simulation. A genuine threat, in a legitimate, albeit patched-together ship, in an authentic remote location, deep in the Lighten desert.

And Clan Timnon was going to have seven different colors of fits when—not if, but when—they found out. It would not be pretty. And they would go after her given half the chance—wait, what was that? "Got approaching vessels from 123—you use a nine-by-nine coordinate grid system, ship centered at 333, right?"

"Yes, right. Heading toward 123." Her left hand danced along the steering panel, her right directed the stick.

"You realize you're headed in the same direction as them, into a canyon now, right?" Phalen sounded more than concerned, more like alarmed.

"They are clumsy-ass fliers. I'm not."

"Can your sensors keep up with your speed?" Phalen's voice tightened, sharp and brittle. Corded muscles stood out on his forearms as he gripped his armrests.

"Doing this visual."

"Visual? No one trains visual, much less flies that way." Phalen looked ready to fight her for control.

"So, you really want to be right?" She waved him off. "Shut up and watch."

Matteo shoved his boots hard into the deck plating and ground his teeth. This was turning into a whole new level of real.

Obstacles approached fast, too fast. From both sides, like they did in simulation games. The kind that didn't actually kill you.

She dipped and wove through the field, hands skating from one panel to another, not blinking—did she even breathe? "What's their distance?"

"Backing off, but still following from above," Matteo stared at his screens, wishing he didn't see what was there.

"Sneaky little trasks. Aren't they going to be surprised?" She dropped even lower but pulled back on the speed.

"Any lower and we're going to eat dirt." Phalen leaned as close as his straps would allow. Was that why she was adamant about having them strap in?

"I've got sufficient clearance, and they don't want to join us down here. Setting cloaks to look like rocks now. Before you ask, look how red the canyon is—iron content that has a distinct magnetic signature—easy to mimic. That, with dropping speed, should make us hard to spot."

Weapons fire exploded above them, the blast wave rocking the little cargo hauler.

"Or completely piss them off. Any sign of your people, Pogo? Now's not the time to be late to the party."

He stabbed at his module. "I got them, about five minutes off."

"Give them our details and remind them of our ID while I play hide-and-seek for a little bit longer."

Matteo clenched his fist, a reminder to keep his mouth shut, too. No comment he could offer would help. Not that he was at a loss for unhelpful things to say. Those abounded.

Including the realization that this was his fault, not hers. This was his errand, not hers. Yes, she'd chosen this route, but he would not play blame-the-pilot. They wouldn't be out here but for him.

Another explosion of dust blossomed beside and behind them.

"I swear those are the same particle beams we use in the mines. First time I've seen them converted to weapons." Phalen muttered more invectives under his breath.

"Well, ain't that a shit-storm in a sollert skin? The nasties are getting better at this. Never seen 'em firing into the canyon, though. Seems we've got a new class of Raiders involved in this mess." She muttered a few more aspersions about the number of dubious reptiles in the Raiders' family lines.

"Two minutes off," Phalen said. "Fork in the canyon coming up, right-hand fork looks clearest."

She veered left. Of course she did.

Matteo dragged his hand down his face.

She rolled the ship forty-five degrees to dodge through a narrow opening, under a rock bridge, and over a large formation. The sort of thing pilots only did in simulation games because trying them in real life was too stupid.

His stomach roiled. He hadn't been flightsick in years. Beny would love this, at least when he was done hating the risks Matteo had just taken.

Above them, the weapons fire whined and bright flashes cast eerie shadows into the canyon. Projectile weapons—had to be Phalen's Enforcers.

"My people have engaged. They want us to hide down here for a bit and stay out of their way."

"To keep from getting shot at? Absolutely. Is that niche in the starboard side wall big enough?"

"For you, yes, for the rest of us, not a lost soul's chance."

"I'll take it." And she did, touching the hauler down in the shadowed niche so softly Matteo wasn't sure when they'd touched down.

"He's right, you've got ice in your veins." Phalen rubbed his hands along his upper arms as if to dispel a chill. "Never seen the like of this before. You do this often?"

"Not when I can avoid it. I'm not stupid. But I like to eat, so I take what I can to keep food on the table."

"That's more than food-on-the-table flying. I get why they call you Arli, though."

She turned and glowered.

Phalen raised open hands. "You ride the edge of the storm like you were born to it. Did you even break a sweat?"

Her expression softened. He'd have to look up what an arli was once he started breathing again.

"I rigged her for this." She patted the dash. "Standard outfitting wouldn't have done us any favors. And you two jumped in to help—I appreciate that."

Phalen's eyebrows rose, and he blinked several times.

He was right. Pilots—normal ones—grandstanded, didn't share the credit for stunts like this with anyone or anything. Interesting.

Phalen's module buzzed, a deep, annoyed rumble that one felt in the deep gut. "We've got the clear. They're going to escort us in. Sending you coordinates now. Can we put out of the canyon at that spot?"

"Can do. But for the love of morning, set up a constant ident broadcast until they get us in their sights. We don't need a trigger-happy friendly ruining our day." She dragged her arm across her forehead, leaving a dark trail of sweat on her flight jacket sleeve.

So, she had broken a sweat.

"Done and done."

She eased the hauler out of its hiding place and poked the nose out at the appointed coordinates. "Paxton 23 to Firen Mine escort, do you see us?"

"Enforcer 1 to Paxton 23, we have you. Sending you flight path coordinates now. We've got four ships to flank you. Stay in our shadows."

"Understood, Enforcer 1." She glanced over her shoulder at Phalen. "Thanks. Nice to have some teeth and claws with us."

"Look, I've got someone who needs to hear about this whole sarding adventure firsthand. Would you mind talking with him? And I'd love you to have a chat with our techies about what you've done with your ship."

"If you throw in a decent meal with that, we have a deal." For a moment, she looked impossibly weary.

Somehow, that was reassuring.

Matteo followed Phalen from the little hauler. The hangar, dug out from the rock under a large overhang, was deeper, better constructed than he would have expected. At home, Firen was thought to be a basic-operations-only mining company, but once again, this trip was rewriting his opinions.

Question was, was that impression managed by Firen, to keep Dextrine interests from interfering, or was it Dextrine prejudice that he'd need to work on changing? Or both, it could be both. It wasn't smart to underestimate anyone, allies or enemies. Interesting.

A four-member, black-uniformed security team, all heavily armed, met them. A typical brute squad, exactly as expected, although their weapons seemed somewhat out of date. No doubt effective, but hardly cutting-edge. He hadn't visited a facility without such a guard ... ever. They used to intimidate him when he was younger, but now they were more or less a part of the background furnishings.

"Lord Heir Timnon, sir." The security lead saluted, snapped his heels together in true Theran fashion, and bowed. Covering all the bases that the encounter might require.

"Escort our esteemed visitor to Lady Iantha's office." Phalen glanced at Matteo.

The man was at home in his element and the security team looked to him for leadership. That was a good sign. A man respected by those he commended was the sort Matteo would rather deal with.

"Yes, sir." The security lead nodded sharply. "Come this way, if you please, sir." He gestured toward a closed door at the deepest point of the cliff side hangar. "Lady Iantha handled all the Record-keeping so we can take you directly to her."

"Excellent." He flexed his shoulders, trying to settle back into his official persona, despite the casual pilot's garb he wore. It wasn't about the clothes, it was the bearing.

Flying in had been a pleasant experience, if one ignored the Raiders, of course. Just being a pilot among other pilots, enjoying the small talk and camaraderie, and even the chance to contribute as an equal was a memorable experience. There was something to be said for that and for not having everyone defer to his rank as though that made everything he said truth. That might not happen again for a long time. He'd miss it.

Chapter 13

ARI LEANED BACK AND gulped several deep breaths. Flying with armed escorts should have been calming. Knowing that no more unfriendlies were lurking behind the rocks or in the depths of the canyon was a good thing. But the sense of being watched, regarded with suspicion, hostility even, didn't settle well. Especially when it came from the heavily-armed enforcers overhead. Hopefully, she could deliver her passenger, answer Pogo's questions from the safety of her own ship, and get back to Anara without Joco never noticing.

What were the chances?

The straps of Joco's worn bag, the one he'd left behind, caught the corner of her eye. Well, that reduced the chances of a happy ending, didn't it? Drown it all.

Firen traffic control directed her to a spacious landing bay tucked into a cliff face in the southernmost peak of the Eternis

Mountain Range. Firen Peak wasn't the most impressive in the range, but it was the site of the first Guild claim, and that made it the right place to put their headquarters.

Rather than a ragged hole blasted in the peak's side, which was what one would have expected from a pack of rugged miners, the Firen Headquarters main landing bay had been carved out beneath a natural overhang, with an eye to preserving the untouched look of the peak. It would have been easy to overlook from the air, making it more secure. And from the ground, one would have to be very close for its true nature to be clear.

Miners were known for being cagey, even paranoid about their claims, not for their appreciation of organic beauty. But perhaps preserving the raw look was one of the most effective ways to hide in plain sight.

Well-maintained beacons and reflective sensor strips guided her under the overhang and into the immense man-made cavern beneath—a modern, efficient hangar facility that seemed to appear out of nowhere. Joco would have called it pretentious and even frivolous, showing off wealth that Firen Mines had accumulated but did not deserve. While some of that might be true, the sentiment would also have been tinged by jealousy over the state-of-the-art systems that Joco refused to invest in.

She brought her battered little hauler down in a feather-light landing that her passengers seemed too preoccupied to notice. Just as well. Next to the other flitters, transports, and haulers beside her, her ship felt like a poor relation invited to, but not welcome at, a family gathering.

"Lady Iantha has arranged your security clearances ... Lord Heir Timnon." Pogo emphasized the title. His entire demeanor had shifted in the moments since they landed. He was in his territory, back straight, shoulders pulled back, eyes sharp, at home and in charge of the bustling enterprise around them. "A security detail is waiting to escort you to her."

Odd that Matté's betrothed would not be there to meet him, but Dextrines had some odd ways about them.

Pogo turned to her. "I'll need to arrange your clearances from my office before we can extend you proper hospitality. This is a Paxton Yard ship and with the upcoming bout with Joco ... people will be a mite twitchy. There's been a lot of trash talk from Joco's supporters and Brels' people are pretty protective of him."

"Hadn't thought of that, but it makes sense. Firen miners haven't exactly been welcome at the Yard since the match was announced."

"If you don't mind waiting here for a few minutes—"

"No need to bother with that. I don't need to leave the ship. I can sit tight and meet with your people here." She patted the armrest and settled in.

"Nonsense. We may be rough about the edges, but common decency isn't too much to expect from us. Not to mention, you promised you would talk with someone for me—"

"You can bring them here. Your techies will want to crawl around the ship, and I'm not having that if I'm not present."

"They will, indeed, and I appreciate you being all right with watching them while they work. But they are not the only ones I'd like you to meet with. I promise, it won't take long."

"And you won't take no for an answer, will you?" Why bother asking when it was clear?

"No. We don't get many unexpected guests out this far. It'll be nice to prove ourselves civilized, even for only an afternoon." Pogo cocked his head and smiled, disarming and a little charming. It was the sort of expression she probably shouldn't trust.

"All right. I'll be here until Matté's done—he booked a round trip. So, there's some time to kill." She brushed dust from her worn flight jacket. Hopefully, Pogo's contact wasn't someone offended by a work worn presentation. And if they were, it wasn't as if there was anything she could do about it. If they couldn't look past maintenance stains and worn elbows, it was more than likely someone who couldn't handle dealing with her, anyway. "I'm sending you our departure window, Matté.

Get back here within that or you'll have to foot the bill for the changes, yes?"

"Understood." Matté tugged his jacket a little straighter. He, too, had changed. Traces of the Dextrine Lord he was supposed to be overtook his humble pilot persona, transforming him into someone much grander, more powerful than before. Best that he hadn't come to her that way to book the job. She would have refused.

Pogo led Matté off, neither one acknowledging her further. Most passengers did that, so it wasn't remarkable. And they both had significant business to attend, so understandable. But they were both pilots, so part of her expected a bit more courtesy.

Foolish little arli.

She powered down the hauler and ran the postflight routines. After that bumpy ride, best not to skip those. Her hand shook as she ran it over the input panels. Her insides were still shaking, too.

She clenched her fists and sucked in deep breaths of mountain air mixed with fuel residue and maintenance grease. The familiar scents should be calming. But calm was not in easy reach.

That was not at all how this flight was supposed to go. A simple in-and-out, nothing fancy. Yes, it was a corridor that had had some problems, but up-close-and-personal with the Raiders should never, never have happened. What were those soul catchers doing this deep in the desert, this close to Firen Headquarters?

Certainly, someone connected to Firen needed to know. That might be the conversation Pogo was so interested in facilitating. And it made sense that it would be the sort of conversation that needed to happen in a proper office setting.

But drown it! It would leave Records. The kind that Joco didn't want her to be a part of. The kind that could come back and reflect badly on the Transport Guild that claimed such things were not happening.

This side job kept getting better and better, leaving her riding the edge of the storm.

Heavy footfalls stormed through the hatch.

She jumped up and turned on the intruders, reaching for the knife that always hung off her belt. "Get out!"

A pair of formidable, well-armed, black-uniformed female enforcers reached for their weapons. Like the rest of the facility, their tactical gear was sleek, state-of-the-art, and not to be underestimated. "Stand down, you're in Firen territory."

"Common courtesy alone says you do not come aboard without permission."

"Arilyn Lysand, pilot designation Paxton 23? Paxton Ship Yard pilot?" The higher-ranking one, or at least the one wearing more insignias on her black leather jacket, barked, weapon—a suppression stunner—freed from its holster and on its way to leveling on Ari's chest.

"Put that drowned thing down! What kind of threat do you expect me to be?"

"You are officially in the custody of the Firen Mine Enforcers. You best come along quietly." She grabbed for Ari's arm.

Ari jumped back, but there was little she could put between herself and them. "Why?"

"You're one of Joco's minions. What business do you have here? No one from the Paxton Ship Yard is welcome here."

"Your own traffic control gave me clearance to land. Check with them. I've made no move to leave my ship. I'm no threat."

"You're a threat if I say you're a threat. Drop that knife, slowly, and submit to our custody." The stunner in the lead enforcer's hand trembled, like she wasn't used to such encounters.

A freshly certified enforcer? Drown it all!

"Wait, we haven't gotten clarification on the orders, yet." The second enforcer backed away.

"What we don't have yet is what detainment area to throw her in."

"The question was if she was to be detained, not where. Traffic control cleared her landing, with no restrictions. We need to wait."

"She's a Paxton Yard Pilot, what else is important here? There's no legitimate reason for her to be here." The decorated enforcer snapped, stunner not leaving its aim at Ari's chest. "Do what you've been told, or I'll write you up for insubordination." She turned back to Ari. "I've been ordered to take you into confinement. Don't make trouble."

"This can't be right. Pogo is arranging security clearances for me."

"Chief Enforcer sent confinement orders." She signaled the other enforcer, who grabbed Ari's arm and tried to pull it up behind her back.

"He wouldn't! That's not right!" Ari twisted and kicked.

"You forced this." A soft, blunt projectile slammed into Ari's chest.

An electric jolt, powerful as Joco's backhand, knocked her to the deck, every muscle spasming so hard she could hardly breathe. Pain, intense like a sollert bite, ran in waves as the shocks continued.

The shocks faded, but the world dimmed, like a ship running on emergency power only. Her vision faded, gray and fuzzy, sounds muffled. Every limb turned clumsy and heavy, like swimming through flood torrents. Hard to move ... to think.

"Plucky little bitch ... suppression effect on full ..."

"Don't ... too much ..."

They dragged her from the ship.

Words, she should say ... should do... something? Fight ... struggle ... get ... away. Breathing took all her strength, energy to remember how.

Shoved through an open door, she fell onto a floor. Cold, smelled, tasted like stone. Sit, she should ... sit. Floor moved, no sit. She curled into a fetal position.

Why?

No sense ... no warning ... no reason.

Fear.

No anger. Anger ... better, but not strong enough.

Afraid.

Cold now, growing ... Suffocating. Chest so heavy. Breathe, had to breathe. Remember breathe.

Weak ... so weak. Sad ... yes. Sadness.

So much to be sad for. Mama ... alone now. Joco ... no, alone now. So alone.

Cold. Cold and dark. No way out—

"Get up." A heavy boot smashed into her hip.

Pain, dull, thudding pain. She curled into herself tighter and struggled to breathe.

Two sets of hands jerked her up. Barking words ... what did they mean?

Walk ... walking ... they forced her ... walking ... long gray hall.

Dark. Cold. Legs, feet, heavy, barely standing.

Open door, bright, so bright. Pushed inside.

Stumble. Falling. Hard floor ... cold ... stone. So much stone. Where was the swamp? The water?

"What soul-catching nightmare is this?" Soft voice. Far away. Angry. Familiar. "Release her now!"

Weight in the center of her chest released, like being dropped into freefall. Light and sound exploded in bright, burning flashes, every nerve tuned to max sensitivity. She shut her eyes, covered her ears, to no avail. Stabbing, shattering, splintering pain, shooting through her skull, through her long bones. Her muscles seized in violent, agonizing spasms, overloaded by stimuli, as she curled into a fetal ball on the stone floor.

Something warm, heavy, very heavy, thrown over her. Warm. Finally warm. Warm pressure embraced her, calming the spasms. Millimeter by millimeter, her limbs, her skin, her body stopped shuddering.

She forced her eyes open. On a stone floor, surrounded by boots, large, heavy boots. One of them had kicked her. Yes, she remembered that. She squeezed her eyes shut. If she pulled hard enough, maybe she could pull all the loose threads together.

A meter away, Pogo—yes, that was Pogo—stood toe-to-toe with heavy black boots. "You never release suppression like that! What sort of rocks for brains stunt was it using it on a guest in the first place?"

Black Boots shifted to an at-attention posture. Ari followed them up—that was the enforcer who shot her. "The prisoner resisted confinement, and she was armed."

What was that woman doing with her belt knife?

"Give me that." Pogo snatched Ari's knife back. "What were you doing in her ship? That was trespassing. She had every right to carry a knife there, and even to use it against you in that context!" Pogo's face darkened into something frightening. "You were to escort her to guest containment, not confinement."

Black Boots pulled out her module. "Chief ordered —"

Pogo snatched the module away, pointed at her module screen, and shoved it back into her hands. "What orders? He hasn't issued any."

"They were verbal—"

Pogo turned to the other enforcer. "What did the chief say?"

"It was ... unclear, sir. Not sure if we were to wait on directions where to detain her or whether to detain her."

Black Boots edged back, one, two, three steps. "Why ... why would a Paxton Yard pilot ever be welcome here? Especially right before the fight? I ... I assumed—"

Ari pushed against the stone beneath her, up and into a blanket-cocooned hunch. At least she was off the floor.

Pogo stomped a hand's breadth closer to Black Boots. "You are paid to follow orders. Not make assumptions."

She stepped back. "I ... I am sorry, sir."

"Sorry is insufficient." A deep voice boomed beside Ari.

She slammed hands over her ears, seized by shivering in every limb, so intense her teeth chattered.

"Forgive me." Large, very large hands held her shoulders. "Close your eyes and breathe." The deep voice whispered now. "I'm going to pull the blanket tight. It'll help."

Her cocoon snugged in close, warmth building, cushioning, easing clenched muscles. Breathe, she was supposed to breathe.

"Arli, are you all right?" She peeked one eye open. Pogo knelt beside her.

"No." She shook her head, but the fog clung like a trask, pumping venom into its prey. "What did they do?"

"Suppression stunner, miserable soul catcher. Might not be lethal, but it's still bad."

"Why? Where am I?"

"You are in the Firen Mine Guild Master's office. This is Guild Master Brels."

She started and pulled away as Brels' larger-than-life face came into focus. "What do you believe I've done? I came with open hands. Pogo knew. Why?" She jammed the heels of her hands against her eyes. "Why?" She huddled into the blanket, rocking—that eased the buzzing static in her nerves.

"This enforcer has violated all the requirements of her office, assuming what you would pay forward, and violated all precepts of hospitality." Brels slowly stood towering over Black Boots, voice expanding to fill the room with each word. "Take your partner to confinement immediately or I will drag you there myself. And tell your chief to report to me in person, now."

The enforcers rushed out.

Brels knelt at her side again. "Please allow us to help you."

She jerked back. Fear—or was it anger, now? Either way, it helped clear her mind. "Don't touch me." She pushed to her feet. The room spun around her.

"A chair, quick!"

Pogo shoved a chair her direction in time for her to catch herself on it. He helped her sit, but his hand at her elbow burned like swamp nettles and her hip ached to the bone. "Kicked, they kicked me," she muttered.

Pogo grimaced and checked his module. Records of the enforcers played barely above a whisper. "Broke nearly every sarding rule of prisoner management."

"Why a prisoner?" Words, sentences, she had been able to use them. Form them. At least she had before.

"You weren't. They saw the Ship Yard's identification and made unforgivable assumptions. And they say people don't get stupid when Kayavan rises." Pogo dragged a chair close to sit beside her.

Brels trundled—he was far too big a man to be able to move so quietly, but he did—to a far corner and returned with a hot mug. He pressed it into her hands. "Drink it, it will help clear the fog."

"Or kill me," she muttered.

"Your sense of humor is back, that's positive." Pogo offered a weak smile.

"Who said I'm joking?"

"Look, I know you feel like sollert shit. I'm sorry. Please, the hot supplements will help." Pogo mimicked taking the mug to her lips.

She sipped the warm, viscous liquid. It slid down her throat, taking its heat deep inside, touching, calming her still shivering insides. Gulping now, rich, savory, salty, her body's need overcame all caution. Large hands replaced the mug with another.

Slowly, the fog cleared. The lights seemed brighter, the room—huge, no, cavernous—came into focus. An arched ceiling reached high overhead, starkly beautiful, designed to evoke the sense of a natural cavern. Deep and wide, with walls mimicking flowstone in caves, water trickled down the farthest wall, masking the sounds of the environmentals that would always hum in the background. Maybe later she'd consider what such a space meant about the man.

"Let me back to my ship. I'll wait for my passenger there. I've had enough of your brand of hospitality for a lifetime. If that's not enough, I'll leave now and never trouble you again. I'm sure you can get my passenger back to Anara. "

Brels huffed and grumbled, rubbing his broad jaw with his fist. She flinched at every move. Drown it, she still wasn't in full control of herself.

"No." Pogo shook his head, lips pressed into a hard line. "In the first place, you can't fly right now. Takes a minimum of six hours for the effects of a suppression stun to fade enough for flight clearance."

"And two," Brels moderated his commanding tone so that it didn't shatter her skull while giving up none of its authority, "we would very much like you to stay. Pogo believes you have some vital information—"

"Should have thought about that before sending your brute squad for me."

"She was at fault and will be dealt with."

Ari snorted. Not the right way to respond to such a statement, even if it was an outright lie. But self-control hadn't quite made it back online yet.

"You doubt my word?" Brels seemed surprised.

"Why wouldn't I? I was told security clearances were being set up, not charges leveled against me. Your people trespassed on my ship and attacked me. Why would it matter to you what they did to me, unless ... Drown it all! You, someone here, thinks this is about the fight. That this might matter to Joco, throw him off his game. Well, it won't, it doesn't, and he won't find out about it through me. Even if he knew, you can't get to Joco through me. I told you—" she stared at Pogo, "he makes no claim to any connection with me. Wasn't I clear enough?"

"That was never our intent." Pogo huffed.

"Really? You have to admit, it explains a great deal." She sat a little straighter, the heavy blanket sliding from her shoulders.

"Sard it all, she's right, it does. In her place, that's what I'd believe." Brels slapped his thighs. Even through his long-sleeve tan shirt and dark slacks, his muscles bulged. Huge, he was huge. Did he cart rocks barehanded all day? "That still does not make it true."

"I believed you once. I'm not making that mistake again." Though her vision still fuzzed at the edges, she looked straight into Brels' eyes.

"Understood. At least allow our medics to—"

Her hands shook so hard, the mug she'd forgotten she held slopped its contents, soaking her pants, puddling on the smooth stone floor. "Absolutely not. Your enforcers were bad enough. I can't imagine what your medics will do to me, oath against harm or not. Let me go back to my ship. Look, I'll give Pogo the information he's asked me for. Let me go back to my ship."

"You are safe, hospitality—" Pogo extended an open hand.

"Hospitality?" She pressed her palms out to stop him. "Don't go there—we're drowning well past that."

"She's right." Brels stood. "Help her return to her ship. Take safe harbor there while your passenger conducts his business. No one will interfere with you. My word as Guild Master."

That should be good for something. She closed her eyes and nodded.

Pogo took the mug and blanket from her, offering to help her stand. She shook her head and braced against the chair for a moment, then stood. This time the room didn't spin, merely wobbled at the edges of her vision. Her knees had all the strength of mud, and she still shook like a leaf in a storm, but she could walk on her own.

He gestured for her to follow.

Out of the cavernous office, into a windowless hall—nothing like the office, smooth metal walls surrounding stone floors, expected and somehow comforting considering the utter strangeness of the day. She fell behind Pogo's brisk pace. Walking should not require so much concentration.

"Sorry." He caught her elbow as she sagged against the wall. "Recovering from a suppression stun is miserable. The effects really do linger the full six hours."

"How would you know?"

"Can't get licensed to use one without going through exactly what you did. Miserable, memorable experience." His face darkened, and he checked his module. "One your enforcer friend missed. Damned mine rat wasn't even licensed for it."

"Then why did she have it in the first place?"

"That's the first thing I'm going to find out after she spends some time in suppression herself. She paid that forward, and if it doesn't come back to her, she's going to do it again to someone else. Or someone else is going to pick up the idea from her, and I'm not having that. Either way, I'm going to make sure our chief pulls her from duty. She can go back to chewing rocks." He paused and looked at her. "I don't know how to apologize to you for this."

"Doesn't matter. You don't have to put on a show. You're going to get what you want, so let it rest."

"And why are you willing to do that?" He folded his arms across his chest and glowered like an interrogator.

"When there's not much in your favor, sometimes paying it forward is the only thing you've got left to try. So, you do that."

"And what happened doesn't change your mind about that?"

"It could, but what does that do for me? The Raiders are a problem for us all. I can't do anything about them, but Firen's got resources. Maybe you can. We all stand to benefit from that."

She pushed off the slick gray wall, and they continued down the hall at a much slower pace than she would have liked, but it was the best she could manage for now.

"Brels will not let this rest. He's going to make this right. I'd like to as well."

"For an unconnected swamp rat? I don't think so. I'm tired, just get me back to my ship. I'll fulfill my promise, and you can forget about this bother." And about her.

"But you won't."

"I'm not stupid. I won't be flying into Firen territories any more."

"And that's going to cost you, won't it?"

"It's not your problem." Anger, there, she felt it. Finally. Yes, that was a good sign. She straightened her shoulders and drew her first steady breath since they'd landed.

"That's a matter of opinion. I think it makes it worse." Pogo punched in a security code and opened a door. The expansive hangar spread out before them.

Cool, fresh air, warmer than inside the hall, caressed her face, soothed her lungs. Almost safe.

"Not the first route I've had to quit. I'll be in the hauler if you want me. Do you plan on putting an enforcer to watch?"

"No, you've had quite enough of them."

"Not wrong."

"Still acceptable if I come by in a bit?"

"I'll have the information you asked for on a Record chip." She glanced at him and headed for her ship. He wasn't following, just watching.

Hopefully, Matté would not want to leave before she was safe to fly.

Chapter 14

THE SECURITY TEAM HEMMED him in, much too close for comfort, as they ushered him through the door into a standard-issue industrial corridor. Were they nervous about something in particular, or was it the presence of High Rank that made them hover so?

The corridor ended in sealed double doors marked with *Evering Industries*—large, etched black letters in a traditional Dextrine font that didn't belong here. Almost like a mark establishing territory.

Perhaps it was. Evering was one of Clan Corbel's major interests. Family Liner managed it, with Trade Minister Lord Josef Liner's direct input. Iantha, his niece, served as Evering's chief local officer. While her appointment looked like a political favor, it only took five minutes with her to recognize that it wasn't only that. Smart, shrewd, and savvy, she had been the making of

Evering's Lighten branch. They claimed the partnership would revolutionize Lighten's mining operations with new, more efficient refining techniques which would allow refined, concentrated ore to be shipped directly from the mines.

Now that he'd seen Lighten for himself, though, he had to wonder. Lightens on the whole seemed capable of figuring out that for themselves. That couldn't be the sole reason Evering was here.

But did he really want to know what else might be going on?

The security lead tapped a signal into his module. The double doors slid open to reveal a pair of security guards, in standard Dextrine uniforms, guarding a long, gray corridor, punctuated by well-labeled doors. More decorative than tactical, but still practical enough, their uniforms were deep Corbel green, accented with black, and their faces were wide and round and soft—hallmarks of the Corbel Clan. Their weapons, though, state-of-the art—nothing decorative about them at all. Odd for such heavily-armed teams to be deployed this deep in a secure installation.

"They will take you from here, Lord Heir Timnon." The security team bowed as he passed through the doors. They were probably relieved to get rid of him.

The formal protocols began as he passed into the custody of the Dextrine team. Bowing, presenting arms, introduction of the guards—they were Corbel Clan as he thought—bowing again. And again. It had been far too easy to get used to traveling like a normal person. He already missed it.

They accompanied him to the first office on the right, marked by an elaborately framed, traditional hinged door, that stood out from the sparse aesthetics that characterized what he'd seen of the mines so far. *Lady Iantha Liner, Chief of Operations,* in the same black font as the hall doors, had been etched at eye level to ensure no one missed it. She was proud of that well-earned door. Matteo was proud of her, too.

The Dextrine guard touched the door signal, and a green light appeared above it. He pushed it open and bowed Matteo through.

An executive-sized office stretched out before him. The false window, which stretched the entire width of the back wall, showed a scene he recognized, the view from an office window in Noreia, Corbel territory's capital city, where the main Evering Headquarters stood. They had signed their betrothal contract there. A faint fragrance of flowers native to Corbel, spicy-sweet with a hint of citrus, danced in the air, just like it had that day. Did she choose that specifically to greet him?

Pictures of Corbel ancestors and achievements lined the right and left walls, reminiscent of the corridors leading to Grandfather's official office at home. Complete with small wall-mounted plaques describing the glories of Clan Corbel and Family Liner. *Duty. Honor. Family.* Indeed. How did that register with the Lightens who met with her here? It would be interesting to discover what they made of it.

Her desk was cast of some sort of clear acrylic resin with amazing optical properties. It disappeared into the room, leaving one with the image of her sitting in front of the window, with nothing between her and her guests. Welcoming, in a way, but distant.

"Lord Heir Timnon, you honor me with your presence." Iantha stood and slipped around her desk to bow. Graceful, and proper, down to the right depth of bow, pause, and return to posture. As much as they annoyed him, the controlled predictability of Dextrine protocols still soothed a few of his ragged edges.

Her long blonde hair had been pulled back from her face, but still flowed down to her shoulders in pristine cascades, a classic Corbel beauty in every sense. The smart, well-tailored dark-blue suit she wore, no doubt bespoke, left him all too aware of her remarkable figure and his own far less polished appearance. But nothing in her serene expression betrayed any reaction. As she had been trained. Ranks, even those on the outer edges of rank, did not reveal their true reactions.

Such a contrast from the plucky little pilot who'd been ready to tell him to get out if he didn't like the terms of her contract.

Still, though, the tiny crease between her eyes suggested she might not be as pleased in his arrival as her words of greeting first suggested.

That was the final confirmation he needed. "You look well, Lady Iantha. As I understand, Evering is prospering under your management."

"Thank you, Lord Heir Timnon. It is gracious of you to be aware of such things. Would you like to sit down?" She gestured to a pair of sleek metal chairs in the corner nearest the door. They did not match the rest of the room, clearly brought in for their encounter. Having her sit behind a desk with him on the other side would disrupt the order of Rank.

"Thank you." He sat down first, as appropriate for the higher-Ranked individual.

She sat across from him, smoothing her skirt. Odd that she would choose that as her working "uniform" in a place like this. Dextrines did love their displays of authority, though.

"Forgive me, I did not realize you would be on Lighten this season. I am rather ... unprepared ... for your call." The barest note of uneasiness colored the edge of her voice.

She was hiding something.

But now was not the time to address it. What would Beny do? "Forgive me for not giving you further notice. Lord Timnon only recently notified me that my presence would be required here. I had little time to prepare."

"Of course, it is our duty to accommodate the requirements of our Clan Lords. May I ask what you are here to do?" She seemed a bit alarmed. Who could blame her, though? It would not be unlike Grandfather to order some sort of audit of her work in order to prove herself worthy of an alliance with Timnon.

"The Lighten Ring Fighting Championships are hosting exhibition bouts this year. I will be participating."

She gasped, then hurried to reassemble her carefully curated composure. "You will be in the ring, fighting?"

"Those were Lord Timnon's orders."

She rose with all the grace and elegance of an image-maker's model and paced the office like a fashion runway. She must have worked diligently to perfect that walk, though it still reflected some agitation. "Are you familiar with the local fighting style?"

"You are well aware I fought while attending Wroxton. I am well-versed in multiple styles, even if I prefer our own."

"Forgive me, I had forgotten." If they had not already discussed it, her expression, the first honest one of their encounter today, would have made her disgust for the sport clear.

"I take it you do not plan to attend."

"If you wish me to attend, then, of course, I will arrange to be there." She tried to maintain eye contact, but that would have been too revealing.

"But if allowed your preference, you would prefer not." He captured her gaze and held it. "Rather like our betrothal."

Her jaw dropped, and she lost color in her face. She hurried back to her seat near him.

Probably not fair of him to drop something on her like that. Beny would never have recommended such a direct approach. But she would otherwise avoid the topic, dancing around any possibility of offending him or his Clan.

"Lord Heir Timnon! How can you say such a thing? I never—"

"No, you have not, and that is quite the issue. We need to discuss it."

She wrapped her ankles so tightly her right foot crossed behind, then in front of her left and she laid clasped hands on her pressed knees. If she wound up any tighter, she might unravel. "What are you implying?"

"Lady Iantha, I am not implying anything. I insist you speak openly with me now." He pulled out his module and set the privacy ware. "Nothing you say will find its way into the Records or the Media."

Her eyes grew still wider. "Are you certain?"

"This is the newest filter, obtained before I left Dextra yesterday, and not widely available, yet."

She seemed to relax. Just a little.

"Perhaps it is best if I start." He swallowed a sigh. This was his job, to be out in front, leading, even in the difficult things. Even if she should have said something, done something long ago. "I am quite aware this betrothal is not what you would prefer."

"It is a stunning match that any woman would be proud to be Considered for." Her face betrayed no real emotion and her words lacked conviction.

"But this is a betrothal, not a Consideration. An arrangement to the mutual benefit of both families. Not between a couple, for their mutual benefit."

"The two are not mutually exclusive."

"They are when your affections lie elsewhere."

"What has that to do with our betrothal?"

"Kayavan's bones!" He slapped the armrest, and she jumped. Finally, an honest reaction from her. "How can you say that?"

"Affections are built after a Bond, not before. They form a poor foundation for a lifetime of working and leading together, do they not?" Her tight smile did not make the traditional position true.

"That is the party line at home, used often to defend undesired betrothals." He leaned back and stared at the sleek, molded panel ceiling. "And maybe it is true, but I have my doubts, especially when there are other affections already in place."

She swallowed hard. "I would never betray you. I never have betrayed you."

And she had just lied to him. Looking him straight in the eye, she lied to him. And he had the Records to prove it. "You are attached to the youngest son of Lord Irdras of Clan Tormeg, Lord Lemos Irdras, I believe his name is."

She dropped her gaze, and shifted in her seat, like a child caught in obvious deception.

Did she believe Matteo so thick he would not discover such a poorly guarded secret?

"As the youngest son, it is unlikely he will inherit any position of importance, though his business acumen is well aligned with yours. You two met first in school, then worked together during your internship years. Sounds like a traditional Consideration in the making to me." He raised his brow.

She squirmed again. "Some might have regarded it that. But that does not mean—"

"I believe your father objected, not finding Lemos' prospects high enough for him, especially when the matchmakers told him Lord Timnon had put a Clan Lordship on the line for the right match."

"You make it sound so cold and calculating."

"It is. Arranging a match for power, status, and pecuniary gain."

"What about our duty to our people? The Raiders have been destabilizing everything around us. Dextrine trade is suffering. It is only a matter of time before they penetrate our defense grid and strike our home itself. Lighten may well end up siding with them before all is said and done, if they don't have some way of defending against them."

"Defending Lighten? I am not sure I understand."

She twitched her head and blinked rapidly. "Defend their economy. The raids on the mines are on the verge of destabilizing their economy. The way the Transport Guild has limited their shipping capabilities and their use of armed vehicles to defend those shipments has not only the mines, but their whole economy, in peril."

"I was not aware that the Transport Guild was such a threat to the supply chains. I will look into that further." He would also need to research the Corbel Clan holdings. Had he read something about military surplus in their business ventures?

"I am surprised that you have not already, given that supply chain security was one of your specialty areas of study."

She might be correct, but that was still a blow a ring official would have declared illegal. But then again, bringing up Lemos wasn't done with the greatest of tact either.

"Do you desire our betrothal?"

"It is what my Family, my Clan, have required of me," she whispered, staring at her hands, as though knowing she was trapped into expressing the truth. "It is in the best interest of Dextra that our families learn how to work together. The questions of Identity and Unity are becoming a dangerous divide."

"On that I agree. But how is a bond between us going to change any of their minds? And when it comes time that my Grandfather is no longer establishing Clan Timnon policy, my views on the matter are well known. They are quite similar to Corbel's, and not dependent on external connections." He pulled a small box, covered with a delicate tapestry woven of the finest precious metals, from his flight jacket pocket and held it out to her.

She opened it with trembling hands, revealing two earrings, one a large filigree gold disk, the other a more elaborate, but matching, dangling affair. "The Promise Rings my Clan gave to yours to celebrate our betrothal?"

"We have not Promised. What we have had is an official betrothal, one that we may dissolve. One that it is time we end."

She nearly dropped the box. "End? What will our families say?"

"I will ensure that it does not damage your reputation. I am the instigator here, not you. I will make it clear that your behavior has been ..." He could not go so far as to say "honorable." Nothing about her secret affair with Lemos was honorable. Disgusting as it was, it was not the reason for his decision. "Is not the basis of my decision. I take full responsibility for dissolving this betrothal."

"I do not understand. Once we are bonded, I would never—"

Did she regard him foolish enough to believe that? "That is not the issue. Lord Timnon has controlled every aspect of my life since my parents died. I will be forced to take his place when he passes, again without choice or options. Something in my life must be under my control. I insist on having my choice of wife."

"And I am not her." The cold words that fell from her lips registered the finality of his decision.

"You do not want to be her." He stood. Yes, it was taking a dominant position, and yes, he was doing it intentionally. "I hired a professional analyst to confirm. Lord Lemos is far more compatible with you than I will ever be. All the years at a Theran military academy have taken their toll. Once you got to know me, you would not find me particularly likable. I do not want to inflict that on anyone."

"You have a mean opinion of yourself." She rose and looked him in the eye, despite having to crane her neck to do so. Confident, defiant, a touch offended and angry. To be expected.

"No, an honest one. I did not say that no woman would have me, just not one who expects a proper High Rank Dextrine heir."

She turned her back on him and returned to her desk, breaching proper protocol. Oh, she was angry and offended. Clearly not accustomed to being told "no." "Are you certain this is what you want?"

"I am certain it is the best for both of us and our Clans. You do not need to do anything. I will manage the press releases and communicate it to our Clans. Be discreet in your communications with Lord Lemos for a few months. For your own sakes, wait until the furor dies down, then pursue your affections. I will publicly support you and attend your ceremonies, if you wish to pursue something official together."

"That is kind of you. Very kind." Everything in her posture declared that was not what she was thinking. "I hardly know what to say."

"I suppose there is a protocol to such things as this, but I am unfamiliar with them as well. Perhaps the best choice is to treat me as an official visitor, not a failed betrothal. You might show me around your operation here? Those images would be helpful in the press releases to quell some suspicions against you."

"A tour?" Complex thoughts twitched across her face, but none of them appeared pleased with the suggestion. "What about an introduction to Guild Master Brels? I am sure you will see him at the Championships. His bout with Guild Master Joco will probably decide who will serve as Chairman of the House of Guilds." A skillful diversion. Had she always been so calculating?

"I have heard that, but I can't say I understand."

"As I understand, it has to do with the way Lighten was settled and the harshness of the environment here. They prefer to trust a person's actions above their words, and the fighting ring allows them to see that more clearly. You will be surprised. Though he is a skilled fighter, Guild Master Brels is a man of deep principles and honor. You will find him a worthy connection if you choose to make it."

Oh, the irony that she was offering worthy connections. "One that Lord Timnon has been unable to obtain. I would appreciate an introduction." It could be quite valuable in the long run. Not as valuable in Grandfather's eyes as a bond with Corbel, but it would be something of a peace offering.

"Let me request a meeting with him, and I will show you around Evering while we wait for his reply."

"Is there anything else to be said before I turn off the privacy shields?"

"Thank you for the courtesy of privacy for this conversation. I hope you are able to find a worthy partner who returns your affections. If you will excuse me a moment to prepare for your tour." A carefully curated tour, no doubt, one designed to keep him out of the places she wanted kept confidential. She hurried out.

He dropped into one of the metal chairs and heaved a great sigh. He tapped out a message to Beny.

Return will be delayed for additional introductions. Otherwise mission accomplished.

By the time he got back to Anara, with any luck Beny would have sent the first round of official announcements Matteo had drafted before he left. He would be free of Iantha, and Grandfather would be livid.

Chapter 15

An hour and a half later, a knock on the hull roused Ari from the Records she was transferring. In the safe confines of her familiar, cluttered little hauler, the lingering buzz had faded from her nerves and the itchy-prickles that had danced along her skin eased to just barely there. The hauler might smell of humidity and lingering traces of sweat, but those spoke of a world she knew and belonged in. Hopefully, she would not have to leave again until she returned to Anara.

Another minute, one more click, and all the chatter feed keywords and filters, sensor and shield specs, and the technical details of her system tweaks that Pogo asked for would be on a chip she could hand him, and his techies wouldn't have to swarm her hauler. Considering what his enforcers felt free to do, the risk with the tech folk was even worse.

Ping. There, it was done, and winds be with her, she could be done with Firen now as well.

Another knock, less polite.

She stood to face the hatch, hand on her knife, as she signaled it to open. Not that she could shut it fast enough if something unexpected happened. At least nothing would catch her unaware. The sun, barely past its zenith now, cascaded into the hangar, backlighting the man who stood at the hatch waiting.

"Who's there?"

"Pogo—permission to come aboard?"

"Yes, come, I've prepared the Records with details you wanted. Call off your techies, though. I don't want anyone else touching my ship."

"Understood." Pogo strode in, carefully, as if approaching an animal that might bolt—or attack. A larger backlit shadow remained outside. "There is another who requests permission to come aboard."

Squalls and storms! Why?

It was hardly as though she could refuse. Not when he was right there, and she was berthed in his hangar. Even if she tried, she wouldn't be able to stop him from entering if he was determined. "Granted."

Pogo nodded with an unexpected solemnity, formality he'd not demonstrated before, and beckoned the other man in.

Brels' posture, his walk, were odd. He moved without the swagger typical of a Guild Master, approaching with eyes downcast. Not a lack of confidence, or a mean self-opinion, but ... yes, it was ... humility; deliberate, and a bit unsettling to watch. A rare expression in a man of such standing.

He stopped before her, dwarfing her in his sheer presence. Reminding her that despite her ready knife, there was no way she could stand against him. Trapped again, as effectively as the enforcers had. Her heart dropped, then raced, even as she searched for an escape route.

He dropped to one knee before her, barely squeezing between the two back passenger seats, his head bowed, sandstone-brown hair fallen to obscure his face, the back of his neck exposed to her.

She gasped and scrambled backward against the dashboard. What could he mean by this? She'd read of this gesture, once. Somewhere in a fable, perhaps. Spoken of as a theoretical, mythical possibility, but nothing done in real life.

What was she supposed to do? The proper response, a light touch of a hand to the back of the neck, seemed far too daring.

How would he respond to such audacity? Only the Arch Key Minder could answer such a question. But surely it would not go well for her if she responded wrongly.

"I approach you wearing my honest name." Brels' shoulders sagged, bathed in cascading shadows. "It is a name of no pride, which I have labored hard to be rid of."

She swallowed hard. What was he about? A man of his standing did not offer his honest name. His reputation and standing ensured he did not need to expose himself that way.

"I was once called Payback."

Definitely a name without honor. "Why present that name to me?"

"In hopes you will hear me out."

She laid her trembling hand on the back of his sweaty neck, close-shaven hair prickling her fingertips. An impulsive move she might well regret. But not trusting instincts got pilots killed more often than not.

"I am honored, Arli." He stood with a grace unusual for a man his size.

"Please, sit down." She dropped into her seat and swiveled it to face them. Looking up at him put a crick in her neck and did nothing to reinforce the air of respect with which he approached her.

Brels sat in the seat nearest her, almost as imposing, wedged into the too-small seat. Pogo sat beside him. The sun had shifted enough, so they were no longer backlit.

But seeing their faces didn't offer the answers she needed. "Why do you come in your honest name? You have earned the right—"

"I have, and it was hard-won with an honest name like mine." The weight of the name seemed to settle on his shoulders, but he lifted his chin, determined, maybe even defiant. "But you refused to hear me out when I approached you without it. I wish to explain myself. I need you to understand who I am. I need you to believe that this unfortunate incident was nothing more than a disgraceful mistake by a badly behaving underling, and not a desire to harm you, or Guild Master Joco." He extended an open hand. "Will you hear me out?"

As much as she wanted to say no, nothing about the situation suggested refusal would be a proper choice. "I will."

He nodded, as though acknowledging the concession, the cost to her. His brows knit as he stared over her shoulder. "Before I was Guild Master, I was a man who answered insult for insult. All offenses were paid back in full, in whatever way was most convenient, with no attention to any but my perception and judgment." His flat tone offered no defense for his self-assessment, only facts of what had been. "How is not important, but I learned it is not the payback that makes a man strong, but how one pays forward." He returned his gaze to her face.

"That is a challenging, difficult lesson." One that ... no, she did not need to go there. She bit her lip.

"Challenging, but crucial, and transformational." He pulled his shoulders back, sat straighter, taller, until he cast a shadow over her. "Paying forward, not back, allowed me to rise to Guild Master. Hospitality I offered returned to me many times over and permitted me to shed an ignoble name as I became a different man."

If that were true, he would be a rare man indeed.

"I am convinced that I cannot afford to ignore what happened today. You came to us with open hands, extended in hospitality, but were paid forward with the worst possible combination of prejudice and malice."

Politeness suggested she should deny that truth. But, then again, no one had ever accused her of being polite.

"I would make that right before that wrong done to you in my house becomes the first rock in a slide that will later bury me." He extended open hands to her.

She squirmed. A favor such as that always came at a price. "I have no such power to bring harm to you. An unconnected, nameless swamp rat is owed no such consideration."

"Yet, you still hold your hands open with hospitality toward us. Are those not the Records Pogo asked you for?" He glanced at her hands.

She stared at the green chip she'd forgotten she held.

"You still pay forward, yet you expect far less than that in return." Clearly, he did not approve. He had a point. Some would consider her expectations of him an outright insult. But she had good reason.

Not a discussion she was about to open.

"I mean no criticism. No doubt there are reasons for your expectation, though I am sorry that is the case. It is a credit to your character that you would go forward with open hands. I would do the same, even go so far as to say what could be a clearer test of one's commitment to our deepest principle of hospitality but to extend it to one who might be considered unworthy of it."

She dropped the chip and wrapped her arms around her waist. According to everyone in the Ship Yard, she was that. Unworthy. Apparently here, too. "There is no need. Just permit me to leave without further issues and any requirement of hospitality will be met."

Brels winced and hung his head. "Forgive me, that came out badly. I did not mean to suggest that you were unworthy. That is not what—"

She clenched her fists in her lap. "Leave it. Just leave it. There is no need to explain yourself, no need for anything. Just stop." Drown it all! Her voice was on the verge of breaking and her eyes burned. She had better control than this. Storm-shorn suppression still hadn't worn off.

"You are not unworthy of hospitality or notice."

"Don't go there. It is unnecessary and ... uncomfortable." Uncomfortable, embarrassing, soul-crushing, any of those words would work.

Brels' perceptive blue eyes studied her. "You make me uncomfortable as well."

"That is not uncommon, sir. I am sorry. Perhaps it is best for you to go."

"Do you know why you make me uncomfortable?"

"No. But I imagine you will find it necessary to tell me. And I will listen politely, and nod my head. Then you can walk away knowing you have done your duty, extended hospitality by giving me actionable advice on how to make myself acceptable in good company like yours." She bit her upper lip and closed her eyes. "But there is no point. I have heard it all before. I am a bringer of storms. That is my honest name, and unlike you, I don't think I will ever leave it behind. So, let us save ourselves the discomfort of that conversation, and pretend we have had it. You have extended your hospitality, I have received it, and our customs have been honored. What more need be said?"

"If that is your expectation of my hospitality, then a great deal." He leaned closer, elbows on knees. "Lecturing you as to how storms are your fault hardly seems like hospitality in such a circumstance."

Forming words around the knot in her throat was impossible.

"My role as Guild Master, and the one I hope to attain in the future, hinges on ensuring I have paid forward nothing I might regret. And I regret what has happened with my enforcers, and what I just said to imply you are less than you are." He picked up the Records chip from the deck and handed it back to her. "And I regret that you so readily believe that my open hand would only contain further disregard of the value that you bring. I know what I want to convey, but it would be easier to carve it into stone than to find the correct words." He sighed as he met her gaze, allowing her to look steadily into him, unflinching.

It seemed like he meant that.

"The enforcer who acted against you has been paid back with the hand she dealt, but that does nothing for you. I want ... I hope you will allow me a second chance, to approach you with the same open hand you offered us."

She tipped her head back, eyes closed, and swallowed hard. How many second chances did life offer? To offer one to a man such as Brels, freely and in good will, was an opportunity to pay forward that should not be set aside lightly.

The fact that he was honored now with the use of his given name suggested he had indeed outgrown "Payback" and was a different man. Perhaps one worth trusting.

She had every right to refuse and to walk away. But ...

"Let us begin again, then, Master Brels." She fingered the Record chip in her hand. Right now, it was all she had to offer, of dubious value, to be sure. But it was what she had. She handed the Record chip to Pogo and offered open hands to Brels.

He pressed them to the hard planes of his angular cheeks.

"Please accept the hospitality of what I have, according to your need." Her whisper barely rose above the hum of the hangar outside.

His face relaxed, and he smiled. "I receive your hospitality with gratitude, and offer what you need according to what I have." He extended open hands to her.

Breath caught in her throat, and she trembled again. When was the last time someone had offered her such a gesture?

Dare she trust it, trust him? From the corner of her eye, Pogo watched, holding his breath. Everything about the way he carried himself insisted he believed his Guild Master's sincerity.

She pressed his huge hands to her cheeks. How vulnerable this position. How much easier to extend hospitality than to receive it. "I receive your hospitality with gratitude."

He leaned his face close to hers, touching his forehead to hers. "It is no small thing to offer trust in such a moment. I do not take it lightly." He released her, and they both leaned back, breathing, and sorting out what had just happened.

Such moments were rare; memories worth keeping, holding onto in the dark moments; reminders that light could penetrate the darkness. Even if Brels forgot, she would not. He looked at her, blinking slowly, and nodded. A promise he would not forget, either?

He nodded again. "Yes. These are memories worth holding."

She blinked back the burning in her eyes.

Brels glanced at Pogo.

"Why don't you explain to him about the Records you gave me." Pogo patted his chest pocket.

She glanced over her shoulder at the control panels of her ship. "I made some modifications to my hauler that he was interested in."

"She has increased several key capacities of this vessel. May I show him the Records?"

She shook her head and shrugged as he handed Brels his module. "Guild Master, you need to understand—"

Brels waved her silent as he stared at the module. "Your modifications allowed this hauler to do ... that?" He pointed at the small screen.

"Yes, those adjustments made it easier, but it is still up to the pilot to make it work."

"Still extraordinary. And well beyond the bounds of hospitality. You must allow us to pay you—"

"No, I can't. Absolutely not." She pushed back all the way in her seat. "Everything in those Records violates Transportation Guild practice and standards. All of this depends on inspectors looking the other way. Selling you untested, unapproved modifications is illegal at best. It is one thing to share them as a matter of hospitality, since you asked. But to sell them would put me in a criminal compromise of Guild regulations. If Joco ever finds out I shared such a thing ..."

Brels muttered something about Joco under his breath. He was not wrong, but her opinions didn't matter right now.

"I can't promise that any of this will work on the models Firen uses. It is all based in an Acoling design that might not be widely applicable. It could be a starting point for your engineers to do something, but it could also be a complete waste of your time. It is important you understand the true, limited value of what I've given you. Please, don't hold me to promises I've never made. And don't let it get out that any of this came from me."

"You have my word, no one will find out this came from you." Brels spoke the words like he meant them. Which was still no guarantee.

How stupid could she be? She should have thought this through much more carefully. Drowned pilot impulsiveness!

"She also has information about Raider encounters in our territory," Pogo said.

"Are you willing to share those?"

"These are unofficial, my personal logs only. Never reported or verified. Information that you must recognize the risks of using." She slid another green Records chip into her module and started the download. "Make what you can of it, I cannot promise what use it will be." She handed it to Pogo.

"I'll add it to our database and see what we can get out of it." He slipped it into his pocket.

"Maybe none of this is useful."

"And yet it might be." Brels leaned back and steepled his hands in front of his chest. "Since you will not accept payment, at least permit me to offer you a proper meal before you leave us? I believe that was part of your arrangement with Pogo, yes? I will be serving guests in my office shortly, and it would be my pleasure to have you join us."

"I am not the sort that belongs in polite company."

"Miners are not known for being polite company, so you will be quite at home." Brels extended his hand to her.

Clearly, she would not get out of this. And she was hungry. "I am grateful to accept your hospitality."

Chapter 16

Iantha presented a tour more cursory than informative. Did she think he failed to notice all the places they did not go, or the curated explanations she gave of Evering's activities on Lighten? How had he missed the signs that she considered him at least inattentive, but more likely stupid?

Too many details did not line up with the rhetoric he'd been given about Evering's Lighten-based activities. As soon as he got back to Anara, he would apply his considerable resources to discovering why he was certain he'd dodged not an inconvenient bond, but a full-on disaster.

On their return to Iantha's office, Guild Master Brels responded to her request to make an introduction with an invitation to join him for an informal meal.

Perfect, just perfect. All Matteo had wanted was a brief meet-and-greet. But now he would be thrown into something sure to be a diplomatic debacle, proving to Grandfather and the rest of the family circle how useless he was. And better still, since he had requested the introduction, he couldn't refuse the invitation.

Beny would never have gotten himself into such a predicament.

"Please convey my thanks for the gracious invitation." Matteo forced his face into something more neutral and fitting for the occasion.

"He wants us there soon, so best head that direction. I'd offer you the use of my garment recycler, but you don't need to be worried about being underdressed. You'll find when Guild Master Brels says informal, he means informal. None of the protocol-laden formalities that the rest of the system considers essential to life and breath. It's rather refreshing, actually." Her tone, this side of scathing, suggested otherwise.

Best ignore that, and the likelihood that denying him the use of the recycler was intentional sabotage. "No trick questions? No political traps?"

"Surprisingly not. It is difficult to believe, but at least Brels, and possibly Lightens as a whole, are far more direct than you or I were prepared for. The first six months I was here were quite challenging, trying to sort out how to respond to what came across as rude and demanding. At times, I still find myself taken aback. Taking things at face value is definitely a learned skill." She stopped at the doors separating Evering from the rest of the Firen Mine complex. "Escorts have been sent to meet us here."

"Directness. That sounds like the sort of thing that would bring Council chambers crashing down around our ears."

"It might, which is why I do not suggest adopting the practice more broadly. But for today, you may find it agreeable, at least more agreeable than the more typical diplomatic dining dance." Mere hours ago, he had considered such a comment from her to be sympathetic. How could he have missed the condescending undertones? Not the kind of revelation to have on the heels of a major diplomatic introduction.

It figured.

"You're sure this," he gestured to his drab and intentionally ill-fitting flight jacket and work pants, "won't be a problem?"

"To him, informal means come as you are. He might find it amusing how informal you are, but that could work to your favor. Dextrines, especially our Ranks, aren't viewed as approachable or sympathetic. Your 'just a pilot' guise might diffuse that. It caught me off-guard." She looked him up and down, judgment in her eyes.

A woman scorned was not to be trifled with. He had dodged disaster. "I appreciate the introduction. None of our Ranks—" yes, he emphasized that word as a not-so-subtle reminder that she clearly needed, "—have been able to get an audience with him until now."

"You are welcome. I am glad to ... offer something of value, despite the way things have sorted out. It would be beneficial for our Clans to remain on good terms. A word of caution though, Brels might appear informal, friendly even, but he's neither a fool nor stupid. Don't underestimate him. He's as zealous for the interests of his people as any Clan Lord."

Don't underestimate—that seemed to be the theme of his visit. One Grandfather would never accept, but there would be some who might. And Matteo would share it with them.

The armed, black-uniformed escort met them outside the Evering doors. Interesting how even though Evering had a presence in the Firen facility, they did not have free access beyond their designated resources. Security wasn't a bad thing, but the well-armed team seemed a little excessive. What statement were they making?

The polite, but ... firm, that seemed the best word for it ... team delivered them to the Guild Master's office. No elaborate doorway and markers of status here. A simple, albeit larger than standard, doorway in the sleek gray metal wall, with a modest plaque featuring small, plain print next to it, to indicate it was indeed the Guild Master's office. The lead escort pressed his hand to the wall plate beside the door, and it slid open.

Iantha stepped back to allow him first entry into the office. It was proper that way. An isolating custom that would not change in his lifetime, so he resigned himself to it and stepped inside.

Kayavan's bones!

The room, softly lit by concealed light sources, opened up before him, much like the hangar had. Far larger and deeper than he expected, the office appeared carved by the natural forces of water through the rock. He sniffed the air, cool humidity with a touch of limestone. A soft trickle of water down the far wall, which seemed to be made of flowstone. This might have been a natural cavern repurposed as an office. What manner of man did that?

The smooth flowstone, slick and shimmering with trickling water, undulated down the walls in shades of beige, red, green, and brown, the colors revealing the minerals the flowing water carried. Narrow stalactites dangled from the ceiling in the right corner, while a massive column where stalactite and stalagmite met and merged into one appeared to hold up the high ceiling dome in the center.

That point divided the room into functional spaces, with a carved stone desk in the far left corner, while the space in front of the column seemed, at least for now, arranged to entertain company. Soft seating and low tables bearing many covered dishes rested on soft, thick woven rugs that dampened the sound, bouncing against the stone walls. Though the fragrances of fresh, if unfamiliar, foods perfumed the air, no dining table seemed evident.

"Not what you were expecting, I imagine?" A mountainous man with a rich, resonant voice approached. He fit in this space like a mythical mountain king. That had to be Guild Master

Brels. "Welcome, welcome, come in." He stopped in front of
Matteo and waited for something to happen.

Iantha scooted in beside them, appearing more flustered than
she had during Matteo's entire visit. Interesting how breaking
a betrothal hardly disturbed her, but this breach of protocol
did. "Guild Master Brels, may I present Lord Heir Timnon of
Dextra?"

"Greetings, Lord Heir Timnon." Brels nodded, not bowed.
As Iantha had warned, he considered himself of equal rank to a
Clan Lord.

Now was not the time to niggle over relative Rank and standing.

"I thank you for your welcome." Matteo mirrored Brels' nod
and held his breath. When in doubt, watch the highest-ranked
local and do the same, Beny's advice for this sort of uncertain
moment.

"I regret not having a proper, formal meal to offer." Brels
lifted an eyebrow over steel-blue eyes. This was a test, but a
good-natured one, intended to set the tone of the meal.

Not quite a trap, but enough to set him on edge. "I apologize
for the last-minute nature of my visit. I hope that has not put
you to any trouble."

"It is no trouble to bring more to my table." He beckoned
them into the room. Not the way a Dextrine Lord would have
done. The gesture was far too familiar for that. But it felt re-
spectful and natural in the context. Matteo was not about to
seek out reasons to be offended, especially when he had too
often been the victim of that brand of hunt.

Several steps led them to the seating area with large soft chairs
and couches, quite the contrast from the surrounding stone. A
broad, low stone table in the center of the seating cluster held
a variety of platters and dishes on a tabletop-sized turntable.
Some ceramic, some glass, a few metal, and a small turntable
made of stone holding numerous smaller vessels in the center of
it all. Definitely informal. Excellent.

"I understand you need no introduction to my other guests, Pilot Lysand and Enforcer Phalen." Brels gestured at two figures seated in chairs upholstered with a stonelike pattern, near the table, whom Matteo had ignored until now. They stood and nodded at him.

Interesting how he introduced them without their nicknames. A nod to Dextrine customs? "Arli, Pogo." Hopefully that wasn't the wrong move.

Brels lifted an eyebrow and indulged in a small smile. Iantha's eye twitched—was that because she did not like him using native customs or she did not like the extra company included with them?

"Sit down, be comfortable." Brels pointed them to an empty couch and sat in the largest chair in the cluster. Once Matteo and Iantha sat side by side on the couch—which was improper—Brels lifted open hands. "Pray partake in the hospitality we freely offer and welcome us someday in the same spirit."

"We receive your hospitality in thanks and anticipate extending ours to you." Phalen—no, it was better to call him Pogo—and Arli replied.

Would have been nice to know the script for that, but then again, maybe Iantha had never paid attention to the formality. Needed to make sure he shared that with Beny and added it to their file on Lighten.

And now things got tricky. How was food to be served? There was always a ceremony attached to such things. Matteo sat back, waiting and watching. With any luck, that read more polite than clueless.

All eyes turned to Brels, who handed around empty plates, then lifted the cloche off the nearest platter and rotated the turntable to Iantha, gesturing for her to serve herself. She forced a smile and looked at the plate. If Matteo could pick up her offense, surely Brels noted it, too.

Brels handed Matteo a teapot, implying he should pass it along after he poured his own cup, and watched for a reaction.

Great. What would Beny do? Go with the tone of the room—so what would Arli or Pogo do? He smiled and nodded as he took the teapot.

Brels glanced at Iantha, eyebrows drawing tighter. Not the reaction Matteo had hoped for, but at least the glower wasn't for him.

Matteo poured his tea as a familiar fragrance from the platter of crusty, fried meat near Iantha invited him to partake. Sollert, a delicacy that appeared at nearly every diplomatic event back home. A show of wealth and refined taste.

Brels handed Iantha a pair of tongs, which she used to take several pieces. She rotated the platter to Matteo, who followed her lead and rotated the tabletop toward Brels.

Brels took a single piece himself. He turned to Pogo and Arli. "No sollert, I imagine?"

"No. Thank you." Her tone was polite, but made her opinion on the delicacy very clear.

"We usually only serve it to off-world guests, you see." Brels uncovered another platter with a different preparation of sollert and sent it toward Iantha. "You may find, Lady Iantha, that you want to avoid putting it on your menu when catering for a group of locals."

The plate in Iantha's hand quivered. "I fear I have made that mistake more than once. Could you help me understand what makes it so unpopular here?" How hard she must have worked for her diplomatic polish to hide the real emotions behind those words.

Brels tipped his chin toward Arli, who looked none too happy about being called upon to answer.

"We only eat sollert when we've had to hunt for our next meal. It's not a luxury, but a sign of particularly hard times. And if you've ever been bitten by one, you want to keep as far away as possible from it, dead or alive." She rubbed her left shoulder.

Iantha squirmed. Was she realizing she needed to have a talk with her catering staff?

Change the topic, change the topic, change the topic. "So then, what are considered delicacies by local standards?" Ask about local pride. Beny said that was always safe.

"I am glad you asked." Brels reached for a painted ceramic dish with a woven basket as a cloche. "Everyone loves fried bread, but we take it to new heights, if I do say so myself." He lifted the cover to reveal a generous dish of fried round balls, dusted with something sweet-and-spicy-smelling. It smelled enough like familiar pastries to be recognizable, but the spice was wholly unique. He offered the dish to Matteo. "Go on, tell me what you think."

The dish had no serving utensil. In fact, there was not an eating utensil anywhere on the table. Only one choice. Mustering his courage, Matteo took one with his fingers—a thing he had never done in any company but Beny's, and even then, it was a complete mockery of proper table manners. Iantha followed suit, perhaps a show of solidarity, perhaps trying not to be rude.

Heavy for its size, still warm and sticky, there must be a dense filling inside. He bit through the crunchy exterior, a fried dough made of a grain similar to Dextrine soft wheat, but with added nuttiness. Then a bubble of salty-sweet-sour fruit puree burst in his mouth. He jumped and puckered.

"You approve?" Brels grinned.

Show appreciation, even if you don't like it. But he did, so it was much easier. "I've never had anything like it. What is that filled with?"

"That's where it takes on its local identity. Anyone can fry up dough and do it well, but marsh fruit is only found in that narrow band of land where the shore blends seamlessly into the desert. The sun makes it sweet, but the salt content of the soil gives it that savory edge that you can't find words to describe." Brels was a man proud of his home.

"I can see why it would be favored. Extraordinary." Iantha tried, but she lacked enthusiasm.

"Are you ready for another?" Brels picked up another bowl of what looked like tiny pickled melons, with green rinds covered in a variety of yellow bumps.

Matteo popped one into his mouth whole. It exploded in a sweet-briny-tart effervescent crunch like nothing else in his experience. "That was amazing. I had no idea what we've been missing. Every caterer insists on featuring sollert eight different ways in every menu, but never anything like this."

Iantha cringed. Probably should not have sounded so surprised, but the melons really were incredible.

"As they should. It is an important export after all. Neither marsh fruit nor pebble melons store well. They are not viable export products. At least not yet." Brels uncovered another platter. There was a lot more to the Mining Guild Master than first met the eye.

Matteo bowed from his shoulders. "Thank you for this rare treat."

Iantha tried to hide her glare at another breach of protocol—a Clan Heir only bowed to a recognized Clan Lord.

Brels looked a little surprised and pleased. Perfect. It was his opinion, not Iantha's, that Brels needed to recognize now. "Not disappointed in the lack of swamp snakes on the table?"

Matteo turned his shoulder to Iantha. "Not in the least."

"I understand you are signed up to experience more of our culture. You are facing our Pogo here in an exhibition bout, yes?" Brels leaned back and stroked his chin.

"I have been cautioned that I might regret that choice." Matteo raised his cup to Pogo.

"I fully intend to convince you of that." Pogo raised his cup and laughed.

"What do you think, little Arli? The Soul Catcher or the Prince?"

Matteo bristled. Not a title he wanted thrown around, but best let it go this time.

"I know storms, not soul catchers, and nothing of princes. Since neither of them fights with wind or rain, my opinion is of little more value than a random guess." Something firm in her voice suggested that was all she would say on the matter.

But that was no simple exchange. There was something more to it. Was it because she did not want to be asked to offer an opinion on the bout between the Guild Masters and feared one opinion would lead to the demand for more? Matteo had found himself caught in that trap more than once.

Brels raised his glass to her, conceding the point, perhaps? "Did you know Fleet is sending representatives for the exhibition bouts as well?"

Iantha twitched.

"Good thing the Ring Officials didn't try setting me up for one of those." Matteo popped several pebble melons in his mouth.

"Forgive my ignorance." Iantha's thin voice oozed her disregard for the sport. "But why?"

Pogo swallowed his mouthful. "Are you familiar with Lighten ring fighting at all?"

"Sadly, I am not." But there was nothing sad about it; she detested fighting for sport as Matteo practiced it. Barbaric and unbecoming his Rank and status.

"Let me see if I can sum it up without getting technical." Pogo dragged one palm against the other, calluses and dry skin rasping. "Dextrines have rules and follow them all—occasionally inventing extras just for the fun of it."

Matteo snickered into his fist. "He's not wrong."

"Lightens believe in hospitality, which requires treating others with honor, and paying forward what we'd like to receive ourselves. Those function similar to your rulebook in that there are some things which you will not do. Therans are forever shouting and stomping their cry of *Vigilance, Valor, and Victory*." Pogo punctuated with upraised hands, mimicking the Therans Matteo had known rather accurately. "And they will do nearly anything for a win, except compromise valor and look cowardly. Since most of them want to give that a wide berth, there are places they won't go, either. They are brutal, don't get me wrong, but won't take a fight past a certain point." He took a long draw from his teacup. "But Fleet, they are the worst of the street brawlers. No holds barred, anything, sarding anything for a win. Look." He used his module to lower a screen from the ceiling and cast images from a fight to it.

"What league is that?" Matteo asked.

"Not a league. One of my old contacts leaked Records from the First Fleet recreation rooms. Watch."

Iantha gasped. "That can't be legal."

"When there are no rules, it devolves to last man standing, or sometimes last man conscious."

"But they are both bleeding!" Iantha's face lost color, and she covered her mouth.

"It gets worse, but you get the point." Pogo flipped off the screencast. "No way I'm getting in a ring with Fleet."

"That's not sport, that's war, and they can have it." Matteo pushed the notion away with an open hand.

"But isn't Fleet made up of representatives from all three homeworlds?" Iantha asked.

"Yes, but the ones who end up in Fleet ... let's put it this way, the honorable, reputable ones end up serving in their home-world forces. It's the thugs that end up in Fleet." Pogo gave Brels an odd glance.

"I don't imagine they are going to garner much favor here, no matter how much the crowds love a brutal fight." Brels passed a dish of bread slices covered in a bright green paste that smelled rich and savory with a hint of heat. "Speaking of brutal fights, you could always try hunting sollert like a native. Right, Arli? I imagine you're the only one of us here who has."

She gave the Guild Master a reproving look—a glare Matteo would never dare offer a Clan Lord in public! "Swamp natives don't need a permit. There's a solid export market for the large teeth as gems, the hides are in demand for fashion, and of course the meat. Hunger's not the only reason to hunt them."

Change the subject! "Are they difficult to hunt? We occasionally hunt game at home, but I have to imagine it's different with a creature in the water."

"Firearms are heavily regulated, so it takes some special expertise." Brels seemed to notice Matteo's perplexed expression and threw back his head to laugh. "A demonstration, yes, that sounds like a prime bit of entertainment. We have a fierce competition around here for bragging rights. Pogo, you care to demonstrate?"

Pogo urged Arli to stand with him.

"Competitive throwing is nothing like hunting, not nearly as interesting to watch." She settled back in her seat.

"What kind of hospitality is that? It's not such a big thing to throw a few knives, is it?" Pogo cocked his head, frowning.

That was uncomfortable.

Arli closed her eyes, shook her head, and joined Pogo at the far side of the room. He opened a storage bin tucked in the shadows of a rocky wall protrusion and produced a large rectangular target bearing three images. One of the sollert in question, snakelike body with a flattened snout and large protruding eyes. Beside the sollert was an unfamiliar, lizardy reptile, and a rodent that, if it had been drawn accurately, would be terrifying to come across. Knife scars punctured the images and the surface surrounding them.

So, the miners, or some subset of them, sat around the Guild Master's office, throwing knives for fun. What could possibly be notable about that?

Brels looked Matteo's way and laughed. "Yes, it is a common game for us to test our skills with one another."

One day, Matteo would learn not to show everything on his face. At least Brels didn't seem offended, even though he was pointedly ignoring Iantha's uncomfortable shiver beside Matteo.

Clearly, she hadn't been subjected to this before. What was Brels trying to accomplish?

Pogo set up the target and retrieved a carved wooden box from the desk. He walked the box to them and opened it to reveal a dozen steel throwing knives, polished to a mirror finish, showing off the blue cast of Firen steel.

"You hunt them with those?" Iantha's tone shouted, "Primitives! Uncivilized!"

Brels ignored her. "Go on, Pogo, show them how it's done."

Pogo counted back ten paces from the target.

"On a sollert, there's a few sweet spots: the eyes; where the skull meets the spine; and right behind their jaw." He removed three knives and threw one into each of the named points on the target.

"You make that look easy." Brels chuckled.

"That was easy," Arli muttered, rolling her eyes.

"You think so?" Pogo crossed his arms and glared good-naturedly. "Can you do better?"

"Sollerts don't stand still on dry land and they sure as sunrise don't hold still in the water." She selected several knives and backed off five more paces, then ten. "Where you want me to put them?"

"Next to his," Brels said.

"Clear the range." Points for safety practices. With no flash or style whatsoever, she cast three knives that landed beside Pogo's. She threw two more, each landing in the head of the smaller targets.

"The little Arli has teeth." Brels applauded.

"The little Arli doesn't like getting bitten by swamp nasties."

Brels and Pogo laughed. "You going to let that challenge stand, Pogo?"

He picked up another pair of knives and threw them, hitting the rodent, but missing the lizard.

Brels snickered.

"You give it a try." Pogo held out the remaining knives to Brels.

Brels ambled to the throwers. He took the knives and backed off two paces beyond Arli. "Right next to hers." The knives landed exactly where he said they would.

Matteo applauded softly. Could be the wrong move, but that was some cracking skill.

"Is that a common expertise on Lighten?" Iantha whispered.

Arli tensed at the judgment in Iantha's voice. "Only in what off-worlders call the 'uncivilized areas' where you need to pick off nasties like that little trask or nutrit—you'd call it a swamp rat—before they ruin your day. Or need to put food on the table." She nodded at Brels and Pogo and retrieved the knives from the target. "You can be certain every Lighten carries a knife, even the most proper-looking ones. It's smart to expect they know how to use it."

"You're all armed?" Iantha squeaked.

"Everyone here carries a similar tool that has many appropriate uses." Brels' slow, deep tone suggested caution was in order. Even Matteo could pick up on that.

"But, it is a weapon." Iantha pulled her arms close to her chest.

"A great many things can be weapons, but are not regulated. Words can be weapons, and are carried by everyone with few restrictions." Arli returned to her seat, bristling with indignation.

She had an excellent point. Matteo had been on the receiving end of that manner of weapon often enough.

"But ..." Iantha struggled to complete her thought.

"It's not like we don't have laws like the 'civilized' worlds." Pogo emphasized the word as he settled the knives back into the case.

"Perhaps we trust our people to follow them more than you do. If you look, you'll find very little violence related to our tool of choice." Brels crossed his meaty arms and met Matteo's gaze, not even bothering with Iantha. "Do you share your betrothed's perspective, Lord Heir Timnon?"

Get this right, he had to get this right. But how?

"Your hesitation suggests you agree with her, but are reluctant to disagree with me to my face."

Honesty was probably a dumb route, but... "No, Guild Master, she is not my betrothed, and she speaks her own opinions. I will speak for myself, and you will have no doubt when I have done so."

Iantha's face flushed first pink, then deep red, her mouth open to speak, but no words formed. At least Brels seemed to appreciate his response.

Arli's module tweedled an alarm. "Return flight window is open now."

Perfect sarding timing!

"Thank you for your generous reception and a memorable meal. I am afraid, though, I need to be back at Anara soon to prepare for my obligations there. Might we continue this conversation at another time?" Preferably one when Beny was around to keep him from causing a diplomatic incident.

"Of course, I would be honored." Brels dipped his head in a polite, and genuine, nod.

Matteo turned to Arli. "How soon can we head out?"

Arli glanced at Pogo, who consulted his module, then nodded.

"We can leave as soon as I get flight clearances with local control."

"Would you have room in your transport to fly me to Anara as well?" Brels asked.

Chapter 17

ARI EDGED BACK. "My hauler is hardly up to the standards of a Guild Master."

Brels snorted. "You flew Joco and Lord Heir Timnon in it. I am sure it will suffice."

How had he known about Joco? "Yes, but—"

"And my pilot approves both your ship and your skills. That is enough for me." The stern note at the end—he would brook no argument and pressing the issue further would only look like she was refusing the hospitality he needed.

She bristled. No one enjoyed being backed into a corner, not even an arli-bug. But he was a Guild Master, accustomed to getting his way. "I am honored by your faith in me, sir. When do you want to depart?" Ari laced her fingers in front of her chest and bowed her head.

Guild Master Brels turned to the Dextrines. "Is your business complete—"

"I would be honored if you would call me Matteo, sir." Dextrines so loved their titles. Matté had to realize what he was doing. He glanced at Lady Iantha. "It is."

The prim, blue-suited woman nodded, but such a strange expression. The two did not feel like they belonged together. How had they come to be betrothed when it seemed they did not even like each other? Odd.

"An hour, then?" Brels turned to Ari. "Will that be sufficient for you?"

"As you say, sir." That might give her time to adjust the passenger seating in the hauler. Not enough to make it as comfortable as even the meanest transport, but a bit more leg and shoulder room for her exceptionally tall dignitaries couldn't hurt.

"A final drink and bite, and we share our farewells." Brels refilled their cups and passed around a plate of delicate pastries topped with sugar threads and candied green mountain berries he had saved until now.

This had not been what she had expected when he offered her a meal. A seat in the miners' dining hall would have sufficed. The invitation to dine with important guests was likely intended to demonstrate how much he'd meant the things he'd said back in the hangar. At the same time, though, he'd clearly used her to nettle Lady Iantha into revealing her ugly true colors, something that, if Ari didn't miss her guess, he'd been trying to do for quite some time. Was the demonstration to confirm Brels' own suspicions, or to ensure they were clear to Matté, a High Ranking Dextrine, that Brels recognized the lady's prejudice and inflexibility? Difficult to tell.

More important, though, was being a tool for Brels' purposes a privilege or a warning that, like Joco, he was a man who would seek his own ends with little regard for those he used along the way? And what would it take to find out?

A quarter of an hour later, Pogo escorted her down the long gray and stone corridor to the hangar.

How was she to keep this journey from Joco? Somehow, he would find out she had piloted for the Firen Mines Guild Master, and Abadon's Gates would demand their toll.

"You feeling all right?" Pogo stopped and peered at her. "You've gotten a little pale since we left the office."

"So that's what that little show was all about! You miserable trask!"

"What are you talking about?" He edged back half a step, guilt in his eyes.

"All that knife throwing and bullying me into that show. You were testing me, making sure I was flight ready."

"It wasn't only that. It made some excellent entertainment for Lady Ice."

"Is that what you call her?"

"Not to her face." Pogo smirked.

"Was that necessary, though?"

"You refused to see medics. Had to be certain somehow. If you couldn't hit those easy marks, you sure as storms wouldn't be ready to fly."

"Then why'd you miss that one?"

"Never a bad thing to give your boss a chance to look good—and the Dextrines didn't know any better." He set off walking again. "Be sure you send me a contract for Brels' flight. He'll be paying you Guild Standard rates, first class, for this trip. He's not up with that rot about flying dignitaries for the value of the reference alone." Pogo unlocked the hangar door and locked it behind them.

She paused inside the hangar, near the rear stone wall, to allow her eyes to adjust to the change in light and the rest of her senses to take in the heat and the industrial smells that hung in the bustle of the immense hangar deck. "For a cargo transport on a vessel that doesn't meet any class rating? That's not right.

If the Guild finds out—" Joco was the kind to check up on the funds passing through her business accounts. Drown it all!

"First class pilot ratings, not ship. You've disclosed your ship's status in good faith. Trust me, all proper forms will be followed. The Guild will be satisfied."

But Joco would not. "I don't have First Class pilot ratings, either. It is too much."

"That you should be paid for your work? Then an additional amount will be added as a gratuity for prompt service."

She squeezed her eyes shut. "You realize it will read like there was some other sort of service rendered."

Pogo tipped his head back and rolled his eyes. "Brels wouldn't ask that of you."

"Not saying he has or he would. But I've been here more than half the day and questions may be asked about how that time was spent. And I doubt either of us is ready for a full disclosure about the party your enforcers threw for me." Hopefully, he didn't notice the involuntary twitch in her shoulders. "I'm not a member of the Comfort Guild—neither my mouth nor my attitude makes me suitable for that profession—and they are zealous in controlling their trade."

Pogo snorted into his fist. "Then send an additional contract, and I will pay you for the trip here and back to Anara, with additional hazard pay for the Raider encounter. That should satisfy anyone looking for irregularities and will make up the difference."

She sighed. "Joco won't be able to argue that."

"What does Joco have against seeing you paid? His reputation as a cheap bastard is as well-known as his standing in the ring. I'd wager your wages aren't extravagant—"

She held up an open hand. "Not your worry. Don't go there."

"Truth be told, Brels wants to hire you away from the Ship Yard." Pogo folded his arms across his chest as though inviting a challenge.

"And you're all right with that? Aren't you his pilot?" She mirrored his posture—if he was challenging, she wasn't backing down.

"Bodyguard. Flying is an extra perk for him."

"And you want to give that away?"

"I'm a better marksman than pilot."

"Sollert shit, and you know it. Might be true, but that's not the reason."

"Those teeth and claws set this little arli apart from her kind." He laughed.

Should she mention she didn't appreciate being laughed at? She shook her head and headed toward her ship.

He stopped her with a hand on her shoulder. "You're a cracking good pilot with a feather-light touch, and you've got some mad skills with your swamp-tech, making that little ship of yours do what any sane man would bet it couldn't. You'd be an asset to our team. Parking ships at the Yard seems a waste of your skills."

"I don't know—"

He stepped very close and pressed his finger to her lips. "None of that. Not now. Think about it. Really think about it." He stepped even nearer. "And take this as it's meant. I sure wouldn't mind the chance to spend some time getting better acquainted."

She gaped, frozen by the heat in his gaze.

He studied her, forehead furrowed, then his brows rose. "Is this fresh territory for you?"

Oh, yes, that was exactly what she was going to admit to him.

He grinned and shook his head. "Should have guessed. Consider it, though. Always the right thing to make a few memories, no?"

A flight deck was her natural environment, where she knew what to expect. Where all the hazards were, and how to avoid them. Except for this one.

"No answers now. Come on." He continued toward her hauler, calm and unhurried, as though conversations like this one were part and parcel of normal life. As if he intended for her to consider his ideas. Both of them.

How did one respond? How did she feel about either suggestion? She would need to come back to that later. Now it was time to fly.

She opened the hatch and settled into her seat. Pogo took the one next to her. "You mind? Figure Brels and Matté will have some kind of business to talk through."

"You going to be all right sitting so close to the control panels? Or planning to wrestle me for the stick along the way?"

His jaw dropped, and he stared at her. "Really?"

"What? Can you handle not flying this one while sitting so close to the pilot's seat?"

"Abadon's Gates! You meant that seriously, did you?" He looked so astonished.

"Of course, I did. What else ..." ... *wrestle the stick* ... storms and squalls! Her cheeks burned, and she looked away.

"I could tell you were ... sweet ... but I didn't realize... Joco doesn't let you out much, does he?"

"He wanted me to stay in the hauler, not the pilots' lounge, while I was in Anara."

"And I suppose he didn't want you talking to anyone, much less taking side jobs, yeah?" He stared at her until she nodded. "Sandstorms, those are some balls he's got. No wonder you've ignored every subtle hint I've dropped."

She squeezed her eyes shut and dropped her chin to her chest.

"I heard he was paranoid about his connections, but I hadn't realized how much." Pogo leaned his head back and sighed.

She began her preflights, keeping her eyes fixed on her controls.

"That's about him and not you, right?"

No, she would not open up that conversation. Especially when she had to focus on flying.

"Hey," he touched her hand enough to prompt her to look at him. "I'm sorry to step on an open sore like that. I've never much liked him when trying to get my flight credentials. And now that I see I've been right about him, I like him even less. But I swear, no one will dress you with those same feathers."

"I'd just as soon no one connect me to him. Without that, there's still going to be enough trouble coming out of what's happened today." She swallowed hard.

"Maybe so, but I still meant what I said. I'd like to see more of you."

She turned a raised eyebrow on him.

"Now you're listening. Finally. It wasn't exactly what I meant right then, but if it goes there, I wouldn't complain." He winked, a touch of mischief in his grin.

Yes, he would. She looked away again. No man like him would have much patience for a naïve, inexperienced, more-girl-than-woman like her. But it was nice that he asked.

"Permission to come aboard," Brels called from outside the open hatch.

"Granted."

He and Matté entered and took their seats.

She wrenched around in her seat to face them. Brels was already struggling to find a place for his bag that didn't interfere with his knees or shoulders. She slipped out of her seat and took the bag from him. "Are you certain you will be comfortable? There is time for you to make other arrangements."

Brels reached for his safety straps. "It was sufficient for Joco, no?"

She slipped behind him and dropped his bag into an empty wall bin behind his seat, securing it as she turned back to her place. "Comfort is not his first priority."

"Nor is it mine. This will suffice."

"That's not what you told me the last time we hit a patch of bumpy air," Pogo muttered under his breath.

"Says the man who flew the worst patch of weather he could find to make a statement. The fact you still had a job after that proves my point. Comfort is not my priority."

"Strap in and get comfortable, then." She settled her safety straps into place. "Obtaining final clearances now. The escort's about to launch. We'll be right behind them. Ready for takeoff? Should be an easy ride, gentlemen."

"After the one we came in on, I should hope so." Matté sounded like he was trying to make a joke, but it wasn't his strong suit. Best ignore it, though.

A moment later, they vaulted from the hangar with hardly a shudder, and that only because of a sneaky updraft from the mountain. Taking off while already up so high was different than from the ground.

"I told you she was good." Pogo looked over his shoulder.

"Why can't you do that?" Brels slapped Pogo's shoulder.

"You hired me to fly like the Arch Soul Catcher out of Abadon, and that's what you got. If you want a dainty little firefly, you should hire yourself one."

"Well, I just may do that." Brels sounded like he'd already made up his mind. "Now, Arli, when we get there, don't bother with any of the main entrances. Straight to the debark field—I prefer to go in the fighter's entrance. Less fuss through there. You all right with that, Matteo?"

"Definitely."

"As you wish, Guild Master. I'll adjust the flight plans and arrange the clearances for that now." Would have been nice to know ahead of time, but no point making an issue of it. Especially when he would pay her for the service.

"So, Matteo, is your schedule full of diplomatic dance partners over the next few days?" Brels said.

"I can always accommodate room for an esteemed connection."

The escort left them as they entered Anara's official airspace. Coming in with an entourage would attract the kind of attention the Guild Master eschewed, and Pogo's people seemed satisfied with Anara's control of its own territory. The extra security over her shoulder had been nice, but there was an itchy-twitchy aspect to having someone watching her every move that she was happy to shed, the way summer beetles were happy to lose their old shell when they molted.

She touched down in the landing field nearest the sporting entrance, so gently it took the jolts and jars of the tires on the uneven pavement to convince them they were out of the air. A few minutes later, she brought the hauler to rest on the debark field. "If you will give me a couple of moments to please the Record Keepers, I'll have you on your way."

"Despite your protests about the insufficiency of your ship, I haven't enjoyed a flight as much in a long time." Brels unfastened his straps and stretched his arms out to touch both sides of the cabin at once.

"I may take that personally." Pogo stood and shook out the knots in his limbs.

"Wasn't it you who suggested soul catchers and arli weren't interchangeable?" Brels fumbled with the catch on the cargo bin behind his seat.

"Oh, drown it all. 'Fraid I need you to be patient a mite longer. There's a bit of a hiccup in your clearances, Guild Master. Someone doesn't like that you're coming in unannounced on a ship out of Paxton Yard."

"Sarding sandstorms. Give me a minute with them." Pogo shouldered her aside from the controls.

"I could switch the controls to you. All you had to do was ask," she muttered.

A shadow appeared on the external visual screen beside her hand and someone banged on the hull.

Stormfall!

"Gotta deal with this." She smashed the hatch control with one hand and snatched Joco's bag from under her seat as she ran for the opening hatch. She stumbled over the threshold into the dangerous, shimmering heat.

Joco's fist pounded the hull near her shoulder. "Where in Laythe's Woods have you been? I told you—"

"Paying my bills. Here, take this and get back to your meetings." She barely caught her footing and shoved his bag at him.

He slung his bag over his shoulder and leaned into her face. "I told you to stay—"

"I can't cover this month's bills, not with Mama's memorial added in. You were the one who refused to contribute—"

"Don't get your mouth going, girl, I ain't gonna have it." He shook his finger in her face. Never a positive sign.

"You've got your bag now. I imagine that's what this storm is all about. Get back to what you were doing, and don't waste time on me." She pushed his shoulder toward the Anara complex.

"I'm not done. When I get you back to the Yard, you're going to settle with Palmer, and we'll be done with the nonsense. He's willing to have a second—"

She jumped back on the ship's threshold, to add a few centimeters to her height. "He doesn't have a first woman, and you expect me to take a place as second?"

"You'll do as I say."

"No."

"What did you say to me?"

"No. I will not be settled for by anyone, much less that drunken excuse for a Yard Master."

"That's the best offer you're ever going to get, and you know it."

"He's a miserable, mean drunk. I'm not going to—"

"You'll do as you're told."

"No."

"I swear, girl, I've had enough out of you. Give me just one reason why I shouldn't take my leather to your back here and now." He tossed his bag to the ground and reached for his belt.

Her heart roared in her ears, a sure sign that she was going to say something she'd regret. "How about three? The last time you did that the medic warned you'd face an assault charge if you did that again since you claimed no connection to me. The enforcer in my hauler isn't the type to sit by and listen to an assault taking place. Second, the Dextrine Rank in there with him might reconsider doing business with a man who commits assault right in front of him. And three, if you do it, Guild Master Brels will jump on the chance to see you disqualified for being out of control."

"Don't you threaten me!" Joco's hand flew.

She hit the ground as she heard the smack of flesh on flesh, and for a moment disconnected from the world around her. Pain exploded across her cheek, her face, her skull, radiating out, burning, blinding. Her heavy flight jacket was wrenched from her shoulders. An iron grip on her wrist yanked her to her feet and slammed her against the hot metal hull. Nausea forced bile into her throat as the desert spun around her.

He was going to take her apart with that drowned belt of his, and there was no way to escape it.

"She's right, you know." Brels' calm, firm voice sounded from somewhere behind her. "Consider your next move carefully."

Joco released her and jumped back. "What sort of Hell Cat's game are you playing? What are you doing with him?"

"Paying my damn bills." She braced against the hull, rolling her shoulders against it to face him. She rubbed away the blurriness in her eyes and wiped her running nose with her sleeve.

Brels stood very close to Joco, Pogo on his other side. "The pilot's done nothing to you. Leave her and get back to your business. If you don't want to concede to me."

"You are going to regret this." Joco shook his fist at her.

"Come along, Guild Master, it will make for good Media Records for us to be seen entering the Stadium complex together." With a hand to Joco's elbow, Brels guided him toward the sporting entrance, Pogo close on the other side.

Her knees gave way, and she sank to the ground, shaking. She'd evaded the storm this time, but she'd pay for it with double measures later, when there was no one around to take her side.

Matté knelt beside her. "Are you all right?"

"Not what I was prepared for. But I knew he'd find out one way or another, so not entirely surprised." She wiped her mouth on her white knit sleeve, leaving a bloody smear.

Where was her flight jacket?

Matté plucked it from the ground and handed it to her. "I don't mean to intrude. But it didn't look like he was holding back when he hit you."

She swallowed hard and shook her head. "Never has." And he wouldn't when they got back to Paxton.

"Would you mind letting my ... my trainer ... have a look at it, make sure there's nothing serious going on. You might have hit your head."

"No, no need. I'm fine." She shrugged on her jacket, falling back against the hull as she struggled to push to her feet. "Just a little dizzy."

"My guy's got a great tonic for bruises, too. Someone's going to notice if you're marked up and might question your flight clearances ..."

"Sollert shit, you're right. I don't need my clearances compromised." Not any more than they had already been today. She shoved the heels of her hands against her temples, but it didn't stop the throbbing. "I'd appreciate the help."

Chapter 18

WHAT DID ONE SAY in such a situation? It wasn't something that any protocol training had covered. He offered his hand and helped her stand. She braced against the hauler for several long breaths, pulling herself together in the blistering desert heat. "Give me a minute to get it all buttoned up." She fumbled for her module, taking far too long at the controls.

Good thing she'd agreed to Beny's help. She needed it more than she was willing to admit. "You all right with taking the service ways in?"

"The fewer people we see, the better. Don't need this getting more notice than can be helped. Bad enough there's Records of all the fields here." She gestured toward the security equipment on the tall poles that dotted this and every field around the Anara complex.

"So, you're not wanting—"

"—any attention paid to this at all. Nothing positive to be had from it. Hopefully Brels and Joco entering together will capture all the notice and this can disappear." She wiped her face on her sleeve and started for the complex, her steps less sure than they had been when they left Anara at first light this morning.

It was hard to argue with her. Grandfather wasn't much different from Joco. How was it that so few were willing to enforce consequences against men like them?

The sun hung midway between its zenith and the horizon, pouring heat into the shimmering air. Heat would always have a smell to him now, pavement, fuel residue, with a touch of sweat and a little blood. And stillness. Heat was still and quiet, like a snake lying in wait for prey. By the time they reached the service doors of Anara, he was ready for climate control.

"Been with your trainer long?" Nice of her to break the awkward silence as he opened the door with a palm print.

"Since I started fighting. He's kin, but the kind you want to have." Oh, that said far more than he intended. Maybe the cool air inside, smelling like all recycled air did, stale and chemically filtered, would clear his mind and help him be more cautious.

She paused, blinking as their eyes adjusted to the softer artificial lights inside the gray-tiled corridor. "Ain't enough of those to go 'round, are there?"

"Not so much." He checked his module to confirm his mental map and gestured for them to follow the first right-hand turn. "You were right to warn him as you did. I don't relish doing business with a man like that."

"Don't be hasty. It's hard to avoid dealing with the Transport Guild here. You can hardly do anything without them. I was hoping to distract him." She turned her face aside, as though trying to keep her bruises hidden.

"Still, I appreciate getting a glimpse at the sort of man he is. Even if he can't be avoided, it does inform other decisions."

"He has positive qualities."

"They all do." That didn't make it any easier to listen to her defend him, even if he'd said the same sorts of things about Lord Timnon years ago. It had taken a long time to stop making excuses for him.

They turned again, this time into a corridor with a green stripe, marking the Lodgings Wing. "Mostly downhill for a while now, but not too far off. Need a pause?"

"Yeah, not long, just need to get my feet under me again." She braced against the wall, breathing harder than she should have been. She wiped her face with her sleeve—sweat, blood, tears, and snot mingling into a smear on the drab flight jacket, from her elbow to her wrist, then shoved herself up straight. "I'm ready."

He continued down the sloping corridor until it ran level again and turned right. "Over here—" He pointed at a gray door that blended into the gray walls, marked only with a small number engraved in the door frame. "Give me a second. Need to give him a heads-up that I'm bringing company." He opened the door and stepped halfway into the expansive, plush, white living area. There was a solid chance she would disappear if he turned his back on her. It's what he would have done. "Beny?"

"In the flesh." Beny called from somewhere deep in the suite.

"Anyone else about? I need you to check out a friend."

Beny peeked out from his room and sauntered toward him, a damp towel over his shoulders, dark hair plastered to the sides of his head. Luckily, he was fully dressed, in a lightweight, light-colored casual shirt and slacks. "Bring him in. What happened? Drunken brawl?"

"Nothing so easy." He ushered Arli inside.

Beny, the unflappable medic, did a double take, which, under other circumstances, Matteo would have enjoyed. "Who is that?"

"Beny, Pilot Lysand, Arli. Arli, this is Beny—my trainer."

Beny's eyebrows rose, and he turned his "I'll bet there's quite a story you're going to tell me later" look on Matteo. There would be no way around a full accounting for bringing a strange woman, not of their circle, into their suite.

She dropped her gaze and edged back toward the service door, as though she could feel Beny's eyes on her. "Maybe this isn't a good idea, I shouldn't bother you. I'm sure you have better things to do." Her protest would have been more believable if she wasn't swaying ever so slightly as she stood.

"Not at all." Beny-the-healer kicked into gear. He grabbed her by the elbow and steered her to the nearest white upholstered chair. "I'm forever patching up some hapless ... fighter pal of his. Give me a moment to retrieve my kit?" He beckoned Matteo to follow him into his bedroom.

"Are you trying to wake the ancestors into knocking some sense into you? What are you doing with her, here?" Beny whispered so softly, Matteo wasn't sure he'd heard it.

"She can't go to the medical wing. There's reasons, ones you'd understand—"

"You didn't—"

"Not remotely. I'll explain everything, and you'll agree. I promise. Just do it." Matteo glanced through the doorway. Arli was eyeing the service door. "She's going to bolt in a minute, and she needs help."

"You owe me for this and you better have a cracking explanation for the risk we're taking having her in here."

"I do."

It was hard to tell whether that made Beny feel better or worse, but he grabbed his kit from a drawer and ambled out, persona shifting from handler back to healer. "Got it. Let's take a peek at what you've got going on. Mind if I set a sensor patch on you?" He pulled a packet from his trusty brown canvas bag and held it up.

"That's not standard trainer's gear." Her swollen eyes narrowed, wary. Her cheek was turning from red to purple. At least one of her eyes was going to be blackened soon.

"I'm wildly overqualified for the job." He shrugged and waved the white packet. "Yes?"

She sighed and closed her eyes. "All right."

Beny knelt before her, wiped the pulse point on her neck with a cleaning swab, and pressed the three-finger-wide white patch onto her pulse point. With two fingers, he turned her chin left and then right. "Doesn't the women's division use gloves?"

She jumped up and away. "Never mind. I'm fine. I'll go. Thank you for the—"

Beny caught her elbow and pulled her back to the chair. "No, no, I shouldn't have pried. No more irrelevant questions." With one hand, he pulled out his module, while the other remained firmly on her elbow. "Fell and hit your head, too?"

"Not positive, but it seems right." She closed her eyes and swallowed hard.

Beny tsk-tsked under his breath. "On the plus side, you're barely on the right side of a concussion. Going to have a killer headache out of this, but not too much worse for the wear."

She opened her eyes and flashed Matteo an "I told you so" look.

"Just guessing by the flight suit, so ignore me if you're not concerned about this, but you're on the edge of losing flight clearances. Anyone looking at you would deny you based on those bruises alone. So he was right to make sure you got checked out."

She sighed and hung her head. "Thanks."

"I'd rather not add anything to Records about this, that's likely to open more questions than you want. But if someone denies you, he can reach out to me, and I'll see what I can do."

"Understood." She pretended not to react, but Matteo felt the sting of Beny's response, too. Not wanting to get too involved, but still trying to come across as a decent person. It was a miserable situation; hard to blame Beny for being cautious. Even so, having been in her place more than once, it was hard to accept. Beny was better than that.

Beny softened. "I can give you a poultice for the swelling, though. And I've got something to help with the bruising, too. That might make for fewer questions. And some tabs for the headache that won't affect your flight status."

She sighed and shook her head, pushing off the chair arms to stand. "No need. I've been enough trouble."

Matteo caught her elbow and her gaze. "Don't. I get it." He glared a little toward Beny. "It's complicated all around, but that doesn't mean you should make it worse on yourself. You took a job for me, and I appreciate that. But things went a little sideways. Let me—let him—do something to make it less awful. I don't want you to lose out because of this. Please."

She frowned. "All right."

To his credit, Beny had the poultice ready and fixed it to her cheek like a bandage, then handed her the pain tabs and waited for her to swallow them. "Life will be easier if folks don't have so many bruises to ask about. If you can find somewhere to keep still for a few hours and let the poultice work, that would be best. It'll evaporate by then and you can take the dressing off and be done with it."

"Understood. Thank you for your hospitality." She slipped away so quickly Matteo couldn't have stopped her if he'd wanted to.

He sank into the chair she had left, raking his hands through his hair. It was almost worse watching this play out from the other side than to have been the one in the chair, desperately wanting to be seen and not seen at the same time.

Beny dropped cross-legged onto the plush white carpet. "I want the story now, not the cleaned-up-for-media version, but the whole, every-minute-detail version, starting with who is she really?"

"She's the pilot I hired to get me to Firen HQ, the one with connections to the Guild Master."

"Okay, I'll circle back to Firen in a moment." Beny balanced his elbows on his knees and laced his hands. Clearly, Matteo would not be allowed to move from this spot until Beny was appeased. "How did she end up like that? Looks like injuries I used to address in the emergency hospital."

"Pretty much that. The details are complicated, but one of her connections met us after we landed, got sideways with her, and backhanded her."

"Kayavan's breath and bones, I hate those cases. But with witnesses?"

"He didn't realize we were inside the ship."

"But he knows you saw?"

Matteo nodded.

"That's not good for any of you. But especially for her. It's a blow to any man to be caught in the act, doubly so when he's a fighter, which I'm assuming is the case. She a bond mate or contracted to him somehow?"

"Definitely not."

"That's positive." Beny leaned a little closer. "How mixed up with her are you?"

"Mixed up? Is that what you think I've been about?" Matteo slapped the armrests. Better than slapping Beny.

"You said you'd accomplished 'your mission,' so someone is going to be asking. Was she the reason for you breaking things off? Did you console yourself with her afterwards? Was she sent to tempt you away from Iantha—the mind boggles with the questions that could come up here. You have no doubt what the Media can be like."

"Yes, I do. But from you? Really?"

"I'm sorry, not trying to be a soul catcher here, just worried about you. How are you doing? Was this a sign of how it all went?"

"It was crazy, Beny. You should have seen the difference in Iantha when she wasn't tied to me anymore. Like the gloves came off, and I saw a different side of her. At best she considers me an idiot, more likely, actively dislikes me. I don't get how the matchmakers put us together, but I'm pretty sure we're as much alike as Lighten and Thera."

"That seriously sucks." Beny stood long enough to pull another plush white chair over and drop into it.

"Yes, it does, but there's no doubt it was for the best. Shackled into a business arrangement is not how I want to find a bond mate. It's the way Ranks have always done it, but no thanks. My wife is going to be the one choice I make for myself."

"No argument from me. I've got my doubts about Mari, these days, but that's for later. If you're not mixed up with that girl, then why bring her here? There's plenty of aid resources in Anara."

"It's complicated."

"I've been making a living tending to complicated, remember? Patching up Ranks who don't want their personal business made public. And let me tell you, most of that 'complicated' makes the Media feed dramas look boring."

Matteo raked his hair back again. "The guy who did it is a popular fighter who stands to lose a lot if this gets out."

"As I understand, they're pretty strict about codes of conduct outside the ring for their fighters. I imagine she'll be blamed if he gets censured?"

"That's what she believes, and I have no reason to doubt it."

"Cracking, splinter shards."

"Call me soft, but—"

"No, I get it. Too close to home." Beny flexed his hands, as if trying to let go of the sense of injustice. "You've got to be careful about picking up strays. Even if you understand where they're coming from."

"She's not a stray, and she's not looking for anything."

"I suppose you'd be able to spot the type, right? You are such an astute judge of character—"

"Not the time for that. She's not looking for anything from me."

"We can come back to that, too." Beny huffed and pulled out his module, cueing up his next points of conversation, no doubt.

"Give me a minute, I need some tea." And he needed not to be backed into the corner. He strode past Beny to the kitchen wall. "You want some?"

"Yeah, that strong black stuff they claim is Dextrine but is definitely homegrown here. Packs a punch. You're going to need it." Beny followed him to the kitchen.

"Great. Hold off until I get my tea."

Beny bit back the frustration that visibly rippled through his body and sprawled on the nearest couch.

At least the kitchen was stocked with decent-sized mugs. Matteo picked the two largest and filled them. Time to face round two. He shoved a second couch closer to Beny's and handed over the tea.

Beny drank several deep swallows. "Hot and bitter. That fits. So, in other news, Grandfather is livid you've missed several of the oh-so-important meetings he scheduled. I am not a suffi-cient stand-in, make no mistake. As I am a mere Family heir, you outrank—"

"Don't go there." Matteo silenced him with an open hand. "That's never been my opinion. You've always been far better suited to that sort of diplomacy."

"You can still rescue yourself by showing up to the dinner meeting tonight and rubbing shoulders with Trade Minister Ducan. If you don't dither about, you've got time to get yourself cleaned up and to that dinner. That way I won't have to spend another meeting explaining why your stomach is so fragile."

"Way to hit me where I live. I'll go. But give me this much credit, I spent a large part of the day with Guild Master Brels himself."

Beny straightened up so fast he nearly spilled his tea. "Seri-ously, the one who has refused to talk to anyone except Evering Industries? Did Iantha arrange that?"

"Yes, as a consolation prize, to offer value to our Clan after I broke things off with her."

"Seems decent of her."

"It was. I wish you'd been there, though. You read these things better than I do. She was on the border of livid by the time all was said and done."

"Tell me about it. I'll want to study your Records of it, but for now, I want the highlights." Beny set his mug on the nearest table and balanced his elbows on his knees.

"It was as informal a meal as you can imagine, on couches, platters on the table, eating with our hands. And the chief entertainment was a display of local knife throwing that was pretty impressive. Apparently, everyone around here carries a blade of some sort. Grandfather would have fallen apart with the offense of it all. Iantha nearly did."

Beny swallowed back something between a laugh and a gasp. "The mind boggles."

"Seemed like a deliberate test. One Iantha may have failed. He showed off local delicacies—not sollert, believe it or not. He seemed to be inviting a reaction from us, and I'm thinking he liked mine. If nothing else, he was chatty on the flight back. Even asked to set up a meeting with me while we're here, and invited me to meet with other mining reps, too."

"Our little boy has finally grown into a diplomat." Beny dabbed at his eyes with the back of his hand.

"Don't push it, buddy. Weird thing, though; Pogo, my fight partner, and Arli were there, not a clue why."

"Pogo? You mean Piers Phalen, the fighter, right? Pogo, as in the Arch Soul Catcher after Kayavan's soul?"

"I know it feels strange. But the nicknames used around here are a lot more important than we realized." He called up a record on his module and sent the link to Beny. "I can't believe I'm saying this to you of all people, but study it. It's a big deal."

Slack-jawed, Beny stared at his pinging module. His turn to rake his now-dried, unruly hair back from his face.

"Anyway, Pogo is Brels' pilot and bodyguard, as well as the guy I'm set to do the exhibition match with tomorrow."

"You do realize how convoluted this is getting. We're heading into media drama territory fast. Is Arli mixed up with Brels, then? Why else would she have been there?"

"No. I don't think Brels leans that direction. He might have been trying to hire her away from her current ... employer."

"Let me guess, the complicated fighter guy?" Beny tapped steepled fingers together.

"That one. She's a cracking good pilot."

"You never say that about anyone."

"I'd be looking to hire her if—"

"Grandfather wouldn't run amok with insinuations and accusations? Speaking of him, how are you going to handle his reactions about Iantha and the connection with Clan Corbel that isn't going to happen?"

"I'll tell him about Brels ... and probably the meeting with Ducan, who you are going to help me impress. Let me get a shower, and you can brief me on what I need to know."

Chapter 19

BETWEEN THE HEADACHE TABS and the poultice, Matté's trainer proved himself overqualified for the title. Definitely more than a trainer, or even a junior medic of some sort. A highly trained nurse, maybe even a physician. Had he come only in capacity as a trainer?

There was a genuine rapport between them. Maybe Beny was there to support Matté. It would be nice if he had that. Poor man was a fish out of water here, though he seemed to try harder to bridge that gap than most Dextrines she'd met. That felt more likely. And it was nice to believe the best of someone today.

She headed through the service corridors for the pilots' lounge. Easy enough to find without resorting to her module's map, up to surface level and follow the green-tiled stripe to the end of Lodgings Wing. Proof that Beny's meds hadn't muddled her sense of direction. That was encouraging. Still, it was for the best she didn't have any flights coming up soon.

She slipped into the pilots' lounge, her entrance un-remarked by the other pilots relaxing there. They played games, watched sports or media feeds, chatted with one another, as though she had not walked in. Perfect.

What was that lingering in the air? Fresh, hot food. They had just begun serving. Something not sollert, thus edible. Her stomach rumbled. Dinner, needed dinner. She retrieved a tray from the mess counter and found a small table in the far corner, near the windows, and away from the media screens, where most congregated.

Though the food might not be the fancy, elegant dishes fed to the guests, the pilots' meals were fresh, homey, welcoming fare that would make Anara a favorite pilots' destination. A business model of hospitality and paying it forward that would serve Anara well in the future.

Her mouth watered as she cut a piece of herbed roast hen. Oh, that roast hen was amazing! Seasoned with familiar savory herbs and local wine, warm, hearty, and soothing. The starchy red tubers mashed, then fried, sated some of the emptiness within. And the unfamiliar, brightly-colored vegetables, so worth risking. Flavor as bright as the color, without the bitterness vegetables often had, they were exact-ly what she needed. Not that the meal with Brels hadn't been memorable, but it hadn't been peaceful. Here, at her favorite spot near the windows, there was peace to savor before the next storm blew in. And she needed that.

The last vestiges of sunset faded into the horizon in bands of rapidly cooling vermillion blending into plum. No one else in the room seemed to notice. Every pilot would have been periph-erally aware of the atmospheric conditions, but they all seemed to be too engrossed in the novelty of other pilots' company to appreciate the spectacle. Piloting could be a lonely business, and where else could one spend time with so many others who understood the wonders and the trials of the enterprise?

The simulation game stations drew many pilots, eager to try their skills in cooperation, or competition, with those who shared their fascination with flight. Then again, nearly every section of the room welcomed those hungry to connect to their own kind, like arlis driven out by the storm fronts to shine and mate before retreating to their isolated existences in the wake of the storms.

Maybe storm-bringer wasn't the only reason Arli was her honest name.

If Joco hadn't come after her this afternoon, she might have had the wherewithal to put herself out and join the conversation. But even if her soul hadn't been too raw and vulnerable, it wouldn't be fair to risk tempting Joco's disfavor on an unexpecting pilot.

She slathered butter and marsh fruit jam on a still-warm fresh roll. She must be hungrier than she realized for that to taste as mouthwateringly good. Almost made eating alone a pleasure. Funny how even a day in the society of those not associated with the Paxton Ship Yard made her hungry for more such company.

And maybe that would happen. Brels might follow through on his hints at hiring her. And if he didn't, he'd given her the confidence to believe someone else might. That alone could make the whole adventure worthwhile. It would give her an interesting memory to look back on.

Staring down at her now-empty tray, weariness descended fast and hard, a burden so heavy on her shoulders, she could hardly stand. If she didn't move now, she might fall asleep sitting here. Not that she would be the first that happened to—it was a common occurrence in the lounge—she'd rather stretch out in a proper sleep pod. But first a shower.

Must be between busy hours—only one shower stall, the one in the far corner, was in use, so she thumbprinted into the one farthest away and slid the door shut behind her.

Alone, she was completely alone—storms and squalls. That felt amazing!

Granted, the shower stall was tight quarters, but a sliding panel on the left hid a small garment recycler that would print garments in a drawer beneath it. Above the printer were access doors for a bin to hold her boots and anything else that might need to keep dry. A ceiling-mounted shower spray allowed for the maximum headroom and shoulder space in the tight compartment. While she had sufficient space to move comfortably, anyone much taller or broader would have to take care with elbows, shoulders, and knees.

She skimmed off her clothes and the bandage that had held the now-evaporated poultice, and dropped them straight into the recycler. Clean, reprinted versions of her garments should be ready by the time she was done. The shower control pad was next to the dry bin. The longest, hottest shower the facility would allow sounded about right.

A quick, just-warm-enough flow doused her from above. Oh, that already felt amazing. She lifted her arms and shut her eyes as a blast of tingly cleansers sprayed from hidden wall jets on all sides. Barely fragranced, the fresh, slippery bubbles sluiced off the sweat and grunge that always came with flying.

The hot water from above and all sides scoured away the itchy-prickly remnants the suppression stunner had left on every handspan of her skin. Being cleared to fly did not mean she felt normal—not being able to avoid Joco's backhand proved that. But between the pain tabs, the poultice, and a solid meal, she almost, almost felt herself.

As the skin-crawl faded, dread and heaviness crept in to replace it. When she returned to Paxton with Joco, nothing would be the same again. Worse, it would be much worse. She may have dodged Joco's leather this time, but he wouldn't forget. And he'd ensure she didn't either.

And once that storm passed, he meant to settle her with Palmer in an unequal partnership like her mother had with

Joco. With the lovely added benefit that Palmer was an ugly, mean drunk who would expect the woman he settled with to do his job along with her own and to be grateful for the opportunity.

No, that was not going to happen. Nothing was worth an unequal partnership. She was better off on her own.

The recycler pinged and her ration of hot water ran out, so she hit the drying jets, twice, to revel in the restorative blast of hot air. Ever the odd one, the heat made her happy, not cross. There was something luxurious about skimming into clothes still warm from recycling right after a hot-water shower. A memory worth savoring.

Dressing sapped her little remaining strength. Probably should have expected that. She needed sleep.

The same inconvenient top-corner sleep pod she had used the night before was still open. So, she tossed her boots into the locker with her rucksack, scaled the wall's handholds and slid into the private cocoon. With the world safely shut out outside, she slept.

Hours later, her module pinged a soft message chime. Drown it all! Who and what now?

Her hands trembled as she checked the message queue. Not from Joco, not from the Ship Yard. So not the worst news. That was positive. Now breathe. Not from anyone connected to the trip to Firen. Disappointing, but not the worst possibility. Another deep breath. She blinked several times until it felt safe to look at the screen again.

She forced her eyes down. Someone wanted to meet with her in the meeting room off the lounge. Not about a side job—just as well; considering how the last one went, another adventure didn't sound promising. It was a meeting request. No ID, no details. Not to communication standards. The sort of invitation that all good judgment required she avoid.

But so far, all her efforts at good judgment had landed her in suppression and at the receiving end of Joco's temper. Her better sense told her to sit tight. Instinct said she should go.

A smart pilot always trusted her instincts. She thumbed "accept" on her module and climbed down from the sleep pod.

Only a few exhausted or drunk—even if Anara wouldn't serve them intoxicants, there was always a way to get them—pilots sprawled on the furniture near the service door, not paying attention to her trek past them. She slipped through the door into the gray-tiled corridor and allowed her eyes to adjust to the harsh, blue-tinged light.

Meeting Room 2. That's where she was supposed to go. Second room on the left. Do it. Any more hesitation and she would give it all up and go back to bed, where she would much rather be. She pressed her thumb to the pad, and it slid open.

Smaller than the room she had met Matté in, it had the same bright white wall tile, white resin table and chairs. The wall display screen took up most of the short side wall on the left. Just enough room for the furnishings, but not enough for that herbal-musky cologne ...

Or the man who wore it.

"Paxton 23?" The familiar, resonant voice left the hair on the back of her neck standing.

"Sander?" Shit-storm in a sollert skin! It was him!

Every bit the man she remembered. He stood behind the table. Not as tall as Joco—few men were—he still took up more space than his mere size would have accounted for. Sander entered a room and commanded it. From the air around him, to the furniture that would support him, to the people who would answer to him, he took charge of it all.

On the one hand, he had hardly changed. He still wore the same style of unmarked flight suit, gray and utilitarian. His dark hair, still in a Theran-style crop with a short queue at the back, once streaked with blond, now had white around the temples. The weather-worn lines on his pale, sand-colored face and brow were deeper, sterner than they had been. His eyes, a peculiar clear golden brown, like a gemstone in a necklace her mother once owned, had become harder than she had ever known before.

She edged back half a step.

"Years past majority and you're still a little bit of a thing, Arli, like your mother was." He studied her up and down, judgmental and cold.

"I thought I saw you, there on the shore, at her last honors."

"Good eyes, girl. I'm impressed. All that hunting must have taught you something."

"Did you know she was happy to be going off with you? Those were some of her last words, wanting me to be sure I told you that." Her throat pinched around the words, as if revealing them would somehow rob her of her mother's memory. "Were you finally going to make a home with her? Was that what she was so looking forward to?"

"She knew and that's all that matters." He walked a circle around her. "Damm, but you look like her. Not a trace of the one who seeded ya."

"Not that there's anyone who admits to that." She pulled her shoulders very straight and sidestepped to stop his circling. "She missed you. It was a bad storm when you up and disappeared."

He stopped midstep. "Some things are for the best. She understood."

"Didn't stop her from crying for you in the middle of the night when she thought I couldn't hear." Mama didn't realize Ari knew about those long, lonely nights.

"Don't judge what you don't understand. Just because Haven didn't like it, didn't mean that she didn't agree with all the reasons." He refused to meet her gaze.

Not what she expected from him. Not that she'd ever expected to meet with him again.

"Why did you call for a meeting with me? Last time I saw you ..." She touched the scar behind her left ear. The sight of him left it burning all over again. "You made it clear you wanted nothing to do with me."

He grabbed her chin and turned her head to examine the scar, his calloused fingers as hard and unforgiving as she remembered them. "And Joco did nothing to lay claim to you, either, I see."

"He's made that very clear." She locked her knees. He would not see her give way to him.

"He made that apparent today, didn't he? Why'd you let him lay you out like that. Not favorable in the Records, you know."

"You're blaming me for that? Why would you even care?"

"You don't need to be connected to him." His jaw tightened and the creases in his face deepened, an expression she had hoped to never see again.

"Why? Why is it so drowning important to you I remain a nameless, unconnected swamp rat?"

"You're too much like your mother."

"Poor and worthless, barely able to scrape by? Without hope of making an equal partnership?" She spat the words in his face. Was that courage or the lingering effects of the suppression stun? Either way, he'd probably make her regret it.

The side of his mouth lifted in an incredulous sneer. "Yet you've been keeping company with three of the most powerful men in Anara right now. I can't understand it. What have you been about?"

"I'm a pilot. My job. What do you think?"

"Your mother had a way of attaching herself to powerful men."

"You?" She fought the urge to jump out of arm's reach.

He raised an eyebrow. The look of a predator—not just a predator, but an apex predator—in his eyes.

"Who—what are you?"

"Someone you do not need to know. Arinel—Haven—should have told you this, but she clearly didn't, and now she can't." He set his jaw, as though chewing on a long-held offense. "Whatever ambitions you have with any of these connections, forget them. Give them up and get away from them as fast as you can. They are not friends to you. Neither am I. You are the only one you can trust to protect your own interest. The more powerful the connection you find, the less you matter. Reaching beyond herself landed your mother in that mudbound shipyard, with few options."

Reaching beyond herself? No one had ever described Mama that way.

"Don't take any favors from any of them. Make your own way. But do it fast. There's a storm gathering, and you don't want to be the arli bringing in this storm."

No point in asking what or why. He wasn't going to answer such a question. "Why bother telling me this?"

"Your mother extracted a promise out of me. I don't want that hanging over my head."

Why would he bother to keep such a promise, though? Had he actually cared for Mama? "You expect me to thank you for this, I suppose?"

"I wouldn't. Either way the storm's coming, and the dead-fall's going to be blown away. You don't want to be part of that, so get out while you can." He shrugged and sidestepped to stand between her and the door. "That's all I've got for you. But for your mother's sake, do as you're told this time, Arli-bug. Stay away from things bigger than you, and away from the Raiders. This ain't the time to be stubborn and ask questions. Take cover and find shelter, and let it blow over you." He marched out, shutting the door behind him.

How had Laythe's Wind blown him here? She clutched the chair for support and sank onto it. Sander, Mama's lover, who wanted no Records of his existence, and was every bit as stern and harsh as Joco, had appeared out of nowhere with a cryptic warning and disappeared again? She knotted her fingers in her hair.

Sander, the man whose honest name was Sand Storm, warning her about storms? Surely this had to be some sort of bad media feed that would fail in the ratings and disappear into obscurity. Wasn't it?

Though Mama had missed him, Ari hadn't. They were better off without his temper and his strict rule, even if his absence made things very lean. While, at times, Ari wished she had a connection with Joco, ties to Sander she could do without.

Still, to have him appear and vanish again like this, on top of what Joco had done ... the aching void of loss reached out to embrace her in cold, unrelenting arms.

Numb, she had to escape before she suffocated. She rushed out of the room and claimed the sleeping pod she had recently left. Perhaps the tiny chamber could shut out the cold, confusing ghost of Sander's presence long enough for it to give up and chase someone else.

Chapter 20

"Does that shirt fit?" Beny called from his bedroom.

The fine white fabric strained as Matteo buttoned the shirt across his chest. He glanced at the wall mirror near his bedroom's polished white dresser. One deep breath from structural failure. "What do you think?" He stalked across the great white—bloody impractical color for a living space—lounge into Beny's bedroom.

"Like you borrowed it from me." Beny, dressed in a perfectly tailored, designer black suit and bare feet, frowned with Grandfather's trademark expression of profound disappointment. "I swear, how can you pilot an aircraft but not be able to manage a cracking recycler? Here, give it to me, and let me tune the settings."

"In my defense, the specs were set for a newer model recycler and the switch plays havoc with the fit. I need to find another designer. There's always problems with this one." Matteo stripped off the offending garment and handed it to Beny. "Too bad I can't go 'generic pilot' for this affair."

"You seem to have impressed Brels that way." Though Beny's room was smaller than his, it still took five long steps for Beny to reach the floor-mounted recycler in the far corner, fling open the wide top, and lay the offending garment flat inside. He studied the top-mounted control panel and punched printing instructions. The machine purred—a sound recyclers never made when Matteo used them. Beny turned, hip parked on the top of the recycler. "Who knows, you might revolutionize Dextrine diplomacy that way. You're already threatening the fashion industry if you abandon Timnon's chosen designer."

"Don't say that too loudly. Grandfather doesn't need another reason to threaten to disinherit me. You know how he hates change." Matteo dropped onto the edge of the plush bed, covered with a tone-on-tone cream-colored velvet coverlet.

"You know he'll never do that." Beny leaned back, crossing his ankles, hands braced on the side edges of the recycler.

"No, I actually don't, and neither should you." Matteo fell back onto the thick mattress. Light from the artificial window behind the bed glinted off the white-tiled ceiling. "You may end up with Grandfather's seat before all is said and done."

"Don't threaten me like that. Dealing with Family headship is more than I want. I've said it at least a hundred times. No more of that now." Beny slid off the recycler and checked the controls. "A couple more minutes on the shirt."

"I suppose I can't avoid it any longer." Matteo pushed back to sitting. "Let's go over the players for tonight's diplomatic dance."

Beny pulled out his module. Not a positive sign when Beny had to consult his notes for a briefing. "Not a mere dance, cousin, this is the ball of the season. So, it's a cracking good thing you've decided to show up for it. No matter what anyone says, trade is king on Lighten and it's the Chief of Trade—"

"Trade Minister Iryna Ducan, right?" Matteo called up the name on his module. The image accompanying the dossier gave him little to go on. A standard-issue political headshot of a professional-looking slightly-past-middle-age woman wearing a standard-issue political smile.

"Most of the locals will refer to her as Iryna, the whole use of the given name thing as an honor around here—and yes, I studied what you sent, and I'm glad you pointed it out. But she'll expect us to call her Minister Ducan. I'm not sure how using her first name will go over, could be a win, could be seen as pretense, so maybe stick with what she's expecting. In either case, it's important to remember it's her, not the President, who has all the power here. Luckily, he won't be here tonight, vying for his chance to rub shoulders with Dextrine Ranks. It's a poorly kept secret that the presidency is where they shunt troublesome players to cut off their power."

"Good to know. I imagine Ducan's eager to strengthen technology import agreements with us—they need to get up to date. You wouldn't believe how much old tech I've seen today."

"You're right, but I think they're even more anxious about improving tourism."

"Which would be why all this is happening here in the Anara complex instead of the capital?" Matteo crossed his legs and looped his hands over his knee.

"That would be my guess. Tourist economy isn't well established yet, but Ducan's very interested in marketing Lighten to Dextra, so that angle is going to be a strong one. She's also a major proponent of the joint venture between Evering and Firen that you visited yesterday. If that experiment works, then she'll be open to more off-world partnerships. Or so the experts back home say."

Matteo scanned the event's attendee list. "Guild Master Brels is attending this one, too."

"He will be. What's more, your recent favor with him could go a long way in establishing you with Ducan. She has a lot of mining connections, especially with Firen. And if Firen likes you, then she'll be predisposed to agree."

"Brels is a decent sort. It said a lot about him to entertain Ranks so informally, while making it feel appropriate at the same time. Seriously, we need to hang onto those Records and study them for future reference. As much as I hate political entertaining, if I could learn to do it the way he did, I might survive it."

Beny didn't bother hiding his surprise. "Tagging those Records with those notes, now. Can't wait for a solid look at them. That could cause a real stir in our circles, you entertaining? The shock! Anyway, several other Guild Masters will be there tonight, too. Be sure you rub shoulders with them as well. Aquaculture Guild Master Dek—the guild that keeps shipping us sollert—is all about pushing Lighten products for export to us. The new Tourism Guild has a rep, Daris, who is expected to become their Guild Master. She'll be another key contact to establish. And of course, the Transport Guild Master, the one fighting Brels."

Matteo looked up from his module and grimaced. "Joco?"

"I don't like that look."

"I don't like the man."

"You need to set that aside." The recycler beeped three times. Beny fished out a crisp new white shirt and walked it to Matteo. "Joco's another major player here. The Mining Guild has most of the power on Lighten, with strong majority representation in both the House of Guilds and House of Regions. So pretty much what they say goes. Except that the Transport Guild has them by the balls in a balance of power that you'll love. Let's say there's no love lost between those guilds. Check if that shirt fits—got enough time to do it again if necessary."

Matteo slipped his arms into the soft fabric, every seam smooth. How did Beny get the recycler to do that? He fastened three buttons across his chest and inhaled deeply. "Perfect. I swear you missed your calling going into medicine."

Beny rolled his eyes and wandered toward his polished black dress shoes on the floor near the recycler. "About the Transport Guild. They've got Lighten buttoned down so hard it's not a joke. With only one primary land mass, I guess it's easier to keep eyes on every mode of transportation. Land, air, and water." He sat on the floor and worked on a long black sock.

"Does that leave the economy as fragile as I think it would? Sounds like the supply chain—"

"Pretty much. You know a lot more than I do on those, but from what I see, they're fragile as a Rank's reputation. Not only does Transport control the licensing of every vehicle and operator on the planet, they control production of every vehicle, and all their parts. And they've got standardizations on all of it that would make a Theran jealous. That's why their tech is so antiquated. The party line is that the stance protects Lighten suppliers and designers and prevents dependence on supplies from Dextra or Thera. But the truth is Transport doesn't let new designs in until they can figure out how to mimic the design themselves and maximize profits on it." He paused to tie his shoe. "It's all locked down tighter than our Prime Minister's daughter."

"The ship I flew to Firen in was anything but standard—"

"Well, that pilot's walking through Laythe's Woods to pull that off, and I'd put money on it all crashing down sooner or later."

And Matteo might have watched the beginning of that this afternoon.

"Without a working arrangement with Transport, the Mines can't get their product out. So there's no choice but to play nice with Transport, which keeps the miners in check. But it's a soul catcher crazy tense situation. Even crazier, their Ministry of Order seems to be going along with Transport for now. Something about Lighten's early charters, I haven't quite sorted it yet. But that renders their Security Corps hobbled with old tech and crazy rules about what's a weapon and what's a vehicle and what clearance is required to operate each." Beny slipped on his other sock. "You can see where this is going. Connections to the Transport Guild, or even better, their Guild Master, are valuable."

"Lovely." Matteo beckoned Beny to follow him to his room for his jacket. "How is that balance going to work with Brels fighting Joco? Sounds like a disaster either way. If Brels wins, won't that threaten the balance of power? And if Joco does, then Brels loses face."

"That's the Key Minder's question these days. No answers, though. Both their reputations are well-known, and if either were to throw the fight, it would be easy to pick up on and a massive insult that would do even more damage. Near as I can tell, no one's going to pull any punches, but it'll be an honest fight. And it needs to happen. If something interferes with it, the Hell Cat herself will roar."

"That explains a lot." Matteo snapped his cravat up from where it lay on the bed and wrapped it around his neck. He stalked toward the full-length wall mirror between the dresser and the recycling unit he officially despised.

Beny sat on the bed to manage his shoes. "Does this have something to do with that pilot you brought in?"

"Did you find the Records?"

"It wasn't easy. They were locked down tight, but since your pretty face appeared in them, Clan Timnon clearances got me in."

"It wasn't a pleasant scene, was it?" He wound the cravat into his favorite knot. Not the most fashionable one of the day, but it was one he could get right without having to drag a valet around to dress him. Or ask for Beny's help, which was even worse.

"Given what I saw, I'm surprised she wasn't hurt worse."

"If Brels hadn't stepped in like he did, I'm sure that's where it would have gone. And no, I'm not sure what I would have done at that point, but more than likely, something stupid." But there weren't a lot of options that wouldn't be considered stupid in some form or fashion.

Beny's calm demeanor slipped and his brow furrowed. "Good thing that Brels defused it. Joco getting disqualified with Brels present could have made things even more complicated. Even you being there could have brought suspicion of Dextrine interference in Lighten affairs."

"Kayavan's bones! I had no idea that it could have been a political move. I thought he was being decent toward the pilot he'd hired."

"Maybe that was part of it, but there was a healthy dose of self-interest there, too. Make no mistake about that. It's possible for the two to overlap—not common, but possible. You should've let me brief you about all this earlier. Just because you didn't wind up face-first in the mud this time doesn't mean it was a smart move, yeah?"

"You're right." Matteo dropped onto the edge of the bed next to Beny. "Just as well I didn't realize how complicated it all was. That would have given me opinions about the way things should be, and you know where that ends up."

"Keep out of that fight. Let the locals sort out their mess. We can't afford a serious gaffe right now. It's enough that you're paired up with Brels' bodyguard for your match and have to navigate that muddle."

Matteo pulled his shoulders back and glared. Nice, neither shirt nor jacket bound when he did that. "You have an opinion about how that should go down?"

"No, I imagine Grandfather has already told you his opinion."

"Gave me his orders."

"I'm not getting involved though it's not too hard to guess about what's going on in your head. And I wouldn't disagree." Beny lifted open hands. "Don't forget, I'm the one who has to patch you up and bring you home to take Grandfather's seat. The one that I'm absolutely not going to fill. So you need to come out of this without permanent damage." He waved Matteo to his feet. "Keep in mind, most of the Lighten economy rests on the mines. So, however it shakes out with this match, you need to do it ... uh ..."

"You're telling me not to be an ass about it. Got it." He straightened his cravat and gave his sleeves a final tug. "How's this?"

"I'm not ashamed to be seen with you."

"I'll take it. Let's go."

Their hospitality team met them at the suite door and guided them to the Conference wing.

Burgundy walls and plush wine-colored carpeting edged with gold and black stripes marked the way to the Diplomatic Dining Room. Open double doors, framed in something that looked like polished hardwood, marked the entry, along with four burly enforcers in black dress uniforms, discreetly armed with some very impressive weaponry, both lethal and not. And probably knives hidden somewhere in their ensemble. Somehow, being in on that secret made him smile.

The hospitality team left them at the door with a promise to wait in the designated suite across the hall so someone would be immediately available if needed. Not far from that suite, a service door blended almost seamlessly into the burgundy wall. Tempting, very tempting, but too many witnesses to make a run for it.

Beny gestured for him to enter first. If Matteo didn't take the hint, Beny might resort to a carefully disguised shove. Not the way to start this show, so Matteo straightened his jacket once more, put on his Lord Heir persona, and strode into the banquet room.

Tracks along the gold ceiling, which supported multiple cascading crystal chandeliers, suggested this room could be divided into three separate spaces, and probably was more often than not, given the pattern of wear on the burgundy-and-gold patterned carpet. Tracks where moveable walls would have slid remained brighter and less tamped down than the broad central areas that marked the centers of each of the three separate rooms.

A plush black-and-gold curtain, designed to dampen sound, hung against the wide back wall. Long banquet tables, heavy with formal linens and elaborate servingware, stood, impressed with themselves, along that same wall, laden with generous platters of small bites reminiscent of Brels' table this afternoon.

Polished white standing tables, metal bases with stone tops, dotted the rest of the room. A few seating clusters sprang up near the shorter, right-hand wall, not nearly enough to accommodate a crowd that would require three ballrooms together. Neat, black-and-gold-uniformed servers circulated with trays of food and drink that were duplicates of what could be had along the back wall. So this was the infamous Lighten Standing Supper.

Grandfather's generation despised the standing supper's informality. They found the insult of not being permitted the seat of honor at a long table nigh on unbearable. Worse still, its burgeoning popularity among Matteo's peers, who brought it home to Dextra, made it harder and harder to avoid.

While it lacked formality, it was convenient for circulating and not getting trapped in conversations one preferred to avoid. A quality that could not be undervalued.

The unmistakable form of Guild Master Brels approached. Draped as he was in a smart black suit with band collar jacket and no cravat, if his size had not made him stand out in the crowd, his movements would. Graceful, economical, sure, and precise, the movements of a man of authority, control, and confidence.

"Good evening, Lord Heir Timnon. I am pleased you have joined us this evening."

"Matteo, if you will, sir."

Beny looked at Matteo with a raised eyebrow, but Brels smiled broadly.

"Guild Master Brels. May I present my friend, trainer, and cousin, Lord Heir Sennet. Beny, this is Guild Master Brels."

Yes, Beny was taken aback by the use of his family-only nickname, but he'd read the material on nicknames; he'd forgive easily enough. After all, Beny was all about making the right impression on new connections. He should have warned Beny beforehand. But occasionally it was nice to be the one making Beny a little twitchy, rather than the other way around. Not to mention, he hadn't planned it either. The name tumbled out since it seemed right.

"Honored to make your acquaintance, sir." Beny bowed from his shoulders.

"Likewise, sir," Brels extended his open hands to Matteo. "Please accept the hospitality of what I have, according to your need."

Matteo took Brels' hands and pressed them to his face, swallowing back the inherent discomfort such contact brought. The fact that Brels was a fighter somehow made it a little easier, bordering on tolerable.

Beny might have passed out there and then if he were not a seasoned veteran of the diplomatic dance. Their debrief later was going to be memorable.

"I receive your hospitality with gratitude, and offer what you need according to what I have." Matteo extended open hands.

Brels placed them along his face. "I receive your hospitality with gratitude."

They both stepped back. Luckily, Brels did not offer the gesture to Beny, who was still too gobsmacked to do anything but stand there dumbly, mouth gaping. It was a great deal for a proper Dextrine Rank to take in.

What Beny would readily understand, though, was that it was a carefully planned maneuver to show mutual respect between two players who had never shared a connection before. Something that would be advantageous all around.

"There's Iryna, that is, Trade Minister Ducan. Come, I will introduce you." Brels parted the crowd as he strode toward the middle of the reception room with an air suggesting he assumed he would be followed. Just like a Clan Lord.

"You're going to have to explain all that, right? And not the least of which, how did you warrant a native greeting from him?" Fortunately, Beny's strained whisper would not carry far in the sound-dampened room.

"Dumb luck?" Matteo winked at his cousin and followed Brels.

Lovely. Why did it have to be *him* there, talking with Ducan?

Brels slid into the conversation between Ducan and Joco. "My honored peers, may I present our most honored guests, Lord Heir Timnon and Lord Heir Sennet."

Matteo and Beny bowed.

"May I present our esteemed Trade Minister Ducan and Transportation Guild Master Joco."

Ducan and Joco also bowed, but did not offer hospitality as Brels had. Considering he had never met either of them, at least not formally, that was to be expected. But then again, it would not have been unheard of for them to follow Brels' lead either. Later, he and Beny would dissect what that meant.

Joco's eyes narrowed slightly, as though he might have recognized Matteo from the debark field. But they had not quite come face-to-face there, so perhaps he didn't.

"Lord Heir Timnon shares common interests with you, Joco." Brels flagged a passing waiter and liberated three crystal glasses. He served Matteo and Beny and kept one for himself. "I understand he is a pilot himself."

"What do you fly?" Joco looked down his nose with the same judgmental expression as many of Matteo's flight instructors.

"I possess ratings on two personal transport models, the most recent models from Skysil Industries and Thyrix Designs."

Matteo sipped the deep orange fluid in his glass. A rich, fruity wine, must be of local vintage. The hint of salt at the end suggested it might have been made with the same marsh fruit he'd had in the pastry this morning. Nothing on Dextra had the same notes.

"Have you clearances for our airspace?" Ducan asked with a meaningful glance at Joco. She was Beny's height, tall for a woman, but short, standing between Joco and Brels. Her blue, almost black, pantsuit looked like it was from the same designer who dressed Brels. Sleek, elegant, authoritative. The way she carried herself between the two larger power-players made it clear she did not consider herself at any disadvantage.

"I am still working to get them. They are rather difficult to come by." He kept his gaze away from Joco.

"I find Dextra is less rigorous in granting such privileges." The way Joco ended the sentence suggested he expected no further discussion.

"As I understand, Dextrine airspace extends reciprocity to most other jurisdictions." Given the glower Beny threw his way, Matteo was going to be on the receiving end of a memorable lecture for laying down that kind of obvious bait.

"I suppose that is one way to do it." Joco clearly did not approve. Of the policy or the statement Matteo was making. "Seems ripe for abuse."

"Quite in the spirit of hospitality, I would say." Ducan smiled tightly at Joco, but tension crackled between them. "Perhaps Dextrines understand the concept better than we expect." There went more bait.

And just like that, Matteo had landed himself in the middle of some well-established conflict between these local dignitaries. Perfect. "We are honored by the compliment." He dipped his head towards her. "I expect we are not so far apart as some might believe. If only our peoples might spend more time together, it would become evident. Having enjoyed Guild Master Brels' hospitality this morning, I am convinced my people would relish further opportunities to have such experiences." He glanced at Brels, who seemed comfortable with the revelation.

"And how did you contrive to spend time with our esteemed guest?" The surprise in Ducan's voice suggested surprise didn't happen often, and she didn't like it when it did.

"I paid a call to Evering Industries."

"That was not on your official itinerary." Of course, Ducan would have been familiar with their official plans.

"No, it was not. But I had personal business to conduct with a member of the Evering staff. Since I was so close, a face-to-face visit was required."

Beny winced.

"Personal business" might not have been the safest way to describe it. That term often led the Media to wild leaps of imagination. "Since I could not obtain local flight clearances, I hired a Paxton Ship Yard pilot for the job. I was very impressed with that pilot's skills. Are all of your pilots as skilled as Paxton 23?"

Joco's glare would have been considered an assault in most polite company. "I would not have recommended that pilot."

"I was given to understand she flew you here."

"She told you that?" Joco's face darkened.

Apparently, this was far more dangerous ground than Matteo had understood. And he'd wandered into it at full speed. "No, the local hearsay suggested it. She did not intimate any such thing, which was odd, as I would have expected that sort of endorsement would be well-advertised. So, she was not your pilot?"

Beny looked ready to kick him. Probably ought to take that hint.

"I would not have recommended her. We have much better." Joco turned his face aside. Clearly unwilling to say more on the matter.

"I understand. I will be sure to go through your Ship Yard channels in the future, then."

Beny kept a straight face, but his hand twitched ever so slightly. Matteo could almost see him thinking '*Change the sarding subject!*'

"Would be best. You shouldn't risk anything that doesn't pass directly through Transport Guild channels."

"About the tourism possibilities, though," Beny stepped in closer, "this sporting complex is first class. I hope these exhibition bouts that have been scheduled are the beginning of a bigger push to share a mutual love of sport."

"I am delighted to hear you say that." Ducan seemed relieved. "The representative from the Tourism Guild, Daris, is over here, if you would permit me to introduce you." Ducan led Beny off across the room. Beny glanced over his shoulder, probably afraid to leave Matteo alone with the rival Guild Masters. Not without reason.

"You ready for your bout with Pogo?" Brels lifted his wineglass to Matteo.

"As ready as one can be for such a thing. I am afraid there are few protocols to prepare one for such a novel experience." Matteo watched Joco's expression over the rim of his wineglass.

"I suppose your Clans don't take it to the ground to settle matters often," Joco said.

"It is discouraged. Though I've wondered more than once if it might be a more expedient way to settle matters."

Brels' jaw dropped, and he laughed, rich and full-bodied as the wine. "We'll see how you do with Pogo. Then we may talk with the Sporting Guild about offering it as a service to your people."

Who knew, someone might make an interesting business venture of it. Matteo chuckled, genuine and unforced, a rare occurrence during a diplomatic affair. "With the greatest of respect, would you permit me a question?"

"You want to know why Joco and I are willing to take it to the ground ourselves, no?" Brels glanced at Joco, who wore a sour look.

"It is a very different practice to our own. I am interested in better understanding it."

Brels studied Matteo, probably judging the sincerity of the request. "You're a fighter, you might actually understand." He extended a hand to invite Joco's response.

"It ain't just about the win or the loss," Joco focused on the back wall, as if weighing his words, "but about how a man fights. When you get in the ring with someone, what do you learn about them?"

Interesting question. "Skill, strength, speed, and strategy to start. Tenacity, endurance, creativity, ability to respond to surprise. Training, preparation, how far a man will go when pushed, and how much he will adhere to the boundaries set. At first it can be a show, but then it gets to a certain point and a man's real character comes out."

"And that's why we do it." Brels lifted his glass to Joco. "A drink to character, gentlemen."

Chapter 21

THE NEXT MORNING, SHE nursed the headache Beny had foretold with pain tabs and a strong, too-bitter cup of dark smoked tea. She curled in a well-worn, well-cushioned chair, pulled near the sports screens, watching six different fights in real time. A dozen other pilots shared the idea, providing a boisterous backdrop for her swirling thoughts.

Why had Sander come to her last night? Why now, of all times? Not during the month of mourning. Not when she might have welcomed the company. But now, when things had taken such a turn with Joco. It had always been that way, with him showing up at the most difficult moments. But his appearances should have ended with the storm that took Mama.

There was something more to all of this, lurking like a sollert in the dark waters, waiting to take its prey to the depths. Such a dramatic image, but then again, things had a way of becoming dramatic when Sander appeared.

The group around her exploded to their feet, decrying a referee's call. One of the local favorites had just lost a highly-contested match, and it looked like the call would be appealed. Even if the fighter won the appeal, it might be a blemish on his reputation.

"Morning, Arli." Pogo perched on the arm of the couch beside her, a steaming mug of tea in one hand and an oversized sticky bun in the other. The only one in the room wearing a Firen rusty-red flight jacket, he stood out. But the way he observed the fights—like he was cataloging and evaluating every fighter on the screens—set him apart even more than the color he wore.

"It is that." She raised her mug toward him.

"Feeling better? Saw someone about that?" He touched his cheek. "Whoever it was did a proper job on you. You can barely tell anything ... happened."

"Just a clumsy moment with some loose cargo." She shrugged and hid behind her mug.

He leaned closer, whispering, "You've got that excuse far too ready."

Drop the subject. Drop the sarding subject! "Occupational hazard."

"Shouldn't be." He frowned and turned back to study the fights until the appeal on the controversial call was denied. "You want to watch one of these in person with me? I've got passes that will get us front-tier seats."

Joco didn't want her keeping company with anyone at all. What would he think of her spending time with Brels' bodyguard? Did she even care anymore? "Sounds nice, thanks. Certainly better than the view here." She craned her neck to look past the three pilots who had jumped to their feet in protest.

"Yeah, this ain't the same as the good seats, come on." He waved her toward the back corridors where the door pings wouldn't alert Joco of her continued disobedience. Pogo took their now-empty mugs to the recycler. "You interested in any particular fights?"

"How about the exhibition series? Those should turn up something interesting." And less personal. She had too many opinions about the local fighters. He might, too, and those opinions might not agree. Too complicated for today.

"Fair enough. They're on the west side." He turned down a narrow gray hall that emptied into a white-tiled one—a main corridor—with a broad yellow Sporting Wing stripe. "The next ones up are the Fleet bouts."

"That will be new. I don't know much about them." Given how much Joco detested Fleet, it would be interesting to get a closer look.

He called them useless interference. Fatherless soul catchers who only got in the way with their own agendas. Ruleless key minders who thought they had answers to things they knew nothing about. He fought them constantly with the way he controlled who could fly in Lighten airspace, striving to keep them out at all costs. Anyone who fought Joco's rule was not only unwelcome, but dangerous.

That was why he disliked miners in general, and Firen, with Brels at the head, in specific. They wanted more control in shipping their products, more armed vehicle options to protect their mines, and improved technology for the vehicles used in the mines themselves. All of which Joco insisted would make Lighten dependent on Dextrine and Theran technology, and he wasn't going to promote anything that tied Lighten to those who had settled her.

At one time she understood, agreed with the wisdom of that. But the more she learned about "big things" that little arlis shouldn't be involved with, like the precarious state of Lighten's economy, the real danger the Raiders posed, and the need for the system to work together to survive the threat, the less she agreed with Joco's perspective. Not that anyone had ever asked her opinions, or that she ever found it a safe option to express them. That would have been like inviting Joco into the ring for a few rounds herself. Leave that for the professional fighters.

The Fleet bouts were assigned to one of the smaller arenas, a third the size of where Joco and Brels' bout would be held. Still, it was huge, with three tiers of seating, plus balcony seating that circled the entire ring. Both the seating, which became roomier and more cushioned as it approached the ring, and the concrete floor were soul-sucking black. The sort of black that drew in all light and made one ignore what was right in front of them. Nearly all the overhead light was focused on the central, round fight ring, encouraging the illusion that it and the fighters within were the only arena occupants worthy of notice. Crowd noise filled every open space like a fog, settling over the audience, thick and heavy, mixed with the smells of many bodies and the air cleansers used to mask it.

An assault on every sense at once.

"It's something, ain't it?" Pogo directed her down to the lowest tier, third row, ring center.

"You weren't kidding, these are pretty fancy." She settled into the lush seat, her feet not quite reaching the floor. She'd ignore how much she hated that feeling until her feet went numb and she pulled them up to sit cross-legged in the seat.

"A perk of winning a championship last year." He pretended to ignore her, but watched for her reaction from the corner of his eye.

So predictable. "Yeah, I saw that match."

"And?"

"Your ego don't need any more feeding, and you know it. You deserved to get the top seed, what more do you need to hear?"

He threw his head back and laughed, a warm, welcoming sound. "Sure as storms, you've lived among ring fighters."

"Strut like cocks, bite like sollerts, and howl like yard hounds for attention."

"Ouch!" He clutched his sides and laughed harder. "Good thing you don't get in the ring, you go straight for the throat." He clasped a hand across his neck.

"I'm just a harmless little arli." She pressed her hand to her chest.

"If there's anything you're not, it's harmless. I saw you throw knives, remember? And outfly some nasty desert birds." He winked and pointed to the ring. "This is the last round of a Theran-Dextrine bout. A couple of the lightweight guys, they've got some local rankings, but not names I recognize."

"The two styles are very similar, aren't they?" Pogo's gaze was too intense, so she turned her focus on the fighters in the ring.

"In theory, yes. They are based on the same tradition. The real difference is in the attitudes. For the Therans, victory, as long as it doesn't compromise valor, is everything. So, they press as close to the tourney rules as they expect officials will tolerate, without going past. Dextrines play for honor, so you'll see them go for style, fancy takedowns, and flashy moves that score high points."

"Neither with a clear advantage?"

The Dextrine fighter, in blue, lunged, trying for one of the fancy takedowns.

"Not really, comes down to the skill of the fighter."

"How does Dextrine honor line up with Lighten's style?"

The Theran fighter, in red, slipped from the Dextrine's hold, throwing a barely legal kick-punch combination.

"You mean Lighten Miners' style?" He flashed his eyebrows.

Begging for attention. Yard hound.

He chuckled. "We've got less polish, more direct to the point, than the average Dextrine. But since none of us wants to pay forward anything that hovers too close to a violation, and we all like a proper strut, flashy moves are not out of the question. Leaving us somewhere between the Therans and Dextrines."

Wouldn't have been the way Joco would have broken it down, but it sounded right. "So, you and Matté should be evenly matched, then?"

"I'm wounded."

"Bookmakers have you with even odds."

"And why would you go believing them?" He pressed his shoulder to hers. "Watch. Next point wins."

Warm and heavy, his touch was impossible to ignore. Distracting. A little disconcerting. How was she supposed to respond? What did he expect? What did she want?

The two fighters, both a weight class or so below Pogo, were locked shoulder to shoulder, on their knees, grunting and scrabbling for advantage. Then the Dextrine flipped over the Theran's hip, thrown to his back with the Theran over him, forcing his shoulders to the mat. The official sounded the buzzer, waded onto the mat, and lifted the Theran fighter's arm in victory.

"Could have gone either way. The Theran was a little faster to the throw." Pogo tapped fingers along his chin, thoughtful, as though considering how he might have handled the same situation.

"No, there was more to it than that." She leaned forward, elbows digging into the soft arms between the seats. "The Dextrine failed to take a questionable shot right before he got thrown. Thera baited him with a dishonorable move to force an opening. Thera won, but I'd bet Dextra gets credit among his own for honor."

He looked at her wide-eyed. "You fly like a hell cat, outsmart Raiders, and now you're analyzing fights? So, what don't you know?"

"Grew up with a professional fighter, remember? I heard fights analyzed as far back as I remember." She shrugged and looked aside before he could catch her gaze. "Anything not related to flying or fighting and I'm just this side of useless."

"I don't know where you heard that nonsense, but you sure as storms aren't useless." He craned around to look at her straight on. "What happened on the debark field, with ... him ... that wasn't unusual?"

"It is what it is."

"So he doesn't limit his bullying to politics."

"Leave it, please." She closed her eyes, the only way to escape his inquisition.

"Why? So he can keep it up? You don't deserve that. You're too sarding good a pilot to have to put up with that nonsense."

"I can't leave until I have somewhere to go."

"Then you'll leave when you can? Seriously, not just trying to make me shut up? Drawing up a formal contract with Firen is a right proper pain in the ass and no one wants to bother if it's only going to be rejected." He squeezed her hand.

Did that mean he thought it was really going to happen? She opened her eyes and nodded the tiniest bit.

He laced his fingers in hers and turned back to the ring, the hint of a smile lifting his thin lips. "The Fleet representatives are coming out. Green's from the First Fleet, Yellow is from the Third. I hear their rivalry's worse than the Firen-Delvin miners."

"That's saying something." It was remarkable Firen and Delvin miners could operate in the same Guild. Said a lot about Brels that he could manage the Guild with that tension going on.

"Good thing you're not squeamish. This is going to get ugly. Nearly everyone in Fleet is running from something worse at home. There's not much honor or concern with paying forward among them. And you can pretty much forget about hospitality."

He was right. From the opening buzzer, the two men flew at each other in a flurry of fists and kicks, most of them barely legal, all of them ferocious.

"I see why no one else will get in the ring with them," she whispered, tempted to turn aside from the bloody spray from Fleet Yellow's busted lip and broken nose.

"A lot of Fleet won't either—their ring fighters are given a wide berth. These guys are a special breed of soul catchers." He turned to look at her again, all levity gone. "Would you want to take me to the ground for saying you need to keep your distance from them?"

"Yes. But you'd still be right."

After the first Fleet bout, which involved far too much bloodshed and far too little honor for the sport, Brels pinged Pogo's module.

"Well, ain't that a dust storm on a sunny day. Boss needs me—he's chairing a meeting between the smaller mining interests and he's gotten wind it might get interesting in all the wrong ways." He lifted their still joined hands. "I'd much rather stay here."

"If he thinks it's going to get interesting, you best get over there quick. You don't want to miss the start of it." She released his hand and waved him off. "Don't risk getting on his wrong side."

"That's one mistake I'm not going to make. I've reserved the seats for the rest of the afternoon if you'd like to stay. Wish I could say I'll be back, but the chances aren't great for it. Sorry."

"I understand. This isn't a pleasure trip for you, so get your body to work. I'll be fine. Go, go!" She waved him off again.

"Fine, fine, get rid of me, why don't you." He chuckled and ambled off.

She had nowhere to be, and hiding in a crowd was a great opportunity to avoid any more complications, so she settled in.

The next match featured a Theran/Lighten pairing. How different they were to the Fleet fighters. Brutal, aggressive, yes, but even the official looked relieved that Fleet was out of the ring. Though he fought well, the Theran was hopelessly outclassed by the Lighten, and the crowd cheered the local victory that cleansed the taste of the Fleet match from their palate.

She'd always found the fights interesting, but now even more than ever. What would Pogo and Matté reveal about themselves in the ring? Some dark hidden flaws, or that they were every bit as much the decent men they appeared to be?

More important, what would happen when Brels and Joco took their places?

Chapter 22

THE ANARA EXHIBITION SERIES was scheduled to end the next afternoon with Pogo and Matteo's much anticipated bout. It was an honor of sorts to be the final big match of the series. Attendance was expected to reach capacity—both those with an allegiance to Firen, and those who wanted to see Firen meet its comeuppance, clamored for the few remaining tickets.

While an honest compliment, the fight's popularity also brought a lot of pressure, far more than any other meet Matteo'd taken part in, including the Wroxton championships. All of which did nothing for Matteo's disposition.

He fiddled with the Timnon-blue, soft jersey robe he wore over the matching Timnon-blue singlet. Though the singlet covered neck to nearly knees, it clung skin-tight, leaving nothing to the imagination. It wasn't as if he hadn't dressed for the ring hundreds of times, yet the sense of naked impropriety still clung as tightly as the Media that followed him trying to get a glimpse of said impropriety.

He had fought at Wroxton Academy, first to annoy Grandfather by taking up a sweaty, brutal, close-contact sport that Ranks avoided. Then he found he enjoyed it. The visceral, competitive nature of the sport filled a void that life in the Ranks never touched. Something about the equality of it, the way he could leave behind his Rank and title and face his opponent on level ground, kept him coming back.

He straddled the line between Theran and Dextrine styles, which set him apart in his division and made him more noticeable in the ring. He could have done without the extra attention, but testing himself against his peers and not being found wanting—the outcome Grandfather always predicted—was worth the price.

And being wrong was one of those things Grandfather hated. That was satisfying, too.

The satisfaction wasn't without cost. Ring fighting was brutal; the injuries and the pain were real. No one left the fighting ring unscathed, and as well-matched as he and Pogo were, they both would pay the price for a long, hard bout. At least he had fulfilled his last diplomatic assignment and could spend the rest of the trip flat on his back if he needed to.

Having Beny in the trainer's pit was encouraging, though. Not only was he wildly overqualified for the job, but he had always had Matteo's back, and in a foreign arena, the power of that couldn't be underestimated.

The diplomatic dinner last night proved that the Lightens would be looking at the fight in a wholly different way to the audiences Matteo was accustomed to. Regarding it as a test of character, and all the judgments that went with that. No pressure there at all. He only had the reputation of Dextra riding on his shoulders.

He really needed to stop reading Media releases before events like this.

He paced the length of the trainer's pit. Six steps below the level of the ring floor, it extended one quarter of the way around the ring. Pogo likely paced the matching one on the opposite side. The designers had left the pit, which had been carved into the deep-gray, almost black, bedrock, raw and unfinished, smelling of stone and earth, strength, and tenacity. By some magic of acoustic design, the pit deadened the crowd noise, kept it swirling overhead, offering an escape from the distracting din.

Anara's publicity materials suggested the design was intended to set the mood for the fighters before they reached the ring. As if the fighters paid attention to such things this close to a match.

Padded black benches, a sink, and a large, well-stocked aid locker lined the inner wall. A cot that could be converted to a stretcher stood against the outer wall, near a very discreet service door that led directly to medical facilities. Points for efficiency.

Beny's kit, a wheeled Timnon-blue bag—the color made it easy to find—stood next to the aid locker, matching its size and shape. Although Beny denied it, he was prepared to manage anything, up to and including minor surgeries, in addition to the usual injuries associated with a ring fight. Madly over-prepared.

"You sure you're ready for this?" Beny eyed the bloodstain on the coarse stone floor as he wrapped Matteo's wrists and hands in Timnon-blue tape.

"This won't be a bloodbath like yesterday's Fleet bout. Pogo's not Fleet. He's a Lighten, a Mining Guild Enforcer, so he holds to rules and principles. It'll be an honest match. He's got as much to lose as I do for fighting dirty."

"I suppose sharing a meal together with Brels puts you on different terms than the two we saw yesterday, but as the guy charged with putting you back together, allow me to be concerned. Have you decided what you're going to do about Grandfather's suggestion—"

"It was an order. Nothing polite or optional about it."

"So you're going to ignore it, then? Let me check the tape."

Matteo extended both hands for Beny's inspection. "I'm playing this straight, make it a clean, honest fight. I'll fight with honor, follow the rules, and what comes of it, comes."

"That takes stone balls, considering how cracked Grandfather's going to be over Iantha." Beny nodded and tucked the tape back into his kit.

"I know. I've given it a lot of thought. Thing is, Pogo would pick up on anything less than a real effort, and he'd be the kind to call it out, too. That would be an even worse look for all of us."

A white-uniformed ring official descended the stairs, halfway into the pit. "They're ready for you."

"For my sake, Matté, keep yourself in one piece." Beny slapped his shoulder. "And don't leave me with a diplomatic incident to clean up."

Exactly what he needed to hear. Matteo straightened his robe and followed the ring official into the lights and noise, like a newly-fledged raptor emerging from its cave, ready to engage its first prey.

He ducked through the thickly-padded ropes, blinking, adjusting to the bright lights trained on the circular ring, fifteen meters in diameter. The padding beneath his feet gave just enough to assure him it met regulation standards, covered in heavy canvas that would offer some traction, even when soaked with sweat. And it had been sweat-soaked. Despite the pungent burn of industrial cleaners, the unmistakable funk of fighters' sweat hung over the ring, an invisible haze marking the space for what it was.

The capacity crowd roared, disordered and loud, not like the rhythmic clapping of Dextrines or metered Theran stomping. But they were excited and receptive, not bloodthirsty, so that was something. The soul-sucking black of the arena helped most of the crowd blend into a faceless mass, much easier to ignore than in other venues. That had to be a good thing.

Brels—Brels?—stood in the center of the ring, wearing a casual suit by the same designer he had worn last night, a microphone in his hand. Pogo, draped in a Firen rusty-red robe, stood lightly on the balls of his feet, just beyond. He acknowledged Matteo with the barest nod, already focused on the fight to come.

Brels beckoned Matteo to take his place beside them. "This year is a first for us—" Whoever ran the sound had done a credible job of making Brels sound like himself when his voice was pushed through the massive speakers. "For the first time ever, Dextra has sent a champion to challenge one of our own."

The crowd roared again, the first several rows near enough to form a sea of unfamiliar faces. Somehow it was a little tough knowing that Beny, watching from the top of stairs leading to the trainer's pit, was the only familiar face there.

Wait, no, there in the center, third row, Arli watched with keen attention. She caught his eye for a moment and offered a wink of encouragement. He nodded and winked back.

And like that, it all felt familiar, almost comfortable again. Funny, that. Brels looked at him with a raised eyebrow. Hopefully, he wouldn't be making the wrong assumptions.

"I present to you the Wroxton Military Academy Champion—" Brels mouthed '*Matteo*'?

Beny caught his eye, nodding, and mouthed '*Local customs—yes.*'

"Lord Heir Timnon, Matteo."

The crowd roared again. Definitely the right move to include his given name along with his title.

"And our own open division champion, Pogo."

Brels ripped the robes off their backs and the crowd jumped to their feet, screaming. One of those Theran-origin traditions that Dextrines had given up. Nothing compared to the feeling of being an attractive piece of meat to put one in the mind to fight.

"Open style rules apply. Three rounds, two minutes each. Points or first full pin."

Brels gestured the fighters together, taking their hands and clasping them to each other with his hand on top.

"Open style" starts like this one weren't used in aggressive Theran matches, where starting combatants too close was a hazard to life and limb. Dextrines preferred the shoulder-to-shoulder "clench" that encouraged quick throws and flashy moves that didn't play to Matteo's preferred endurance game. Would be interesting to see how this start influenced the fight.

Brels pushed down on their hands. "Fight on!" He released their hands and sprang out of their way.

Locking eyes with Pogo, Matteo stilled his thoughts and moved into a place that only he and his opponent occupied. The arena noise faded into the background. All that mattered was in the ring.

Pogo gripped Matteo's hand harder. "Enjoying your little vacation on Anara? Planning to drag this out as long as you can?"

So he knew something about Matteo's fighting style. But Matteo had done his homework, too. Only question was, would he let Pogo believe he fell for the bait? Pouncing into Pogo's throwing range wouldn't have been a bad move—Matteo's ground game was as strong as Pogo's.

Not yet.

Matteo tightened his grip on Pogo's hand and took a half-step closer. Smirking, Pogo mirrored Matteo's move. The smirk faded as Pogo realized Matteo's bigger frame gave him the advantage in this close space.

A drunk Theran accent shouted, "I didn't pay to see no rutting! Put the rock chewer on his ass!"

Pogo spun, breaking Matteo's grip as he brought Matteo's arm over his shoulder and levered him up and over.

Matteo twisted enough to avoid landing flat on his back, but not enough to land on his feet. He used the ring floor's slight bounce to make a seamless spring back to his feet.

Matteo lowered his fists and charged like a Theran, a good way to land a few strikes, the distracting kind, not the sort of strikes that lead to points or pins. But distraction was a legitimate tactic, not to be underestimated.

Pogo feinted, stopping Matteo's charge with a stomp. A classically trained response. But would Pogo go on with the expected reprisal or try something unpredictable?

Matteo stepped in with an uppercut. That should leave Pogo nicely unbalanced.

If it landed.

Pogo hopped back to avoid the strike. But Matteo pivoted to land a spin kick to the jaw. A solid strike, but didn't feel like it broke anything, except maybe Pogo's concentration, giving Matteo the opening to lunge his shoulder into Pogo's forward hip.

Fists rained down on Matteo's back and shoulders, a few landing, illegally, to the back of his head. Weak strikes, at bad angles, worth no points, so he'd ignore them, dropping Pogo to the mat hard.

But Pogo managed to land seated, not flat. So much for a quick pin.

He could abandon the pin and earn a few points for the throw, then try for another takedown, or go for some flashy high-point moves, or attempt the pin from the current awkward position.

Don't be an ass about it. Beny's voice in his head. He was right.

Matteo yanked Pogo's leg and drove in with his shoulder.

Pogo threw his locked arm behind him, holding him up while hammering Matteo with the other fist. Ineffective blows at the tight angle.

"Break! Round one over. Back to your corners." Brels stomped toward them, ready to break them apart himself if necessary.

Matteo released Pogo and offered his hand. Pogo smirked, rolled backwards, and sprang to his feet.

Fancy hell cat's move. Let him keep his dignity. That's what Beny would say.

Beny met him at the top of the stairs above the trainer's pit, a bottle of water in hand, his best game face in place. "Almost looks like he's properly trained." He poked at Matteo's sides, checking for injuries.

"Not trained. Well-read but not practiced against anyone trained. He knows what he should do, but it hasn't turned into reflex." Matteo gulped the water. "My count says I'm slightly up on points, yours?"

"Up by half a takedown, but he's still fresh. Lightens don't burn hard in the early rounds like the Therans you're used to. Expect more feints from him. You giving any more thought to Grandfather's—"

"No. I'm sticking to my plans. Brels would never respect us if we did anything less."

"You sure?"

"Fighters to the center for round two."

"No doubts." Matteo tossed the water to Beny and trudged to ring center.

Between them, Brels clapped twice. "Fight on."

Both fighters hopped back to create space as Brels dodged away.

Dextrine fighters would circle about now. So, not that.

Double-leg takedown. Much better.

Matteo dropped his body low and charged, while Pogo bounced on the balls of his feet, ready for a strike. Dropping lower as he closed on Pogo, Matteo aimed to bind his legs.

The classical defense for the takedown would be a sprawl, drop weight on the opponent to reverse the takedown.

Matteo braced for Pogo's weight, ready to counter with his own throw.

The crowd exploded.

Matteo had missed Pogo entirely. The soul-catching little rock chewer leapfrogged and landed behind Matteo.

No points for that, but it put him in an excellent position and worked up the crowd, convincing them they'd gotten their money's worth.

Matteo kept his stance low as he whipped around to find his opponent. Before he worked out his next attack, a powerful kick to his ankle took out his forward leg, driving him to his knee.

Pogo launched his full body weight into Matteo, intent on taking him to the ground.

Matteo locked up Pogo's arms by bringing his own down to clamp Pogo in place and added his momentum into launching both of them backward. Uncontrolled, but worth the advantage if it worked.

Matteo managed a near-full backflip, landing both himself and Pogo out of position. Pogo broke out of Matteo's tenuous grip, foiling the takedown.

Pogo smirked as they regained their footing. Taunting, self-important little upstart. Trying to get in Matteo's head.

Matteo charged. Not angry, but it would look that way. Now was the right time to be angry. What Pogo would expect, what the Media would want to write about, something Grandfather would rage against.

But Matteo was playing his own head game.

Pogo mirrored the charge. Several crossbody shots flew, barely blocked, before they slammed into one another. Pogo twisted sharply, landing a solid kick to Matteo's ribs. Ducking in to guard his ribs, Matteo shouldered Pogo off balance.

Matteo followed him down, trapping Pogo's head and near shoulder. Somehow, Pogo levered his opposite shoulder off the mat, frustrating the pin.

So close—so sarding close!

"Break! Round two over. Back to your corners."

Matteo staggered to the training pit stairs, gulped air into his burning lungs. "What's the point count looking like?"

Beny tossed him a water bottle. "You might have a little bit of margin after the last throw, but not much. I do not know how that leapfrog-backflip thing gets scored. From where I sit, I think you can play to your strength and wear him out. I know that's not terribly satisfying when you've got more skin in this game than simply beating that miner." He poked at a rib Pogo had been focusing on. "That's cracked and won't take too much more to break. Adrenaline's been covering it, but you'll feel it soon."

"Yeah, I noticed that."

Beny leaned back, arms crossed—his thinking face. "Pogo knows it, too. You could trap him with it."

"That's new. Haven't known you to coach me to get injured. Grandfather's really pissed you off, huh?" Matteo struggled to hold the water bottle in his trembling hand.

"If you're going to win this thing, you need to get it done and reduce the wear and tear I'm going to have to patch up. Don't make my job more difficult."

"You can fix the rib when we're done?"

"Of course I can fix the rib, what do you think my kit's for? But don't make it worse than it needs to be." He slapped Matteo's shoulder and took the water bottle back.

"Fighters in for the final round."

Matteo swaggered to the center of the ring, a solid way to cover the searing pain in his ribs. Pogo moved similarly, controlling his breath to hide his exhaustion from the crowd, perhaps himself.

Two minutes left. Matteo could do anything for two minutes.

And he might have to.

The pair lined up, got into stance—

"Fight!"

Pogo launched forward, leading with a powerful cross to Matteo's head.

Can't fight a pin if you're unconscious. Solid strategy. Matteo leaned back just enough to feel the wind from the strike, countering with an uppercut to Pogo's center of mass. Matteo's strike landed hard. Pogo brushed off the blow.

Probably the adrenaline. He had to have felt that.

Pogo backed off, intentionally taking one of Matteo's strikes, then shoved him back, opening an arm's length of distance. Setting up for a kick.

That cracking smirk, again. Rock-chewer thought the ploy worked.

Enough.

Matteo lifted the arm he had been using to protect his cracked rib as if to launch a leaping cross punch. A subtle tell, but Pogo was sharp.

Hopefully not sharp enough to see the trap.

Pogo shifted his weight and launched from the mat like a flitter with escape velocity. Bait taken.

Time slowed.

Matteo braced for Pogo's kick. Pain, like a spearhead, lanced through Matteo's chest from the point of contact, snapping the cracked rib.

Autopilot took over. Matteo wrapped and trapped the striking leg, stepped in, swept the other leg, dropping Pogo to the mat. Release Pogo's trapped leg halfway down. Land his knee above Pogo's swept leg. Pressure on the chest. Grab a wrist.

Pogo broke Matteo's fugue with a powerful cross to Matteo's jaw. Pogo grinned wildly—adrenaline-fueled mind game. Cocky little soul catcher.

Couldn't be more than half the round left. Matteo could win by simply holding the position. Like Beny had first suggested ...

Not good enough. If he was going to win, he was really going to win.

Matteo shifted his weight towards Pogo's unpinned shoulder. Pogo fought him with a flurry of blows from his single free arm, arching his back off the mat with his head.

Seconds left.

Matteo wove his free arm into an arm bar around Pogo's. Risky, very risky. But too little time, too much pain to try anything else.

He wrenched Pogo's elbow forward while shoving his weight against Pogo's unpinned shoulder, increasing the pressure, slow, steady...

Pop!

Pogo grunted, face contorted, and dropped to the mat.

Brels acknowledged the pin as the buzzer signaled the end of the match.

The crowd, which had seemed strangely silent and distant until now, exploded into a roar to rival the Hell Cat calling back lost souls.

Matteo backed off, bracing hands on knees, bent over gasping for breath, knees quaking. Pogo rolled to his side, then up, throwing his injured arm up with a stomach-churning pop. He grunted and grimaced, but seemed relieved when the dislocated joint returned to its place.

"Sarding good match." Pogo staggered to Matteo and offered a fist—with the uninjured arm—to bump Matteo's in a sign of respect and honor every fighter in the system, regardless of style, recognized. Matteo returned the gesture. The crowd roared approval.

Brels met them in the middle and encouraged both to stand upright. He lifted Matteo's hands, and the crowd lauded the hard-fought win.

Grandfather was going to be livid.

Chapter 23

ARI LEAPT TO HER feet, adding her voice to the arena's cacophony. Despite the rumors that one or the other had been ordered to throw the match, Matté and Pogo both fought with honor and passion and the respect due from one fighter to another, and even more from one pilot to another.

Which none had actually expected. All things considered, that was more important than who won. Not that anyone would admit to such a thing—except the few who'd bet on that result and were pulling in the best profits from the day.

Their styles were entirely different, with Pogo all offensive and rush and Matté patient, waiting and observing—a much more strategic approach. But neither had a clear advantage. Made for a fascinating match, one worth studying, if anyone would bother to study a mere exhibition match.

She sat back down to allow the crowd to trickle out around her. She had nowhere to be but the pilots' lounge, so why rush?

Both men cut fine forms in the ring. Pogo, with his lean wiry muscles and sure, bordering on cocky, swagger, would be fighting off willing partners tonight, even if he restricted himself to the pilots' lounge. He seemed the type who'd enjoy celebrating that way.

Matté, not so much, though. Taller, more heavily muscled than Pogo, he avoided that hulking, brutish look that many fighters acquired. It was in the way he carried himself, like a man worthy of respect, who respected himself. He'd probably hide in his suite to avoid the attention that was likely coming his direction this evening. Poor man, but he needed to be careful about his connections.

Connections could come back and bite one later, like a sollert lying in the deadfall. That was one of Joco's favorite warnings. Joco had such a strange approach to connections. Cautious, to the point of almost paranoid.

He'd chosen Bithy so carefully, more for connections that she brought than affection or compatibility. Hence his need for Mama—his Haven, he called her—to fill those places Bithy left empty. Still made so little sense why Mama would choose that kind of life.

The crowd trickled away to make merry until the final championship rounds started again tomorrow, taking with them the oppressive cloud of noisy intensity, leaving the arena echoing and empty, save for the crew coming to prepare for the next event. It was a positive note to end today's sport.

Much better than yesterday's bloodbath with Fleet. Even the most bloodthirsty fight fans swore off further Fleet bouts. They weren't likely to be invited to exhibitions again. Though the Dextrines and Therans would. There was even some talk about adding an off-world division to the league. Pogo and Matté made that look like a good idea.

She started the long climb to the exit doors. Her module pinged. An invitation from Firen Mines to a reception to honor Pogo and Matté celebrating a well-fought fight. Brels wasted no time in capitalizing on the match regardless of the winner. Not a bad strategy, one in line with the man she had met earlier. Nice to see his generosity was more real than an affectation for publicity.

Interesting, though, that he would include someone like her, not only the important types who were tucked into their suites and private boxes. Maybe it was an actual celebration, not a hastily-disguised political opportunity.

Dress code said to "come as you are," so it was not a formal event. Fortunate that she'd ditched her flight gear for a simple black shirt and slacks. Plain, but a tiny step up from her work gear.

Joco would forbid her to go, no doubt, wouldn't want the possibility of her being mistaken as a way to get to him. Wouldn't want her making any connections of her own either, though he'd never admit to that. But Joco would be at a dinner with the fledgling Tourism Guild's representative, so he would not be there.

Good sense insisted she return to the pilots' lounge and not give Joco one more thing to hold against her. But good sense hadn't served her well recently. So, she made her way to the room listed on the invitation.

Not in the VIP section of the burgundy-striped Conference spoke, so that was another positive. The large conference room already had a line forming outside the door. She would just as soon avoid a crowd of so many people, with so few who looked familiar. But she did not want to offend the man who, according to Pogo, was interested in hiring her. That was reason enough to endure the crowd and stay.

Wait, she peered at the door number, then at the invitation. She was in the wrong place. The invitation listed a door beyond this one. Strange—comforting, but strange. Right now, strange seemed far more tolerable than the crowd.

A door monitor—oh wait, that was Marsh. Suddenly, things felt far less threatening.

"Well, look at you, Arli, rating an invitation to this little party." Marsh grinned like a man who had won a bet. Wonder which one that would have been. He checked his module, eyebrow rising. "The Guild Master has asked that you go directly to him. He's in the receiving line, there."

Dozens of people stood in line, waiting on the Guild Master's attention. She grimaced.

"Don't worry, you don't have to go through the line. I'll take you." Marsh waved at her to follow him, shutting the door behind them as they entered the conference room.

The expansive chamber had been transformed for a real Lighten-style celebration. Dining tables for six and eight filled a third of the space. What looked like gaming tables still being set up took up another section, while a large area of the floor, in front of a small stage with musicians, remained open. Modest centerpieces, attractive mineral formations, graced the tables—a signature Firen touch in their entertaining. The only flowers in the room were from the sparse, leggy canera bush, native to the Firen region. Long branches, smothered in clusters of little copper-red blossoms, gathered in tall vases near the musicians' stage, the doors, and to mark the gaming area. Their rusty, floral fragrance perfumed the room, much stronger than one would expect from such modest flowers.

Marsh led her to Brels. "Excuse me, Guild Master."

"Arli-bug!" He extended both hands and drew her a step nearer, studying her face, his eyes narrowing.

She blushed and turned the still somewhat bruised side of her face away.

His voice dropped to something only she could hear. "You had someone look over you?"

"Matté's trainer. It's fine."

"Nothing serious when you hit your head, then?"

"He said I avoided a concussion."

Brels turned her chin back with two fingers to examine her cheek. "Looks like he did something for the bruises, too."

"Thank you for stepping in as you did."

"Too little, too late. You paid the price for me avoiding standard passenger protocols. I didn't expect that. Second time since we met that things have gone sideways for you. Do such things happen often with you?" His tone was teasing, but the words landed hard.

"What's an arli for but to lead in a storm?" she shrugged.

Brels sighed. "I'm glad you came tonight. Would you be up to doing me a small favor?"

That explained the invitation. "If you need transport, you could have sent a message."

"We can talk about transport more later. But that's not what I need right now. Matté there has never been to a proper Lighten celebration, and he looks like a frightened puppy turned out among the hounds. He's at loose ends at an event with no written protocols, especially when he's got to be cautious about the appearance of connection. If you'll accept a spot on my staff for the evening, then I can assign you to be his assistant for the event. Will make it far easier on both of us."

"What sort of assistance do you expect?" She slipped back half a step. "I am a pilot, not connected with the Comfort Guild, despite my mother's affiliations. Those are not services I offer—"

"That is not what I meant. Give me a moment." He tapped his module, and hers pinged. "Check the contract I sent you. The parameters are clear. Stand with him, explain what is going on so the stick up his Dextrine ass doesn't create offense. Help him participate in the festivities. He honored us in the fight, and I want to help him save face here. Dextrines are notoriously bad at these events."

"Wouldn't one of the arena hospitality specialists be more appropriate?"

"Many of them have affiliations with the Comfort Guild. He made it clear he does not want to be Recorded in that company. You'll help me with this, yes?" Brels gestured to her module.

He was right, the contract was very clear. No "services" outside the event proper were required. Even the requirements within the conference room were spelled out clearly, with no doubt that she was acting in the capacity of Brels' administrative assistant. Not a role she had ever considered, but for one night, it would be acceptable. Moreover, he offered an acceptable rate for the service, which would go a long way to making life more comfortable while she sorted out her future. She signed the contract and sent it back.

Brels smiled broadly and waved Matté toward them. "Here you go, Matté, a familiar face, as promised." Brels pointed to Ari, then wandered back to the receiving line.

Matté had not come as he had been in the ring. He couldn't have tolerated the attention his wrestling singlet would have earned him. He was well-looking enough in his casual, sand-colored suit and open-neck shirt.

"Congratulations on an excellent match. I imagine your trainer has done a proper job putting you back together afterwards. Your ribs took a real pounding. Nice touch that he even left you with a few bruises for show."

"Thanks, I'll tell Beny you approved. It was an excellent match, all around. Pogo proved his honest name in the ring." He avoided looking her in the eye.

"Are you comfortable with this arrangement? For what it's worth, he caught me as off-guard as you."

"He told me he'd ensure there would be someone I was comfortable with to walk me through this."

"Do I count for that? He's added me to his staff for the purpose, but if you don't want that, I'm sure the contract can be canceled."

"You're on his staff for this event?"

"Here, you can look at the specifics if you're interested." She offered her module.

The tense lines on his face eased as he read. "He is specific about the boundaries of your ... uh ... responsibilities and services rendered."

"I would not be standing here talking about it if he weren't." She stared straight into his eyes. "Look, Joco is crazy strict about who he admits as connections. Maybe to the point of ridiculousness. I'm used to that. I understand how complex such things can get when you're in a position like yours."

"I suppose you do." He scratched the back of his head, as though he were thinking it over. "It isn't a personal statement, you understand?"

"We all have to protect ourselves the best we can. People are often not what they seem. It is better for both of us that everything is spelled out clearly. I don't need people thinking that they can get to you through me, either."

"That's a solid point." Matteo frowned and sighed. "The contract is absolutely clear on the nature of our interactions, and without a handler I am likely to offend someone—"

"So that's what Beny is really here for." She laughed. "He's overqualified to be a trainer."

"I'd deny it, but you're right. I'm not good in these settings, and worse at doing what I'm told."

"Joco says the same thing about me." She glanced back at her module. "You ready to do this, then?"

"If the terms are favorable for you, yes."

She tapped a quick message to Brels. A moment later, he patted his module and glanced at her with a nod. "I think it is settled, then. You ought to return to the reception line. It seems a bit of a crowd has gathered to wait for you."

He groaned, but made his way to the line. She followed in his shadow.

"Wondered if you'd ditched us entirely." Pogo, also out of his wrestling gear and in a casual suit, stepped back to allow him space through the waiting throng. "I present to you, Matteo, Lord Heir Timnon of Dextra."

Matté bowed, and the surrounding group made their introductions.

Pogo turned to Ari, head cocked and eyebrow raised. He too sported decorative bruises, and he pulled his arm a little closer to his chest. The question—was it really sore or was that reflex in memory of the pain from the injury?

"You put Brels up to this, didn't you?" Ari asked.

"Look at him. Matté wouldn't survive an hour in these hostile waters without help."

"And you thought I could be of help? You know how many parties I attend?"

"You're a native, this is informal, you'll be fine. The important thing is that it keeps you in Brels' eye a little longer. You need to work for him." Pogo leaned closer and whispered, "I'm supposed to take a remote assignment soon, and I need a replacement."

"I'm no bodyguard and not interested in that assignment."

"Already got someone to fill the bodyguard spot. Trouble is, Joco's got such a lock on pilots, assigning them all himself now, that it's damn near impossible to get someone who meets our quals. You impressed me and drowning few do."

Her cheeks burned. "Brels said he wants to talk to me. And when he does, I'll listen."

"Good enough. Reception lines closing now. The main meal won't be out for an hour; grab Matté and help me open up the entertainment."

Brels made his way to the front of the room, with Pogo close behind.

"They want you to go, too." Ari tapped Matté's shoulder and whispered, "It's time for the entertainment to begin."

He disengaged himself from the conversation and followed her toward the stage. "Dare I ask what that looks like in this sort of event?"

"I haven't been given a schedule or much of any information, but I've got some solid guesses on what to expect. And before you ask, yes, you do have to participate in at least some of it. I can help you figure out the most important bit, and the ones that will make you the least miserable."

"That's kind of you." Matté stalked past her, then paused. "Okay, that sounded really pissy, but I do appreciate it."

"If you lose a little of the stick up your ass you might even enjoy some of this. It might not be what you're used to, but not everything has to be pomp and protocol to be fun." She folded her arms across her chest and not-quite glared at him.

"I don't know the rules—"

"If you mean expectations and how to succeed, or at least be looked upon favorably, you're already doing better than you think with that fight. That's why you got invited to this. You've got solid instincts if you let go and trust them a little."

His brow furrowed as if she'd tried to explain the physics of getting into low planetary orbit.

"It's going to be fine, just breathe. I won't let you drown in all this, now that I have a sense of what you need. No one here is looking for you to trip up. This is meant to be fun and to celebrate something that should be good for all of us."

He blinked several times, as if the concept was utterly foreign to him. "I'll try." He continued up to the front with her half a step behind and to the side.

Brels stood at a podium on the stage and turned on the microphone. "Firen Mines welcomes all of you to celebrate with us. To new connections and new understandings." He raised an opened hand in the air.

"New connections and understanding," the crowd echoed.

"Dinner will be set out in an hour. In the meantime let's show our guest some true Lighten hospitality! The card and game tables will be open shortly, but first, let's teach Matté how to bring in the storm."

The crowd applauded.

"Arli—fitting we have an arli to lead the storm, no?—" Brels chuckled.

Ari cringed and suppressed the urge to glare. It wasn't Brels' fault the joke was old and tired beyond reason. To him, it was new and humorous. She'd have to remember to include a clause against that in any contracts she made in the future.

"Arli, grab Pogo there, and you six there, demonstrate how it's done for our guest."

Pogo offered his hand.

She looked over her shoulder at Matté. "Pay attention. It's not hard, but you're going to have to join in after the demo. I'll partner with you and help you out."

Pogo took her arm and ushered her into a clearing on the floor.

The group of eight arranged themselves into two lines, facing each other. She with her partner, Pogo, across from her, headed the two lines. Brels signaled three musicians, on keyboard, strings, and wind, who sat on the platform behind him, and they launched into the familiar spritely tune that went with this dance ... game ... competition ... how did one describe this?

Pogo extended his right hand, and she took it in her right. They turned halfway around until facing the next dancer on the opposite side. She extended her left hand, and that dancer took it, turning her back to the middle in time with the music. She took Pogo's right hand once again to repeat the moves and turned halfway until she could take hands with the next dancer down the line with her left hand.

The simple version would have had her and Pogo progress all the way to the end of the line, before the next couple would take their turn down the line. Instead, though, the second couple began their progression as she and Pogo joined right hands to turn the second time. That was the beginning of the "storm" that would follow them all the way down the line. When she and Pogo turned the last couple in line, they rejoined the line at the end just in time to turn the couple coming down the line behind them.

When done as a dance, the music would end when she and Pogo made their way back up to the front of the line again. This, however, wouldn't be the dance version, but the competitive one. So, if a pair of dancers made a mistake, they would exit the set when they reached the end. And the music would continue, increasing in tempo until only four pairs of dancers remained.

As Pogo and Ari made it back to the head of the lines, Brels signaled the musicians to pick up the tempo. All the dancers crossed their hands and took hands with their partners in tight grasps, elbows held close to their bodies. They turned in pace with the music, faster and faster, until only one couple remained standing.

She locked hands and eyes with Pogo, as they spun with the music, the room behind them turning into a shimmering blur, meshing with the music, until the music cut and the audience clapped wildly. Apparently, they were the ones left standing.

They dropped hands panting, hands braced on thighs, the room still swirling. Pilots, with better-than-average equilibrium, had an advantage in Bringing the Storm. Ironic, that.

"Now you've seen how it's done, Matté, take Arli there, and try it yourself. Storm-bringers, line up behind them." Brels waved the group into motion.

A partner claimed Pogo, and Matté took his place across from her. She blinked, willing the room to stop moving. "Did you catch the steps well enough?"

"I think so. You going to keep me from making a fool of myself?"

"Depends on how hard you try."

He laughed. "Not what makes its way through the events I get invited to."

"All the more reason to try it. Maybe bring it back home and horrify a few of the proper types."

He laughed harder. Seemed like the sort of thing he didn't do often enough.

The music started. "Here we go." She extended her right hand, and they began.

Chapter 24

TAKING ARLI'S HAND WAS strange enough. The way she smiled set his teeth on edge, with alarms of danger all around. But he had the assurance of her contract with Brels. She was not trying to entrap him into anything. She was there to help him not look like an idiot. Something he very much needed.

Dextrines of his Rank rarely touched those outside their close circles, and even then, only in ways tightly governed by clear protocols. Which he shattered in the bout with Pogo, offering a given name, touching hands and fists outside of the actual fight itself. No doubt those would make the news feeds and provide him no end of grief.

But if he balked at her offer, it would give offense. Probably embarrass her and worse still, Brels. Too late to back out now.

He took her hand—small and calloused, but delicate, dainty even, not what he'd have expected for a pilot. She guided him as they turned to the music, slow and lyrical. It might have been proper in an elegant ballroom at home.

Surprisingly graceful, she floated through the turn as though her feet did not touch the floor. Luckily, the next dancer extended a hand toward him, just in time to snap him out of his distracted reverie. Focus! Concentrate on not being an embarrassment to his entire planet by disqualifying them from the dance-game, whatever this was, in the first few moments.

Arli met him in the middle with an extended hand. Back home, the faraway look she wore would have suggested she was well on her way to hoping for a betrothal. More likely, she was getting lost in the dance. He couldn't fault her for that. There was something hypnotic about the repetition of the music, the steps, turn after turn, meeting each new dancer to return to a familiar face, with eyes so soulful and deep. How unusual they were, a unique clear brown like the crystals on the dining tables.

A third of the way down the line, the music's tempo picked up. He stumbled when he noticed, but extended hands and the reassurance of those familiar eyes brought him into the new rhythm. Still elegant, but more energetic, they twirled down to meet more dancers.

He glanced up the line as the tempo changed again. Already a fair number of dancers had dropped out. Had he picked up the simple repetition that easily, or was Arli that adept at cueing him that she kept his steps right without him noticing?

Probably the latter.

The next tempo change hit as they reached the end of the line and had a moment's pause.

"You need to pay attention to the new beat. This is faster than you expect. It works best if we switch to a firm, full-handed grip. Pull your elbows close to your body to keep the turn tight. And if you focus your eyes on mine you won't get so dizzy." She extended her hand, easing him into the new pace. She was right, it was fast and the secure hold helped.

But more secure meant more personal. Keeping elbows close meant they stood much closer, giving the appearance she was more than his handler here. But she knew that wasn't true, and there were Records and paperwork to prove the case. This was not a trap. Even if he couldn't relax, this wasn't the fight ring where he was waiting for the next assault.

The next dancer he met offered a fully-extended arm, and he barely made it around in time to catch Arli's hand. She locked eyes with him, elbows in tight, and held him firm as they spun, releasing him just in time to catch the next dancer.

No more elegant floating to the music, spinning and twirling one after the other—they were flying, feet barely touching the floor. She, his copilot, navigating him through unfamiliar terrain. But not heavy-handed—an equal in the endeavor—something he had never felt before. Always, his Rank set him apart, but here, where he allowed the movement and rhythm to write their own rules and protocols for all to follow, he was among equals.

Free. It felt so free. The thought caught in his throat, leaving it almost too full to breathe.

"We're down to four pairs now." She spoke through their next turn. "Follow me, take a tight grip, elbows in, and keep up with the music." She crossed her hands and grabbed his in a secure grip. From the corner of his eyes, he made out Pogo, taking hands with his partner the same way. The first rotation, he failed to focus on Arli's eyes. Big mistake. He found her gaze and held on for survival.

Few people looked him in the eye—it was considered rude, even arrogant, to look someone of higher Rank in the eye. When was the last time—had there ever been a time when he had permitted such an unfiltered personal connection? Not even Iantha looked him full in the face like this.

The couple at the far end stumbled and staggered away. And another. Now it was only them and Pogo and his partner. Twice more around and the music shifted again, to a pace more sustainable. The crowd gathered around, clapping in time with the music, each beat driving them on past exhaustion and dizziness and good sense.

Without warning, the music stopped, the clapping stopped, leaving an aching void into which all four dancers fell into each other, holding each other, laughing, as the room continued to whirl around them.

Something in the back of his mind screamed in horror at the personal proximity and informality of it all. But splintering shards. This had actually been fun! What would happen when Beny coaxed that truth out of him?

"Two winners tonight!" Brels cried into the microphone. "Fitting, so fitting. The game tables are open and first bites are with the circulating servers. Enjoy! Make merry and celebrate with us." Brels dismissed the crowd with a wave and made his way down to them. "Well done, all of you. So, Matté, how did you like 'Bringing in the Storm'?"

"Something I will never forget. Thank you for including me." He caught Arli's gaze—such a look of pleasure and abandon on her face. "Thank you for taking me under your wing. I'm sure I would have embarrassed all of us without your help."

She ducked her head, embarrassed and awkward, blushing, and drew back half a step. "You are welcome."

Had he said something wrong? Was he not supposed to voice such things? No, that didn't seem to line up with what Beny had told him …

In some ways, it looked as if she were on as unfamiliar ground as he. She might be a native, but not to big celebrations and important company. And if anyone could understand the awkwardness associated with that, it was him.

"Have you found your footing yet?" Brels examined them carefully. "We are far from finished. There is much more to come."

Brels led him through a dizzying array of introductions, for which he would never remember the names, food tastings even more impressive than what he'd enjoyed at Firen HQ, and even an impromptu lesson in knife throwing as Pogo and Arli were drawn into a competition with several of the local champions. Arli surprised him with the competitive nature the contest drew out of her. Neither she nor Pogo won, but they made a good showing for themselves. And Matteo hadn't made a fool of himself when he conceded to be tutored through his first knife throws.

Another dancing game started up, but after Arli warned him it was too complex for a beginner, he resigned himself to observe as she and Pogo took to the floor. That was harder to watch than it had any reason being. Must be the effects of trying to force far too much into the day. At least the feelings were fleeting and quickly brought under proper regulation.

Finally, though, the adrenaline from the fight and the celebration ran out, and Brels put him in the care of his hospitality team to get him to his suite before he fell down.

He hardly noticed the hospitality specialist who escorted him back and implied she and her associates were available for his comfort if he wished.

He did not.

He staggered inside and locked the door behind him. Then checked the lock twice to be sure.

Soul-crushing exhaustion descended. Which might well have laid him out on the ridiculous white floor near the door except for the bewildering realization that he'd had more fun in the last few hours than he had in years. He leaned hard against the white wall and raked unkempt hair back from his face.

"I was wondering when you'd return." Beny sat, stiff and straight, on the couch near the kitchen and looked up from his module.

"I'm sorry you missed it. Brels is an excellent host." Matteo staggered into the lounge space, struck by the night landscape displayed on the false windows across the back wall. How had it gotten so late? "You did a solid job on the ribs. Didn't notice them most of the night. I'd never have made it through the first hour without that help." He fell onto the plush white couch across from Beny. "Brels hired a handler to get me through the event. It went well, though our Media is going to have a field day, no matter what."

"That was considerate—but he could have saved the effort and had me do the job." So Beny was indeed pissed not to have been included in the invitation.

"You'd never have gotten me through that." Matteo cued his module to "Bringing in the Storm" and handed it to Beny.

His brows climbed higher and higher as he watched. "That's quite the party game, isn't it? Your pilot friend cleans up pretty well."

"I hadn't noticed."

"I'm calling shit on that. Of course you did. I caught the way you looked at her."

Later, he'd chew on that more later.

Matteo trudged through the thick carpet, feet nearly too heavy to lift high enough to get to Beny's couch, and pulled the module out of Beny's hands. "Here's her contract with Brels. No services outside that event room."

"That's a well-written contract. I'm impressed." He scrolled through more of the event Records. "Seems like she did a decent job making you look open and personable. You even looked like you were having fun."

"Would you believe it if I said I was?"

"I'd say you were drunk, except I can tell you heeded my warning not to drink after the osteogen on your ribs." Beny handed the module back. "You need to watch yourself with her. Even with that contract, it's not hard to imagine what our Media is going to do with those images of you two dancing or competing or whatever it was."

"What can we do to lock those down?"

"I've been working on those options all evening, just in case. There's a fair chance it'll work, but something's going to leak.

It always does. And yes, as soon as it does, I'll make sure that contract is public as well. That's the best we can do. It helps that she'll stay out here, out of the way of all but our most determined Media."

"She was decent. Don't want to see her hurt for that."

"That's why I should have been there with you. This sort of thing makes my job exponentially more difficult." Beny leveled an "*I told you so*" glare to emphasize the point.

"I only received the invitation after you finished patching me up. It's not like I was trying to ditch you like the rest of the babysitters."

"I know, but we've got to be careful. Things are complicated." Beny's glare softened. "Still, I'm glad you enjoyed yourself a bit. That doesn't happen often."

"Sounds like you're about to burst that bubble with bad news." Matteo pressed his temples; there was a headache somewhere in there waiting to break out.

"There's a strong pot of java waiting in the kitchen. There's a lot to talk about."

"Any chance that can wait until morning?"

"You're not drunk, so no, it shouldn't wait." Beny headed to the kitchen wall and poured two generous mugs. "Should I study that celebration for tips for our party planners?"

"Right after we schedule an informal supper. That would probably bring an end to proper civilization. I will give them credit, though, they know how to have fun."

"There's something in the Lighten information packet about 'making memories,' they call it. Seems that they are keen to create memorable experiences in the good times, so when it all goes to shit in the next storm, there's something to remember."

"Not the worst tradition I've ever heard."

Beny handed Matteo a cup. Strong, bitter, and not sweet enough. Beny never added enough sweetening. "I suppose you can't fault wanting pleasant memories."

Something about the way Beny emphasized the last word. "I'm not kidding, get over it. I'm not mixed up with her. And I'm not planning for it either."

"But the Records leave me wondering. And if I'm wondering ... you know what the Media can do with that. The way you looked at her, the way she looked at you, you'll claim it was dizziness, but still. You're killing me, cousin, you're killing me. Couldn't you have gotten, I don't know, Pogo to coach you through it?"

"One, there's no way this side of Laythe's Woods that soul-catching pilot-enforcer would ever consent to being my handler. And two—"

"She is a much better dance partner, for sure. Yeah, you and Pogo would have turned it into another bout. Not that anyone else will understand that ..."

"Don't you have more important news than that to torment me with?" Matteo took a deep draw from his mug. "You need to learn how to brew this stuff, Beny. It's just this side of un-drinkable."

"It'll keep you awake if my news doesn't. That's all I care about."

"Okay, you've got my attention." Matteo sat up straight, back screaming with the effort. "What has our ancestors' bones in such a knot that it can't wait?"

"Where do you want me to start, close to home or across the system?"

"Sarding shit." Matteo slammed down his mug on the nearby table. "Thera?"

"The media releases or the short form?"

"What do you think?"

"Short form, then. The biggest news of the day is that the Conservatives have made a strong showing in this week's elections, ousting some of our strongest allies from their seats."

Now he was awake. With a thundering headache joining the party for good measure. "How bad?"

"Not enough to have a majority, not yet anyway, but the Progressive majority is pretty slim now, and a handful could shift Thera back to their old policies. The Conquest Manifesto doesn't seem far from making a glorious return."

"Damn. That's going to make a mess of things."

"No one's going to escape untouched at this rate. Our Unity Bloc's going to suffer, Lighten economy is going to take a hit, Fleet defenses against the Raiders are going to turn inside out, since they'll be pulling resources out of Fleet to concentrate them around Thera. And that's scratching the surface."

Matteo picked up the mug and rolled it between his hands. "There's a solid chance the Conservatives are going to have enough trouble consolidating power, so they are just as likely to ignore Fleet until they sort themselves out."

"And that could give us and Lighten enough time to organize ourselves to deal with the Raiders?"

"That's my theory." Matteo ventured another gulp of the bitter java. It burned all the way down. "I'm worried that the Traditional Old Guard are going to recruit the Raiders to their cause with promises that making conquests on Lighten and Dextra will restore their honor as Therans."

"You're the one who studied military strategy, not me, so I don't have a clue. But considering how the Raiders stole the Celios Station from its orbit around Thera and it still hasn't been found, they've got the chops to deal some real damage to us, especially if the Old Guard is funding them."

"That's why we need the Progressives to keep power. They're the ones who put up the orbital stations in the first place, which was supposed to have proven to the Old Guard that the Conquest Manifesto could be turned to space exploration instead of conquering and reconquering the same territory over and over." Matteo's head pounded in time with each word. Talking about Therans and their bloodlust for conquest did that.

"Which leads me to problem number two."

"Thera wasn't enough?"

"Council has their knickers in a knot about the Theran shake-up and has gotten very interested in our defense against the Raiders and all things military. Which turned up some interesting information about those two Guild Masters out there itching to beat the ever-loving crap out of each other."

Matteo rubbed his temples. "Get me something for this headache before you start that story?"

"One step ahead of you." Beny pulled a packet of red and blue headache tabs from his pocket and tossed them to Matteo. Sometimes it was scary how well Beny knew him. "You've already figured out that the Mining Guild and the Transport Guild aren't the best of friends. The miners have the controlling interest in both the House of Guilds and the House of Regions around here, and the Trade Minister is one of theirs."

"Old news."

"Here's the new part. The latest bone of contention is that the Transport Guild has a lock on all transport and flight credentials, vehicles, and parts. They control all of it. Nothing lifts off or moves around here without Guild clearance. So, all the miners' pilots are Transport Guild loyal—or at least they say they are to keep their credentials. However, anything with weapons has to be staffed with Enforcers who answer to the Ministry of Order. They are the only ones cleared to manage the weapons. The miners want better weapons to protect their claims and their shipments. So, pilot-enforcers like your friend Pogo there are incredibly valuable to the miners—and in short supply. As are armed vehicles."

Matteo covered his eyes with his hand and squeezed his temples. "And you're about to tell me Iantha's involved because of the military surplus Evering deals in?"

"Evering isn't cleared to sell weapons but—I'll come back to that in a minute. But remember, the Transport Guild controls every damn vehicle in the place. No one is supposed to be selling anything that moves, or parts for them, without it going through Transport. Now for the fun part—there's a major debate going on in the Lighten legislature about what constitutes a vehicle."

"You mean like an armed transport?"

"That would be one possibility, but it isn't a huge leap to believe the mines might jump at the chance of getting their hands on mobile weaponry, like military fighters, classed as weapons, not vehicles, so that they could be staffed by their own Enforcers, not Transport-Guild-loyal pilots." Beny tapped fingertips together before his chest.

"And that's what their fight is really about?"

"Sure looks like it to me. If Joco gets the seat as Chairman of House of Guilds, he'll have the power to block the classification measure and keep control as it is now. But if Brels wins, then things get interesting."

"So, then Lighten could be acquiring arms at a whole new level, maybe even establish a proper military, and the whole balance of power in the system could shift away from the Raiders—and the Old Guard Therans. Damn."

"It gets even better." Beny's brows flashed high on his forehead.

"I swear you're writing this to sell as a drama to the media feeds."

"I wouldn't come up with this. I'd stick to hospital drama."

Matteo threw a decorative white pillow at him.

Beny batted it away. "If you're going to be that way about it, then I'll let you find out about Corbel on your own."

Matteo screwed his eyes shut and scratched his head. "Can't I skip that?"

"I know how you feel about Lord Timmi's—"

"Lord Timmi?" Matteo laughed until he couldn't breathe. "You didn't just say that."

"Apparently that's what Lightens call him, and following local customs is polite, right?" Beny chuckled. "In any case, you are well aware of how he carries a grudge."

"A grudge? A single grudge? Take your pick. He has something against Lord Pandier because he got himself named Second Minister when Grandfather wanted the position. He resents Lord Routel for supporting Lord Pandier's bid despite the fact that Grandfather challenged Routel's ascension to Clan Lordship when his sister Lady Routel proved herself unfit." Matteo stood and paced the length of the lounge. "Let's see. He resents the entire existence of Clan Ravas, having informed Lord Ravas that his Clan was too small to be recognized as a clan and should be a small family under Tormeg. And when Lord Tormeg had the wisdom and diplomacy not to agree, he took up a grudge against Tormeg, too."

"Lord Timmi is a touchy old rock troll with a long memory. We've established that. But regarding Corbel—whom you have not yet mentioned in your list of offenses—he may have a point there. Corbel manipulated those trade negotiations to put Timnon in an unfavorable position with Lighten's Delvin mines."

"Yes, that was a bad spell, especially with the grudge being mutual. I can see Grandfather's point on that one, though if you ever tell him such a thing, I will deny it with your dying breath."

Beny snorted and raised open hands. "Threat understood. No worries."

"Trouble is he needs Corbel in order to make up a majority voting bloc in the High Council. Which is why he pressed so hard on that damned betrothal with Iantha after Firen started paying attention to Evering. Trying to get in bed with Corbel and Firen in one masterful stroke of the matchmaker's pen."

"You're sarding kidding me." Beny's entire countenance shifted, eyes wide and grim.

"What did you think it was about?"

"I feel like such an idiot." Beny's head fell back against the couch and he laid his arm across his face. "I swear by the ancestral crypt, I had no idea it was solely a political machination."

"What would give you the idea that it was anything else?"

"Dad. He gave me this long diatribe about what an ungrateful wretch you were, not appreciating all the effort Grandfather had gone to with the best matchmakers on the planet to find a suitable woman with whom you would be compatible and likely to develop a long-term affection."

Matteo laughed, but it only brought a bitter taste to his mouth. "Of all people, you believed that?"

"I wanted to. With the situation I'm stuck in with Marietta, sure as the Key Minder's question, I wanted to."

"It's that bad with her?"

"I've gotten word from some pals at the hospital that could spell the end of the betrothal."

Matteo grimaced, the hair on the back of his neck prickling. "*That* sort of news? And I assume that means it can't be yours?"

Beny shook his head.

"Kayavan's bones! Beny, I had no idea. I'm so sorry."

"Maybe just as well, she and I are not as compatible as the matchmakers suggested. It's best that there's a clear reason to draw a line under it and consider it done."

"The matchmakers had to have been paid off to declare Iantha and I were a sound prospect. At the best of times, she was so diffident, I wanted to scream. No, she isn't our Rank, but if we bonded, she would be. But even then, I think she'd still be walking behind me and agreeing with everything I said, at least in public."

"Which is of course what Lord Timmi says is your due."

"Except I now know full well she'd be working her own networks and contacts to do her own thing behind my back rather than risk having me disagree with her. I can't live like that. I need someone to walk beside me, as an equal, who I can trust to have my back when someone's gunning for it, who can help me lead the sarding mess I'm going to inherit when it's least auspicious."

"Iantha was never that person." Beny scrubbed his face with his hands.

"What did you uncover?"

"Beyond the issues with Lord Lemos?" Beny's lip curled up in a sneer, probably as much about his betrothal as about Matteo's. "Some strange stuff going on with Corbel. It's hard to put my finger on, but you remember how I get twitchy when stories don't line up? I've been seeing quite a bit that doesn't quite match where it should. I haven't been able to get into Grandfather's files—"

"Yet?"

"I'll get there, but no, not yet." Beny took a long draw from his mug. "I have been digging through what I can access and I've got some serious questions about what Corbel is about."

"Lord Corbel, or Evering Industries?"

"Is there a difference?"

"I had thought so. I was under the impression that Evering was Iantha's pet project to prove herself to Lord Liner. She wants him to support her to Lord Corbel. She claimed it was because she wanted to be a more worthy partner in—" Matteo used his fingers to draw quotes in the air—"our bond."

"A convenient story. What do you understand about Evering's business with Firen?" Beny stared into his mug, brow furrowing.

"She hasn't told me too much about it, just that they were supplying essential mining equipment to Firen."

"Makes me wonder what that essential equipment might be. Protection seems essential, doesn't it?"

"After what happened on our way to Firen, it does." Matteo tried to wash away the acrid taste in his mouth with more java. It didn't help.

"Yeah, I didn't like those Records at all."

"Is there anything about me you don't study?"

"Don't ask questions you don't want answers to." Beny dodged Matteo's gaze.

Yeah, he probably didn't want a better idea of how much his cousin, handler, and friend knew about him. Even the illusion of a little privacy was comforting.

"Given where this could go, it could be for the best that you've broken things off. Timnon doesn't need to be in bed, literally or figuratively, with Corbel, for all that Lord Timmi is going to lose his mind over it."

"How long do you think it's going to take to figure Corbel and Evering out?"

"I've been working on this for nearly a month. I'm pretty close."

"And you didn't tell me?" Matteo slapped the couch beside him. What an unsatisfying thud.

"Look, I bought my Dad's rhetoric on it being a great match for you, and I didn't want to throw fire on it without being absolutely certain of things. I didn't want to take something from you that would be good for you."

"I can't hate you for that," but it was a little tempting. Sometimes, Beny really took too much upon himself. "But if things are that serious, we need to move faster on finding out what's going on there. And I know how to do it."

Chapter 25

Ari turned off all her alarms and collapsed into the inconvenient little sleep pod in the pilots' lounge that always seemed available when she needed one. She slept long and hard until her rumbling stomach forced her to give up her sanctuary in search of sustenance.

Muzzy fog circled around her head, and her body ached being too many hours abed. But alarms wouldn't have woken her, given her level of exhaustion last night. Brels knew how to throw a party and make people feel at home. Yes, he had planners hired for the event, but it bore his signature.

Matté seemed to enjoy himself with more than a little coaching. Once he stopped being so afraid of making some unforgivable mistake, he proved to be personable and in possession of a good sense of humor. Brels, Matté, and Pogo all came away from the evening looking good. What was more, she had enjoyed herself, too, and had been paid as agreed after the party wrapped up. What more success could she have asked for?

She gathered a tray from the mess counter and curled up at her favorite table near the window with honey-sweetened fruit-and-nut-laden porridge and heavily sweetened tea. Well past sunrise now, halfway through the morning, heat shimmered off the paved vehicle parking fields around Anara. Kayavan's star—yes, it was a comet, but everyone called it a star—hung in the morning sky, an omen of storms on the horizon.

A tiny glimmer of hope rose, though, that one day she might be working for Brels. He ended the night with a reminder that he had something to discuss with her after his bout with Joco. Of course, it made sense that such a thing would have to wait until the fight was over. Even so, knowing he hadn't forgotten was encouraging.

And it would give her a little time to consider her response.

Brels was a man who got things done, which meant he would have big expectations of all who worked for him. He seemed to demand a lot of his people, but not unreasonably so. On the whole, his people seemed not only to respect him, but to like him. But she'd seen his response with the mistakes made by his enforcers and it was a little intimidating. He didn't lose control of his temper, though, and that was significant.

But she had a long history of getting under Joco's skin, and eventually she'd find herself sideways with Brels, too. It was inevitable. What then? What would he be like when she stepped too far over his lines? More importantly, would it be worse than Joco?

It shouldn't be so hard to consider leaving Joco's dominion. A sensible and reasonable decision—that scared her senseless at the same time. What if he was right? She was too rebellious, too irregular, not up to the "big things" he worked so hard to keep her out of. What if Brels didn't need a storm-bringer on his staff and cut her loose?... What if—

Her module trilled with an incoming message.

It wasn't Brels or Joco. Good, good. She needed to break that train of thought, though. Maybe breakfast would help—she'd been so wrapped up in her own head she'd neglected the tray in front of her.

She took her time eating, but the module buzzed a reminder of an unread message in queue. Time to get on with things. She shoved her tray in the recycler and checked the incoming message stack.

A summons to the Sporting Officials' office? Drown it all! That couldn't be good. Joco had to be involved. That was the only thing that made sense. There was only one Joco-related reason that they would want to talk to her.

And it would be a sarding shit-storm in a sollert skin.

Breathe, just breathe. No amount of panic would help now, but a calm, careful course might.

Breathe.

And get down to the Officials' office as fast as possible. She'd already kept them waiting too long.

She followed the yellow Sporting Wing stripe all the way to the end of the wing, where she'd been ordered to report: a tall door, surrounded by a black frame, with an access pad to the left and signal lights above. And nothing but a door number to indicate its identity. Exactly the sort of portal to make her feel welcome and safe.

She tapped her invitation code into the access pad. The door slid open, revealing a waiting room. Chairs, all metal with no padding, lined gray-tiled walls that matched the larger gray tiles on the floor. Gray on gray on gray—the color of an incoming storm. A tall, black-lined door opposite the one she'd entered barred her from moving farther into the offices. A frosted reception window beside that door was tightly shut as well, almost as though she was an unwelcome guest.

Pogo, in his signature Firen-red flight suit, and Matté, in a light-colored casual suit, sat along the shorter left-hand wall.

Neither appeared at ease. There was only one reason that would bring them all together here. A level five shit-storm.

They both turned to look at her.

"I'm so sorry. It wasn't either of us. Or Brels." Pogo huffed under his breath and gestured to the chair between them.

"Beny didn't report it either." Matté grimaced. "The field is covered by Records equipment, one end to the other."

Yes, it was, but that didn't mean the automated reviews would have flagged the event. It wasn't the level of incident that would trigger an inquiry. Someone had to have nudged the algorithm along.

She sank into the hard, cold seat between them, hiding her face in her hands. With so much riding on the fight between the Guild Masters, far too many would be happy to see Joco disqualified.

Especially when he'd made it so easy.

She'd warned him. But why would he listen to a worthless little arli-bug?

The inner doors slid open, revealing a stocky, white-haired woman in a gray and yellow League Official's uniform. She hurried toward them with her module held ahead of her, like some sort of shield to distance her from the entire affair. "Thumbprints." She shoved the module at them.

They obliged, and the module pinged approval. Nice that someone was happy.

"Follow me." She led them through the inner doors, down a short, gray-tiled corridor and into a large, cold meeting room.

A U-shaped, white resin table that could seat twelve, maybe even sixteen, dominated the middle of the room. High-backed white chairs with gray padding lined the outside edge of the table. Two gray metal podiums faced each other, one inside the table U, one outside, as though the table were there to separate two complainants likely to come to blows. Considering how many fighters might have stood there, it wasn't a bad assumption.

Three stern, uniformed Sporting League senior officials, two men and a woman, sat to the left of the outer podium. They represented the three major sports leagues who competed at Anara, the Fighting League, the Ball Sports League, and the Athletics League, and wore insignias to identify their affiliations. They had all been champions in their own sports, making them uniquely able to adjudicate matters between competitors. Maybe that meant they would also be fair.

Joco, in a gray-brown suit, which hung off his lanky frame like a flag left out on a pole after a storm, sat to the right of the podium, a storm cloud ready to burst. His hands flexed in and out of fists and he ground his teeth when he caught sight of her. Not good signs.

Brels sat along the left-hand outside of the table, face chiseled in a dangerously neutral expression. His casual suit seemed far more formal when worn with that expression. Probably wise to keep the distance between Brels and Joco.

The white-haired junior official directed them to take their seats beside Brels. Pogo sat nearest, with Matté next, then Ari. She was happy to keep as much distance between her and Joco as she could.

The man wearing the crossed-fists insignia of the Fighting League on his tailored white jacket over gray pants rose. The jacket's garish yellow trim clashed with his deep olive-toned skin. Broad-shouldered and heavily muscled despite his approaching middle age, he wore five championship pins, one for each of the major Lighten fighting styles, under his insignia. Fighter's-style close-cropped, straight black hair framed his stern features. If anyone was going to preside over a matter involving Joco and Brels, he was by far the most appropriate choice.

"We will convene." The Fighting League representative's deep, resonant voice rang with an air of authority that did not bear questioning. "I am Risse, Chief of the Fighting League." He gestured at the officials beside him.

The woman wearing the symbol for level five storm winds on her jacket stood. Tall, lean, and very pale, her blonde, nearly white, hair was pulled back from her face in a high ponytail. "I am Nabil, Chief of the Athletics League."

Beside her, the wiry, golden-tan Ball Sports representative stood. "I am Ven, of the Ball Sports League. We will judge the complaint."

Nabil and Ven sat and looked at Risse. "Guild Masters, have you any objection to the council chosen to hear this matter?"

"And if I do?" Joco glared at Risse. He had lost to Risse in the ring the year before Risse retired to become a league official. Joco still resented the loss and Risse for dealing it.

"That is your prerogative. The matter can be referred to the local Enforcers' office for investigation, but they cannot hear it before the championship bout. As the one accused, Joco, you will be disqualified from the match as a result, unable to fight again until the matter is resolved. Is that agreeable?" So controlled and level, Risse's demeanor matched his style in the ring.

Joco grumbled. "No."

"And you, Guild Master Brels?"

"I am satisfied with the chosen council." Only the deepened creases beside Brels' eyes, and the deepening flush that glowed against his light, warm-toned skin, hinted at any disquiet.

"The Records will show both Guild Masters have accepted the arrangement." Risse nodded to the white-haired junior official who still stood at the far end of the U-shaped table, with formal Recording equipment in hand.

How had Ari missed her presence? She drew several deep breaths. Focus, don't allow Joco's ire to distract.

"Sources unconnected to any in this room have registered a complaint against Guild Master Joco, flagging Records from the Anara complex for review." Risse gestured to the junior official, probably to make sure the Records were ready to cast to the screen lowering behind him.

"False accusation to distract from the fight." Joco stared, narrow-eyed, at Ari. "Nothing has happened."

Ari rubbed her hand over her shoulders—was the chill from the climate control, or the tone of Joco's voice?

"The Records suggest otherwise, with initial automated reviews applying a charge of assault to the matter."

Joco rose, pounding the table. "You know this is a ploy to disrupt the fight. How dare—"

"An accusation for which you have no proof," Brels said mildly, eyes on Risse. "It is much better for me to win our bout, clearly and decisively. I don't want you disqualified, I want you pinned to the mat, preferably unconscious."

"Which sure as storms and Laythe's Wind ain't happening," Joco snarled.

"You will cease this behavior now, or risk proving the charge of being out of control, Guild Master. As I have already said, the Records were flagged by an individual unconnected to any of the parties related to the complaint, with no stake in the results of your bout with Guild Master Brels. Any reprisals on your part stemming from this inquiry will result in immediate disqualification from the Fighting League and legal charges being filed with the regional Enforcers." Risse spoke the words as though he meant them.

And he probably did, now. But, without an enforcement body to do the job attached to the Sporting Leagues, the chances of any follow-through actually happening were slim. Especially once they were back at the Ship Yard where Joco controlled all the Records.

"We will review the Records, then proceed with the inquiry." Risse gestured to the junior official at the back and took his seat.

The room lights nearest the screen behind Risse dimmed, and the familiar worn hull of her hauler on the debark field outside the Anara complex came into view. Doubtless caught from an automated Recorder, given the angle of the composite image.

Even though Records were a part of life, Joco kept such tight rein on everything in the Yard, she had never seen Records of herself before. The image of herself standing up to Joco felt surreal. A little arli flying straight into the face of a storm.

Foolish. It had been foolish to provoke him like that. She knew better. How else would he have responded when challenged?

She winced at the sound of flesh striking flesh and again at the way she cried out and cringed as he tore off her jacket, reaching for his belt. She fought to suppress a shudder.

Pogo leaned his shoulder into hers and Matté offered a quick glance, concern and encouragement in his eyes.

Was it possible—yes, this was the first time she'd ever seen anyone disapprove of the way Joco treated her. She'd have to think about that more later.

Joco snorted as they watched Brels and Pogo rush out of the hauler, to stand between her and Joco, and lead him off to the Anara complex. Matté exited in their wake and helped her up. The room lights brightened, and the Records faded away.

Just as well, she would rather never relive that experience again.

Risse stood. "Committee, you have seen compiled, but otherwise unaltered Records. Joco, take your place at the podium beside me. Witnesses, take the inner podium. Council, you may ask your questions."

Brels led the way to the podium inside the U-shaped table. They arranged themselves around the podium, with Brels in the center. Joco glowered at them all, but let his fiery gaze rest on her.

What chance she could avoid speaking?

Ven glanced at Risse and Nabil, who gestured for him to begin. "Why were the witnesses in the hauler in the first place?"

"We," Pogo glanced at Matté, "individually contracted her to fly us from Firen Headquarters to the arena. Sending you the contract now." He pulled out his module.

"Mine as well." Matté followed suit.

"Distributed to the evidence folder," the junior official muttered.

"I forbade you—" Joco looked like he was ready to jump over the table to get to her.

"Was there a contractual stipulation against taking outside work?" Nabil asked, glancing at her module. "Can you provide the contract to document the assertion?"

Joco appeared to send something, and the three officials stared at their module.

"We need the signed contract, not a blank generic form," Risse muttered and looked at Ari. "Can you provide that?"

"No, sir."

"You are required to provide all requested evidence, either here or in the Enforcers' court."

"I understand, sir. The contract does not exist." She swallowed hard and braced herself.

"You have it right there." Joco pointed at the council's modules.

"I was never offered a contract to sign. And if he believed a contract was in force, he would have paid me the initial down payment by now," Ari said. "Yard Records, if you could get them, will verify there was no contract drawn up for this trip. I have not been paid or compensated in any way."

"Yes, you have. The privilege of having me fly with you—"

"No, sir. You do not want me advertising that fact, or have you forgotten that conversation?" Breathe, remember to breathe.

Joco growled under his breath.

"Records will show no evidence of the alleged contract has been received." Risse turned his attention from the junior officer back to the witnesses. "Why were your passengers waiting in the hauler instead of immediately debarking as is the standard protocol?"

"Records were delayed at traffic control." Nice of Pogo to spare her from explaining. "Traffic control will confirm."

Nabil cleared her throat and looked at Ari. "You brought out a bag to Joco after he ... uh ... knocked on the hull. How did you know what he was after?"

"I flew him from the Paxton Ship Yard to the arena. He left his bag in the hauler when he debarked. I figured that was the only reason he'd be looking for me. I hoped to prevent ..." She sighed and touched her cheek.

Ven frowned—the first official to show some definite re-action. "Joco, the Records showed you threatened her be-fore you struck her. 'To leather her back' were your words. Why?"

Joco sneered. "You heard her insolence."

Lines creased Risse's forehead. "Insolence is not consid-ered a threat. Nor is it sufficient provocation for an assault."

"There was no assault." Joco threw open hands high.

Nabil knocked on the table. "You struck her, you cannot deny that. There was no self-defense involved."

"You heard the mouth on her. What would you do?" Joco pointed at Ari, hand shaking.

Nabil rolled her eyes. "Not that."

Ven traded sympathetic glances with Nabil. "Guild Mas-ter Brels, why did you leave the transport, knowing you were not cleared for debark?"

"I heard the altercation—"

"There was no altercation." Joco pressed both hands on the podium and leaned toward Brels.

"Forgive me, you are correct, an altercation is not one-sided." Brels' face darkened. "We heard her cry out and went to see what sort of threat might await us."

"Enforcer's job." Pogo pointed toward himself.

"But you?" Ven gestured at Brels. "Why? She is no con-nection to you."

"Simple hospitality requires no connection." Brels shot such a look at Joco! "It sounded like she might need help. I, we, were in a capacity to answer that need."

"Do you have a connection to Joco?" Risse tried to look Ari in the eyes.

"I work at the Yard. Joco claims no connection to me beyond my employment." Trying to force her into a settlement with Palmer didn't count as a connection.

"Is that true, Joco?"

"I recognize no connection to her."

"Despite her being the offspring of your officially-designated second woman, born well after the establishment of your relationship." Clearly Nabil did not approve of something about that arrangement. Not everyone was comfortable bringing in a second when an equal partnership was in place. After what she'd lived through, Ari had come to agree with that opinion.

"Her mother would not submit to proving paternity, so there was no reason to recognize her spawn." Joco looked past her, as though she did not exist. Not the first time she had endured that.

"But it is standard practice." Nabil was like a sollert on a carcass, now. Lovely.

"I do not recognize a connection to her."

"The lack of contract or payment for the flight, and your threat of ... correction, I suppose you would call it." Nabil rolled her eyes. "All imply a connection."

"I do not claim her. She told you herself." Joco punctuated the statement with his fist on the desk.

"He does not claim me, never has, and I have no expectation that he will." Ari turned her head and pulled her hair aside to reveal the scar behind her ear. "My mother's second man gave me this mark. Joco did not choose to alter it."

Brels gasped, and muttered something she could not make out under his breath, but it sounded disapproving.

Risse cleared his throat. "In that case, we have no alternative but to deem this an assault—"

"What!" Joco was shouting now. "There was no assault. Her mouth—"

"She is unconnected to you. She can say near anything she likes, and it gives you no right to raise a hand to her. Your actions against her are governed by laws of hospitality and civility, not domestic law." Risse seemed to struggle to maintain his composure.

Joco stepped back. "Connection changes that?"

"In this case, one connected to you by kinship might opt to ignore the matter as part of established domestic agreements."

"You engineered this to force my hand." Joco's face turned deep red beneath his dark, weathered tan. "You know what this will cost me?"

She closed her eyes and turned away. There was no reasoning with him in this state. "This isn't my fault. I warned you—"

"You disobeyed me, provoked me to this. Do you understand what this will mean—"

"I would have them ignore all this." She stared at her hands. No point in explaining the price she was going to pay for this inquiry. No matter how it turned out, it would only make it worse.

"Do you claim her as kin?" Nabil asked. "It is the only way for this event to be considered under domestic law and thus dismiss it."

Joco growled. "She is kin."

"Do you recognize the connection?" Risse turned to her and sighed. "It is your choice. You do not have to accept it."

And have Joco's ruin on her head? Oh yes, that was an appealing option. And it wasn't just Joco but the entire Guild that would suffer. Whether she liked the way he ran the Guild, the abrupt and contentious transitions that could ensue from Brels simply walking into the Chairman of Guilds' position would hurt real people who were trying to put food on the table and keep a roof over their heads.

That was not the hand she would pay forward.

Besides, no matter what she said, Joco was going to take her apart as soon as they returned to the yard where he could control the Records and there was no one to hold him accountable. And for now, at least, she had nowhere else to go. Maybe she would soon, but it wasn't safe to count on that now.

"You owe me, girl," Joco snarled.

Unfortunately, he was right. She did. He didn't have to tolerate a child who might have been seeded by another. He didn't have to teach her to fly, to give her a trade, or employ her. He'd offered hospitality. Meager though it was, it was hospitality. If she claimed to believe in paying things forward, she was obliged to do the same. "I accept the connection," she whispered.

Not that it would ever be a genuine connection. In name only. She knew better than to believe she could rely upon it or count it among her connections.

Brels looked at the floor, head shaking, and Pogo bristled. But they didn't want Joco disqualified any more than she did. They had a lot riding on the outcome of an honest fight, too.

Joco blew out a coarse breath.

"We will deliberate." The officials huddled together.

"Clear duress ..."

"... danger to the House of Guilds ..."

"Risk of reprisals ..."

"Under domestic laws ..."

Why did they put on this show? The need to properly establish the Chairman of Guilds was far more important than a few more bruises to a nameless pilot.

The council broke apart and Risse stood. "The committee accepts the petition. But consider yourself warned. The committee retains the right to disqualify the fight upon any further Record of out-of-control behavior." Words they had to say, but everyone knew had no teeth. Once Joco won and was installed as Chairman of the House of Guilds, Joco would retire from the ring and the Sporting Guild would have no influence over him.

"Understood."

"Inquiry dismissed. Joco, if you would remain a moment for Records to be completed. The rest of you—" Risse looked meaningfully at Ari, "may leave."

She bolted for the door like the frightened little arli-bug she was. Where was the nearest entry to those service corridors?

"Are you all right?" Pogo appeared at her shoulder.

"What do you think?" She walked faster.

There, the service door. She slammed her hand on the panel and it slid open. She ducked inside.

"You can slow down now, he's not going to follow. He won't jeopardize tomorrow's bout. He's not stupid."

She paused, sucking in a shuddering breath. Pogo was right. "I did what had to be done. There was no other choice, but it don't mean I won."

"You're right. There was no choice. You were set up. Why are you looking at me like that? You think I'd missed that?"

"Never thought anyone would say it out loud." She dragged her face across her flight jacket sleeve. "As soon as the fight is over and the Sporting Guild has no more hold on him, he's going to take me apart. Now that he's claimed me as kin, he's my leading connection. Are you familiar with what domestic law says about that?"

Pogo muttered under his breath. "Far too well. It happens in the mines, too. What do you think he's going to do?"

"He's going to strip me of all flight credentials and force me to settle with his partner's useless son, like my mother settled with Joco. I can't work without those clearances."

"I know Brels is interested in more than just your flying. The things you've done with your ship ... I'm sure—"

"Of what? Let me tell you what I'm sure of. I've got the man who controls my only hope of being independent waiting to swat me like a worthless little insect. And it doesn't matter how right it was to do as I did, there's going to be no one there to offer me hospitality when he strips me of the only resource I have." Her voice broke. Saying it made it so awful, so real. "Please, I really need some space right now." She waved him off and hurried to the pilots' lounge.

Chapter 26

MATTEO DID NOT SPEAK to his hospitality escort on the way back to his suite. What had just happened there was so ... unconscionable, yes, that was the word for it. His self-control wouldn't hold out in the face of small talk. And the hospitality team did not need to hear his opinions.

From all Beny had said and Matteo's own hurried study after the Trade Commission dinner, keeping Joco in the fight was critical to the perception of an informed election which maintained the fragile balance of power. If Arli's choices forced the Transport Guild Master to concede, it could, and probably would, result in severe retaliation against the entire mining industry.

Joco had a history of such things. One might argue such powerful reactions were essential to keeping the miners from running roughshod over all other concerns on Lighten. But Matteo questioned the long-run benefits of such tactics.

Though, technically, Arli walked away from the encounter with a valuable connection, the look on her face suggested she didn't believe it was a genuine connection. And he couldn't blame her for that. Worse, she would pay dearly for the "favor."

She was an insignificant pilot caught in the middle of a grudge match between two powerful forces unconnected to her. Bloody unfair and typical of the power games played at that level. Watching it unfold, all the while unable to do anything that wouldn't make things worse, could tear one apart. One reason so many Ranks kept their distance from "regular" folk.

He'd never wanted to be one of those, but this made it tempting.

"Do you require anything further?" The lead hospitality specialist, a fresh addition to his hospitality team, an attractive young woman with big green eyes, asked as they arrived at the decorative door to his dignitary suite. The equally attractive man and woman behind her seemed poised to respond.

"No." At least nothing they could provide.

"Very good, sir. Just let us know what events you wish to attend, and your hospitality staff will be ready to assist." She bowed and stepped back, probably to wait there until he shut the door behind him.

He waited for the door to latch shut and set the lock. The last thing he needed was for anything else to become more complicated. He tossed his jacket aside and dropped onto the plush white couch, throwing his arm over his eyes.

It was interesting, the subtle change in the way he was received here in Anara since the fight with Pogo. He had always been treated with respect, but it had been the grudging sort that was paid for. But now, there was something genuine there. It didn't seem it was his victory that made the difference. There seemed to be an appreciation for the fight itself, that he and Pogo had respected the sport for what it was, and each other, revealing a key component of their character people wanted to know ...

... and that's what these fights were really about. Matteo would never, never look at the sport the same way again. Or at Lighten the same way, either.

And that only made watching the power plays around him more intolerable.

His module pinged.

Speaking of intolerable ... "Good afternoon, sir."

Lord Timnon scowled from his module's screen. His hair was disheveled, or at least what was disheveled for him, and he looked as though he had been up all night, his blue eyes bloodshot. Oh, this was going to be a lovely conversation. "That is what you have to say to me?" And he was already shouting.

Reflex forced Matteo to sit up straighter, draw his shoulders back, and moderate his tone. Wasn't he the well-trained little heir? "What would you have me say?"

"You have betrayed your Clan. You have betrayed me, and you wonder what to say?" Was it the screen or was Grandfather's face really turning that color? "Explain yourself. Explain this."

The display switched to a series of Records—him helping Arli off the ground and handing her jacket to her. It flipped to a brief image of her in the suite with Beny and him. Then an image of her teaching him "Bringing in the Storm" from the celebration after the fight.

Splintering shards off the Timnon name! How had Records from the suite—Records guaranteed to be private—gotten out? He should have kept his privacy ware set all the time. Sloppy, stupid, he knew better ...

"What is that slut doing in your rooms?" Grandfather pounded the table so hard his module fell over and his image glowered at Matteo sideways. It seemed his hands shook as he righted the module. "What were you doing with her in public? Is she the one you betrayed Iantha with? How many others have there been?"

No, that had been Iantha's tactic. "I did not betray Iantha with her or anyone else."

Grandfather sneered. "Just because you have not left a string of bastards in your wake does not mean you have been faithful to your promise to Clan Corbel."

"I will not dignify that accusation with a response. And if that is all you have to say to me, this conversation—"

"What am I to think? You have thrown away a betrothal that took a year of negotiations to bring about. You threw it away, and then you are seen in the company of that ... that thing? How could you jeopardize our alliance with Corbel like that? I have told you all your life, keep it in your pants until after the bonding, then you can find whatever side piece you like to satisfy yourself on. Your bond is for the boardroom, not the bedroom."

"And yet my choice to end the betrothal has probably won us a lifelong alliance with Lady Iantha."

"Fine words from her, I am sure, but there is no contract, no blood to back up the alliance. Not to mention, that stupid girl is not in line for enough power to be worth an alliance apart from Clan Corbel—whom you have irreparably offended."

"She is a brilliant and innovative leader who has made great strides in building connections in a place we could never touch." Until now, of course. Matteo had built his own personal connections to Guild Master Brels, but he wasn't going to give that to Grandfather, not yet.

"Which is why the match was necessary, you ungrateful, unlicked cub."

"She and I are not well-suited for one another and her affections—"

"No. I will hear nothing about feelings and affections. They are irrelevant to your bonding. You need a political ally and lack the sense to find one, which is why I chose for you from Corbel."

"You chose, sir," Matteo's voice lowered half an octave, "but I did not. In fact, I was hardly consulted at all."

"You chose that Lighten slut—"

"I chose a pilot, not a partner, in bed or otherwise."

"So, she was the one who took you on the journey of betrayal? I will have her clearances—"

"She had nothing to do with my business. And there was no betrayal. I made a valuable connection with the Mining Guild Master who you have been trying to court for years now." So much for keeping that information to himself.

"You arrogant little fool, disregarding my plans again. That's what your mishandled fight was intended to buy us. What better way to open relations than to give him the idea they had some sort of upper hand on us? I needed that as a bargaining tool. But, no, you chose yet another betrayal instead. You had one simple instruction. One even you could understand, and you bumbled that, too. I am ashamed of you."

He had heard that so many times, it shouldn't bother him anymore. Little chance that would happen. "Did you even see the bout?"

"Every disgraceful moment."

"Where was the disgrace?" Matteo fought to keep his seat and not pace the room. "What precisely was disgraceful? We fought with honor and respect and showed ourselves ..."

"Disobedience is disrespect. I told you to—"

"To behave in a way contrary to your goals—your goals! Throwing the fight would not have gone unnoticed. It would be seen as an insult to the sport, my opponent, and all his connections. We won greater favor with Brels with what I did—"

"Arrogant, ungrateful, power-hungry soul catcher. You confuse popular opinion with actual power and undermine me at every turn. I should—"

"Disown and disinherit me?" Matteo sprang to his feet. Better that than throwing the module against the false window next to him. "I've heard that threat every day since Father died. The problem with your threat is, none of your other options are prepared to take my place. You've seen to that."

"You think far too well of yourself ..."

"You are the one who groomed me for your role, with my education, my connections, all my training. And you kept the rest of your potential heirs as far away from useful training as you could, lest their fathers get the idea they could gain power from having an eligible heir for you." It was a clever strategy, in a made-for-media-drama sort of way.

"Benton—"

"Is heir to the Family and will be a bloody good one. But if you take him as your heir, then one of his sisters, Patryce or Cortly most likely, will take the Family seat. And you have said there wasn't a lick of sense between the two of them. Either of them leading the Family ensures Family Sennet will lose control of Clan Timnon in a generation."

If Grandfather's eyes bulged any more, he would do himself a serious injury. "How would you know? Your idea of leadership—"

"Was acquired at Wroxton Academy, the most brutal military academy that you could sequester me off-planet, according to a curriculum you yourself established." Matteo folded his arms and glared, a lifetime's resentment threatening to explode. It had been a good education, but one he would see no one else forced to endure.

"If it was so adequate, why did you supplement it with your own additions?"

"To balance your biases! I am far more prepared and educated than you were when you took the Clan seat."

"How dare you!" Now it was Grandfather's turn to look ready to throw his module.

"Perhaps because I know something about leadership and where yours has been wanting. You only have yourself to blame. It was you that ensured every hour of my life for the last fifteen years, since the accident, has been spent in preparation to lead this bloody Clan. Leaving me with some little understanding of what that requires."

"Little good it has done." Grandfather slapped the table again. "You will do as you are told or—"

"Go ahead, disinherit me."

"No, not now. Not yet. You cannot force my hand. I have something else in mind."

"What are you talking about?"

"I am aware of Lady Iantha's infidelities against you with Lord Lemos. There is incontrovertible proof. I expect that is the real reason you ended the betrothal."

Of course, the fatherless soul catcher knew. May his name be forgotten from among the ancestors.

"And if her infidelity is not enough to ruin her, the truth of what she is doing on Lighten will ruin them both, and leave me in the enviable position of having brought the truth to light."

The hair on the back of Matteo's neck rose with an icy chill. "What do you think she is doing here on Lighten?"

"Oh, so there is something you don't know." Grandfather crossed his arms over his chest. Disgustingly self-satisfied. "So much the better. You can come away from this clean, ignorant of her schemes, and preserve the high-minded moral reputation you seem to enjoy so much. You wouldn't much like being connected to accused of high treason."

"That's ridiculous! There is no way—" Whatever Beny suspected Iantha of, it certainly could not be treason. That was bait.

"You were in the position to save them this ignominy. This was your choice. I hope you are satisfied with your decisions." Grandfather cut the feed.

Matteo swept his module aside and slammed both fists on the table.

"Well, that was pleasant," Beny said.

Matteo jumped. "When did you get here?"

"Somewhere around 'power-hungry soul catcher,' I think." Beny sat down on the opposite couch. "For what it's worth, you were right. None of us is being prepared to step into his seat. It's a relief to see you understand that, given how often you threaten to step down."

"You could do it. I know you don't want it, but you could do it. Your sisters—"

"I agree, the thought of them in headship is a little terrifying. I'm not even sure I want the Family, but I love them and you too well to leave it in my sisters' hands." Beny leaned elbows on knees and stared at him with a penetrating glance that Matteo couldn't hide from. "You holding together all right?"

Matteo laced his fingers behind his neck and leaned back to stare at the ceiling. "Thanks for the warning about Iantha. I'd hate to have heard it first from him."

"Still sucks, though, especially with how hard you lean into your monkish persona."

"Not like I enjoy it, but the thought of how anyone I dally with will get treated—can't do that to someone. Until I find the one who's going to go the distance with me and understands what they're signing on for, then, just call me Brother Matteo."

"We already do." Beny chuckled. "The treason charge, though—do you think Lord Timmi is actually going to do it, or is it all enticement to get you back in line?"

"If it were a lure, he would have offered sordid details to hook me. It's when he mentions something in passing like that I get alarmed. It'll take him a little time to make the formal accusation, but not much."

"What do you want to do about it?"

"Can't chance the conversation getting into Records. I need to get out there myself and warn her what he's up to, give her and Corbel a chance to brace for it."

"But we know something's going on out there—"

"Whatever she and Evering are doing out there with Firen, I can't believe it's treason. She's squirrelly, to be sure, but treason is a whole different level. And if I'm wrong, I'll find out soon enough."

Chapter 27

SHE NEEDED SPACE AND time to figure out her next move, and she couldn't do that with Pogo breathing down her neck. She all but ran down the gray-tiled service corridor. He meant well, but he didn't seem to accept how much power Joco had to ruin her and that, so far at least, all Brels had done was talk about making her a job offer. Reed had been right when she warned that Ari had been skirting the edges of the Transport Guild rules for a very long time, and all that she'd paid forward was coming back to her now.

It didn't matter that Joco's policies were selfish and short-sighted. It didn't matter he had been stingy and even cruel to her. It didn't matter her intentions had been—well, perhaps not the time to examine those. They didn't matter. Someday, it would come back to him, somehow.

Just as it was all coming back to her. Drown it! Drown it! Drown it!

She burst into the pilots' lounge at a full run. Several gaming pilots turned to look at her, but returned to their amusements as she waved them down with a forced laugh. It was easy enough to convince people not to see what they didn't want to pay attention to in the first place.

Savory, inviting lunch smells wafted from the mess counter. No, she wasn't hungry, but she took a lunch tray plus several prepackaged meals. No telling where her next meal would come from. Nothing would be helped by going hungry before she had to.

She tucked into the little table she preferred and forced herself to eat. A vegetable omelet, rolled in a thick flatbread. Hot and fresh, mild-tasting, so it went down easily. Cold red fruit juice helped.

Options, what options did she have? Not much. Joco's reach extended to all the pilots, all of Lighten. How was she going to get out from under his shadow?

An impertinent ping jogged her from her thoughts. A message, not a call. That was something. She couldn't trust herself to be in control of her words right now. That was far too much to expect at a time like this. Sunlight hit her module, making the screen difficult to read.

Lovely. The top message on the incoming stack was from Joco. She'd wait 'til later to deal with it ... except reflex took over and she opened the message, anyway.

Blistering language usually reserved for Guild matters seemed even louder when it was written rather than spoken. Her eyes lingered over the soul-singeing words as she touched the scar behind her ear, the one Sander had branded her with. The one message not much different from the other.

Someday, maybe, she would confront Joco with what he had said, and he would mutter something about "only a fool would take such words seriously." And then he would ignore any ramifications those words might have had. And that would be it.

Maybe.

Sometimes it happened that way. But even if it did, she would save this message as a reminder. Maybe she wouldn't forget this time, wouldn't make excuses for all the reasons he might have said what he did, wouldn't pretend that it was all right and didn't shred her soul into a thousand tiny shards.

Maybe she had gotten smarter this time. That happened sometimes, when one hurt enough.

"Sarding Laythe's Woods!" She nearly knocked her tray off the table.

Palmer was flying in, would arrive right before the pre-fight festivities began. He was to collect her and take her back to the Yard. Be ready to go with him; leave the hauler here; Joco would fly it back himself.

No. Not a lost soul's chance that she'd leave her ship in Joco's hands. He'd find some way to wrest it from her, payment for all the illegal maintenance and modifications she had done. Without it, she would be trapped.

When she got back to the Yard she was to move in with Palmer. Settlement papers, already signed by Joco and Palmer, were attached. She would—an imperative, a demand, not a request—sign them and return them to Joco before the start of the fight. The "or else" was implied, not said, but it was there.

Joco must think that recognizing her as kin now gave him the right to force Bithy's worthless son on her. Shouldn't be a surprise—and Palmer had been trying to push the issue for longer than she wanted to think about it.

One glance at the papers and it was clear it was as far from an equal partnership as any legal agreement could be. Exactly what she needed to see. She needed to be angry, not afraid. And she was angry.

She'd outrun the soul catchers barefooted and blindfolded before signing anything less than an equal partnership! She closed the documents and ordered them to the recycle stack.

Dropping her face into her hands, her heart raced to get ahead of the storm. She panted to keep pace. Reed had been right. The terms of this settlement were indeed a reckoning for her stubborn willfulness, paid forward to Joco all this time.

Exactly as she should have expected.

But expected did not mean accepted.

Even if Joco claimed her as kin, he could not force her into this. Not legally. Both parties had to consent to settlement terms, especially because they called out the inequality of the parties involved. And this one was breathtakingly unequal.

But if she saw Joco, would she be able to stand up to him? He had a way ...

No. Not this time.

She had her ship and a potential job offer—Pogo had said Brels wanted to hire her. Even the hint of a job offer was better than that joke of a settlement. But only if she was gone before Palmer arrived. She couldn't risk seeing him being swayed by the old forces that kept her under Joco's control. Distance would be her greatest ally.

She had an hour before the first moment he could land.

That would be enough. She established her flight plan and sent it to traffic control and headed for the showers.

Fifteen minutes later, her rucksack over her shoulder, she returned to the pilots' lounge, damp hair clinging to her neck. She settled at a small table, with a cup of too strong, not sweet enough java, her module already open to a blank message to Pogo.

She didn't need to say too much. Just say that she was interested in Brels' offer and ask him to approve her arrival at Firen HQ to discuss the terms of employment. Surely, he would read between the lines and would approve her visit? He had been at the inquiry with Joco, after all.

It wasn't as though the details wouldn't come out soon enough, but those could wait until she wasn't trying to outrun Joco and the trask he was sending after her.

"Arli?"

She jumped and nearly spilled her java on Matté, wearing a drab flight suit, with his bag in hand.

"Are you all right?" he asked.

"I'm on my way out. I don't have time—" She stood and pushed past him.

He kept pace at her side. "Any chance you're passing by Firen territories? I need to get to their HQ as soon as—"

"Yes." She stopped to stare at him. No questions now. Enjoy the fortunate coincidence. If she could get in a little more paid work with no extra trouble to herself, she couldn't refuse. "I'm sending you a contract. Can you fill it out on the way to my hauler?"

He looked like he was about to ask something that she wouldn't have answered, but merely nodded. "Will do." He pulled out his module and opened the contract.

"I'm leaving now. Can you keep up?" She shoved her module into its holster and slung her rucksack over her shoulder.

Her module trilled. Damn, it was Palmer, not Pogo. Keep the distance, keep the distance.

She broke into a run and used voice mode to check her flight request at traffic control. Approved, and the flight window was opening soon.

Matté kept pace beside her. The advantage of height and long legs.

Ship in view, voice mode unlocked and opened the hatches, so all they had to do was run straight inside the cramped and cluttered little hauler, and avoid the hatch hitting them as it shut behind them.

A green light blinked on her dashboard. "That's the way now. Clearances are through, and launch window's open. Strap in and we're off."

"Talk about efficiency!" Matté dropped into the seat beside her and fastened his safety webbing tight.

She opened her flight control comm. "Proceeding to takeoff field, runway five." Tighten the safety straps and reset display panels to her preferred takeoff configuration—done. And the drowning module trilled again. Distance. Keep the distance.

"Paxton 23 cleared for takeoff."

"Acknowledged." She accelerated down the runway and lifted off with barely more bounce than usual, but she could tell she wasn't at her best. She needed to shake that clumsiness off before they got into the deep desert, where things could get interesting.

As they eased into the open sky, she leaned back and gulped air, hands trembling as they danced along the touchscreens, resetting it to her preferred in-flight displays. They were away from Anara and safe now, beyond Joco's hand, beyond Palmer's reach.

The module trilled.

"Who's calling you?" Matté asked.

Sorry, storm-shorn piece of sollert shit! "What do you want, Palmer?"

"Where are you? I heard you left the complex." Drown it! She'd sent it through the ship's speakers. His was one of those voices that sounded even more threatening through speakers than it did in person. "He told you to wait there for me."

"Actually, he didn't. And if he had, he doesn't have that right."

"You're making this more difficult than it needs to be, Arli-bug. If you knew what was good for you—"

"I do, and it ain't you or that drowned settlement." She narrowly avoided slamming her fist on one of her display screens and hit the armrest instead.

"The one you haven't signed. Joco said you'd have it done by now. This isn't the right way for us to start."

"There's no start. I am not signing that. I am not settling with you. Neither you nor Joco can force me."

"You're kin to him now. You have to—" Palmer had to recognize Joco's kinship to her was a sham as much as she did.

"Chief Connection or not, I have final say in any domestic contracts, whether equal partnerships or settlements. You can check the domestic law code."

"He's going to take you apart for that. And for what you've already done to him. You really want to make this worse?" Palmer's voice dropped into low warning notes. "I don't much like what I'm seeing, either. Once you're in my house, domestic law applies."

"So, you're saying once he's done with me, you'll try your hand at making sure I'll never forget?" How kind of him to shine a light on the final, inarguable reason she would never, never sign that document.

"Can you blame us? Not like you're giving us much choice."

"Go drown yourself."

"He'll revoke your flight clearances if you don't, and your membership in the Transport Guild after that. Then what will you have?" Palmer tried to sound persuasive, but it was more petulant whining than compelling. "He's going to deny your connection to him."

"You think I didn't know that from the start? I might be a worthless little insect, but I'm not stupid."

She shut off the comm and leaned back hard in her seat, gripping the armrests to conceal her shaking hands. Every joint was primed to run, but with nowhere to go, the urge itched and prickled like swarming insects on bare skin.

That happened faster than she'd expected. Was he already in Anara or still in the air? Did it matter? She couldn't, wouldn't, go back to Anara. None of this was unexpected, but she had a plan; at least for now, she had a plan. Flight control wouldn't reveal her flight registrations to him, and by the time he found someone to unlock them, hopefully Firen would offer some refuge. Either way, she'd still be away from them.

Matté cleared his throat. Storms and squalls, let him not ask any stupid questions! "I didn't mean to be intrusive. I asked you who was calling so my voice would be part of those Records. Which means I can put a lock on them—diplomatic privilege. He won't be able to unlock them, at least not for a good while. Even Joco shouldn't be able to get into them."

She exhaled hard, panting. "Thank you." She forced the words out, not because she didn't mean them, but the lump in her throat hadn't faded yet.

"It's not like I particularly want this trip in the public eye, either."

"Your family?"

"How did you guess?"

"Stupidity isn't limited to Guild Masters."

"And not all of the stupidity needs to be up for public display in the Records." He laughed like he needed something to laugh at.

"I can't go back to Anara after this. So you'll have to find your own way back. I'm sorry."

"After what I heard, I wouldn't want you to. I'll sort that out when it comes to it." Matté drummed his fingers on the armrest.

"Interested in running the comm and getting the clearances into Firen territory sorted out?"

"Happy to. Sitting duffer isn't exactly my happy place."

"I get twitchy as a bag of bait-bugs sitting in that seat." She giggled as she set his screen to display the communications panel.

"Requests sent." He tapped the screen with a flourish. "Just have to wait on them now."

"I can make time out here until they come in. Don't want to push my luck with Firen. With all the Raider activity recently,

I can see their enforcers shooting first and asking permission after."

"Don't know how long it'll take to hear back." He drummed faster.

"Won't get an answer from them any sooner." Distraction, she needed to distract him ... "You fought a good match with Pogo yesterday."

"Thanks. I haven't gotten to fight outside my own style often and it was nice to hold my own against one of your best. You ever get in the ring yourself?"

The drumming stopped.

"Can't say I ever thought about it. And I doubt Joco would have appreciated it." That was an understatement. She was already far too insolent and bold as it was. He would not have approved anything that encouraged those traits.

"Seems like you'd be really solid in the ring. The way you stood up to Joco yesterday—"

She shrugged. "Still ended up giving him what he wanted. Can't be too many points scored for that sort of move."

He sighed sadly, knowingly. "Maybe, but ... I understand. It's harder than it ought to be." The comm panel buzzed. "Got clearances in, but they're insisting on an alternate flight path. Raider trouble on the standard approach."

Of course. Sard it all. "You interested in managing nav now, too?"

"I wouldn't mind the distraction. But tell me I haven't been so much of a pain in the ass that you want to keep me quietly occupied and out of your hair." He glanced at her, one eyebrow raised.

"I'd offer you the media feeds for that. The big fight's set to start soon and the commentators will have started their chatter by now." She added the navigation panel to his display screen. "Seriously, I wouldn't mind the extra hands and eyes. Something doesn't feel right. My skin's crawling—"

"Like a fight got called off right before the first round?" He ran his hands up and down his arms.

"Yeah. I don't like it. Doesn't make sense, I can't quite put my finger on it, but something isn't adding up."

"Want me to scan the pilots' chatter feed for something?"

"Do it." Her module pinged. Pogo finally answered and gave the same instructions as Matté had received. At least it was consistent. That was reassuring. A little.

"I'm not getting anything in the chatter except that everyone is being routed around those primary routes right now." Matté bounced his fist off his chin.

"Happens sometimes. I suppose that should make me feel better—"

"—but it doesn't, unless I miss my bet. What do you want to do about it?"

"Gonna tune the sensors up high." She set the pollution sensors as high as they would go and increased the range on the navigation marker sensor. Those three-cycle pings would rattle their bones now. "She'll be screaming at every shadow, though, so get ready."

"Better than getting surprised. Plotted in the recommended course, ready for you."

She double-checked his course, not exactly what she would have set, but close enough. "We should have at least half an hour of quiet running before things could get weird."

"You interested in tuning in the fight feed?"

"You can if you want, but I'd prefer not to follow it in real time." Distance, keep the distance. She didn't need Joco in the cockpit with her now, even if it was third-hand through the commentators' prattle.

"What will happen if Joco wins? I don't understand the subtleties of how that works."

"Despite what is squawked on the media feeds, the fights do not actually decide anything. Another yard master challenged Joco for the Transport Guild Master seat about six months ago.

Technically, the other guy pinned him, and won the fight." She caught Matté's gaze for a moment. "The winning move was a barely legal choke that the Guild members didn't like. Made them nervous about what the guy would do in office, so Joco kept the seat. Joco's a cheap, controlling soul catcher, but he's always been that way and will always be. A known quantity. Before people vote for someone, they want a strong sense of what to expect from a man and figure a fight brings that out. But you showed that, given the way you and Pogo fought." She cocked her head, then turned back to the dashboard.

"I knew that was important, but not how it would come into play with the governmental seats."

"It's more significant when the elections are as close as Brels and Joco's. The undecided folks are paying close attention to inform their final votes. The election is set for the day after the fight."

"It sounds like your fights serve the same role as the debates for our elected roles. That's really interesting." His forehead creased as though he were thinking very hard.

"Not as savage and backward as you expected?"

"No, not at all. And for what it's worth, those things have been said often about Lighten, but hearing them and believing them are two different things."

"Fair enough. There are a lot of things said about Dextrines that you seem to contradict, too."

The sensors screamed.

Chapter 28

MATTEO GASPED AND JUMPED against his straps. Not that there was much room to jump in them. That was going to leave some noticeable strap burns.

She turned down the alert volume and adjusted the read-out panels. "Sorry. That was one of the shadows I warned you about."

"Still better than missing something. You still looking for fuel residue?"

"Among other things." She seemed to be debating a confession. "You'll figure this out for yourself, so I may as well tell you. I also scan for Raider hull composition—it's got a magnetic signature I can pick up off the—you're going to think I've lost it, but it really does work—the docking assist sensors can pick it up, when you get them tuned the right way. And I'm also scanning for the three-cycle nav ping I mentioned before, the one I think they're using in their comms. It turns up a lot of false positives, though. It makes little sense to put up with all the false alarms when you're not expecting company. But out here ..." She shrugged far too apologetically.

Granted, the arrangement was unorthodox, and the results were difficult to make sense out of. But given the level of tech on Lighten at the moment, it was cracking amazing to see what she'd developed actually working in the field, not in a hypothetical paper.

"How did you come up with the parking sensor arrangement?" Naturally, at right that moment, Matteo's module pinged.

She nodded and turned her attention to her readouts, offering the illusion of privacy.

Iantha's face appeared on the module's screen, all but hissing and spitting. "I got your message. I cannot see you today. You cannot come."

That tone of hers clicked his Lord Heir persona into place. "A little late for that."

"No! You can't be. You're not already on the way? Why didn't you wait? How dare you—" Her voice became colder with each sentence.

"I've already received clearances from Firen HQ."

"How could they? Those idiots! I forbade it." Her Hell Cat incarnate expression was one he could live happily, never seeing again. "Turn around and go back. I will pay your pilot double for the trouble. Triple if necessary. Just get out of Firen airspace."

"Enough!" He boomed in his Clan Lord voice, one he avoided resorting to. But it got her attention. "Let us be clear here, Lady Iantha. I am not asking permission. I do not require your permission to visit Firen. I do not answer to Clan Corbel, and I do not answer to you. If you choose not to receive me when I arrive, that is your prerogative. I will not force my unwanted presence upon you. However, the insult you offer to Clan Tim-non may have far longer reach than you expect."

"Is that a threat?" Her face matched the color of Grandfa-ther's at their last conversation.

"If you knew me at all, you would realize I do not, I will not, make threats. I am reminding you there will be witnesses when you refuse to receive me. And it will be effectively impossible to pay every one of them off for their silence."

"You manipulative soul catcher—I'm warning you, stay away from Firen. I'll meet you at Anara tomorrow."

"You may choose to go to Anara tomorrow, but that does nothing to change my own plans. I will be at Firen HQ shortly, to see you, or not. Good day, Lady Iantha." He flipped the call off. "Splintering shards! It never even occurs to her there may be a bloody good reason I'm trying to get to her."

"You can be seriously intimidating." Arli glanced at him with raised eyebrows. Respect, not derision, in her eyes. He wasn't used to that.

"It has its uses." Matteo shoved the module back into his pocket. So much for trying to do Iantha a favor.

"I'm not asking questions, just offering a small suggestion. Don't go chasing off the ship once we land. Their enforcers can get overzealous, and suppression stunners live up to all the rumors." She twisted away, but the shudder coursing down her back revealed the full story.

"Sarding soul catchers—seriously?" So much he wanted to ask.

She squared her shoulders. "Some of them might not be as well-trained as one would hope."

"Thanks for the warning." He cupped his jaw with his hand and dragged it down his chin. "That's the sort of thing that could ... the mind boggles to consider it."

"Neither you nor Firen need that kind of problem to deal with."

"Neither did you."

"No, I didn't." She swallowed hard and lifted her chin. "But, Brels did right by me, and the matter is behind us. It would be much harder for him to do the same for you."

She was right—he, no one really, would have known what happened to her. In the grand scheme of things, it didn't matter. Many would say she didn't matter. That Brels made amends she was satisfied with said a very great deal about him—and her—but he would have to consider that later.

If the same thing happened to him, though—he shook his head. There would be no way to keep that quiet, and the diplomatic incident coming out of that boggled the mind.

The sensors screamed again.

She shifted her display screens, studying one in particular—maybe the parking sensors? The ancestors might shudder, but it was a sarding brilliant use for those.

"Drown it all! I'm seeing something, I think. Tighten down your straps hard. This may get rough before we're done."

He tightened his safety webbing until it chafed.

"Get me options: course alternatives, hiding spots, places I can fly that they can't negotiate, anything in your wildest imagination that could be useful."

She had already stretched his imagination as it was. How much farther could it go? "Parameters?"

"They're in the nav panel. Search for the specs file."

"Got it." He entered the parameters into a geographic survey search and added his favorite display structure. "Putting up a map overlay. I've color-coded by type of option. Color intensity indicates level of accessibility."

"Sarding brilliant!" Her jaw dropped, and she shot him a look of such admiration his skin tingled. No one had ever paid him such a heartfelt compliment. "Later, I'll ask you about how to add that into my next display update."

And, for that look alone, he would give her those routines and program them for her if she asked.

"What are those?" She pointed to vague shapes on the viewscreen above the dashboard. "I've never seen that ship configuration before. Whatever those are, they're chasing a pair of Raiders right into us."

She was right.

Those shapes were familiar, though … and impossible. "Anticipating their most likely course and plotting alternatives."

Arli swung the ship around to one of his suggestions.

"Is that weapons fire?" Arli pointed at a distant dust cloud and turned up the viewscreen magnification. "That doesn't make sense. We don't have armed ships that look like that."

When did the Hell Cat roar and let them out? "I have. Looks like a fighter, a Raptor."

"Fighter ships? Like the ones Fleet uses?"

"Yeah, but not just Fleet. All the militaries have them."

"We don't. Our military is a joke, and Joco's hold over it doesn't help. He's locked down their access to new vehicles and technology. He says it's to make sure we only use the specs we control. Says he's afraid of licensing stuff from off-world because that's a sure way to lose independence—claims we can get locked out of specs we're dependent on."

"I suppose he has a point. But there's other ways—"

"He's been told, but he's attached to his ways."

"Wouldn't be the first Clan Lord I've met who's like that." He chewed the inside of his cheek. "Old style Raptors have a fault in their sensors … you willing to let me re-tune the cloaking to take advantage of that? I'm not sure what model they've got out there—"

"I'll want to know how you came by that information, later. You have control, do it."

"They've also got a blind spot—"

"Later. Get it into the system." Her fingers danced over her displays and shifted his again, giving him access.

Should that feel like such an honor?

She slammed the heel of her hand on her armrest. "Not finding any hidey-holes along the way. Drown it all! I'm guessing the Raiders have seen us now, too. Going to take it through the canyon."

"But how fast—"

"You might want to close your eyes."

She was right, but he didn't look away. He kept one eye on her and one on the viewscreen.

She didn't flinch, maybe didn't even breathe. The woman had ice in her veins. That was the only explanation for the way she darted through the significant obstacles like she was playing a ship-sim game.

"Sending our details to Firen HQ," Matteo said. Whether they could help was another thing.

"Raiders about to come right over our heads."

"My guess is they're looking to get a weapons lock on us."

"Maybe we can confuse them. Set the cloaking to send a magnetic signature like these rocks and keep close to them." Weapons fire exploded overhead, projectile weapons, knocking several large rocks loose to bounce off the reactive shielding.

"Told you you'd need that webbing." She steadied the ship. "Shields can dissipate their first couple shots if they hit us."

"And the third?"

"Don't ask. Don't intend to get hit the first time." She pulled hard to port to hide in the shadow of a ledge, pulling back hard on the speed, throwing him into his seat.

"I didn't know this class of transport could decel like that."

"They can't."

"You customized that, too? Is the Guild aware?"

"Yes, I did, and no, and I'd just as soon they don't find out."

"If we live through this, they won't hear it from me." He clutched his armrests, feet braced hard on the decking.

Another explosion rocked overhead, raining debris down over them.

"Raider ship down, I think." She deftly avoided another mass of falling debris.

The comms crackled to life. "Unidentified craft, identify yourself, or we will be forced to shoot you. You are trespassing on Firen Mine Territory."

"Read my ID beacon, you drowning trask-brained reptile. Paxton 23, Paxton 23, with territory clearances. Check with Firen HQ base. Repeat, clearance code can be verified by Firen HQ."

"Show yourselves, or we'll be forced to shoot."

"And what soul catcher are you? I'm not moving until Firen confirms your sarding identity."

"This is your last warning."

"Incoming from Firen HQ." Matteo shifted the incoming message to play on the main speakers.

"Paxton 23, comply with instructions from Interceptor team. They will escort you to base." Good thing that was Pogo's voice, something they could trust. "They've been told to disengage weapons."

"I'm still reading them hot."

"You can't—" Pogo snapped.

"Confirm my reading."

How—-wait, she was bluffing. She had to be.

"Thundering dust storms, Interceptor One. Paxton 23's cleared. Weapons offline, now."

"We don't have visual confirmation."

"I've confirmed—offline now, or you pay the Soul Catcher when you return to base."

"Affirmative. Down powering weapons. Satisfied?"

"I read no weapons, Paxton 23. Accept their escort to base." Pogo softened his tone, maybe enough not to raise Arli's hackles this time.

"Acknowledged." Arli huffed out a ragged breath. "We'll clear the canyon at the following coordinates. Don't shoot. I repeat, don't shoot."

Matteo gripped the armrests hard enough to tear the fabric as she peeked the nose of the hauler over the rim of the canyon.

"Visual confirmed, Paxton 23." A Raptor, probably Interceptor One, hovered above them.

"Follow Interceptor One in. Interceptor Two will cover from behind," Pogo said, in the same not-so-authoritative voice.

"Acknowledged." She flipped off the comm. "I suppose that explains why my skin was crawling. Not the sort of bird that's native around here at all."

And not the welcome Matteo expected. What was Iantha involved with?

Chapter 29

"TOLD YOU THEIR WEAPONS were hot," Ari muttered.

"Could you really tell their weapons were charged?" Matté's gaze shifted from the viewscreen to her and back again.

"Does it matter? I was right." She stared at Interceptor One. Storms and squalls! That was a beautiful ship. How could she get a closer look?

"Just curious. Trying to figure out if you're a cracking good engineer or have a pair of stone balls."

"Both." She snorted—they were both a compliment when one thought about it. "I haven't figured out how to read their weapons status—not yet at least. If you've got any ideas for that, I'd love to hear 'em. Still, though, it isn't hard to take an educated guess on what they were up to. And if I was wrong, blame my kludged-together systems for wonky readings. I prefer to assume things are dicey and find out I'm wrong, than the other way around."

"Bet you're a hell cat at the card table, huh?" He laughed.

"I don't play. Not a hobby I can afford, especially if I started liking it too much." She couldn't help it. She winked at him.

The barest smile lifted his lips. "I've got landing directions from Firen coming in. Plotting the course, now."

"Instructions received, Firen Base. On final approach. Landing in five minutes." She leaned back and willed her heart to settle. "After that welcome, you still have business there?"

"Absolutely. Got a whole slew of new mission parameters now. Excuse me a minute, need to make some notes on a few things." He pulled out his module and started tapping at it.

Nice that he had so many things he wanted to remember. She probably had at least as many that she wanted to forget, and a real chance there would be more soon.

Did she even want to know what was going on here? Was it as complicated as it looked? How did it look now that the first shock was wearing off?

An impressive fighter ship was cruising the desert, in Firen territory, shooting down Raiders. All legalities aside, was it actually a bad thing? It probably depended on which side of the Transport Guild one was on, but it wasn't difficult to see how it could be positive for Lighten, maybe even the Kayavan System.

More important: whatever Firen Mines was involved with, was it worse than returning to Joco and Palmer?

Hard to imagine what could be worse than that.

It didn't matter, though. She'd made her choice to leave them behind and had to stick with it now. Returning would only make things worse.

Good thing she kept that list of options she'd made during the storm, though. She might need it soon.

Firen's secondary hangar, on the back side of the second peak in the Eternis Mountain Range, appeared on the viewscreen. A difficult approach, limited visibility, subject to sudden updrafts.

It was secondary for a solid reason. Not as bad as flying through a level three storm, but something she'd have to pay attention to.

"Paxton 23, clear for landing, hangar pad five." That was the one dead center in the hangar, the one security could most easily surround. Hopefully, Pogo had a tight rein on the enforcers this time.

"Paxton 23 on final approach, landing in three minutes." And it would be a textbook perfect, passenger-wouldn't-feel-it landing, one that she would be proud of. If she was going to be watched, then she would give them something to see.

And she did.

"If I hadn't seen you actually set down, I wouldn't believe that we were on the ground. You've got a real touch for that." Matté released his safety webbing and drew a deep breath. Probably hadn't been able to do that since things got interesting.

"Paxton 23, debark not cleared, pilot or passenger. Do not debark until your security escort arrives." Pogo's warning filled every corner of the hauler.

"Understood." She checked the locks on the hatches, just in case, fighting the urge to reach for her belt knife. Not that it would have much effect against armed enforcers, but the reflex kicked in, regardless.

Every nerve thrummed like it had when the suppression stun had been abruptly shut off. Every sound, every shadow screamed alarm and danger.

"You all right?" Matté whispered, watching the hatches.

"One grumpy greeting is enough to sour you for a place." She tried to laugh, but failed.

"The mind boggles."

Maybe his did. She had a crystal-clear idea of what to expect.

"Cleared for debark. Repeat, cleared for debark, Paxton 23." That was Pogo again.

Ari flipped on the external cameras. Half a dozen uniformed enforcers swarmed around her ship. "Where are you, Pogo? All I see is the enforcer team outside."

"Pilot and passenger, debark now." Exasperation colored Pogo's voice. Too bad for him.

"Not unless you're out there to manage that brute squad. I don't trust your people. Not after—"

"Drown it, Arli! Please." His fist hit something unforgiving. "This is complicated enough. I don't need you getting stubborn on me."

"It's my nerves on the line, not yours. I'm sitting tight. I'll send Matté out, though. I'm sure no one is going to stun him." She slapped the console and turned to Matté. "Use the front hatch and only open it enough to slip out. I'm locking it behind you."

"Got it." He pulled his bag out from under his seat and checked his module. "Payment for the trip's cleared, including the hazard contingencies and gratuities. Thanks for everything." He paused and turned to meet her gaze. "I mean that, it's been memorable working with you, and I appreciate all of it. Thank you." He cracked open the hatch.

She watched the hatch as he slipped out. He was good company. She'd miss him. The door latched with a distinct click, and she returned to the external camera feeds.

A pair of guards greeted Matté with a bow. Several more took their places as the rest of the squad surrounded the hauler, weapons ready.

Why? Was it her now "official" connection to Joco that made her such a threat?

She pulled up her employment options list on her module and set another search to run in the background. The faster she could get away from Firen, the better.

Fifteen minutes later, her module pinged.

"Let me in?" Pogo waved to the outside camera.

"You alone?"

"Shredding sarding sandstorms, Arli, don't you trust me?" He held up open hands to the camera and waved the squad back until they disappeared from view.

She punched the lock, and the hatch rose. Dry, dusty air with traces of chemical scents rushed in, carrying a keenly honed edge of threatening desert heat.

He stepped inside with slow, deliberate footsteps, hands still held wide and open. "There's no one with me. I didn't bring a team. They will stay back unless I call for them."

"Even so, I'd like to shut the hatch."

He tapped something into his module. "Go ahead, then."

"I'm not a threat to you or anyone else." She watched the hatch until it shut behind him and locked it. "What in Laythe's Woods is going on?"

"This wasn't supposed to happen." Pogo dropped into the seat behind hers, his Firen-red flight suit dusty brown in the shadows.

"Those Interceptors—that's why flight control had me take the alternate flight path."

"They weren't supposed to be anywhere near the alternate path, near you or anyone else heading for us today. Rock for brains tunnel-snakes got a couple of Raiders in their sights and lost their crunchy little minds." He pinched the bridge of his nose. "I'm gonna need some time to work this out."

"Some time? What does that mean?" She clutched the edge of her seat, prepared to bolt, but where would, where could, she go?

"I need to sort this out. We didn't have contingency plans for ... this." He looked like a man about to say something she didn't want to hear.

"Get out of my ship, and I'll get out of your territory. I'll sort out a destination along the way. I can spend a couple days in the deep desert if I need to. But I'll be out of your way." That was why she picked up the extra rations ...

"That's not going to happen." His words were slow and deliberate, but his hands, his arms tensed. "I've got to tell Brels about this, but not until after the fight."

"You intend to hold me a prisoner here until you decide ... something?" She turned halfway to check her display screens.

"Sard it, no! You're not a prisoner. A guest. A guest of Firen until—"

"Until you let me go? How is that different from being a drowning prisoner?" She fell back against her seat. "I'm trapped here as surely as I'd be if I went back to the Yard with Joco and signed that drowned settlement with Palmer."

Pogo jumped, eyes wide. "Settlement? Palmer, Bithy's son? Joco recognized you as kin, why would he try to partner—"

"Not partner. Settle. Settle to keep me there, under his control. Like you're threatening me with now." Every bit of warmth drained away, scouring her skin like marsh nettles as it went.

"I had no idea he'd do such a thing. It's not legal."

"Oh, I am well aware of what is legal. I am also only hours away from having all my flight clearances canceled and my Guild membership revoked, of having all my options taken from me. And now you're threatening to take my very last one."

"I'm not threatening you. I'm trying to sort a way out of this." He raked his hair back.

"Accepting the position Brels offered isn't enough?" Technically, it wasn't even an offer, it was the suggestion of one, but it was all she had.

"He'll be pleased to hear that when he gets back after the fight. And that will probably settle the matter. I expect it will. But right now, it's complicated, more than you realize. Please, let me take you to some guest quarters, and you can be a little more comfortable than being stuck here on this ship."

She folded her arms over her chest. Better to keep them well away from her knife. "And you're going to drag me out of here with suppression stuns if I don't."

"That wouldn't be my choice of how to do it."

"But if I refuse, that's what it is going to come to, isn't it?"

"I don't want that."

"You're not saying it won't."

"You know me, you know Brels, well enough at this point to know that's not the way either of us want to work. I'd have hoped you've got some reason to trust us."

"Maybe you," she sighed. He was right, he and Brels had done right by her. "But not your brute squad."

"I can understand that. What if I escort you to guest quarters myself? I'll handpick your escort team, and make stone sure they're aware of what happens to inhospitable enforcers, paying a little visit to the one you remember who's still in confinement. Will that make this less awful?" He pressed his lips together tightly. "I hate this, really, I do. But, please, make this easy. For all of us."

So many things she wanted to say, but what was the point? Was there another option? She grabbed her rucksack and followed him out.

Chapter 30

THE BRUTE SQUAD PARTED as Matteo stepped out of the hauler. He squared his shoulders and adjusted his Lord Heir persona. So cracking wrong that he had nothing to fear from them, when he was the real threat to whatever was going on here. Arli was just the innocent caught in the crossfire, and there wasn't a cracking thing he could do to change that.

Iantha appeared in the guards' wake, a seething mass of blonde fury in a black pantsuit and work boots. She leveled a weapons-grade glare at him, a side of her he'd never seen before, and would be happy to avoid seeing again.

Behind Iantha's guard, a second squad milled, ready to swarm Arli's hauler if called to it. Maybe even if not. Kaya-van's bones! He hated this and the fact there was nothing he could do about it. At least he could turn his anger to use.

Beyond them, in the darkest shadows of the deep mountain-side hangar, at least half a dozen Raptors stood in a single row. The shine on their hulls was still fresh, as though they hadn't had their maiden flights yet. From this angle, he couldn't see the telltale signs that would indicate whether they were older models, legal for military surplus sale, or newer, still proprietary technology. Either would be problematic for Lighten's laws, but the former would keep Evering within Dextrine strictures.

No wonder Iantha was touchy.

She muttered something unpleasant under her breath and waved for him and the guards to follow as she stalked off toward the rear of the hangar. They moved too fast, and still at the wrong angle, to give him the necessary details on the Raptors, but they were freshly assembled from newly-printed parts. That explained the security and the odd, cursory tour he had encountered in his earlier visit to Evering.

Sometimes he hated it when all the pieces started coming together.

He paused for a moment to get a better look at the sleek, single-man fighters, with the profile of a bird of prey diving for a kill. Stunning, simply stunning. The sort of ship he'd love to get his hands on.

She glowered at him without a single word and motioned for him to move on. Gone was the respect and courtesy she had always extended toward him. Now she behaved with all the disdain of a High Lord thwarted in her designs.

The last remaining fragment of trust he had for Lord Timnon twisted and crumbled like a dry leaf in his hand. Not that he had expected a bond with Iantha would be similar to what his parents had enjoyed, but Grandfather had led him to believe life with his betrothed would be amicable, and the matchmakers agreed. Never, he would never trust matchmakers, or Lord Timnon, again.

If he ever chose a partner, the affair would be of his making, and not from the Ranks of Dextra. And it wouldn't be with someone he could tolerate, but someone he couldn't tolerate to be without. Such defiance would rattle the ancestors' crypt good and proper.

Iantha stormed through an open door onto a huge manufacturing floor. The air swirled with metallic and chemical scents associated with aircraft part printing, circulated by loud factory fans overhead. Farthest from them, a wall of huge, glistening white industrial printers hummed and whirred. Half a dozen printing techs, wearing clean suits, tended the printers like oversized bees hovering around a field of strange square flowers.

Closer to them, three partially-finished Raptors stood, eerie, skeletal birds, in a strange half-alive state, waiting for the moment of their birth. Flight techs in dusty, gray jumpsuits, two or three to a ship, crawled in, on, and through the unalive carcasses, working to bring them to life.

Iantha waved the guard to stay in the hangar, while she led Matteo to a small nearby room, complete with several chairs, a worktable, and display screens.

The door slid shut, and she whirled on him like a hell cat, claws and teeth bared. "In the name of all the ancestors, what are you doing here?"

Despite his casual garb, he pulled himself up to his full height and loomed over her. One of those skills he'd picked up from watching Lord Timnon. "First, Lady, I will remind you, it is not your place to speak to me in such a fashion."

"We are not on Dextra, your Rank has little meaning here." Her fine blue eyes narrowed into a sneer.

"While that might be strictly true, you and I both know that is not the case. You will eventually return to Dextra and be reminded of the strength of Clan Timnon."

"So you came to intimidate me? Now that you have Brels' regard, you want to get your piece of this endeavor, make your mark to impress your Grandfather so he will finally acknowledge you as his Second?" She rolled her eyes and paced to the other side of the table. With a fresh glare, she slammed her hands on the tabletop. "This is none of your business. Forget what you have seen. Go back to your sport and carousing, and leave me to my work."

"Sport and carousing?" That barb met its mark. "You think that's what I have been about? Yes, I have been in the ring, but not for sport. If that is all you can see, then you know less about Lighten than you think. As for carousing—I will remind you, I was not the one trying to cover indiscretions. As I understand, Lord Lemos paid dearly to bring your excursion with him out of the Media's attention. With questionable success."

"I imagine Lord Timnon has found those Records and sent you to ruin me, then? How much does he know?" She leaned back against the wall beside the display screen, arms crossed.

"Your affair with Lemos is well known. As for what Lord Timnon knows of your business with Firen, he has not confided in me. "

"But he intends to get the Media involved. Everyone knows that's his favorite weapon."

"Be that as it may, I believe he intends to level much more serious charges against you and Evering."

"Evering?" Her face lost color and her posture shifted from defiant to determined. "Do you understand what that will do to me, to Family Liner, to Clan Corbel? Not to mention all the people we employ? You must stop him."

The order in which she mentioned those affected was telling. "I have no control—"

"Oh, yes, you do. You can't play the cracking victim with me." She marched toward him, stopping well within his comfort radius.

Reflex insisted he step back, increase the distance. He stepped closer and stared down at her.

She blinked, but held her ground. "Do what he wants, and he'll back off. I've studied the Records and seen the dance you do with him."

Sard it all! She was right. He'd capitulated too many times, now he apparently had a reputation. One that was about to change.

"We can manage this." She chewed her upper lip and exhaled heavily. "How about this? I'll publicly take the blame, confess my affair with Lemos, and declare it is entirely my responsibility. We both will. I'll apologize and extol your virtues to the Media in any way you want. You'll look like the wronged, principled hero you have always strived to make yourself out to be. The public will love it. Your image will shine, especially when you take back the repentant, errant Lady. Then, this will all go away as if none of it ever happened." She extended her hands as if to invite an embrace.

Matteo backed away. "No."

"What, then? Do you want a full ceremonial apology? It can be done. I did not think you were the type to need the formal rites, but it can be arranged."

"No."

"What, then? What will it take?" Her eyes widened as if imagining the disgraceful demands he could make of her.

He lifted open hands as if to push her away. "Absolutely nothing. I am not interested in you taking the blame, in restoring the betrothal, in any sort of connection with you. And I am certainly not going to be a cover for what you are doing here."

"You must. Don't you understand what's at stake?"

"I am not offering my future life as some sort of tool for you to use for your benefit."

"I am helping my Clan establish their role—"

"By interfering with the fabric of another society? You have no right, we have no right, to meddle in the working of other people's ways. I still haven't sorted out if what you're doing is legal by Dextrine standards, but I know without a doubt that it is not by Lighten's laws. I cannot support violating local law, even for a cause I might believe in."

"Stopping the Raiders isn't important enough? Lighten can't or won't do it on their own. They need our help. Kayavan's bones! They choose their leaders in the fighting ring. How can you respect that?"

"Even if that's actually what they did, they are an independent people. Whose autonomy we must respect."

"Lighten is a moon colonized by the dregs of good society, many of them criminals. They are brutes who don't know how to function with more sophisticated cultures. We're doing them a favor—"

"No. This is for your shortsighted benefit alone, and I will not be a part of it."

"How nice for you. But that leaves us both with a problem. I know you won't be able to keep your mouth shut, and I still have business to conduct. Once the handovers are completed, then I expect word is going to get out, no matter what we do. But until then, my transactions with Firen can have no interference. And you would try to do just that."

"You mean to hold me—"

"You will be a guest until our business is complete. Perhaps you can even make some agreements with Brels yourself during this time. He seems favorably disposed to you. After Firen takes full possession of the product, then you will be released to do as you will. Evering's business on Lighten will be complete and we will remove ourselves from this forsaken mudball."

No wonder Brels seemed to have such distaste for her. But what did he have in mind that would have driven him to make such a deal with Evering?

"Need I mention such detainment is wholly illegal and could prove the charge of high treason that Lord Timnon intends to level against you."

"High treason? That is Timnon's plan, treason?" Her voice wavered on the word.

"That is what I came here to warn you about."

Her eyes darted back and forth, processing that information. "There has been no treason in any of our actions."

"Much as I disagree with your dealings here, I concur. However, if you detain me, then—"

Her brow furrowed, then she brightened. "I do not have to detain you, only the pilot who flew you here."

"You would illegally detain someone unconnected with this matter?"

"The pilot is responsible for your being here. That is not my problem."

"You disgust me."

"I will also ensure you have no interactions with any other pilot here. But that won't take much. It is not detainment, after all, if you cannot find a way back to Anara until it suits me." A saccharine-sweet smile lit her face.

His hands knotted into fists, shaking at his sides.

"Nonetheless, I appreciate your warning. I will begin damage control efforts immediately."

"You play a dangerous game." More dangerous because she was involving people unrelated to the situation. "There's an old adage: if you have a choice, offend the Lord, not the heir, as they will be around much longer."

"Have I offended you, my dear Lord Heir Timnon?" She smirked and patted his cheek.

"Never take such liberties with me again, Lady. Remember your place." He grabbed her wrist and forced her to step back. "Lord Timnon will be offended. I am not. I am not easily offended. I am disgusted—disgusted by your arrogance, by your failure to care for anything beyond the end of your nose. Shortsighted pride that trades the illusion of profit for the values of Duty, Honor, and Family."

"You self-righteous, overbearing prick. As if Timnon is so perfect—"

"Do not mistake me for my grandfather. While I respect his legacy, you will find I am not he."

"Big words for a man who may never step into his own. With so many cousins—" She wrinkled her nose and sniffed.

"I am finished with this interview. Are you?"

"Entirely. The security team will show you to your guest quarters until a pilot is available and able to get flight clearance back to Anara. After the election, to be sure. But I do not think it will take very long after that. I expect Firen will do everything possible to make your stay comfortable; Evering has other, more important concerns to attend to."

"I would say good day, Lady, but it is not." He turned on his heel and strode out to the waiting brute squad.

Chapter 31

TRUE TO HIS WORD, the brute squad stayed away as Pogo led Ari down the long, gray stone and steel corridor to an intersection marked with a carved limestone arch. Beyond the arch, the walls were lined with limestone tiles, their natural subtle patterns creating an interesting abstract mosaic. This had to be for the benefit of guests. So at least he'd meant that much. These were guest rooms, not a euphemism for confinement.

He'd be offended if he realized she'd thought that. But then again, he wasn't stupid; he knew.

They stopped at a door with a simple, dark polished stone arch around it. "These will be your quarters for the time being." Pogo opened the door to a modest-sized lounge area, with a small tan couch and chair, low table, and media screen on the wall. A built-in desk and matching chair tucked in beside the media screen. An open door to the right revealed a bedroom and bath beyond. The furnishings looked well-maintained and comfortable, though efficient and without unnecessary decoration or false windows to ease the inherent tension in the enclosed space. Not the worst accommodations she had ever experienced. But at least those she had been free to leave.

"There's a common room through that door on the left, if you're in mind for some company. I expect Matté's been escorted to the quarters on the other side by now. You are free to interact with him, or not, as you like."

"I'm surprised you're not worried about allowing us contact with each other. No telling what kind of trouble we could make." Venom dripped from her voice. She would have liked to control it better, but it wasn't going to happen.

"Solitary confinement is cruel. I told you, you're not a prisoner. Don't make this out as worse than it is. Get a cold drink, watch the fights, try to think of it as unscheduled downtime." His frayed nerves crackled in his voice.

"I imagine you've restricted my module." She patted her hip pocket. No, she would not let him out of this easily.

"No outgoing signals. Limited incoming. You can still get media." He sighed, shaking his head. "And don't try to get around the systems. Someone will notice and come apart at the seams. No one wants that."

"Understood."

"If you need anything, your escorts ..."

"You mean the guards who won't hesitate to use whatever force they find amusing in a given situation."

"No, they won't. They're handpicked, properly trained, and not looking for an excuse to flex muscle." He muttered under his breath and squeezed his eyes shut. "Look, give me your module, and I'll program a one-touch emergency call, straight to me. I promise, if you call, I'll drop everything and be here. Short of sitting here myself, which I can't do, it's all I've got."

She handed him her module. He programmed it, then hit the emergency signal. His module screeched until he turned it off.

"I won't ignore that." He pushed her module back into her hands. "Let my team know if you need anything. I'll be by later to check in with you and bring some dinner." He laid a heavy hand on her shoulder. "We'll get this sorted out."

She refused to look him in the eye as he left. It wasn't fair to blame him for being the bearer of such news, but she'd reached her limit, and he'd have to deal with it.

Checking out the bedroom revealed a clean and reasonably comfortable bed. She hung her rucksack in the narrow closet, over a tiny clothing recycler. Seemed a newer model, but it would take a solid hour or more to print up a clean flight suit. It wasn't as if she had to be anywhere in a hurry, though.

She left the bedroom and paced the lounge like a trapped animal, which she was. What if ... What if ... What if ... all questions. No answers.

Surprisingly, the common-room door actually opened, revealing a seating area furnished for four, perhaps six, with a large media screen and a small kitchen alcove. The flush-mounted cold box was stocked with fruit, cheese, and non-intoxicating beverages. A box of assorted crackers and a teapot sat on a sliver of metal countertop next to the cold box. She took a bottle of chilled tea. Maybe she could choke down some fruit later. Starving herself wouldn't make things better.

What would, though? What could?

The far door slipped open. She jumped, reaching for her knife.

"Oh! Didn't expect company, but it's nice to see a friendly face." Matté stopped as he saw her, a sad smile blooming. Even a sad smile made a very attractive picture. "Sure as my ancestors' disapproval, it's been a day, hasn't it?"

"Your meeting with Lady Iantha didn't go well?" Ari perched on the arm of the couch.

"That's putting it mildly. She seems to think nothing of illegal weapons sales and how they might affect more than her Clan's bottom line." He dropped onto the other end of the couch, leaning his head back to stare at the ceiling. "Probably shouldn't have said that, but I'm sure you'd have put it together yourself."

"At least they're for use against the Raiders. Not like Firen's staging a coup." She stared at the tea bottle as she rolled it between her palms.

"They could be."

"I don't know if that would be a bad thing."

He turned to her with a start.

"Not what you expected to hear from me, I'm sure. There's a lot of folks who question Joco's transport policies, though, even within the Guild. Six months ago, he had to fight off a rival for the role as Guild Master, who voiced concerns with his policies. The election after wasn't pretty. Joco held the seat, but not by the majority he expected."

"If those decisions come from within Lighten, fine. I just don't think Dextrines, or anyone else for that matter, have any business meddling in those decisions."

"Good luck making that happen, though. Apparently, we are too ignorant and savage to manage our own affairs. Seems like Thera and Dextra feel they've got a moral obligation to interfere." She checked the time on her module. "You want to see the big fight?"

"Do you?"

"Not especially, but not much else to do. Every time I look at my module I get reminded we're stuck here and want to start climbing the walls looking for loose maintenance panels."

He laughed like he might have considered the same thing. "That's making me a little loose around the edges, too. I guess the fight, it is." He turned on a feed that opened with a close-up of Brels.

Grim and determined, Brels' face seemed locked in that expression, as though he did not relish the opportunity, but had a job to do. Maybe that was how he felt. But was it only the fight he wanted to win? Clearly, he wanted the Chairmanship, but there seemed to be further agendas behind that than she had thought possible.

The image panned to include Joco, also grim and determined, but there was something else in his eyes, too—anger, and a little desperation, perhaps? Good chance some of it was still directed at her, but Joco detested being challenged, especially when there was a risk he'd lose.

Matté traipsed to the kitchen, returning with a bottle of tea and a handful of crackers. "No offense, but it seems strange to see men their age take it to the ground."

"It is. Few choose to keep fighting past the general senior divisions. But they were both on the professional circuit when they were younger, and I think people expect it of them. Or they expect it of themselves." Ari took a long draw of her tea, cold, sweet, but with a slightly bitter tang. "You may not realize, but not all our elections include a fight. It's common practice because it's pretty popular with people, but especially as contenders get older, they don't keep it up."

"Really? It seemed like such an entrenched practice with all I've been hearing, I had no idea." His wide eyes asked her to explain further.

"This is a major election and people are excited that they're willing to take it to the ring, that's why all the media feeds are talking about it like the fight is the most important thing on the planet. So much so that they aren't focusing on coverage of the real issues of the election. And after the fight and election are done, there will be endless analysis of how the coverage made things better or worse—and they'll never come to an answer. What everyone agrees on is that the fights encourage people to be interested in the election and the more people who vote the better. What happens in the ring itself is likely to influence the undecided voters, and it looks like it's that group who will swing the election."

An announcer went over the rules, what few of them there were: no illegal shots, two long rounds. In case of a tie, the second round would continue until there was a winner.

"They're so evenly matched, it could be a long bout." Matté settled on the couch near her, crunching on delicate, seed-topped crackers, crumbs falling into his lap.

"Bookies are taking bets on that, too. Besides the kind of pin that might win, points or pins, the point spread, and the outcome of the elections afterwards. There's going to be a lot of money changing hands after this, no matter what."

"I know the same sort of thing happens at home when there's a contentious inheritance to be decided in the courts. That sort of thing tears Families and Clans apart."

"Isn't that—I'm sorry—but isn't it a rather primitive way to install leaders, to blindly pass it down because of an accident of birth?"

Matté laughed hard enough he nearly spilled his tea. "Never thought I'd hear the day Dextrine ways were called primitive, no offense, but especially by a Lighten."

He might have meant no offense, but really? "I suppose it is usually the other way around, isn't it?" Rolling her eyes did little to control the acid in her voice. She rose from her perch on the edge of the couch to move to the far side of the room.

"Stuck my foot in my mouth, didn't I? I'm sorry. I'm not even going to try to explain what I was trying to say 'cause it will only come out even worse. Lightens aren't primitive, and I find it offensive when I hear it being bandied about like fact. You can ask Iantha about that." He glanced back at her with a genuinely recalcitrant expression. "And you're absolutely right, Dextra's had some terrible leaders installed simply because of the accidents of birth. I'm trying hard not to be one of those." He nodded at the seat next to him, then at her.

She sighed and returned to the couch.

The first-round buzzer sounded. Joco leapt out to take control of the center—he was lightning fast and needed to secure a win early. Brels fought the long game.

"Honest question here, I promise. What are undecided voters looking for when watching this sort of fight?"

How to explain what she knew at a gut level, but didn't really consider in words? "A lot of things: skill and dedication to the sport; tolerance for discomfort; strength of purpose. Their strategies reveal their personality and style. What they're going to do when they hit adversity. Watch, see how Joco jumps in hard and fast. He's like that, a pilot who jumps to conclusions, trusts his intuition, and never wavers from his conclusions."

"You described a good pilot."

"Right, but not everyone understands that. In the ring they can see it for themselves. Even if they can't call it exactly that, they understand in their gut."

"What about Brels?"

"He's patient and adaptable. He watches and learns, conceding points to gain understanding of his opponent. He builds a strategy over the first round, and in the second, he'll pour everything into it. That's why he is seen as more progressive, he changes, he learns. He took Firen Mines from being a struggling enterprise, to a solid company, to being top of the Guild. That's how he took Guild Master."

"Sounds like you respect him." Matté tipped his bottle toward the screen where Brels was throwing Joco over his hip.

She winced as Joco landed hard on his shoulder and rolled up to his feet. "I'm not ashamed to admit that."

"Who do you favor? Who's best for the House of Guilds?"

"No good can come from me saying, no matter how tight Pogo has things locked down." She pushed the thought away with an open hand.

"I respect that. Not everyone understands how Records like that can ruin your day."

"Joco hates 'em. Keeps the Yard buttoned up tighter than the Key Minder's gate."

"My Grandfather wishes he could do that. I dread to think how this complete debacle is going to play out in the media." Matté actually shuddered.

"Funny to think Joco and your grandfather have that much in common."

The first round ended with a long buzzer and the commentators jumped in to analyze the fight.

Both their modules pinged.

She pulled hers out and checked the incoming message stack. The time stamp suggested the message was sent right before Joco entered the trainer's pit before the fight.

Monitored message approved.

Transcript follows, video withheld. Content may have been redacted. Those portions will be indicated with —...—

Lovely, not only was the message not private, but it was edited into something Firen Mines approved. Mangy trasks. But then again, it was likely Pogo's approval that got it through to her. She should be grateful.

But the message was from Joco. What chance she would be grateful for anything coming from him?

You stupid worthless little bug, can't you do as you're told and come in outta that storm?

She gasped, hands trembling. Probably should stop there and cut her losses. It wasn't going to get any more pleasant.

I told you to sign that drowned agreement and let Palmer settle for you. It was good enough for your mother. When did you start thinking so well of yourself?

When indeed? So full of herself with ideas like a life of her own, with a career of her choosing, and the chance of an equal partnership. Radical, ridiculous ideas, to be sure.

You're not getting the chance to insult either of us again. You hear? The offer is canceled and you'll never hear of it again.

What was the other half of that promise? Surely there had to be a sollert lying in wait to attack.

I'm done with ya, girl. You hear that? Done. You never been kin. You're no connection to me. Never have been, never will be. Won't speak your name again.

And there were the fangs and the venom. No surprise, he'd been manipulated into recognizing that connection. Still hurt like a sollert bite to hear.

I warned you, there's been enough playing fast and loose with my rules, with Guild rules. All your flight credentials are canceled and your Guild membership revoked. Don't even dream of touching a Guild vehicle on Lighten. Don't set foot on the Yard again. I've had enough of your storms.

The words ended, cold and abrupt, leaving her trembling and gasping for breath.

Chapter 32

MATTEO MOVED TO A chair across the room near the media screen. She probably wanted a little privacy as much as he did. He opened his incoming message stack to find two messages waiting. Both had been sent well over an hour ago, but only now made it through to him. One from Beny, the other from Uncle Wentforth, Beny's father, Lord Sennet.

Lovely. Best read Beny's first. He might not have the where-withal after seeing what Uncle had to say.

Monitored messages approved.

How dare they! Did Firen, no, more likely Pogo himself, realize how many laws they had broken getting into his personal messages?

Dextrine laws, not Lighten ones. And he was a prisoner here—what did he expect? They would think it a privilege to allow him access to messages at all.

Transcript follows, video withheld. Content may have been redacted. Those portions will be indicated with —...—

He flexed his hands in and out of fists. What were the chances of getting Pogo into the ring again?

What's going on, Matté? I just got the strangest message from Iantha. She was near hysterical and making no sense. Just going on and on about you being in danger. There were Raiders involved, and she feared the worst. I've never seen her like this. I'm worried. Really worried.

Get back with me and tell me what's going on before I send a brute squad after you. If she somehow gets to Grandfather, you know he won't hesitate to do something dramatic, and possibly dangerous.

Matteo had half a mind to let that happen.

Automated response text sent: I'm fine, Beny. Things just got a little complicated, but no brute squad needed. I'll get back to you soon.

Forgery, that was forgery!

Splintering soul catchers. He jumped to his feet, barely registering the second round of the fight starting, and stalked the perimeter of the room. Firen was going to regret crossing that line.

But that might not be his biggest problem. That message Iantha sent—when he'd left her. She wasn't hysterical or even worried about Matteo. That had to be the first of her attempts at damage control. And she was warning Beny that he was in danger, possibly from Raiders.

More likely, the danger was from her. What would it take to have the ship he traveled in shot out from under him and the Raiders blamed? That would distract Grandfather from his attempts to ruin her, her Family, and Clan. That would create enough chaos in Timnon to sideline them from any real influence for quite some time. All the while focusing attention on the genuine danger to the system, the Raiders. Might even help to solidify more support for the Unity movement.

Which he believed in, but wasn't ready to be a martyr for.

Maybe he was overreacting, but instinct said he wasn't. Smart pilots always trusted their instincts. And his instincts said Iantha was a clever, dangerous, and angry foe.

His hands trembled as he switched to the second message.

How could you do this, Matteo? How? You have forced Lord Timnon's hand to do the unthinkable and expose Corbel's plot to the media, who has now dubbed you an unfit heir for being taken in by Iantha's schemes.

You can't show your face on Dextra again until you have proven yourself worthy.

In hopes of salvaging this debacle, Lord Timnon has arranged for a tour of duty in the Dextrine Planetary Guard for you. Attached, you will find your commission papers for the Planetary Guard. Return them to me, signed, and report directly to the Capital Guard Base.

Don't call me to whine about this and don't bother coming home. Neither Lord Timnon nor I have any intention of seeing or supporting you until you prove you won't be an embarrassment to us all. And don't bring Benton into this. He has his own problems to focus on.

Iantha was probably trying to kill him, and Grandfather was all but abandoning him to another stint in military training. This was rich, absolutely rich. Matteo threw back his head and laughed long and hard and slightly unhinged.

Arli looked at him, eyes glistening with tears. "Bad news?"

"Pretty awful." Seemed a reasonable way to describe things when your former betrothed was more than likely planning your assassination. "You, too?"

"I knew it was coming. Just thought I had a little longer. He's cut me off, with nothing, not even my flight clearances. I'm well and truly stuck here now. No flight control will approve flight plans from me without those clearances."

"Sarding soul catchers, all of them." He stalked back to the couch and dropped so hard Arli bounced beside him. "This isn't what I came to Anara, to Lighten, for."

Arli pulled her knees to her chest and rested her chin on her knees. "I was just looking for a job."

"Better reason than me. This all started 'cause I was ditching an arranged betrothal."

She covered her face with her hands and laughed with a touch of hysteria. "You're kidding. I just refused to settle with Joco's partner's son, that was the final straw. I guess your decision was just about as popular. You get thrown out of the family, too?"

"Close to it. They're not currently speaking to me, and I'm not welcome to come back home. Does that count?"

"Close enough to say I know what it feels like." How small and alone she looked, huddled on the couch, knees tucked under her chin.

He rubbed his forehead with his palm. "That's too strange for words, you know? Beny scolds me regularly for bitching that no one understands the crap I have to deal with. It seems like I only had to get to a different sarding planet to find someone who is nothing like me, while at the same time being everything like me, to understand it all." He laced his hands behind his neck and pulled down until his neck popped. "I can't wrap my head around it."

"I can't wrap my head around that—" she gasped and pointed at the viewscreen.

Brels and Joco, both on their knees, locked shoulder to shoulder, unmoving.

"Clock says they've been like that for over three minutes now." She bit her knuckle.

"One of them is going to have a heart attack or stroke out if they keep that up."

"They're not going to call it, though—"

One of them, he couldn't tell which, slipped in a slick of sweat. They went to the ground, rolling in a frenzy of fists and feet and elbows and knees.

"That downward elbow was an illegal shot—" Matteo jumped to his feet, pointing at the screen. "Joco's disqualified himself."

"Or it was an accident. He might have slipped. The mat's covered in sweat." She stood beside him, eyes fixed on the screen. "The officials could go either way with the call."

"No, it was clearly illegal—"

The buzzer sounded, ending the round, and no call was made. Joco was hauled to his feet, declared the winner by points.

Arli stared at the screen for several more moments, then staggered back to the couch.

"What does that mean?"

She hugged herself hard. "No telling. Usually the winner takes the election, but it's going to depend on how the media portrays that last move, and if people believe them or not. It could go either way at this point. I don't know."

"They both look in pretty rough shape." Matteo retrieved her tea from across the room and handed it to her as he sat beside her.

She offered a look of thanks and clutched the bottle in both hands. "Neither one is going to rest before the final vote count. They'll go straight to interviews and appearances from here. Don't ask me how, though."

"Campaigning until the very end?"

"More or less, yeah."

"I hate waiting for all the detritus to fall from these things."

"We call it deadfall. Some say the storm will blow the deadfall away, but somehow it always seems to end up in my path." She traced condensation trickling down the bottle with her fingertip.

"And you're expected to clean it up?"

"Every drowning time."

One more thing they shared in common.

The door slid open and Pogo stepped in, full of authority and himself. At least he left the swagger on the other side of the door.

Pogo glanced at the screen. "Only the Arch Key Minder knows what's to come from that storm."

"Not what anyone expected, was it?" Arli avoided looking at Pogo, almost as though she expected him to resent her for the fight's outcome.

"None of this is." Pogo dragged the corner chair toward the couch, until it was right in front of them, and dropped into it. "You already know the messages you got were monitored. For what it's worth, and I doubt it's much, I was the only one who saw them."

Not the time to lose his temper. Pogo wasn't responsible for the content of the messages, just for breaking into his private communications and forgery. That was all. "You know how many laws you broke?"

"Mostly Dextrine laws, which don't apply here." Pogo shrugged with a self-assurance that made Matteo want to do something that would bring the brute squad running in. "And yes, I can recite each one, as well as the counter legal arguments for what I did. Will take the barristers years to sort it all out."

Unfortunately, he was right.

"What do you want from me? From us?" Arli pushed back to sit on the arm of the couch, gaining a little more distance from Pogo. Good chance she'd be standing behind it the next time Pogo opened his mouth.

"Look," Pogo extended open hands, "I know you've both slid face-first into a storm front no one could have prepared for. It should never have happened. I know now what I would have done differently to prevent it, but that's as helpful as closing the shutters in the middle of a dust storm. And the pilots whose poor judgment caused all this have been appropriately dealt with."

What exactly was appropriate in this context? He wanted to ask, but Pogo's tight expression made it clear he wouldn't be answering.

"But we're stuck in the situation we have with only a very few choices. You can both wait it out here until the information you have is all public knowledge. You'll be guests of Firen, and we'll extend all the hospitality we can. The accommodations aren't luxurious, to be sure, but they're comfortable and safe." Pogo emphasized the word and cast a quick look at Matteo. "But that's only delaying when you'll be facing the debris from those storms. I'm sorry that I've got a better idea of what that will be than I'm sure either of you would have liked. Apart from what's happened here, both of you have level five storms coming at you I wouldn't wish on anyone."

Was that a hint that Pogo also saw Iantha as a threat to Matteo? A stint in the Dextrine Planetary Guard wasn't the sort of thing to be called a level five storm, was it?

"Things are what they are," Arli murmured, poised to spring back for distance again.

"Maybe not." Pogo tried to catch Arli's gaze, but she refused the contact.

Matteo leaned forward, elbows on knees. "You imply there's another reasonable alternative."

"Yes. But I'll be up front with you, I'm not so certain about the reasonable aspect. What I propose is extreme, even insane, and could make things worse. But that's all I have to offer, so I will."

"Offer?" Arli didn't slip behind the couch. Still perched on the armrest, she straightened her back as she hugged her knees to her chest.

"Yes, offer. You can hear it out, or not; take it or not. No pressure, no reprisals for refusing. If you say no, you're our guest until you're no longer a danger to us or yourself for what you know. If you are interested, we can work out the details." Pogo tried again to catch her gaze.

This time, she allowed it. "I'm listening."

"I suppose it doesn't make things worse to hear you out." Matteo kept his tone mild. It wouldn't do to reveal too much interest at this stage.

"Excellent." Pogo rubbed his hands together and stood. "Give me a minute to get someone who can explain it much better than I can." He left.

Arli unfurled and pressed her feet to the floor. "When all is said and done, you're going to take legal action against Firen, aren't you?"

"It doesn't matter whether or not I do. The Clan, my Grandfather, or one of the Lords on the High Council will. Unlawful detainment, maybe even kidnapping, are pretty difficult to deny."

"Whatever the charge is, it's going to be bad for both sides. Drown it all." She rubbed her shoulders. "Firen and Timnon will both be seen as villains. We'll be looking at each other instead of the Raiders. That hurts everyone."

At least Iantha's plot would put everyone's eyes on the Raiders. "As pissed as I am about all this, and you can be sure I'm seriously pissed, I don't want your people or mine paying the price for it." Matteo bounced his heel rapidly. "But I don't know how to stop it. It's like stopping a rockslide once it starts. Not much can hold it back. I'll try, but I don't hold out much hope."

She stood and paced behind the couch. "This last week has felt like constantly trying to outrun the soul catchers, with so much riding on every move!"

"That's exactly what it's been like for far too long for me. But outside of my family, you're the first person I've known who has understood that." And that made him feel far too many confusing things. Later, deal with those later.

"I guess you're your own kind of storm-bringer, too."

"Never thought of it that way. But maybe you're right." The way she looked at him made his vow of "later" even harder to take seriously.

The door slid open. Good, he needed the distraction.

Chapter 33

ARI JUMPED AND GASPED. "Sander?"

"You know him?" Pogo asked, slack-jawed.

"I knew her mother." Sander said with his air of "*That's all I'll say, so don't ask.*" He wore an unfamiliar dark-gray military duty uniform. Difficult to sort out what his rank was, but it had to be some sort of senior officer. He stared at her with the sort of long-suffering frustration that usually exploded in a memorable show of temper.

Pogo looked back and forth between her and Sander as though struggling to fit pieces together.

She touched the scar behind her left ear. "There's no connection."

Matté's and Pogo's eyebrows shot up. They could think what they would about the matter. She wouldn't say any more. Nor would Sander. After all, there was no connection.

"This is Colonel Castanel of the Theran Armada, Liaison to Fleet." Pogo gestured toward Sander.

So that was the uniform he was wearing.

"Apparently, you already know Arli." Pogo's brow knotted again. "This is Matteo Sennet."

"Heir of Clan Timnon, late of Wroxton Academy, as I understand." Sander focused on Matté, not quite pointedly ignoring Ari, but close.

"I imagine you've already investigated my academic records, then." Matté bristled.

"Naturally. Impressive, both in academic achievement and prowess in flight." Sander's quick glance her way seemed intent on reminding her she lacked any sort of relevant credential for much of anything, especially now.

Pogo cleared his throat, breaking the already stifling tension between them. "You have already seen the Raptors we're purchasing, but they are useless without trained pilots."

"And you've made a deal with Fleet to train them?" Ari gasped. Brels' agenda far exceeded her imagination.

"As weapons operators. By the end of the next term of the House of Guilds, those birds will be classed as weapons, not vehicles, and no longer under Transport Guild control."

How was he so certain? Brels had lost the fight, after all. The election was no sure thing.

Then again, did she even want to know?

"I told you I had a remote assignment and was hoping to hire you as my replacement here." Pogo shot a meaningful look at Sander, who acknowledged it with a twitch of his heavy eyebrows. "That's going to be difficult now that Joco's canceled all your clearances."

"Canceled them? That's quite the tantrum on his part, isn't it?" Sander chuckled under his breath. "You finally stood up to him, didn't you? Bet that was a level five shit-storm in a sollert skin."

She shrugged.

Pogo coughed softly. "We need a company of pilots, trained as weapons operators, to defend the mines and our products against the Raiders. Colonel Castanel has agreed to allow you to join that company, if you so choose. Six months' combat flight school, a year's tour of duty with Fleet, and after that a three-year renewable contract with Firen as a weapons operator."

"And if the legislation isn't changed?" Ari asked.

"An alternate position with Firen will be made available, or you can cut ties and take the Fleet experience and flight clearance to work elsewhere." He turned to Matté. "You don't need a job with Firen, but you're about to be shipped off to the Dextrine Guard under your Grandfather's microscope. He claims you need military experience. You've got the chance to get a similar experience under your own terms. Take control back from Lord Timnon and prove yourself in a place where no one can argue it was favoritism that got you there. Not to mention it would keep you clear of the other storm that may be gathering on the horizon."

Did Iantha and the broken betrothal have something to do with that rather unsubtle hint?

"Why invite us to be a part of this? What's in it for you?" Matté squared his shoulders and looked at Sander as one regards an equal—clearly not something Sander was accustomed to.

That was a little too satisfying to watch.

"Fleet needs pilots," Sander said.

Fleet was also the backwater of all backwaters, where those who didn't want to be found hid. There was a reason they needed pilots—on the whole, pilots were less likely to have a solid reason to seek refuge in Fleet.

"That's a lot of resources to spend on a one-year commitment from me, especially when I am unlikely to work for Firen afterwards."

"Perhaps so, but then again, what better way to secure a friend to Fleet and Thera in the Dextrine High Council? Your politics are well known, Lord Heir Timnon, and in that, we are allies."

Matté had never mentioned his political views, but it suddenly felt very important to understand them. Surely, it would not be difficult to find Records of what Matté believed.

"And you think I will be such a friend after my tour of duty? That's a significant risk, considering Fleet's colorful reputation."

Colorful was a unique definition, but then again, blood was colorful.

"I have every faith in my organization. Fleet ring fighters have created a reputation for Fleet that is perhaps exaggerated." Sander's imperious posture dared anyone to disagree with him. "It is exactly the experience a young heir who supports the Unity party should want to lend credence to his claims. You were trained up at Wroxton, a premier Theran academy. What more reasonable next step for your career?"

"It is an interesting thought." Matté nodded like a card player trying to decide what to do with his hand.

"You, on the other hand—" Sander turned to her, "it is hard to fathom how it might be reasonable for you. You are hardly the sort that makes their way into Fleet. Unless it is on her back."

She twitched as though she'd been slapped, but his words didn't land as hard as Joco's hand. "I did not follow my mother's career choice. As you well know, I followed yours. And that's what Fleet seems in need of."

Pogo's jaw dropped and the corners of Matté's lips turned up a mite, though he tried to hide it.

"You don't have to do this, either of you. It is just an alternative that seemed worth putting up for consideration." Pogo looked as though he was questioning the wisdom of that decision.

"Fleet will train your pilots to fly Raptors?" Ari licked her lips, hopefully not salivating visibly.

"That is the agreement." Sander closed his eyes and twitched his head "*no*," but that only encouraged her.

"Can we see them, the Raptors, first? I need to sit in the cockpit and know they aren't going to disqualify me because I'm too short. No point in agreeing to this, only to be sent back for not qualifying."

"She's right. I'd like to see them as well." Matté might be worried about being too tall, or broad in the shoulder to fit the cockpit, but more likely, he was as eager to get his hands on one as she.

"That sounds reasonable to me." Pogo actually agreed—or maybe he wanted an up-close-and-personal look himself. "It is in my jurisdiction, so I'll approve that. Colonel, do you care to join us?"

Chapter 34

MATTEO STOOD WITH POGO. Sander seemed to mull over
the thought while staring at Arli. How were those two connected? Clearly, he knew her mother in more than a casual
sense. The way she kept touching the little scar behind her
left ear suggested he was connected to it. And Sander went
too far in saying they were not connected. All of which
screamed they were connected.

But this was neither the time nor the place to press for
information that was none of his business.

"I will join you." Sander rose and allowed Pogo to lead
them out.

Pogo spoke briefly to the guards outside the door. No
telling what he'd said, but the effect was that the guards
remained behind as they returned to the hangar.

Sander dropped back to walk alongside Arli, close enough that Matteo could hear their conversation. No, he shouldn't listen, but to do that effectively, he'd have to make small talk with Pogo, and that was simply beyond him.

"What did you do to make Joco clip your wings?"

"Refused a settlement with Palmer." How did she say that so nonchalantly?

"That's all? Seems extreme for that."

"You taught me to fly and how to keep that damn bird of yours in the air with spit and good intentions. That's not the way the Guild works."

Sander had taught her to fly? And her ship was or had been his. Definitely connected ...

"And it took until now for him to crack down on it? Interesting ..."

"What's interesting?"

"That it all came apart just after you committed your mother to the sunrise."

"Are you saying Joco looked the other way because of her?" Arli's voice became strained.

Was Sander intentionally unnerving her? Dumb question, of course he was.

"There was a reason she put up with so much from him for so long. Things were rough long before she and I reconnected." Sander tsk-tsked; nothing subtle about him.

"It wasn't my fault that she made those choices."

"Fault, perhaps not. But reason? I cannot say, it was not the sort of thing she discussed with me ..."

Why was Sander so intent on rattling her?

They stopped inside the hangar, near the line of newly-assembled Raptors. Sleek, deep gray, steel birds of prey, waiting, watching for their chance. Amazing to be so close to one. At Wroxton, the ships were held up as the pinnacle of Theran engineering—although more than Therans had contributed to the design. The height of flight technology that only the most select few would ever get to experience.

And he had not been one of those. He had put his application in for combat training, but it was summarily denied because of his Rank at home. Grandfather had made sure of that. This opportunity seemed tailor-made to thwart Grandfather's designs while offering him the kind of real-world experience he desperately needed. Pogo had been right.

"They're something, aren't they?" Pogo pulled a set of mounting steps to the nearest Raptor and tapped a code into a panel on the stairs that raised the cockpit. "Go ahead, have a look, sit down and see how it feels in there."

Matteo all but ran up the steps to the cockpit that would seat only a single pilot. There was something about flying entirely alone, the challenge of it, that made his skin tingle. With little backup or support, it would be on him alone to make it work, or, literally, die trying. Success would be on his merit alone. Embarrassing how much he wanted, needed that.

"Mount up." Pogo called.

It would be a tight fit, for certain. Maybe too tight to make it work. But now was the time to find out, not when he could be sent back in what Grandfather would consider disgrace, only to be shunted into a meaningless make-work position in the Dextrine Guard.

He climbed in slowly, avoiding the myriad of controls and displays that seemed to cover every inch of the cockpit. Somehow it was reminiscent of Arli's hauler, compact and efficient, and an even tighter squeeze.

There, he'd wedged his shoulders in with a bit of clearance. Hurdle one conquered. But it wasn't enough to wedge himself inside. He needed to be able to function.

He scanned the control panels, recognizing a reassuring number of them. And there it was. The proof he needed, a model number at the top of the control stick. This was not old tech, nothing that could be categorized as military surplus.

The Dextrine military would not have sanctioned the sale of the specs to print these ships. Grandfather's accusations of treason wouldn't stick, but illegal weapons trade would, especially if a few discreet Records made their way out. Which they most definitely would, filtered through enough layers that they would not be traced back to him.

Even so, things were going to get cracking ugly over this. He didn't want to be involved in the whole affair to begin with, but Iantha's cavalier attitude toward interfering with Lighten was insupportable, and that made it his responsibility to deal with. Even so, it would be best for all if he stayed out of the Media's range while this all shook out. Which would be the case if he was conveniently away training with Fleet. That alone made the opportunity more appealing.

He drew several deep breaths and systematically reached for every control, tested the view on every readout, stretched, twisted, reached, and sometimes contorted to ensure he had access to everything. Therans might slap down an arbitrary rule about a pilot's dimensions he would not be able to argue, but Fleet? All they would care about was that he could do the job. And he definitely could.

But did he dare? He leaned hard into the seat and exhaled slowly, counting ... seven ... eight ... nine ...ten. Breathe in four ... five ... six. Out ... eight ... nine ... ten.

For the better part of a decade, he'd been threatening to wrest his life out of Grandfather's control. To prove beyond any doubt that he was capable, without his Clan's name, without his Rank, but on his personal merit alone, to rise beyond the insignificant duties and built-for-media opportunities given to him, to be the man his people needed him to be. With Thera in turmoil and the Raiders on the move, Dextra needed leaders who could do more than posture and argue.

Now that he had the chance to do that, would he dare?

"You fall asleep in there? Give someone else a chance," Pogo called up from the steps.

"As soon as I can extricate myself, I'll be there."

Said extrication proved less difficult than he'd anticipated, and he made his way down the steps only a little stiff and scraped from the adventure.

"You see what you needed to?" Pogo asked.

"I did."

"I'll take you back to quarters, then. Sander and Arli seem to need ..." Pogo tipped his head toward them.

"Lead on. I need some time to think. This is a soul catcher crazy idea, you know that, right?" He walked shoulder to shoulder with Pogo back to the guest quarters.

"That pretty well sums it up. Figured it might be hard to swallow. But it also might be exactly what you need. Just to be clear, you don't have to work for Firen after the tour, like I said before. I know a lot of lines got crossed today—we're not crossing that one."

"For now, we can focus on the one you're not crossing rather than the ones you did." Matteo bit back far too many things he'd be quite happy to say about those very transgressions.

Pogo paused at the guest quarters' doorway. "Think about it, combat training and firsthand knowledge of both Fleet and the Raiders in exchange for a one-year tour in Fleet, which is a joint venture you claim to believe in. Sard it all, if it doesn't sound tailor-made for your situation."

"I'd accuse you of manufacturing it to manipulate Dextrine politics as much as Iantha is trying to do on Lighten, but you're not good enough to have put all this together."

"I hate to admit it, but no, no sarding way I could manage that. I'll give you some time to think. Page me when you've decided. Either yes or no, it won't be mentioned again." Pogo tossed a salute and headed down the hall.

So, a limited-time, once-only offer. Made sense.

Matteo entered his quarters and paced. Somehow, he thought better while moving, but there was little space to do that in these guest quarters. Four steps forward, three across, four more back while dodging the small table. He'd half a mind to go out and pace the hall, but there were some very touchy guard-types around who wouldn't find that amusing.

The most upsetting thing in all this was that Pogo was right. It was a perfect counter to Grandfather's plan to shunt him to the Dextrine Guard. A tour of duty with them had always been in his plans, but knowing no one would ever forget who he was haunted him. Never knowing if any accomplishment was earned or a political favor left a bitter taste in his mouth. As did the certainty that he'd never be given anything meaningful to contribute—the risk of him cracking something wide open and word getting out about it was too great.

If he did this thing, it could be eighteen months walking in Laythe's Woods, but when he was done—assuming he didn't splinter things down to bedrock—he'd have solid experience behind him that would give him credibility to oppose Grandfather's dangerous notions.

Sard it all! It was a cracking good offer. One he should be thoroughly suspicious of. Except that it seemed Pogo was signing up for the same experience. And Arli might, too. That gave it all an air of credibility. His module pinged.

Pogo had sent him a list of the exact terms and conditions of his attachment to Fleet. Including Fleet verification code. Either this was the real thing, or a damn impressive forgery.

Splintering shards! What was one supposed to do when gut instincts and common sense screamed the opposite answers in his face?

Chapter 35

ARI WATCHED AS POGO brought the stairs and allowed Matté to examine the Raptor's cockpit while trying to ignore Sander standing beside her. She'd done a very great deal of watching in her life. Watching others pursuing their goals, their dreams, helped by their connections. Watching others succeed, become worthy connections in their own right, while she stood by, with all her efforts to do the same squashed by those around her with more power and influence than she would ever have.

But now she stood here, watching again, as an impossible desire dangled before her and a powerful man stood beside her, with the control to squash it all again, as things had always been.

But perhaps they were different this time. Somehow, those stairs made it different, as though there might be a path to the impossible.

As soon as Matté and Pogo stepped away, she ran up to the top of the stairs, leaving Sander behind. Storms and squalls! It was gorgeous!

She dropped into the cockpit in a single leap. Compact and efficient, not cobbled together, but designed to do ... it seemed designed to do everything. She scanned the displays, the controls. All signs screamed of something designed by Acoling Flight Design. She felt along the edge of the control stick for the maker's mark. Yes, it was an Acoling design.

Her hands trembled as she caressed the dashboard. "You are a pretty bird, aren't you? I'll bet you aren't balky like my hauler, complaining at everything she's asked to do. No, Acoling's ships are willing partners. A joy to fly. I bet you'd enjoy dancing through the air with me. And I certainly could make you dance."

A few settings were difficult to reach, but Acoling always included a few extra adjustment options in their cockpits. She reached under the dashboard—yes, right where she expected it to be. With a click of a lever, she brought the panel to a better angle. A few more tweaks—perfect! As if it were made for her. Acoling didn't have the standard prejudices about who was tall enough to be a pilot that other designers did.

She leaned back and closed her eyes as a shiver coursed from head to toe and back again. She might be a little arli, but that was enough. This really was possible.

"Aren't you the little hell cat, sitting there like you belong in that cockpit?" It was hard to tell whether Sander's tone was admiration or disregard. He had this way of walking a line between the two that made him difficult to read. He stared down at her from the top of the stairs.

"I do belong here. What do you want to know about the flight specifications of this ship? Or would you rather me tell you about its flight characteristics instead?"

"This design is military-access only. What can you possibly know about it?"

"Where do you want me to start?" She listed the flight characteristics common to all the Acoling models, guessing at a few as seemed appropriate for the style of vessel and the military capabilities that would have been built into it.

Sander listened silently, but one eyebrow crept higher and higher.

"Not perfect, I'm sure, but I'd bet money I don't have that I'm better than seventy-five percent accurate."

"Closer to eighty. Clever party trick, but it don't prove you can manage a vessel like this. Get out of there, we need to talk." He waved her up. "Privately."

Not a word that boded well for her. There were only two things Sander ever required privacy for: comfort and correction. One of those was absolutely not a possibility; the other could make her decision very clear.

She followed him back to her guest quarters, fighting the urge to run the other direction the whole way there.

He immediately stalked to the common-room door and locked it, then removed his module from its holster and stabbed at it, probably setting some sort of military privacy ware, and placed it on the low table in front of the couch.

How was it possible a single man could take up so much space in the room? Somehow, he dominated every corner, every shadow. All the air belonged to him. "I told you not to get mixed up in this."

"What is 'this' that I'm not supposed to get mixed up in? You make it sound as though there's been some intentional plot on my part to become involved in things bigger than myself. Well, there's not. I've been trying to earn a living while Joco keeps trying to make it impossible. That's how I got here. Following up on a job lead with Firen. How is it my fault a couple of storm-addled pilots, that you probably had some command over, failed to follow orders?"

"What part of avoiding connections to powerful men did not make sense to you?" His voice had that low, dangerous edge to it and his face flushed.

"I was trying to get away from Joco. What about that is not clear to you?" She clenched her fists, leaning in toward him.

"And you ran straight into the company of Brels and Timnon's spawn."

"I've been working, under contract, for both of them. Do you want to see the contracts? That doesn't make them connections! Why is it you and Joco are so obsessed with any connections I might make? You both have disavowed any connection to me. Why does it matter so much to you?"

"You should avoid your mother's habit of getting mixed up in things much bigger than herself."

"You know, that's not exactly helpful. What does that even mean?"

"All of this—Brels, Joco, Timnon, they're all so much bigger than you—you have no idea just how much is tied up with those three. You need to get away. Go back to where you belong." He looked over his shoulder toward the door, his tightly-bound queue bobbing as he did.

"At the moment I don't belong anywhere. Going back to the Yard would be leaping from this storm to another one, which, from where I'm standing, looks even worse than this one."

"That's what arlis do, isn't it? Ride on the edge of the storm, leading in one storm or another?" He rolled his eyes.

"Do you know how tired I am of hearing that?"

"Sometimes an honest name can fit too well." He leaned, looming over her.

"Is that why you hated being called Sand Storm?" She stared directly into his clear brown, angry eyes.

"Nice try, but no. It's a Lighten name that never fit the world I actually live in." He broke eye contact and looked off to the side, into another time and place. "Lighten was where I paused between storms."

"Is that why you called Mama Haven? How did she come by that as her honest name?"

"She was that." He nodded, just barely, then returned his gaze to her. "You're a lot like her, but maybe not enough for your own good."

"You know I don't have a lot of options. The swamp won't have me. Brels might, but if I can't fly for him, then this is my best alternative. What do you want me to do?"

"I told you before. I'm not your friend—don't ask me for advice."

"That sounds very much like a man who doesn't want to be blamed if everything goes sideways."

Sander flinched, as though he were to be blamed for something already ... miserable soul catcher was probably the one who flagged the Records that started the inquiry back in Anara. "I may be the Liaison to Fleet, but that doesn't mean that I don't realize that Fleet gets the dregs of society, Theran, Dextrine, Lighten. Everyone there is running from someone bigger than themselves—"

"Sounds like I'd fit in well, then."

"I agreed to entertain this scheme of Pogo's because Brels has offered to supply a dozen decent pilots who don't carry the baggage the rest of Fleet does. I'll get a year's service out of them and that's in my interest. Frankly, I'd sooner see you in the Theran Forces than in Fleet. But they wouldn't take you now, not after Joco's stripped your clearances."

"You just made my point for me."

"Sure as the Hell Cat's roar, you need to get out of the storm that's about to make landfall here. You might have nothing to do with what's going on, but storms blow away everything in their path." Sander muttered under his breath and strode a brisk twelve-step circuit around the small room. "There's a reason the Fleet training base is called Laythe's Woods."

Of course it was. "So, I'll know what I'm walking into. That seems to be an advantage."

He growled deep in his throat, a sound she hadn't heard in five years. "Do you remember what I taught you when you were growing up?"

"Your Theran Precepts and Codes and Protocols? The ones you insisted we live by when you were in residence?" Her stomach churned, and she edged half a step back. Those had been memorable lessons.

"Do you remember them?" He stood nearly toe-to-toe with her, as he had in those days. Harsh, critical, painful days.

"I can't forget them."

"Can you follow them?" The accusing look he gave her. What did he suspect her to be guilty of this time?

There, she'd found the anger she needed to straighten her shoulders and strengthen her voice. "Not sure I can help it. Not when they're sitting in the back of my head screaming at me most of the time."

"You've been flying since I sat you on my lap in the cockpit the first time, nearly twenty years ago. Having your wings clipped will smother you." He studied her, nodding. "If you take this offer, what you learned from me will serve you well. But if you do this, nothing is going to be given to you. There'll be no favors or quarter given. You will stand on your own merit or not at all."

In other words, joining Fleet was going to be like living with him. "My own merit is all I've ever had."

"You could stay here with Firen, though grounded, of course. But you'll find something to do with yourself. You've proven you can do that. No doubt Brels will have you re-engineering his mine equipment or some such. Entirely respectable."

He was right. It would be safer and sensible. And better than living with Palmer. "That would be settling, though."

"Sounds as if you've made a decision I'm not going to like."

"I'm not going to settle. I wouldn't settle for Palmer. Waiting to take whatever the mines can give without flight clearances would be settling in a different way. I'll take Fleet."

"Remember, for all the talk of it being a joint venture, Theran standards run Fleet. They don't approve of women in combat of any form, and they don't like anything that smells of innovation or independence." Sander looked at her as if to ask if he needed to go into detail. "You'll be going in with serious marks against you."

"Joco never much liked it either. I'll get by. And if I do, at the end of it I'll have earned something even Joco can't take from me. I'll take Fleet."

"Understood." Sander seemed resigned, but he wasn't fighting her, so that was something. "Two pieces of advice. Don't get into the fight ring with any of them. And don't let any of them in your bed."

The first of those made sense. The latter stung, but given Mama's situation, he was one of the few with the right to say such a thing. "Seems sound advice."

He muttered under his breath. No, she wasn't going to make it easy. Why should she? "Let's see what the lordling has decided."

Chapter 36

MATTEO PACED THE COMMON room, five steps across and four wide. Only a little larger than his quarters, but easier to skirt the furniture as he paced.

The door from Arli's side slid open and Sander entered first, with Arli trailing a healthy distance behind.

"She's in." Sander pointed back at Arli.

"I can speak for myself," she snapped.

Sander's eyes widened, and one corner of his mouth rose. "You've grown teeth."

"And claws. And a spine."

"Good, you'll need them." Sander pointed to Matteo. "And you?"

"I'd like a few minutes to talk with her first," Matteo said.

"I thought you said you weren't mixed up with him." Sander turned to her, glowering.

"She's not." Her look suggested that maybe Matteo shouldn't have spoken for her, but it might have been as much about Sander's question. "One doesn't need to be 'mixed up' to have a conversation."

Sander rolled his eyes. "I'll go find Pogo so we can complete whatever needs to be done to put an end to this dithering about." He stalked out.

A weight seemed to slip from Arli's shoulders as the door shut. "Been better than five years since the last time he darkened Lighten's door. He hasn't changed much."

"Is that good or bad?" Matteo perched on the back of the couch.

"Hard to say. What'd you want to talk about?" She dropped onto the couch, head leaning back, eyes closed.

"This is going to sound stupid, but I need someone to help me process this. Usually I'd call Beny, but that's not going to work. You've already kept my ass out of the fire twice now, so I have some reason to think you don't have a vested interest in seeing me fail, which makes you the best option available."

She opened her eyes, brows knitted in an attractive expression of puzzlement.

"Is that asking too much?"

"I'm not exactly a fount of wisdom, but I can listen if that's what you need." She leaned forward, elbows on knees, in a classic posture of I'm-paying-attention-now.

"I don't need you to tell me what to do. Just listen, ask questions. I need to get my thoughts sorted out and my head's a jumble right now." He set off on his first circuit around the room. Kayavan's bones! If only he could talk to Beny! "So, if I don't take this offer, I'm going to be forced into a tour with the Dextrine Guard."

"Doesn't sound like a bad gig. They've got a solid reputation. I'm guessing that keeps you away from home until tempers cool down, too. What are the downsides?"

"Grandfather will interfere at every turn, so I'll be shunted to meaningless work that won't be affected by his games." He raked his hair as he strode past the couch. "Upside is that it'll keep the Family happy, the Media happy, and I'm not likely to get shot at."

"You think that latter bit is true?"

He pulled up short and stared at her, prickling tension creeping up the back of his neck. "What do you mean?"

"Not trying to pry, but it seemed like Pogo hinted that you might be in some sort of danger, and I leapt to the conclusion that it might be of the ... 'friendly fire' sort."

What had she just said? His stomach flipped and nearly landed in his boots. "Splintering shards, you don't miss much, do you?"

"Necessary skill living around Joco. So, if I'm right, would serving in the Guard make you an easy target for them, more so than flying with Fleet?"

"That's a key minder's question for sure, but one I hadn't thought of. Not used to worrying about 'friendly fire,' as you put it." He set off on another lap around the room. "Now you've got me thinking, I'll keep that in mind. What else?"

"Fleet's essentially Theran, you've lived under that at school. Is going back to that worse than your grandfather's interference?"

"Been giving that some thought. Keep going."

"Those Raptors—how much do you want to fly?"

He couldn't suppress the foolish grin. "Probably about as much as you. Sitting in one was amazing—"

"I think I drooled on the dashboard. But only another pilot would understand that."

"Damn straight, so yes, I really want to fly one."

"I don't know about you, but for me, this is a once-in-a-lifetime chance."

"Hard to see how it wouldn't be for anyone. I know it's only the best of the best who get the chance ... and ..." he swallowed hard. Getting that rejection stung more than he wanted to admit, even to himself.

"Not the sort of thing you'd be tagged for, is it?"

"It would probably rouse the ancestors from their crypt."

"One more question, then, and it's the most important one. What does your instinct tell you?"

He looked her straight in the eye. She was completely serious, nothing mocking about that question at all.

But of course, another pilot would understand. "That's exactly what I needed to hear. Thanks, seriously, thanks." He pulled out his module and sent a page.

As quickly as Pogo appeared, he must have been waiting outside the door. "And?"

"Looks like I'm in, too."

"I'll get the Records work arranged, then. Ship-out date depends on the elections, but it'll be a few days. That also means you're technically working on a Firen contract, so if you're willing to sign a full NDA, I can let you have some outside contact to make whatever necessary arrangements you might need to make." Tension seemed to flow away from him, almost puddling on the floor around him. "Yes, there will be some limits, but I can put filters on the conversations to cut them if necessary. I won't need to do a live monitor of the conversation. You need anything sent in from Anara? I don't think I'm going to be able to allow you to head back there."

Matteo glanced back at Arli, who nodded. "All things considered, I think it's best to stay here. As long as I can talk to Beny, I should be able to manage everything I need."

Pogo turned to Arli, who shrugged. "Mostly need a spot to leave my ship for the duration."

"I'll see what can be arranged."

"That is kind of you."

He patted her shoulder. "That's hospitality, and it's about time you saw a little of it come your way after all you've shown us. If there's more we can do, say the word. This whole day has been a shit-storm, and I'd like to turn it over to the sunrise and be done with it. Matté, it'll take a bit to get all the Records processed through, but after that, tell me when you want to make those calls. In the meantime, dinner will be here soon and the post-fight commentaries are being posted. Might be interesting to hear the analysis and the pre-election polls." Pogo turned on the media feeds and dropped onto the couch beside Arli.

She seemed uncomfortable, so Matteo sat on her other side, closer to her than he had ever been permitted to sit with Iantha. She gave him a quick sidelong glance and a little smile.

There was definitely something to be said for being ordinary, even if only for a little while.

The fight commentaries continued until the voting opened at midnight, then the news feeds switched to exit polls and political commentary. At which time, they sent Pogo on his way for an all-night vigil with other miners, and called it a night themselves.

It should have been more difficult to get to sleep than it was, with his future making a sharp, unexpected pivot today. But exhaustion—and maybe a touch of relief that he would not be headed straight into Grandfather's clutches again—served him well, and he fell into a blissfully dreamless sleep.

First thing the next morning, Pogo delivered breakfast and announced he and Arli both had clearance to make calls, provided they stuck to the NDAs they had signed yesterday. Of course, filters would be in place to cut off the call if they even seemed to transgress, and the offer to head to Fleet would also be rescinded in that case. A bit heavy-handed, but given the situation, it was not unexpected. Realistically, being able to make calls was generous ... had to keep reminding himself of that.

Matteo hurried back to his guest quarters to call Beny.

Poor man looked like he hadn't slept since Iantha's call came in. He probably hadn't. "What's going on? And don't play games. If I don't get a satisfying answer, then this key minder," he pointed to his chest, "is sending troops to drag you back here, today."

Matteo laced his fingers behind his neck and pulled his elbows together, not quite meeting in front of his chin. "I get it. I'm sorry, things have been so sarding complicated."

"So, I gathered. Now spill," Beny leaned into his module until his face took up the entire screen. "I'm not exactly a well of patience here."

Matteo chuckled, mostly because he was supposed to at that face. "First, I'm safe and not currently in any imminent risk of harm."

"Were you, though?"

"On the way here, things got interesting." A yellow light blinked in the upper corner of the module viewscreen. Probably a warning that he was skirting close to the filters. Nice touch, that. "But since we landed, no, not at risk."

"Care to fill that out a bit?"

"Sorry, I can't. But I am safe and don't expect that to change while I'm with Firen."

Beny pinched the bridge of his nose, eyes rolling in a look of well-earned long-suffering. "We'll come back to that last bit there, but go on."

"Iantha and Evering are not guilty of treason. But they aren't in the clear, either." Another yellow blinking light.

"Going to tell me what that looks like?"

"I can't, not yet. But as soon as I can, you'll be the first."

Beny raked both hands through his hair. He might be ready to pull it all out at this point. "And the danger Iantha alluded to you being in?"

"In a word, yes. And it's *not only* because I've accepted an offer to the Fleet Training Academy on Laythe Base."

"You what?" Beny slammed his hand on the table hard enough to bounce his module.

"I'll be training to fly combat raptors, then do a one-year tour in Fleet."

"Seriously, Matté, have you lost your mind? Is there some coercion involved?"

"I can see why you'd think that, but no. Absolutely not. I have rarely been more certain of anything."

"Fleet? That makes no sense. You've got a commission with the Guard waiting for you—or even with the Theran Armada since you graduated Wroxton. Why that cobbled-together band of—"

"How better can I show support for the Unity Bloc?"

"What's wrong with the Dextrine Guard?"

"We've talked about it, you know—it would be like having Grandfather looking over my shoulder day and night. They can't risk me screwing up something, or worse, getting hurt. They'll be babysitting me, not letting me do anything useful."

Beny muttered under his breath, but they had talked about it often enough that the argument was nothing new.

"This stint is a proper opportunity to take a stand that I believe in and to prove myself apart from his influence."

"But you could get yourself killed out there. A combat pilot? Do you know their mortality rate?" Beny screwed his eyes shut and shook his head.

"Better than you do. And if I didn't have a solid heir in you, I wouldn't chance it. I've filed the paperwork to make you my second and hit submit on it all. So, it's official—you're now my designated heir. Not that Lord Timmi won't try to manipulate things, but what other viable choice is there?"

"I don't want this."

"I know. And if it were only for my sake, then honestly, I wouldn't do this to you. But you know this is bigger than either of us. Getting out there and serving with Fleet will put more than lip service behind my support—our support—for the Unity Bloc. I know you see the need for that as much as I do. Besides, I plan on coming back."

"You best do, or I swear I'll send the Arch Soul Catcher, Pogo himself, after your soul."

"Think I've met him already. He's going to be going with us, too. Don't know if that makes it better or worse, though." And there went the yellow light again.

"That's not the sort of joke I need right now. You said 'us.' Who exactly is an 'us'?"

"One more of those things I'm not allowed to talk about now. But as soon as I'm allowed to, I will."

"How much do I need to worry about this 'us'?"

Matteo pulled his shoulders back and stared straight into the viewscreen. "You don't."

"And that in itself worries me. You're always worried about who you're seen with."

"That's the beauty here. Fleet security clearances will control Records, which means I won't be seen, and I'm going to enjoy that while I can. For a year and a half, I'll get to be unabashedly ordinary."

"I'm not sure you're going to like that as much as you think you will. Or that you'll be as ordinary as you hope."

"It's as close as I'm ever going to get in my lifetime. And yes, that is part of the appeal for me, but if that were all, I wouldn't do it."

They stared at each other for several long, silent moments. Finally, Beny sighed. "Any chance I can sign up, too?"

"I'll ask if Fleet needs medics as much as pilots." Good, it looked like Beny understood. "Hold down the fort for me. Things are going to get rougher than you imagine, and no, I can't explain now, but I will."

"Are you absolutely certain? No Dextrine Rank has ever served in such a position in Fleet."

"It's time for a first, then. I'll be in touch when I can."

"May Kayavan himself guide you out of Laythe."

He might need that, considering Pogo, the Arch Soul Catcher himself, was guiding him in.

Chapter 37

ARI TOUCHED HER THUMB to the panel beside the door to Brels' office. It slid open with the barest whoosh. The cavernous space had been transformed, with most of the usual furnishings replaced by fittings for the evening's celebration, but the fresh, clean scent of stone remained. A long serving table had been stationed near the far wall where the water trickled down the flowstone. Standing tables dotted the area near the serving tables, while clusters of chairs and small low tables spread out along the adjacent wall towards the doorway. Game tables with cards and other accessories took up the third corner nearest the doorway, while the floor beyond the majestic stalactite-stalagmite column was left open, probably for dancing. A smaller version of the celebration at Anara.

"Arli! Come in, come in!" Brels smiled broadly and waved her to join him at the long table. He stood at the center of the table, arranging dainty orange canera bush flowers among a formation of tall brown-gold crystals that would serve as a centerpiece for the serving table. His informal, dark-brown suit somehow seemed more formal than it was. Maybe it was in how well it fit his broad frame. "What do you think?" He gestured to the centerpiece.

"I can't imagine anything more fitting for your celebration. Congratulations on your election, Chairman of Guilds." She smiled as she spoke the title, a little chill chasing down her spine.

"We have a great deal to celebrate. Come, sit with me." He tucked a last flower into place and headed to his substantial, carved stone desk, tucked in its usual far corner, the only remaining piece of office furniture left in the room. Two smaller chairs that matched others throughout the room had been arranged near a bottle of wine and two glasses. He sat down and gestured for Ari to do the same. "Share a glass of wine with me. Once the rest of my guests arrive, I imagine you'll do your best to blend into the furniture, and I'll hardly see you. Unless, of course Matté, has asked you to assist him through the festivities again."

"He has." Heat rose in her cheeks.

"Good, good, he'll help you have some well-earned fun. Although I'm certain Pogo would not mind keeping company with you either. You danced together well at Anara." He poured two glasses of wine.

"I expect he has plenty of ready company to enjoy." She sat down, avoiding his gaze.

"He'd be willing to forgo other company, for you. But then again, so would Matté." Brels winked as though pleased with his observations.

"Is who I keep company with important to you?"

"You are a valuable connection. It is fitting I should know those who would seek to connect themselves to you."

He was, of course, correct, at least in being concerned about who would connect themselves with him through her. But pan-

ic threatened to grab her throat. "You have far more important connections to be concerned with than mine. Besides,
Pogo is not interested in more than a comfortable playmate,
which I could hardly be, and Matté's Rank makes any connection between us impossible."

Brels leaned back, head cocked, and studied her. "You
have a rather mean opinion of yourself."

"Not mean. Realistic, sir."

"No, it is not realistic, and I do not approve." Stern notes
crept into his voice.

She gripped the edges of her seat. Brels was not Sander,
was not Joco, she did not need to escape. "I don't know what
you want from me."

"It is as big a mistake to underestimate yourself as it is to
overestimate. You make both errors at once."

"I suppose if one is going to make a mistake, it is good to
do it properly, then."

She tried to laugh, but Brels shook his head, frowning. "I
am very serious. Do not make light of this. You are a valuable
asset to me, and I do not want to suffer loss because you have
not managed that asset correctly."

"I still don't know what you want."

He huffed and stared at the stalactite-covered ceiling, each
one ending in a tiny bead of water. "Do you understand
what shifted the election?"

"Joco's last move in the fight was highly questionable,
despite the officials not making a call against it."

"That was not the move that changed public opinion.
This was." He called something up on his module and handed it to her, volume set very low.

A news feed, with two reporters pointing to an image of Joco
making a statement in the background. She held the module
close to her ear. Joco's voice repeating the words of his last
message to her: *I'm done with ya, girl. You hear that? Done. You*

never been kin. You're no connection to me. Never have been, never will be. Won't speak your name again.

She tried to push it at Brels, but he resisted. "Listen to what they are saying about that. You need to hear it."

Her stomach knotted, and she swallowed back the bitter taste in her mouth. There had been too many things she had "needed to hear" that left their scars upon her soul.

She pushed off the desk to stand, but Brels caught her hand. "Please, trust me. This is important." He stood beside her and took the module, turning up the volume and holding it where she had no choice but to watch.

The reporters recounted the Anara Sports League inquiry, and the accusations made against Joco. At least the winds were with her enough that they didn't show the Records from the debark field. But they explained in detail how it came to be that he claimed her as a kin connection, grudgingly and only under duress.

They went on with blistering opinions that Joco claimed the connection for his advantage alone, and that was a clear indicator of how he would keep promises made in his campaign. Further, his move to disavow himself of her, not even waiting until after the fight was over to send the message she would never forget, suggested how he would treat his allies in the future. Voters beware.

She pushed the module away, her hands cold and shaking. "How did that message get into the hands of the media?"

He laid gentle hands on her shoulders. "It was not through Firen channels, I have made sure of that. It was sent from Anara, though."

"How? I thought Records made there were locked down."

"Records compiled entirely from within Anara grounds are locked down by their own Enforcers and only released by petition. But Anara cannot guarantee privacy on any transmission that is intentionally sent out of the complex. And that is made very clear in all Anara's documentation. So Joco had no reason—except his own hubris, I suppose—to expect the message to you would be private."

She grabbed the back of her chair for support. "Even so, who would have looked at it, unless it was flagged?"

"It isn't difficult to imagine many news outlets submitting flags on anything Joco or I would have sent, just in case there would be something newsworthy there."

"Or it was Sand Storm." Her knees melted, and she collapsed into the seat. "It was him, it had to be. I'm certain that he was the one who set the flags that triggered the inquiry. He called me to meet with him just after it happened, so I know he was there. And he'd have reason to look for something to bring Joco down."

"It could have been him." Brels returned to his seat. "He has said nothing of it, and it is better if I do not know such information. But it wouldn't matter who it was. The way Joco treated you was entirely of his own volition, and I'd say an accurate reflection of his character."

She hid her face in her hands. "I'm sure my image got attached to that somehow, too."

"I am sorry that it did. We were approached for an image, but did not provide it."

She wrapped her arms around her waist. Ironic that her connection to Joco would stain her reputation, when he had always been so concerned about how being connected to the wrong people would damage him. "It is a good thing I'll be leaving here for a while. I am sure there are many who hold me accountable for Joco's loss."

"That is true. I certainly do."

She winced and turned her face away.

"Don't hide, look at me. You need to hear this. For all the preparation that went into the campaign and the fight, it all came down to opinions changed because of choices you made. Choices to allow Joco to show himself for who he really was. You accepted him as a connection because you wanted to allow the fight to happen, for him to have the chance, for both of us, to show ourselves honestly in the ring. He did that in the fight and beyond."

"It seemed like the right thing to pay forward," she whispered.

"Of course, you know I think it was. Those choices changed everything. But it cost you a price few can fathom." He contorted himself to catch her gaze. "I'm not even sure I understand it all."

She swallowed hard, eyes prickling. "Why should that matter to you? Now that you are Chairman, you have so many more important things to concern yourself with. And with the invitation to join your Interceptor program with Fleet, I have a place to go, out of Joco's reach, and a promise of credentials that he cannot touch. That is more than I ever expected."

"Still, that seems very little, and at no cost to myself. I am not comfortable with that."

"You have been dedicated to pay forward, and it has served you well."

"But you are still waiting for the same. And I don't like it. What more can I do for you?" He looked at her with such intensity—he would not go without an answer.

"There is one favor I would ask."

"How might I show you hospitality?"

"Pogo hasn't been able to make arrangements yet, but he said it could be done. My cargo hauler will need storage while I am away."

"Firen has space for that." He sat back, arms crossed over his chest. "It is still a very small thing, considering the hospitality that you have given me."

"But it is what I need right now."

"No, that's not all you need. You need to recognize that I see you as a valuable connection. One to whom hospitality will always be available whenever you have need. Will you please embrace that?" He extended open hands.

But that would require trust. How did one trust? ... Then again, in a way, she had trusted Joco and Sander. Trusted in their untrustworthiness, and that had served her well. She knew how to trust that way. But this was different.

So was Brels, though. There was no reason for him to take notice of her when his enforcers hurt her. He could have washed his hands of it, delegated the matter to those under him. But he didn't. Over and over, he made choices to show himself different.

She pressed his large, rough hands, hands which had chosen to help her when she was most vulnerable, to her cheeks. "Thank you for your hospitality, sir."

His eyes lit as he took her hands in his and did the same. "You have given to me when I have needed, I look forward to doing the same for you. Now, drink with me, knowing this celebration is as much for you and what you have done, as it is for me." He lifted his glass and raised it to her.

Mirroring his actions, she sipped the rich, fruity orange wine. It tasted of canera flowers, red swamp fruit, and desert wind. "I have never had anything like this."

"I have long dabbled in winemaking. This is the first vintage that I have been satisfied with. I am glad you approve." The office door slid open, and guests trickled in. "I must be the host now, you will excuse me. And you will remember what I said, yes, that this is your celebration, too. So, enjoy it, however you can."

With sure, bold steps, he approached his guests, who mobbed him with enthusiastic bear hugs. Clearly, his people loved him. Hard to find better validation than that. And now she was one of Brels' people.

"Mind if I sit with you?" Matté stood near the chair Brels had used. "It's a bit overwhelming over there."

"Go ahead. You have to give him credit, Guild Master Brels isn't afraid to embrace a good celebration."

"As I understand, this election has been tough for Firen, so they definitely need this."

"I imagine you've done a deep dive through all the Records during all our downtime."

"I suppose I'm not hard to predict, am I?" He laughed.

"You know you really don't need my help for this event. You did well at the Anara celebration, and Firen controls the Records here and isn't about to let anything out that could be embarrassing. Brels hasn't hired me as your handler for this, so being seen together ..."

"I know. It could lead to speculation about—how does Beny put it? About whether I'm mixed up with you."

"That's one way to put it, isn't it? But still, it's something—"

"It's not something I want to avoid right now."

"Even though Firen controls are pretty solid, do you want to take that chance?"

He looked at her with a peculiar sort of determination. "If you don't mind being seen with me, yes, I do."

"Not as your handler?"

"No." He bit his upper lip, as what he wanted to say was risky. "As someone I'd like to know a little better. Would that be agreeable?" He looked so out of his element. For a man who had suffered an arranged betrothal, he probably was.

And so was she. But maybe, just maybe, that was a good thing. She glanced over her shoulder toward Pogo, standing near Brels, surrounded by a knot of other Firen miners. Something about the way he stood with them suggested he had more than a passing acquaintance with at least a few of them. He caught her eyes and winked, eyebrows raised. An invitation.

Two of the miners next to him followed his glance and stared at her. Studying, not sure what to make of her. But the woman beside Pogo pressed in a little closer to him and flashed her eyebrows before turning back to the rest. The man on his other side winked at her.

Drowning, she was drowning, even from this distance, too deep in over her head.

She turned back to Matté, who had clearly watched the entire exchange. A little crestfallen, but concealing it admirably. "I think I'd like that very much."

"Really?"

Brels suddenly appeared—how could a man that size move so stealthily? "We're about to 'Bring in the Storm.' Do you have partners for that, or shall I lend a hand?"

"I think we do." Matté stood and offered her his hand.

She took it and they followed Brels to the dance floor.

"Form up, Firen. I've found our storm-bringer! We have a genuine arli to lead in the storm!"

The room laughed as dancers assembled.

And for once, she didn't mind being the storm-bringer.

Book 2 of the Kayavan Chronicles, *Laythe's Own* is coming soon!

Sign up for my newsletter for the latest updates and get this exclusive bonus chapter!

Scan the QR Code
to sign up and get
the chapter!

Why not try out another of my series for free?

__The Wright Way to Begin__ Scan the QR Code to sign up and get the book!

__The Buttercross Dragon__ Scan the QR Code to sign up and get the book!

For book news and other random bits sc*an the QR Code* visit my website.

Also By Maria Grace

The Kayavan Chronicles Series
Kayavan Rising

World Wrights Series:
The Wright Way to Begin
Wrighting Old Wrongs

Jane Austen's Dragons Series:
Pemberley: Mr. Darcy's Dragon
Longbourn: Dragon Entail
Netherfield: Rogue Dragon
A Proper Introduction to Dragons

The Dragons of Kellynch
Kellynch: Dragon Persuasion
Dragons Beyond the Pale
Dragon Keepers' Cotillion
The Turnspit Dragon
Dragons of Pemberley
Miss Georgiana and the Dragon
Here There Be Dragons
Secrets of the Dragon Archives
Dragons at Land's End

The Queen of Rosings Park Series:
Mistaking Her Character
The Trouble to Check Her
A Less Agreeable Man

Sweet Tea Stories:
A Spot of Sweet Tea: Hopes and Beginnings
Snowbound at Hartfield
A Most Affectionate Mother
Inspiration

Darcy Family Christmas Series
Darcy & Elizabeth: Christmas 1811
The Darcy's First Christmas
From Admiration to Love
Unexpected Gifts

Given Good Principles Series:
Darcy's Decision
The Future Mrs. Darcy
All the Appearance of Goodness
Twelfth Night at Longbourn

Fine Eyes and Pert Opinions

Remember the Past
The Darcy Brothers

Regency Life (Nonfiction) Series:
A Jane Austen Christmas: Regency Christmas
Traditions
Courtship and Marriage in Jane Austen's World
How Jane Austen Kept her Cool: An A to Z History of Georgian
Ice Cream

Anthologies
Pride and Prejudice: Behind the Scenes
Persuasion: Behind the Scenes
Dragon Dreams
Christmas Celebrations: Stories of Jane Austen Fan Fiction

Non-fiction Anthologies
Castles, Customs, and Kings Vol. 1
Castles, Customs, and Kings Vol. 2
Putting the Science in Fiction

Available in e-book, audiobook and paperback

About the Author

Six-time BRAG Medallion Honoree, #1 Best-selling Historical Fantasy author Maria Grace has her PhD in Educational Psychology and is a 16-year veteran of the university classroom where she taught courses in human growth and development, learning, test development and counseling. None of which have anything to do with her undergraduate studies in economics/sociology/managerial studies/behavior sciences. She pretends to be a mild-mannered writer/cat-lady, but most of her vacations require helmets and waivers or historical costumes, usually not at the same time.

She writes Gaslamp fantasy, science fiction, historical romance and non-fiction to help justify her research addiction.

Contacted her at:

author.MariaGrace@gmail.com

Thank You!

So many people have helped me along the journey, taking this from an idea to a reality.

Leslie, Marci, Linda, Linda, Lynda, Ruth and my whole Beta team—thank you so much for reading, proofing, and especially being honest!

Friends of the Blue Order, your unflagging encouragement and imagination has been inspirational.

Thank you to those who read and encouraged me in the very first incarnation of this series, *The Storm Series*. Both the story and I have grown alot since those days!

My dear friend Cathy, my biggest cheerleader, you have kept me from chickening out more than once!

Thank you!